THE PHOENIX'S
UNLIKELY PRODIGY

"Though, at first, the book appears to be a classic take on the enemies-to-lovers trope (my favourite trope by the way); it was so much more. I cannot believe how well the author conveyed all of the characters' emotions and struggles. The writing style was profound and pulled at my heartstrings more than I can describe. This book has so many things going for it: how Alexa's and Bruce's chemistry evolves, their relationship with the children and their emotional and professional growth. The reader (just like the characters) is not the same after reading this story."

Reedsy Reviewer Karla Danklu for Making Room For You

THE PHOENIX'S UNLIKELY PRODIGY

Most UNLIKELY To Book 2

MARYANN CLARKE

Want to connect with me?
www.maryannclarkescott.com
maryann@maryannclarkescott.com

For Romance Readers Everywhere in search of a friendly place to call home, where everyone knows your name, and you are always welcome. I hope you find your next book boyfriend, or girlfriend, between the covers of these books.

Foreword

The Most UNLIKELY To Series of Contemporary Romance novels.

Get to know this close knit group of twenty-something friends while they learn to cope and grow as their expectations are turned on their heads.

The Most UNLIKELY To series books are full-length, character-driven, adult contemporary romance novels. They can each be read as stand-alones, or read in order to experience the story chronologically. More rom than com, with a little steam, they're perfect for fans of Christina Lauren, Mhairi Macfarlane or Helena Hunting's single-titles!

Welcome to Port Camosun

an idyllic historic small town on the West Coast of Canada.

When you've given it all you've got, and are tired of life's hard knocks, it helps to have a place to return where everyone knows your name and is glad to see your face. Sometimes the answer is going back to the one place in the world you can always call home. And sometimes your happily ever after can be found in the most *unlikely* place.

Chapter 1

Jeannie

My moment of hesitation before joining my welcome back party at Millhouse Coffee was just long enough to notice that my hand on the old brass door handle trembled uncontrollably. I pulled my hand away, clenching it into a fist. My feet stayed cemented to the sidewalk while I gathered my thoughts and my courage. Filling my lungs, I braced myself for what lay ahead.

Not just the next few minutes, but the next few days, weeks, and months.

Until last week, I hadn't been home for ten years. I hadn't seen my group of closest friends from high school in a decade. Even I could hardly believe it, and I'm the only one, except for my best friend Quinn, who knew what I'd been through since graduation. My road had been long and strewn with obstacles.

I was nervous enough returning to my hometown. Nervous enough that I'd conveniently-oh-so-strategically missed the ten-year Port Camosun High School reunion last weekend. That felt like more than I could handle all at once. A soft re-entry was what I needed, and the casual after-the-party gathering at my best friend's new café had seemed like the perfect speed. Or so I'd assumed.

Despite avoiding the reunion, I'd ended up reconnecting with pretty much everyone in our group a few days later instead of individually the way I wanted. It transpired that the biggest event at the reunion was Julian and Ruby getting together again. I thought my own history was fraught. But those two, it seemed, had it… Well, at least as bad.

Everyone assumed that from the moment Julian and Ruby set eyes on each other the summer before tenth grade, they'd be together forever. They were that rare couple who seemed like soulmates. But something happened the summer after grad that tore them apart, and broke Julian's heart, according to Quinn.

I realized that what I found inside Quinn's café might be hard to recognize. Everyone else would have changed, too. For better, or, like me, for worse. The girl voted 'Most Likely to Succeed' had become the 'Prodigal Daughter' returning from exile with her tail firmly tucked between her legs. I dreaded being the focus of everyone's attention. Fortunately, that day, I was able to reconnect with just a few friends at a time as people wandered in and gathered around the battered old wooden coffee table. For a while, I'd thought maybe it'd all be okay.

Until he walked in.

Initially, I felt most nervous seeing Zach Chapman, my high school boyfriend, after all this time, especially after the catastrophic way our relationship imploded on grad night.

But the incredibly hot, intense guy Zach came in with stole my attention instantly, casting a large shadow over my old beau. Taller, wider, with an imposing presence, his sweat-dampened t-shirt clung to impressive bulging muscles covered in ink like a *Men's Health* cover model. He was pure man-candy and sucked the breath from my lungs.

I honestly didn't know who he was. Just the most perfectly exquisite man to melt my inhibitions and distract me from my restorative mission—exactly the type of man who haunted my pathetic, lonely single-mom dreams.

My belly had swirled with heat and a shiver of excitement at the idea that maybe my future, now that I was home, might include something beyond motherhood, endless study, and hard work. Something decadent and delicious just for me. Now that I'd have my family's support while I was going to school, maybe there'd be time for a little dating, at last.

When his warm, steady gaze made its way across the room to me time and again, setting my face on fire, I finally leaned over to whisper in Ruby's ear.

"Who *is* that tall guy with Zach? He keeps staring at me."

"Who? Phoenix?" She laughed. "Yeah, he changed a lot, hey? And surprised the hell out of us all when he showed up at the reunion last week."

"I don't remember anyone named Phoenix," I said, mentally scrolling our grad class list.

Her reply turned that thrill of attraction and hope into a solid wall of fiery dread. "Oh, that's just a nickname he picked up in The Navy. You knew him. I'm pretty sure you took honours math together," Ruby said. "You used to talk about him sometimes. Had a really rough family situation? His real name's Peter. Peter Corbin."

In a nanosecond, everything I knew—about my past, my present, and most certainly my hopeful future—irrevocably changed.

Phoenix

Jeannie hadn't yet shown up to her own party. Her late arrival had me rethinking my approach. She was obviously gun-shy about being with our group of old friends. I could relate, sort of, but it didn't scare or inhibit me. She was different, and I needed to find out more about her before approaching her. I didn't want to overwhelm her by coming on too strong, too soon.

Within about fifteen minutes of arriving, Quinn asked Zach and me to get a load of liquor from Parker's truck, parked just down the block. We lifted the cases of beer, and boxes of wine and tequila bottles, into two piles. I could see Zach fighting the urge to compete with me, and failing.

"Don't overdo it, Chapman. You don't want to overwork your muscles so soon after an intense workout."

We'd already spent hours at the gym today, Zach watching my routine and quizzing me on how to improve. Considering he'd been training and playing professional ball for a long time, I was frankly surprised at his desire to get stronger now.

"I'm good," he insisted. "I'm recovering nicely."

Having watched him lift weights, I knew this was patently untrue. He nursed his lumbar and was obviously in pain.

"I can take another one," I said.

"What about you?"

I shook my head. "I'm not nursing a sore back. And this is well within my normal load." I routinely ran twelve kilometres with a thirty-five-kilo pack plus gear, so I could easily carry a few more pounds a half a block.

Zach tentatively added another case onto the stack in my arms.

I hardly felt it. "One more."

Scowling, he piled it on, and I shifted it and reconsidered. "Nah. Take it off. I don't want to get my shirt sweaty."

Scoffing, he removed it, setting it down inside the truck. "Show off."

"We can get more later if we run low."

"So what's with the new shirt? I swear you've never bought new clothes. You tried on maybe twenty options this afternoon and fussed like a girl going to prom."

He wasn't wrong. After our morning workout, I'd talked Zach into showing me a couple of local places to shop for clothes, and made him sit and rate me. Because I seriously didn't have a clue.

"I haven't bought civvies, except to work out or hang out. Other than that, I'm on duty, so I have uniforms for… stuff." So many uniforms.

"Huh."

I hesitated. Technically, I didn't have to say anything to Zach, but we were rebuilding some kind of friendship here. "Have you talked to Jeannie yet?"

He straightened his stack of cases, not looking up at me. "No. Why should I?"

I continued staring at him until he looked up, and I held his gaze. "Because you owe it to her? Because it's the right thing to do."

His gaze narrowed, then darted away. "It's been for-fuckin-ever. I dunno. S'pose." He jerked his chin at me. "Why do you care?"

I tongued a tooth, twisting my mouth to the side. "Jeannie and I were good friends in school." I waited for a beat. "I, uh, might be interested."

Zach's face brightened as he processed what I meant. "No shit. Huh." He coughed. "So…the new shirt." He tilted his head towards the café where we headed, and I quirked a small smile. His next shrug conveyed permission, of sorts. "Not my business, man."

"Still. You ought to talk to her. Once. Clear up old hurts."

We carried our loads towards the café entrance. I could practically hear the gears working in Zach's brain.

"Hey, Big P."

"Yep?"

"I was wondering. If maybe you can walk me through your routine. Take me through it step by step."

He'd obviously finished thinking about Jeannie. "You planning on enlisting? It'll just make you hurt."

His mouth flattened, and his brow quirked. "I just want to try it."

I scoffed. Guys were always curious about what it took to train for special forces. Wondering if they had what it took. They usually didn't.

"Yeah, sure. I'll watch you sweat and beg to stop and then kiss my ass."

We laughed, and as we neared the door, Julian arrived at the same time with a stack of food trays from his van.

"Guys."

"Hey, man."

Zach set down his load to grab the door, and I followed Julian inside, where the party crowd had thickened.

***

Jeannie

I ripped off the Band-Aid and finally hauled the café door open, a wall of music and voices enveloping me. On the other side, I waded into a miasma of rich scents—coffee, spicy food, and beer—that pushed my queasy stomach further to the edge. The chill café that now served as our gang's daily hangout, which I'd avoided since that encounter last week, had been transformed into a sparkling bar scene with a standing crowd of people all talking at once.

It had been a struggle to stay away until now, but I was getting good at excuses. My first task, scanning for Peter Corbin, turned up nothing, and I breathed a sigh of relief. I was safe for now. I squinted into the dimly lit space, eager to find and attach myself to Quinn.

Seeing Quinn again had been—continued to be— amazing. She was the only one of our rag-tag and unlikely group of friends who I stayed in touch with all this time, keeping me from desperation, though a long-distance friendship just wasn't the same. Even during those first few years when I barely called my parents because I was so devastatingly ashamed. She was the only one who knew my secret.

And even Quinn didn't know *all* my secrets.

Quinn and I were honour roll geeks, math whizzes, and popular but nerdy good girls. Unlike many in our group, she took a different path. She didn't go to uni either, though everyone expected her to as well. But she knew what she wanted, and she went out and grabbed it by the throat.

Quinn's twin brother, goofy Parker, was not the brilliant student his sister was, but clever enough, combined with athletic ability, to get a scholarship to the uni here in town. I laughed, recalling he'd been voted 'Most Likely to be a Justin Bieber Impersonator in Vegas' because of his glib tongue and boyish good looks. That family never had the patience for desk jobs, more hands-on and pragmatic in their skills and passions than bookish, like me. Instead, Quinn took business classes at the local college, worked a long but strategic series of grunt jobs at shops, restaurants, and cafés and saved her money.

Two years ago, she bought this historic brick building in Old Town before anyone else fully realized how valuable and popular this blue-collar warehouse waterfront district next to the downtown would become.

But Quinn the entrepreneur knew. She had her finger on the pulse of the city. At least a third of the old warehouses were already converted to trendy lofts, and new construction was happening everywhere. So now the girl voted 'Most Likely to Own a Café' was finally the proprietor of the trendiest café in the trendiest neighbourhood, at only twenty-eight years of age.

She told me her dream was to make a place where people could hang out and feel at home. Where people could have a superior cuppa ethically sourced joe and a delicious healthy snack and chill with their friends. Where have you heard that before? *Starbunckles ain't got nothin' on this place*, she told me in her emails.

And in spite of my deep desire to run and hide from the inevitable, Quinn, along with Deanna, had insisted on throwing a proper welcome back party at the café just for me. How could I say no when I was the guest of honour? Not something I could get out of.

And I knew that, along with everyone else, Peter would be here.

And so, here I was. Now my girl squad was all together again. Even the famous war correspondent, ambitious and elusive Ruby Zimmer, had returned to our hometown, apparently to stay.

I spotted Ruby, Rainy, and Quinn near the bar, where Jae Soo leaned at the front, and Parker served as bartender behind. I cut a beeline through the crowd before anyone else noticed me arrive.

"Here she is!" JJ called, spotting me first as I neared.

Quinn's face opened in a rare but broad and welcoming smile. She stepped towards me and enveloped me in her arms, murmuring in my ear, "I'm so glad you came."

As if I wouldn't, but she had excellent people senses and, being my bestie, obviously noticed my reluctance to be with people.

Rainy kissed my cheek, and Parker offered me a glass of wine, which I accepted only too happily. I needed that and something stronger to calm my nerves.

"Thought we'd see more of you before now," JJ said, sipping his beer. "I have so many questions."

I sighed, smiling at him. Jay-Soo the Suit, voted 'Most Likely to be on the Cover of Forbes,' proud owner of the MBA I should have had. That I still wanted. He used to have a floppy mop of beautiful silky black hair. Now, severe chiselled cheeks and trendy hair dyed all shades of burgundy and pink, with sculpted sides, slicked on top.

Seriously though, everyone thought he'd have been whisked home to Korea long ago, swallowed up by the mega family business that supplied him with money to burn. And according to Quinn, he did disappear for years at a time. Some kind of apprenticeship, we supposed. Yet he was here again.

He still wore expensive fashionable clothes, but now he seemed harder, like a buttoned-up, no-nonsense business-man. Until he opened his mouth and laughed that ridiculous donkey bray, flashing those million-dollar white teeth and you realized that inside he was still the same old crazy rebel he'd always been. Yet tempered somehow, with a quiet determination.

My smile tightened, and panic swelled in my chest. This was the part I dreaded. The questions.

I replied, "Of course, sure, JJ. I can't wait to hear everything that you've done during the last ten years. I'm so excited to be here. I'll make the rounds first, say hello to a few people, and catch up with you, okay?" I was babbling. I always babbled when I was nervous.

He nodded, grinning, and turned to say something to Parker.

I'm sure by now word had got around, and everyone knew I had a nine-year-old son. I just hoped they were too polite to ask too many questions about him, though I doubted that very much.

As if to underscore my concern, as I turned the door opened and Julian entered carrying covered trays, presumably of his yummy food, while Zach held the door open for him. On Julian's heels, entered Peter—or Phoenix, I guess I had to get used to calling him that—his short dark hair gelled, his muscles straining against a dark-coloured short-sleeved shirt, sending my pulse hammering in my chest, like a prisoner demanding escape. I could relate. But there was no escape.

I spun towards Quinn. I needed time to sort out this crisis—and get my story straight. Yet first, somehow, I had to get through this night.

I didn't know how I would, but I'd survived worse, and I had to trust myself. I filled my lungs, setting my teeth. *I will get through it. I will find a way.*

Phoenix

I didn't recognize half the people here and assumed our friends had brought friends, and probably dates or partners.

We hauled the cases of liquor behind the counter and

set them down. Parker dumped a bucket of ice cubes into a half-full tub on the counter.

"Rip a couple of cases open and toss some bottles in here," he said. "We need to cool them down."

Jae Soo, glass in hand, leaned on the counter. "Fried chicken once a week isn't going to kill me," he drawled.

"But think of the poor chickens!" Quinn prodded his arm, grinning.

Once Parker was satisfied, Zach and I each grabbed a fresh cold one and circled the counter to hover near Jae Soo, watching the crowd. It was curious, observing how certain pairs of people related to each other, especially old friends or siblings like Parker and Quinn. The subtext. The habits. The emotional shifts were visible to me now, after running missions and leading units of soldiers for years. The dynamic between Jae Soo, Parker, and Quinn was complex and fascinating.

Ruby, as usual, caught my eye. She had an air of exhaustion about her that I'd noted before. But now, standing next to Julian, one or the other of them always touching the other, with a glow of elation and…relief, like a marathon runner who'd finally reached the finish line, like she'd been pushing through with her last ounce of energy.

I could wish my love life sorted itself out as quickly as theirs did, but I knew it couldn't have been easy with what Ruby had gone through. I could never let on all that I knew. But she'd suffered a lot. I'd seen people do much worse, really, after experiences like that.

She'd made the tough call, stepping away from her war correspondent work to stay here with Julian, near her family and friends. It was the right one. Going out on assignment, again and again, was no life. She'd used herself up that way. Even though she was smiling now, I knew from experience her battle with PTSD wouldn't be over any time soon. I had Dad to thank for that knowledge.

She was here now—Jeannie. A shrinking violet next to Quinn and Rainy, trying not to take up too much space. I wondered where the self-assured girl that I knew was hiding. Ten years ago, I'd found her pretty and poised, but also envied the shit out of her. She had her family, and lived in that big old heritage house at the crest of the rise a few blocks beyond the house I'd grown up in before we had to move to the trailer park. Everyone knew her mom who had taught at the elementary school nearby.

It was only after we'd been in the same classes for a couple of years, and become friendlier, that she confided in me about her little sister drowning when she was twelve. My baby sister Bess was only six at the time, and the thought of losing her killed me. But even then, Jeannie rose above it and was so strong and determined to succeed, and she believed she would.

She'd been an inspiration to me. I never got the chance to tell her, but I could start now.

Even though there was a brittle edge to her that hadn't been there before, there was also a ripe softness that had come with maturity. I found I liked it very much, my body responding with a rush of blood, and twitching fingers whenever my gaze traced her curves, or the soft blush of her freckled cheeks whenever I caught her looking at me.

I'd be a fool to think she was unchanged, unaffected by the past decade. I was hardly the angry scrawny teenager I was then. I'd heard she had a child, and that meant a complicated story. I needed to know more. To understand what had happened to her. No better time to start than now.

More than just Jeannie was glancing my way, so I figured this was my moment. I pushed away from the counter and strode towards her. Her eyes widened when I stopped in front of her, leaving no ambiguity that I was there to speak with her.

"Hey, Jeannie. Welcome back. It's really great to see you again."

"Uh-um. Yes! Peter. I heard you were home too. Nice to— You too," she stuttered, her blush ramping up to a cotton candy pink as she fumbled with her purse. The bright colour on her cheeks made her golden freckles pop. "I mean, it's nice to see you, too."

Her embarrassment was too sweet. She was eyeing me like I was a bag of licky-chewies. *She likes you, sailor.*

I couldn't stop my face from twisting into a smile. "Nobody but my mom calls me Peter anymore. Everyone calls me Phoenix now."

"Right. Of course. Sorry."

I hadn't meant to embarrass her further, but it was damned weird hearing my old name on her lips. Like I'd time-travelled back to high school.

"No problem. It takes getting used to. I hear you're going to school."

It wasn't a hard question. I was trying to put her at ease. But she was completely flustered. Her lake-blue eyes darkened to navy as her pupils grew large, and I pretended not to notice her gaze dart over my chest and arms and down my body, avoiding my face.

"Uh-huh. Yes. I'm finally going to get my MBA," she choked out.

"I hope we can reconnect this summer. Spend some time catching up before you get too busy." I took a small step away to give her a bit of breathing room, my smile growing at how flustered she was. I wanted to wrap her in my arms and give her a bear hug. Reaching forwards, I satisfied the impulse by setting my fingertips against her arm.

She squeaked and recoiled as if I'd set a torch to her smooth pale skin. *Sensitive.*

I took a deep breath and let it out slowly, picturing her response if I touched her all over the way I wanted to, my chest filling as if I'd come upon a secret buried treasure. It felt like I'd breached a fortress she'd built around herself, catching her off-guard. Her fine smooth cheeks flared an even brighter shade of pink like summer rose petals.

With a sputter of nervous laughter, she replied, "Sure. Yup. Maybe. Um. I'll have to see. Busy schedule. Busy."

Okay. *Back away, dude.* She was really delicate. Even more than I thought. Or maybe it was just me that rattled her. This thought both thrilled and concerned me. I hoped her memories of grad night were not unpleasant.

Shit. Is it possible she didn't even remember our stolen night of intimacy? That night, she'd been upset, and did have a lot to drink, and hadn't appeared used to it. But I hoped her memories were as pleasant as mine. Despite everything that happened before, and afterwards, I still held that secret memory close to my heart, treasuring it like a precious jewel. I'd had dreams of Jeannie.

Well, I didn't want to pressure her. This wasn't the time. I'd catch up with her later, when she wasn't on the spot, and give her my number. I'd make sure she felt in control.

Smiling, I bent forwards to kiss her cheek lightly, straightened, winked, and returned to my post at the bar. I took the beer Parker handed to me and ignored the knowing stare Zach angled my way.

"Obvious, much?" he muttered under his breath, nudging me with his elbow.

I chuckled. "What's wrong with that? I know what I want, and I'm going for it."

Jeannie

My pulse skittered wildly as I watched Phoenix walk over to his friends at the bar. I tried so hard to stay in the moment, to follow the conversations all around me, enjoy the party and pay attention to my lovely friends. But my mind had withdrawn, turned inward, drilled down on my own situation in a buzz of panic and worry.

What was I going to do? How had the universe turned against me once more? Would nothing ever be easy?

My body felt numb and tingly, and spots danced in front of my eyes. I couldn't let it get the better of me. I had to stay calm. At least this time, I knew what I was getting into.

Last Sunday, the day Ruby returned to say she was staying in town, and she and Julian got together, was my first time at the café, and everything had been going so well. I thought.

I was happy for them. Ruby was going to write a book or something. And I guess she was going to live with Julian on his farm. Unlike me, who would be stuck for the foreseeable future living with my parents. But then that gathering had turned into an impromptu party to celebrate them. That's when everything went sideways.

That's when Peter walked in, and the floor fell out from under me.

I wasn't faking to get away when I excused myself early, feeling sick. I truly was sick to my stomach, sweating, with a splitting headache. Stress and anxiety will do that. And shock.

Now the dizziness and nausea were returning, despite my being prepared. This stress sickness was new. I'd already been through so much, and managed everything just fine. I was strong. I was in control. I could do anything. But lately, I seemed to be losing my composure.

Maybe I was exhausted and overwhelmed by all I had to do to make the move west. There'd been so many affairs to wrap up in Kingston. Everything to sell, give away, or pack up. And Will. Managing his expectations, stress, and resentment at having to leave his home, his school, and his friends. But I'd done it. And I'd dealt with far worse in my life. Why was I so frazzled now?

I couldn't stop myself from stealing glances at Phoenix, compulsively searching for the boy Peter that I knew in his unrecognizable masculine face, with its hard jaw, chiselled cheekbones, and thick neck. And that body, a huge wall of solid muscle, bore no resemblance to the gangly teen I'd known. From time to time I caught a twinge of something familiar—his straight nose was the same shape maybe, and why wouldn't it be? The whorls of his ears seemed familiar, though why I even knew that, I'm not sure. A tiny mole on his cheek. And most importantly, his eyes. The intense, serious, intelligence of his eyes, and their colour—a deep fathomless bottle green like the sea. Somehow, I remembered that.

An image flashed through my mind. A visceral memory, old and buried. The intense focus and wonder in those green eyes as they looked into mine. That wasn't a memory from math class. Shivering, I blinked the picture away.

Now he reminded me of a big cat—watching everyone with those feline eyes. You just knew he saw things others missed. Watching and waiting. Waiting for the right moment, but for what?

When he looked at me, which I couldn't help but notice was often, I felt naked. Whether it was because he was mentally peeling off my clothes, or because he could see right through me, right into me, I didn't know. One thing I knew in my bones was that he was dangerous.

It wasn't just his massive size or his solid muscles, or the intriguing ink that decorated his skin and drew my gaze over each bulging curve and hard plane, making me want more, though they were as intimidating as they were appealing. There was also his dark hair, cut short, and the intimate fit of his clothes, close but roomy enough for instant, powerful movement.

My body seemed to react to his presence with an agenda all its own. My skin tingled, my pulse raced, and my brain turned to mush. Just that, alone, set alarm bells ringing in my head.

It was him. Who he was. Who he was to me, and to my son, made him a ticking bomb.

I knew virtually nothing about him. And what I did know didn't put my mind at rest. He'd changed so much, it felt like the past meant nothing. I was starting from scratch.

What could I know, based on the past? His rough life as a teen had made me feel so sorry for him. Under the brittle toughness that he showed everyone else, once I'd got to know him a little better, I saw his kindness, his vulnerability, his will to survive, and his drive to succeed. His love and loyalty for his broken father that kept him close when a better life became available. It was those things that had made me the most sad when I'd learned he'd died with his father in the trailer fire. What a waste. It was one of those moments in life when something happens that felt both tragic and inevitable. I was hardly surprised, and maybe wouldn't have given it much thought, if it hadn't been for that one night we'd spent together.

Beyond that, I hadn't mourned him. I hadn't the luxury of time or attention to dwell on him later. If he hadn't died, I'm not sure how I would have handled the pregnancy differently. Would I have reached out and told him? What could I have expected from him in the way of help? The fact that he was gone was, in a small way, a blessing. I had enough problems on my own without getting tangled up in his.

Of course, I'd wondered who he might have become if he'd lived. His blood flowed in my son's veins, so I was curious. Now, I'd find out.

My God, so many of the facts had changed in a flash. I could hardly trust the ground I stood on. I felt dizzy with the need to rearrange my whole view of the world. Before long, I'd have to come to terms with these changes and face up to my moral duty. But I wasn't ready for that yet.

What I didn't understand was why he'd singled me out. Why was he staring at me? Why would he come over just to talk to me when he was so cool to everyone else? And how could I resist my attraction to the sexy wall of hunky man he'd become? How long could I hold out?

Chapter 2

Phoenix

COMPLETING A SET OF SHOULDER PRESSES, I set the weight bar back on its supports. "Then we add weight for the dead-lift," I told Zach, and we swapped out the weights. "Start with what you can comfortably handle, and add a bit for each of the five rounds."

Once loaded up, I demoed the proper posture for a safe deadlift a few times and set the bar down, drawing in a deep breath, and along with it the familiar scents of rubber, oiled steel and sweat.

"So you do a different routine each day?" Zach asked.

"Pretty much, we rotate," I confirmed. "Core, basic 101 and then strength. Plus runs. Let's start with the core today. It's the most fundamental."

I'd gone through all three routines for him, talking him through each step and focussing on safety. "You start on the back extensions like I showed you, and I'll do squats and watch you." I set my watch timer for twenty minutes as he climbed onto the glute and ham machine. "Go."

I was glad Zach had attached himself to me and pushed me to guide his training. It gave me something to do every day and eased my transition back into the group since we often ended up at Quinn's café afterwards.

When I returned to Port Camosun after ten years away, I knew my return would cause a disturbance. I was aware, complicit even, that almost everyone who'd known me then believed me dead. Would my friends, who'd thought me dead, accept me again? Could we, who'd lived such different lives, find common ground?

Just a week ago, I'd cracked the seal on the door to my childhood home with a sense of purpose but no clear mission plan. Unlike most of my missions, I'd not been briefed. I had insufficient intel to know what to expect, beyond memories, hopes, and maybe unspoken fears.

But now? Now I had one more piece of data that changed everything. The ten-year reunion last week had been a revelation, my welcome warmer than I could have imagined. What I hadn't seen coming?

Jeannie van Bellen.

That my old friend and secret high school crush would be single and moving back to Port Cam, too? I hoped it was a sign that we were meant to reconnect.

We swapped places after Zach had completed his ten reps, and I'd done fifty squats. By the time he'd grunted his way through fifty squats, I'd completed both my back extensions and sit-ups and waited for him. We'd both worked up a sweat, but Zach was gasping and groaning. Already.

"You asked for it, bud." With a chuckle, I slapped his back to encourage him, and we started on our second round.

When I say I opened the door, I don't mean literally to the shabby trailer I'd lived in with my father from the age of twelve to seventeen, because that structure had burned to ash long ago.

Instead, I meant to the life, the identity, and the community that I'd abandoned when I ran away. Even though I'd only run through a gate, into another world: my new life, and my new identity, as an enlisted officer in the Canadian Navy.

My decision to return to my hometown had been twofold. To be closer to my mother and younger sister Bess, who I'd seen little of for far too long, despite calling, occasionally visiting, and sending money regularly. Because they needed me.

But also, to find a place where I could settle down and call home, something I'd not had all these years. Even growing up. Because it's what *I* needed now.

We swapped places again, Zach breathing pretty heavily now, his face and chest flushed. My own heart rate was elevated, as it should be, but this was routine for me. We continued, our breathing and the clank of the machines and weights the only sounds in the room.

My career in the military, while not barely half over, had by necessity been nomadic, more so than most of my colleagues, since I had nowhere to return to, and nowhere to miss.

Or at least nobody had been missing me.

Now though, my two closest friends from my unit, who'd gone through basic and advanced training with me, and survived countless covert missions, had dispersed. I was at loose ends, feeling at a disadvantage for the first time in years.

As we approached our thirtieth birthdays, they'd each chosen to make a change, returning to their families, and their respective quieter futures. Lt. Damien Meskew settled in Ottawa with his wife Brianna, where they were raising their new baby, Mellie. Second-Lt. Carter Robinson had joined his fiancée Ciara and extended family in Halifax and whatever that brought. Even Monty Borges, after transferring to the US Navy four years ago, was closer to his home and family in San Diego. My thoughts inevitably included Russell, the fifth in our group, who'd come home from Libya in a body bag three years before.

My dream was to make a new family and home here like my friends had in other places. If I could figure out how. I had wondered if I would be happier settling near one of my buddies, or feel like a fifth wheel if I followed them.

Despite Carter's arguments, if I wanted to stay with JTF 2—Canada's elite joint task force, similar to the US's Seal Team Six—Halifax wasn't an option. And for the foreseeable future, I did. For him, it made sense to go home, but he'd made career sacrifices to do it.

Perhaps starting over in a semi-familiar place like Ottawa, near the Dwyer Hill Training Base, where I could transition into tactical development and training and still jump into the Canadian Special Operations Regiment—CSOR—as needed, and as I aged out of active duty, would be better.

So I'd returned to Port Camosun with questions, but no firm direction. Could I call this place home again? Underlying all these life questions was a silent one that ate at me, causing my heart to race more than a workout could. Would this aching sense of loneliness follow me everywhere? Well, I'd find out soon enough. Sooner or later, I had to put down roots.

When we'd done all our reps and rounds, and Zach lay on the mat for five minutes catching his breath, we grabbed a drink of water and headed out.

"You think you can run to the café and back now?" I asked him.

"Running…I can do," he grumbled as we hit the pavement. "I am a midfielder. I can run all day."

"It'll get better," I reassured him, keeping pace on the way, wondering if I'd see Jeannie at the café today.

Now I had both a clear sense of purpose and my North Star. Because if there was a chance I could be with Jeannie, who I still held up as the ideal against which every woman I met was measured, then this mission would be more successful than my wildest dream.

Jeannie

I pranced down the worn wine-red-carpeted stairs, spun on the ball of my foot on the polished fir boards at the bottom, and took three long strides through the front hall to the kitchen door. These movements were automatic—muscle memory if there's such a thing. The product of a thousand mornings growing up in this big, creaky heritage house. This time, my mind twinged uncomfortably, because despite being back, I didn't belong here anymore.

"Morning, Mom," I said, entering the kitchen to find her stumbling in backwards from the porch, carrying a heavy load.

"Oh, there you are, sweetheart," she mumbled absently. "Excellent timing. Can you take this?" She thrust the box she carried into my arms, and I nearly buckled under the weight, grunting.

"Oh, my, God. This weighs a ton! Why don't you get Dad to do it?"

"Take it to my car." She flicked a garden-gloved hand and headed outside. "Dad's busy in his shop."

I'd only been here a week and a half, and I'd already

learned two important things that both negated and intensi-fied my concerns about this plan.

The first was that my parents hadn't changed in the ten years I'd been living out East. If anything, they'd become *more*. More absent-minded, preoccupied, and absorbed in their respective passions. Mom with her gardening world. Dad with his whirligigs. They were both retired now, leaving more time for their passions, therefore, somehow busier than ever.

And secondly, it seemed that my moving in—and bringing with me my nine-year-old son Will, who they had never met before our arrival— would hardly make a dent in their self-absorbed lives. In fact, I felt almost invisible.

I worried about how this peculiar household made my shy, anxious kid feel. It was not the warm grandparently welcome I'd hoped for—for him, anyway. I hadn't expected much for myself. Still, they never ceased to astonish me, and being here made my stomach pinch in a familiar and unwel-come way.

Will sauntered into the front hall as I passed through with Mom's box, opening the front door at the lift of my chin. At least someone in this family was thoughtful.

"Thanks, my love." Setting the box next to Mom's station wagon, I returned. "You hungry?"

Will shrugged. "A bit."

"Let's find something." I stroked his velvety freckled cheek, straightened his glasses, and led the way to the kitchen as Mom returned with stuffed shopping bags in each hand. "How about a grilled—?"

"Oh! Here. Will. So glad to have an extra set of hands. Be a dear and take these." Mom shoved the bags in Will's direction, and he took them without a word.

I caught his eye and smiled. We'd already had a couple of dozen conversations, both to prepare him for my family before we came and to debrief after disorienting encounters with them. But every day brought new weirdness that needed explaining.

I pulled some cheddar out of the fridge and started prepping grilled cheese sandwiches. Mom stomped in yet again with another open box, this one filled with teetering stacks of small plastic pots.

"Why don't you put that stuff in the wheelbarrow and take it all to the car in one load?" I asked, knowing that common sense had little bearing on my mother's relentless movements. "Why drag it all through the house?"

She hummed absent-mindedly, chewing the inside of her cheek. "Oh, that thing has a wobbly wheel. And it was piled up by the back…um, door…anyway…" Her voice tapered off as her mind drifted onward.

I pushed the sandwiches around the buttered pan as the cheese softened. "You heading to the garden centre today?"

"I'm visiting a new garden. Someone who came in last week looking for…" Her sentence faded out as they often did.

My mother was not practical, despite being an in-demand Master Gardener who taught popular workshops at the local garden centre and volunteered her time to answer questions from local residents. Even though she was a fount of knowledge when it came to plants, soil, irrigation, or pests—and had been a well-loved and competent school teacher until a few years ago—other aspects of life escaped her notice or were largely uninteresting.

She relied on Dad for many practical things. He was better. But Dad too was absorbed with designing and building the whirligigs that he loved so much, and donated to local charity auctions, schools, and such. Instead of being a weekend escape from his rigorous accounting practice, now that he was retired, he seemed to have lost himself in his projects and often disappeared into his backyard shop for hours on end. Or maybe he just needed time away from Mom.

It was hard to resent anyone who was so involved in their community, so generous with their time, and so warm and friendly to everyone they met. I'd always assumed it was me that was deficient in some way—and worked hard to overcome this shortcoming. And succeeded. Up to a point.

But now, seeing the alienating effect their doddering ways had on my sweet son, I was beginning to see them in a different light.

I desperately needed their support, both financial and practical, to get through my MBA program as quickly as possible. Will needed more of my attention now than ever, and relocating to a new city and school wouldn't make this any easier. Working full-time while juggling these two things was more than I could handle. Thus the move.

Thus my dependence on my parents.

Sighing as I plated the sandwiches and added a few carrot sticks, I wondered how we'd make it through the next two years.

***

Phoenix

My buddies Damien and Carter were bickering like two raccoons in heat when I joined the online chat on the non-military computer in the open office area.

"Hey, guys."

"Ottawa is *not* colder than Halifax!" Carter snapped.

"More sub-zero temps. More snow," barked Damien, immovable.

"Dry cold's better'n wet cold, any day. Halifax winters are fucking miserable, and you know it."

They didn't stop, so I raised my voice.

"Hey! Gentlemen!" Their argument petered out, their gazes shifting to, presumably, my face on their screens. They sat up straighter.

"Good Morning, sir!" Carter barked, saluting.

"Sir, Commander, sir!" echoed Damien.

I took a moment to study their faces. Despite their apparent formality, their eyes sparkled and their firm mouths twitched with suppressed humour.

This ritual was some perverse combination of our rigorous training and habit from field missions, and a kind of passive-aggressive dig that I'd been promoted a rank higher than them, that they never tired of.

We all knew this was largely because I was Task Force Commander, despite having gone through training with them all at Dwyer Hill and Valcartier. We all had type-A personalities, spines of steel, were invincible fighters and irreplaceable team members hugely committed to success, and were keen to serve, protect, and defend our country. You didn't make JTF 2 if you weren't.

My promotion to Commander was largely due to my versatility, I figured. And my leadership skills. I was the brains of the unit and always had been. We were all specialists within the Special Forces, of course. It's just that with my engineering degree, my communications and IT training as well as my tactical, intelligence, and strategic strengths, I'd grown into that role. There were other reasons, too. My Navy background. And though we were all by necessity physical badasses, I still had six inches and fifty pounds on them. And of course, I was a know-it-all bossy fuck. There was that.

At their erect posture and alert expressions, I remembered how my habitual disciplined straight spine and focus looked to others. I wondered what my old high school friends saw when they looked at the new-and-improved me. I'd been doing it so long, it was my skin now.

After another beat, I smirked and said, "At ease, sailors. This is a social call." I reclined in my desk chair with a squeak, folding my arms, and felt my mouth pull into a grin. I'd missed them. It had been weird hanging out with civilians these past few weeks, and these guys put me at ease.

They relaxed, too, smiling.

"How you doin', sir?" ventured Damien, jerking his chin at the screen. "Looks like you're at work."

I nodded, acknowledging the room they could see behind me, the standard issue grey JTF 2 Pacific HQ office space where I'd been assigned a desk while staying here on base. "Still on leave. "

We weren't always together, but we'd been together more than apart these past six years. I knew, despite the choices they'd made and the damned good reasons why, that this transition to separate lives would be tough on them.

"You guys happy to be home?"

"Can't beat it." Carter's grin said it all. "Got my own fan club here. Between Ciara, my mom, and my grandma, I've gained five kilos already, and it ain't muscle."

"You fat fuck. You always did eat more'n your share," grumbled Damien.

I smiled. "Just because you're regular now is no excuse to slack on fitness, Carter. You're trained to lead, so be a leader."

"Yeah, yeah. I'm just enjoying it for a minute. Mostly I'm just…you know. I feel like I can exhale."

I nodded, knowing exactly what he meant. Even though on leave, my antennae were forever tingling, expecting to be called out any second. And my check-in with JTF 2 HQ brass Lieutenant-Commander Unger was coming up fast. I needed a plan.

"Don't relax too much, Carter. You can still get called to sub. Damien? You a happy little pig in shit, too?"

He grinned and held his phone up to the camera, showing off a blurry picture of a drooly-faced toothless baby. Carter guffawed, and I shook my head as a wave of nostalgia and a weird twang of jealousy twisted in my gut. Though Damien was still in the unit, he was withdrawing from the frequent deployment demands of JTF 2, the unspoken reality that he'd reapply to CSOR and would no longer join me on missions. However, once JTF 2, always JTF 2. He'd always be special. In an ideal world, soldiers would marry after thirty, and delay kids till closer to thirty-five, when we'd age out of direct-action missions.

"Congratulations, man," I said, wondering if there was still a chance for me. "Must be nice to be with your family."

He bobbed his head, his lips pulled into a flat smile of agreement. "The brass at Dwyer keeps me hopping. Onboarding newbies."

"How do the new units look?"

"Not bad. Good batch of guys."

I could lead any team. Any unit would pull together under strong leadership. But not having my guys at my side. That fucking sucked.

"How'd the shindig go?" Carter asked, changing the subject, and I knew it hurt him to step away from our life together.

"Aw, yeah. Did everyone shit when you walked in?" Damien added.

I nodded. "You could say that." I let out a small huff of laughter. "People were shocked. But really welcoming."

Damien added, "That's great, man."

Carter tilted his head and lifted a brow. "And now you're

finally coming back to Dwyer, right?" I knew he was only half teasing. He really did want me there. "Your god-daughter wants to meet you," he added for good measure.

"Shut your pie-hole. Why would Phoenix want to live in your ball-freezing part of the country when he could join me here in—?"

I laughed, as if Halifax was any better. "If weather was my primary concern, I'd stay right here in Port Cam, turkey."

"Truth." Damien's pout twisted into a frown. And if you can make searing eye contact through a video call, then he came damned close. "Any progress, though, really?"

My hands dropped, and I stared at them, lying relaxed in front of the keyboard. Both men fell silent, waiting.

"Something…significant happened."

They leaned closer to their screens, alert. After a few tense moments of silence, while I let their imaginations run, and their expressions morphed from puzzled to curious to concerned, I cleared my throat.

"Is it your mom? Is she okay?" whispered Damien, the sensitive one, despite his gruff manners.

My mouth pulled slightly to the side in acknowledgment of the way his mind worked. I knew my guys, my unit, as well as I knew myself. I knew where they'd go and what they were capable of. Quickly, I put a stop to his downward spiral.

"No. No. Nothing bad. It's all right. Good even."

Suddenly, I felt my face warm, and glanced to the side, drawing a breath. If I said this aloud, it would be real.

"Remember that girl I told you about? The one I…had a crush on?"

"The brainy one? From honours math?" Carter asked.

"The girl you hooked up with at grad?"

I nodded. It was funny that they remembered these weird details from my life, but when you're on a mission—and you're huddled in the desert dust behind a rock outcropping waiting for a target, or gathering intel for days on end in an abandoned warehouse, or on long overseas flights—there are thousands of idle hours to exchange life stories.

I swallowed. "Yeah. Jeannie."

Carter's eyes bugged. "You hooked up again? At the reunion?"

"Whoa," Damien breathed, and if we were in the same room, I knew he'd be punching my shoulder in congratulations. "Dude!"

That shocked a huff of laughter from my throat. "No. God."

Embarrassed at the admission, I felt my brows itch, and swept my fingertips across them, rubbing. "She didn't make it to the party. But she is here. She's moved back here, and…" A half cough, half laugh of embarrassment swelled in my throat, choking me. "She's single." I shrugged, my voice weirdly soft, an echo of the insecure teenager that had been half in love with her for years.

I remembered her, of course. You didn't forget a girl like Jeannie van Bellen. You never forgot your first crush. I'd thought of her often over the years, but I'd imagined she'd got her degrees and was settled somewhere, having the brilliant career and life she'd been destined to have. Likely in a committed relationship if not married. But when I saw her the day after the party and learned that she was not only moved home but was single, all the variables rearranged themselves in my mind.

The excitement in their faces reflected the thrill that thrummed in my veins, validating my feelings. I sensed a trace of disappointment, too, as if they knew this meant my first choice would not be to join them when I made my decision.

"You know there are women in Ottawa, too. You'd get some no matter where you were," Carter tried.

"Uh, no. This isn't that. This girl… She's more."

That didn't stop them from ribbing me.

"Ah, too bad, so sad. That you're not gonna get some," Damien sang. "She won't be interested in your hairy ass," he joked.

"Uh. I've got a helluva lot more to offer her than I did ten years ago, asshole. How can she resist?"

"Well," Carter spat. "Women, you know." As if that explained everything.

"That's nice, coming from a married man," I said.

"Don't even."

Since I'd learned at the reunion party that Jeannie was returning to town, I'd been on edge, tightly wound as if I were heading out on a mission, senses tingling.

I wasn't worried, though. I saw the way she checked me out at the café the first time she saw me. She was interested, all right. I just had to execute the mission. Something, as it happened, I was pretty damned good at.

I didn't believe in signs. I was a data man, and there were such things as patterns. As Task Force Commander, sometimes I was faced with a shit pile of facts, no patterns, no clear path, and a ticking clock. At times like that, I relied on my gut. And if I were having a good mission, a good day even, one extra piece of data dropped in my lap and made my next step crystal clear.

Today was such a day.

Chapter 3

Phoenix

Lieutenant-Commander Brun Unger was JTF 2 Chief of the Pacific HQ, under the overall naval base commander. I'd met him a few times but knew him more by reputation than personal experience since I'd worked out of the eastern HQ for the past five years. He'd be my superior at the Naval Base here in Port Cam if I stayed, and it was with him I needed to discuss my career situation—and my goals. Kitted out in my freshly pressed NECU, I reported in early for my appointment with Unger, easy to do since I was living on base while on leave.

I knew there'd be guys I wanted to chat with on the way to my meeting, so I left time to stop at my own desk, check my email, then head over.

"Hey, Corbin," called out Robbins, a guppy bin kicker whose desk was opposite mine, among a gaggle of other pencil pushers and paper clips. "You back on duty?"

"No. Checking in with my career mangler."

"Got your orders yet?"

"Still waiting," I said. It was nobody's business that I was a ninja and didn't get placements like regular anchor crankers.

I knocked on Unger's door.

By now, I was sure I'd have a definitive answer for Unger when he asked me what I'd decided. It was a privilege to have a say in it at all. But that was a perk of my position, my seniority, and my status. My job would take me wherever I was needed. But being stationed on the Pacific meant I'd be less likely to get diplomatic escort duty unless the Prime Minister or some other brass were heading to Asia. Though I never knew until they called me.

After a moment, I heard a gruff, "Enter," from within, and turned the knob.

"Sir." I stood to attention, saluting. "Lieutenant-Commander, sir."

After another minute of paper shuffling, the block-jawed fifty-something man with shorn grey-brown hair lifted his head. "Corbin." He saluted. "At ease. Take a seat."

I sat in front of him, removing my ball cap and setting it on my lap.

"How's your leave going?"

"Very well, sir. So far."

"You haven't been out West for a while now. Spending time with your family, are you?"

"I'm heading to the mainland to visit my mother and sister this weekend."

"Good. Good. We all need family, Corbin. Important to have that support outside of work." He nodded, twisting his mouth while scanning the paperwork in front of him.

"Says here you've got another four weeks to go. That's a long break for someone of your value, Corbin."

"I appreciate that, sir." I swallowed. I knew this would come up. My time was short.

"Have you made a selection?"

I cleared my throat. "Not quite, sir. Getting there."

Unger dipped his chin and scowled at me, studying my face. "It's not like you to waffle over anything. As you know, we'd very much like to have a leader of your calibre on the Pacific."

I nodded, glancing down at my glossy black Cadillacs. "Yes, sir. I have a few personal matters yet to resolve before finalizing my choice."

"You say the word, I sign this form." He adds, "Though once this admin is settled, I will call on you at any time. Be prepared."

I nodded. I was always prepared. But I wanted more time with Jeannie before I got shipped off for weeks. Anything could happen in that time. "I realize that. I'd appreciate staying in town until after Labour Day, though, if possible."

His scowl deepened, the creases in his brow and cheeks deep as the Kabul canyons. "I can't guarantee that, if a critical situation comes up and your skills are needed."

It was more likely that I'd be sent out on SIGINT or TECHINT missions, or training in Ukraine or Libya. These days, the hot spots for terrorism tended to be the Sahel and a few spots in south Asia, as well as the usual suspects. I was up to speed on where the currently deployed units were. Carter was out, and there were new guys to coordinate with, but I'd work more with the team here if we trained and planned missions together. I had to adjust to being away from the centre of things. I wondered if I ought to suggest a shift towards more cyber-terrorism work, which was a specialty of mine, anyway. I didn't want to get stuck being a pencil pusher, though. My expertise was field comm, recon, logistics, surveillance, and intelligence. But then, Unger likely knew my strengths better than I did.

Reluctantly, I nodded again, but my teeth were grinding with frustration. I'd never assumed my generous seven weeks of leave was a guaranteed thing. But for the first time in my life, I had something other than my job that felt critical.

"Let's talk again in a couple of weeks, Corbin. If you're leaning this way, I'd like you to be involved in strategy and staffing meetings so you know what's on the horizon."

"Yes, sir. Thank you."

***

Jeannie

I found Will hiding out in his room, flopped on his bed with his nose buried in a book.

"I want to take you out to buy new clothes for the school year."

He crossed an ankle over his knee, exposing the holey bottom of his sock. "Why? What I already have is fine. It's comfortable. I hate shopping."

Patience. "You want to make a good impression at your new school. You want your teacher to like you. You want to make new friends, don't you?"

"I like the clothes I have. They're soft and comfortable." Then he added, his tone belligerent, "And I liked my old friends just fine. I don't need new ones."

My heart squeezed in sympathy. I knew he was lonely. "I know you miss Dak. Have you heard from him?"

"Sure. We message."

"Does he miss you?"

Will shrugged. "Dunno. He's busy."

"Well, we're busy too. We have so many things to get ready."

"You're busy," he grumbled. "I'm bored. I'm stuck at home while you run errands."

I opened my bag and rummaged for the list of supplies I'd downloaded from the school site. "We should pick up the school supplies, too. I need a few new notepads and pens."

"Mhm. What am I supposed to do for the rest of the summer?"

"You're meeting your cousins next weekend. Logan's nearly your age. That'll be fun. And don't forget, your assessment meeting's at the school next week."

He groaned, dropping his arm over his face, muffling his speech. "I don't need math tutoring, Jeannie."

Attitude! I glared at him until he relented, lifting his head and shoving his glasses up his nose.

"I don't need math tutoring. Mom."

Jeez, Louise. He was only nine. What was he going to be like at fifteen? "It doesn't hurt to find out," I said in a small voice. I couldn't let him know how worried I was about his math.

"I hate that. All the kids will think I'm slow. That'll be a great first impression."

"You are most definitely not slow. No one who met you would think that."

He sighed dramatically. "You obviously forget what it's like to be nine."

"I just don't want you to fall behind in the math curriculum."

"I'll work hard. I'll be okay. Stop worrying."

"Put your shoes on. Let's go."

"Can we go to the café and see your friends?"

"No."

"But you go there."

"I could hardly skip the party they threw for me. And I

see Quinn for a few minutes when I stop in to get a coffee, that's all."

"When are you going to take me with you?"

"Um. I will. I'm just not ready to show you off yet. Besides, you met Quinn already."

He rolled over, propping his chin on his hands and staring at the headboard. "You're embarrassed of me. 'Cause I have no dad."

I gasped and launched myself onto his bed, sitting down beside him. My gut pinched. I set a hand on his warm back and rubbed. "Honey, no! Of course, I'm not. It's just these are friends I knew in high school, and none of them have kids yet. I'm getting to know them again. I'll take you soon."

If only Will knew the truth. What lay ahead would be so disruptive for him. I couldn't even imagine what the fallout would be. That was one reason I was stalling on talking to Phoenix. It was a great big can of worms I'd rather not open at all. I had everything figured out. I didn't need or want this. But I knew I had to deal with it soon. This was not news I wanted to drop on Will after he started school. It was just too much.

"When?"

"Soon! And the Farm-to-Table Faire is starting soon. You'll get to meet everyone and hang out at the park then. Right now, we just have a lot of things to get organized."

"We stay here with Grandma and Grandpa too much."

"I thought you were helping Grandpa in the shop with his whirligigs. You were interested."

"They're weird."

I knew he meant my parents, not the whirligigs. I shushed him, and he dropped his voice to a hiss.

"Grandpa just ignores me. And Grandma's always making me do stuff when I'd rather be left alone. I want to play games. Read. A-ny-thing. Or go out with you." He shot me a coy glance.

I knew he was curious about my old friends.

"Well then, stop complaining about going shopping with me. We can get out of the house together. Let's go. I'll buy you a burger and ice cream. I know a great place, if it's still there."

"Eating out is a waste of money," he mumbled, but followed me downstairs, anyway.

Phoenix

A half block from Millhouse Coffee, I spotted Jeannie, laden with shopping bags, shuffling along the sidewalk, looking sweaty and tired.

"Hey! Jeannie," I called out, jogging to catch up with her.

"Oh! Pe-Phoenix! Um. Hi." She was flushed, distracted, struggling with her heavy purchases. She fumbled, her bags slipping and falling open. One ripped at the corner.

I leapt to catch the books that tumbled out and her purse strap before it slid off her shoulder as she bent to retrieve a notebook. Hooking her purse strap on, I was getting the picture that my lovely girl carried a lot on those soft-sloping shoulders of hers.

"Thank you so much!" She adjusted the handles of the bags she still held. "I bought more than I intended to and got overloaded." She puffed out a breath. "Obviously."

I was mesmerized by the sparkle in her deep-blue eyes, and the bloom of rosy colour on her cheeks and neck, where her pulse fluttered like a moth's wing. Her heightened colour and fast breathing resembled a woman sexually aroused, and my dick got the wrong message, responding with an eager twitch. Being close to her, catching her sweet floral scent and hint of womanly musk, scrambled my normally disciplined brain.

Moving to add the fallen books into one of the intact bags, I noticed a Grade Four math workbook. Chuckling, I held it up and said, "I remember this fondly," and tucked it in.

"Oh, my God, yes." She laughed breathily, but I picked up a hint of strain in her voice. "Fractions and ratios and problems. Will hates them with a passion." As if she hadn't meant to reveal that, her colour intensified and her gaze darted bashfully to the ground amid rapid blinking.

The son of the math whiz hated math? "Where are you headed?"

"I was planning to drop my shopping behind the counter at Quinn's so I could get my car and pick them up."

"Do you want to have a coffee or something?"

"I'm sorry. I don't have time. I promised my mom I'd return her car so she can go out to a meeting, and I'm running late."

"Let me help you get all this straight to your car then," I said. "Save you the trip."

"Oh, no, no. No need! I'm fine," she insisted. "I'm sure you're busy."

I smirked and shook my head. "Jeannie. Let me help. It's nothing." I took her bags from her hands. "I was only going to the café to see if anyone was around, anyway." To see if she was around, to be exact.

Conceding, she flexed her hands, and I noted the red lines cutting into her palms from the bag handles. I tilted my head. "Lead the way."

She headed down Store Street, her strides long and frenetic. "I'm parked in the big Union Ironworks lot."

"What is all this stuff?" I peeked into the bags that gaped. "Was there a sale at Staples?"

"Exactly!" She took a beeline towards an older model silver Honda Accord while rummaging in her purse for the keys. "I had this huge list of school supplies for Will that I downloaded, but when I got there, everything was on sale, so I went a bit mad." The car beeped, and she popped open the trunk. As I dropped all the bags in, she babbled on. "I didn't think I could aff— I mean, I wasn't planning on getting a new laptop for either Will or me, though we both desperately need them. But there was such a great two-for-one deal I couldn't resist."

"I see. That's why you have so many heavy bags."

"That and a ton of notebooks, pens, highlighters, sticky notes, binders, you name it. Since I'm starting school too, I got some of everything."

I closed the trunk. "Did they set up the laptops for you?"

She paused with her hand on the driver's door, her face blank. "No?"

I smiled. "It's fairly easy if you've done it recently. Have you?" I knew better than to mansplain.

"Well. Um. Not really. I haven't had a new computer… ever, really. Money's been tight, so we had to make do with hand-me-downs from friends."

I had to work to keep the smile on my face, but it felt tight. Why was she alone? Where was her kid's fucking dad and why wasn't he helping with expenses? And her parents? They had enough money, I thought.

"Your parents didn't…" I shrugged.

Her lips gathered into a sweet-and-sour little purse of disapproval as her chin lifted stubbornly. "No. I don't take money from them. It's bad enough we're living there. I already spent…anyway, no. I pay my own way. And

Will's." She nodded and turned to slide into the driver's seat.

Skipping over the money issue, I offered, "I'd be happy to set them up for you, if you like. The laptops."

"Um…" She glanced at the dash clock, colour rising in her cheeks again. "I…uh, don't know. I can't think. I have to run. I've got to get this car back and then pick up Will, and I'm so, so late already."

"Where is he? How are you getting him if you're dropping the car?"

"Um. A fast walk, I guess?"

Her reply broke my heart.

She twisted to set her purse on the passenger seat and turned the key in the ignition.

I grabbed the top of her door to stop her from racing off. "I'll give you a lift. Wherever. Then you'll get there in time. I'll meet you at your house."

"Uh…" I could see the distressed thoughts whirling in her head. She didn't want to keep her kid waiting, but didn't want to impose. "I…well…okay. It's on…"

"I remember where you live." I smiled. "I'll be right behind you." I gently closed her door.

Fifteen minutes later, I pulled up in front of Jeannie's parents' house in my rental truck and stepped out. She was at the trunk, fighting with the bags again. I nudged her aside and lifted the whole lot into my arms.

She led the way to the front door, opening it so I could step in and set everything down.

"There you are, sweetheart," her mother swept into the front hall. "I was frantic you wouldn't make it home in time. Oh, my!" she exclaimed, stopping in her tracks when she saw me.

Jeannie handed the keys to her mother. "You remember Peter Corbin, Mom? From school?"

I stepped closer to the wall to make room space for them.

Her mother's face clouded in confusion as her gaze swept over me. "Um. I… Of course! Hello, Peter. Nice to see you again. How are you?"

"Very well, Mrs. van Bellen, thank you. How have you been?"

"Excellent, thank you." She grabbed some overstuffed cloth bags and scurried out the door, waving a hand over her shoulder. "I'm so sorry I can't stop to chat. I'm late for my shift at the garden centre."

I smiled, watching her go. In about half an hour, the penny would drop, and she'd remember that I'd supposedly died ten years ago. And probably quiz Jeannie tonight.

Standing on the front stoop, we watched her mother pull away from the curb.

"Thank you," Jeannie said, with a sigh of relief.

"No problem. Let's head out, eh?"

She locked and closed the door behind us, and I led her to my truck.

On the way to the elementary school a few blocks away, I said, "You know, math was always my favourite subject."

"Mine too, of course." She blushed, as if embarrassed to recall that she was the smartest math student in the school, celebrated for her high grades.

I risked a little more. "Not just because I loved math. I mean, I did. I went on to study engineering. But because you were there. We had a good time."

She blushed and stuttered. "W-we did. I-I remember." She paused, smiling, and changed the subject. "How's your mom doing? And your little sister?"

"Good. I'm heading to Vancouver to see them this weekend. Bess is starting university this year."

"Oh! She's eighteen, already. Wow. Starting university.

Just like I'm doing at twenty-eight." She laughed nervously, her face flushing pink again.

"Yeah." I hesitated. I could see she felt bad about that. "Life throws some curveballs at you, hey?"

She smiled gratefully, nodding with a little sound, almost like a whimper of agreement.

At the school, I pulled into the drop-off and got out, circling the car to open her door. She was half out by the time I got there, and our hands clashed on the edge of the door. The touch thrilled me, and I held still for a second, relishing the feel of her soft hand, my blood thrumming.

Again, she twitched and pulled away, blushing, avoiding my face.

"Thank you so much. I appreciate your help, Peter."

She forgot my nickname again, and the way she reverted so easily to high school made something warm bloom in my chest. I licked my lips, my mouth suddenly dry, my thoughts a bit scattered.

"I'll wait for you. Drive you two home."

"No!" She looked at me finally, the expression in her blue eyes genuinely distressed. "You've done enough. Thank you, but. Um. We have somewhere we have to go." She cast her hand out in an arc. "Somewhere near…here."

I didn't believe her for a minute, but I knew not to push. I was already on cloud nine for having spent the past few minutes in her company. I wasn't mistaken. It was still there. The feeling. Though my circumstances made me undesirable in high school, at least for someone like Jeannie, there'd been chemistry between us.

I nodded. "We really ought to chat. One-on-one, you know. About stuff. About…grad night?"

That sent her into a tailspin. "Mhm. Yup. Definitely. You're right. We ought to do that. Soon. But I'm super busy this week."

"O-kay. Maybe I can help with those new laptops later in the week. I'm sure your son will want to try his out."

"Well. We'll see. There's just a lot, you know. New town. New school. Got to head out to the university to meet with my advisor and…"

I chuckled as she edged towards the school door, and I hoped she didn't trip over a crack in the sidewalk.

"I'd love to meet your kid some time. Bring him by the café. Introduce him to everyone."

"Right, maybe, yes. I'll do that. Oh, look at the time. I have to pick him up right now. Thanks for your help. Phoenix. Bye. Bye. Goodbye."

She was so flustered and shy; it was adorable. If she felt even half the electricity I did when I was near her, her insides were sparking. And I got it. Everything was new for her. She felt awkward returning after all that had happened. She had a lot to do and her son to think about. Somehow, I had to win her trust and get her to relax. I just wished I had the time to court her properly. Slowly and gently, the way she deserved.

But I didn't.

Chapter 4

Phoenix

"Mom! You'll smother him!" cried Bess.

I laughed, my cheeks pushing against Mom's palms, which framed my face in a soft vice-like clamp.

Mom made a series of unintelligible smooshy lovey noises and planted five or six more sloppy kisses all over my face. "I'm just so happy to see him, Bessie. I can't help myself."

I gently peeled her off of me. "Okay. Enough. I'm happy to see you, too." I lifted my mug as a shield against any more overt displays of affection.

She hugged my head and sat down, and I ran a hand through my hair to fix whatever she'd done to it.

We three sat around my mom's kitchen table drinking tea and catching up. I'd called them when I landed in Port Cam and a couple of times since, but this was my first time visiting, and I'd arrived midday in my rental truck, having caught the early ferry across the strait. It was a clear, warm summer day, and I'd spent the crossing sitting outside on the deck, soaking in the sun, the clean breeze, and absorbing the unmatched blue-green of British Columbia. Another perk of being based out here, instead of the sweaty, humid middle of the country. On top of being able to see these two beautiful women more often. Or let them see me, as it happened, since they spent an inordinate amount of time just staring at me and grinning like monkeys.

"Have another piece of banana bread. I made it especially for you."

"Oh, that's very nice," Bess whined, her tone sarcastic. "It's *my* favourite too, you know. I guess I'm not special enough to inspire you to bake."

"You're just as special, baby, but I see you every day."

"All the more reason for me to live on campus. More baking when I come home." Bess lifted a fist to bump mine in triumph at her wit and I gave my head a small shake.

"That," snipped Mom, "is a closed subject."

Bess flopped her arms and head down on the table in a melodramatic faint, her long black hair spread in a curtain, a curly strand of it bouncing over the plate of banana bread. "Pe-ter! Tell her, puh-lease."

I chuckled. I'd missed so much of Bess' growing up, the flamboyant and outspoken young woman in front of me felt like a virtual stranger, even though she wrote long and frequent emails, venting to me every thought and experience, especially those not deemed suitable for Mom's ears or eyes. And I agreed with Bess, actually, that moving out would be a good thing. As if to compensate for leaving me behind years ago, Mom was overprotective of Bess.

"Get your hair out of the food, young lady!" Mom barked.

Bess straightened, tilted her head to one shoulder, and

cast me a plaintive silent appeal, with sad, puppy dog eyes and an exaggerated pout. *Help me*, she mouthed.

"Okay. Seriously. Why can't she live in residence? It's perfectly safe."

"It's already settled, Peter."

"Apparently not. Is it about money? You know I'll cover all of Bess' expenses."

"I *want* her to live at home with me." Mom's dark eyes were like green-black lasers drilling into my face, dramatic with long, black lashes that I doubted were natural. I guess maybe that's where I got my eyes, and why my subordinates cowered when I gave them my famous death stare. Except without mascara.

"Let's pick this up again later," I said, standing to dispel the mounting tension. I didn't want to spend my first visit in a war zone. "I want to hear about your job, Mom, and talk about your math grades, Bess." I gave her a hint of stink eye. "And also go over your course registration and extracurriculars. Then I'm taking you out to a nice restaurant for dinner."

AFTER A LATE DINNER, we returned to the apartment, groaning with full bellies. I was fine with a big steak dinner, but I wasn't used to indulging in dessert, and that massive slice of cheesecake put me over the top. I could tell Mom was exhausted—and had had a little too much wine. At my urging, she agreed to turn in. But she refused to go unless Bess went first, and I sensed she wanted a few minutes alone with me.

While Bess was in her room, Mom sat with me. She held my hand between hers as if I were still twelve. Except my giant callused paw dwarfed her petite soft hands with their glossy red polish.

"Thanks for the lovely dinner, honey." She sniffled, and I bent my head to peer at her face in the dim glow of the table lamp.

"What's the matter?"

"Nothing. I'm happy you're here, that's all."

I lifted her hand to my lips and kissed it.

"Why won't you let Bess stretch her wings? She'll be better for it."

A quavering hum preceded her answer. "You were away so much I want to keep her close. Is that a crime?"

"No. I understand. But…" Parenting was strange. I wondered when it was my turn if I could make choices that were best for my child ahead of my own needs.

"I'm happy you look so strong and well."

"But?" I chuckled at her preamble.

"But. I worry about you. Why do you have to have such a dangerous job?"

"Because I'm dangerous. I'm among the most highly trained warriors in the world. My job is keeping other people safe."

"I wasn't born yesterday, Peter. I've been military family all my life."

This was true. "That's why I did my engineering degree and all the comm tech specialization. I'm too valuable to send to combat zones. They need me for my brains, not my brawn." That's how I framed it for her, anyway. She didn't need to know where or how I used my brains.

"I know what JTF 2 personnel do, Peter."

"And I'm trained for it. When there's a SNAFU, there's no one you want on your team more than me."

"I know. Okay," she conceded in a tiny voice.

It hurt that she had to bear the burden of fear. I had to remind myself that Dad was a badass too, and things didn't go so well for him.

Later, when Mom and Bess had gone to bed, I rolled out my bedding on the sofa and flipped through my phone, thinking about Jeannie, mostly. I wished I could take her and her kid out for a nice dinner, too. I wished being home with her family gave her the feeling of comfort that visiting Mom and Bess gave me, but I had my doubts. She was too on edge. Too defensive.

I thumbed a text.

HEY, *Jeannie. Phoenix here. How's your weekend going?*

BUT I HELD off pressing send.

I wanted to ask her out on a proper date, but my gut told me it was too soon. Too fast. I had to suss out her reasons for being so shy. Was she really just busy and stressed out? Or did she feel awkward about dating when she had a child? Was the father still in the picture in some way? Maybe she felt self-conscious about my interest in her because of Zach?

He seemed completely disinterested, but maybe Jeannie still held a candle for her old high school boyfriend. I frowned. It didn't seem like it, but women could play it pretty cool when they had a crush. Hm.

Too many possibilities; not enough data.

I deleted the last bits of my text and instead volleyed something super simple.

. . .

HEY, *Jeannie.*

SHE WAS PROBABLY SLEEPING. Though it wasn't that late. A minute or two later, I finally saw blinking dots. But still, no response.

ANY CHANCE *we could connect next week? I have a question for you.*

THERE. No pressure. Just a friend with a question. Or ten. The fact that my main question was, will you have dinner with me, well, I'd figure out how to spin that later.

And then Bess snuck out of her room as I knew she would.

"Who are you texting?" whispered Bess, tiptoeing out to curl up next to me on my bedding, tucking her bare feet under my quilt, and leaning against my side.

If a smile can start in your belly and radiate out to your fingers and toes, that's what I felt.

Well, I was not going to talk about my fledgling love life with my kid sister. "Hey, kiddo."

"Whatever Mom told you, it's not true."

"She didn't say anything about you. She trusts you. Why, what have you done?"

"It's not that. It's her. She has a boyfriend."

"What?"

"She feels guilty about it. And I think she wants to keep me at home, so she has an excuse to keep him at arm's length."

"Wow. I did not expect to hear that. Is it serious?"

She nodded. "She's trying to keep their relationship

from progressing to the next step. But it's happening, anyway. I think she's in love with him. He's definitely besotted with her."

I chuckled. Besotted. My baby sister was definitely destined to be an English major. No science in her head. "Have you met him? What's he like?"

"He's the principal at my high school. Mr. Barnes took the position during my last year there."

"Huh." This came as a surprise. I was half expecting Mom to tell me she was worried about Bess dating boys, and keeping her home to keep her out of trouble.

"They try to play it cool, like it's casual dating. But they're so incredibly bad at hiding their feelings. I've seen him sneaking out in the wee hours a couple of times."

"How does that make you feel?"

"It's cute actually, and I'm cool with it. She needs this, Peter. She's sacrificed so much for me. I want her to have this."

I caressed her hair. "You've really grown up, Bessie. I'm proud of you. And I'm so happy you're going to university. I want you to have everything you dream of."

"And I can. Thanks to you."

I gave her a side hug, pulling her tight to me.

Then she added, half-jokingly, "And you know, I wouldn't mind so much having a little independence and privacy, for fuck's sake."

"Watch your mouth, miss."

She rebutted, sarcastically, "Who do you think you are anyway, my father?"

We laughed. It was an old joke.

"Okay. Leave it with me. I'll see what I can do about residence." The independence was, of course, something my little sister would have to achieve on her own.

Jeannie

"They're mostly charged up now," I said, checking my new laptop screen.

Turning from his old laptop, Will said, "This guy Nick on YouTube says not to click on the *continue with limited setup* button because you'll have to enter a license agreement or something."

I had no idea. "What's this for?" I held up an unfamiliar cable from the box.

Will shrugged, pulling his mouth down. "Peripherals? Do we have peripherals?"

"Um. Well, we ditched our old printer in Kingston. So…not yet?" I grimaced, wishing this was a skill I'd had an opportunity to acquire. I had learned to do so many things, to survive independently. I could model maternity wear, do basic plumbing and household electrical stuff, negotiate rental contracts, barter and trade for all kinds of services, manage finances, of course, do first aid, sew on buttons and hem pants, make grilled cheese sandwiches, and stay fit on a budget. But computers… Other than using spreadsheets and accounting software, not so much.

Extra money for brand new computers was never available, so the second-hand ones we'd always used came ready to go, pretty much. Or at least we'd made do with whatever we found.

"The wi-fi part is easy," Will mumbled, clicking keys on his laptop. "What about antivirus malware? It says here, turn on encryption for your system drive. What's that?"

I sighed. "No idea, honey. I'm afraid we're in over our heads here."

My dream was to have enough money not to have to worry about such things, and I hoped once I had my MBA I'd be able to earn a decent salary so I could provide Will with all the things he needed. My guilt at his being deprived of what his peers had, because of choices I'd made, rode me like a cattle prod. I was tough, but I was also tired.

If I hadn't gotten pregnant at eighteen and dropped out of university, I'd be there by now, instead of dreading dinner with my social-climbing brother and elitist sister-in-law.

But then I wouldn't have my lovely Will. I watched him scowling over the online installation guide, his blunt little boy fingers hovering over the keyboard, and smiled.

Starting with a home of our own. My parents were quickly driving us both crazy, and it was still August. I only hoped when we were both busy with the school year, things would settle down. At least we'd both have the excuse to stay in our rooms studying.

"Ever heard of bloatware? It says remove it."

I grunted softly. Maybe some computer tech help, then a home.

Which reminded me to check my phone again. I was disoriented when Phoenix texted me last night, after not hearing from him since our encounter Monday. He'd been so attentive, and keen to help me, I'd half expected him to call me before now. Against my better judgement, I felt a little abandoned. I'd caught myself looking forward to seeing him again. Or being seen by him.

I'd been in the middle of saying goodnight to Will and getting him settled for the night when Phoenix's text arrived. By the time I'd thought to send a reply, an hour or so later, a second text had come in that unsettled me.

Instead of repeating his offer to help set up our new

computers, or ask me out, Phoenix had, somewhat crypti-cally, said he wanted to meet to ask me a question. That had sent me into a tailspin of panic. What could he possibly want to ask me? Was he just interested in me, or…? Was it about Will? Did he suspect the truth? Earlier, he'd said we should talk about grad night.

My stomach roiled. I wasn't ready to face this. I hadn't even begun to sort out my own feelings about Phoenix in relation to Will and our life. How could I answer his ques-tions? I needed more time.

I glanced at the time on my laptop.

"They'll be here soon. I'd better get to the kitchen to help Grandma."

Will flopped on his bed, sulking like only a nine-year-old can.

"You'll be fine." I squeezed his leg. "Lucas is young and innocent. Be patient with him. Try to remember what you were like when you were six."

"I know."

"Just be the kind, mature, and wise older cousin and you'll be fine." I smiled at him. "And Logan is nearly your age, so he should be fun to hang out with. Grandma says he's super smart. Try to find common interests, and that'll help you bond. Okay?"

"I highly doubt that, Mom. He's eight. It's his literal job to be annoying."

I choked on a laugh as I left his room.

Naturally, since we were living here, Mom expected me to help prepare and serve dinner. I didn't mind that. We lived rent-free. But Mom was distracted, swanning around the living room, telling my sister-in-law Stephanie some story, and leaving me to pull together the meal she'd planned. If there's one thing I hadn't learned how to do in the past ten years, it was entertain. Anything more than two servings or two dishes overwhelmed me.

I stepped into the living room. "Mom, could you help please?"

"Oh, oh, oh, of course, dear. Just drain the potatoes. I'll be right there." But it took her another ten minutes to sail in and help pull dinner together while I'd been fretting about burning the roast and not timing the veggies right while dicing the salad.

Not surprisingly, the stylish Stephanie didn't offer to help. Nor did Brandon or Dad, who sat in the corner drinking whiskey while discussing the economy.

Once at the table, snobby Stephanie humble-bragged about Logan's grades and his accomplishments at their chichi private school. That he won a spelling bee and debate competition and was now on the team representing the school at the regional competition. I kept a smile on my face and interspersed sounds of being impressed with mouthfuls of food.

They'd done incredibly well the last few years with the booming real-estate market, but you'd think they'd be sensitive to my situation.

Brandon blustered in his know-it-all tone, "I was saying to Steph on the way here, you really should consider enrolling Will at West Bay College with our boys. He'll get a far better start in life with a private school education."

I bristled. As if we had choices. And way to make my kid feel crappy, bro. "Will's new school has an excellent academic reputation. We'll be perfectly happy there."

"Yes, but who are his classmates?" Brandon pressed on, oblivious to my situation. "Who will he graduate with? What can they do for him?"

"That's a long way off. Will's not even in middle school

yet. I'm sure he will be just fine no matter where he goes." I sent him a supportive smile across the table.

I didn't even know how I felt about private school. Brandon and I had both graduated from the regular old Port Cam high. I'd been top of the class and got all kinds of scholarships for first year. But that didn't stop him from going on and on about private school's superior qualities. I think it was Stephanie who changed him. I don't know. We were never that close, really. Even before Bonnie died, when he and I were closer in age, he'd still been the eldest and the only son. He'd lived in a world of his own. Or he'd lived in a world where he was boss, anyway.

"Jeannie!"

I looked up. Mom was glaring at me with her pinched face of disapproval.

"Yes?"

"You forgot the gravy boat. Run and get it."

"Yeah, Dreamy Jeannie. You forgot the gravy boat," taunted Brandon, and I glared at him on my way to the kitchen. What a tool. I returned and passed the gravy to Mom.

Suddenly, Will squeaked and jumped in his chair, like he'd been shocked, drawing everyone's attention, and not a few frowns from the family. I sent a questioning glance his way—and got bugged eyes in response, telling me nothing.

I reached for my wine glass—and discretely shaped my hand into an American Sign Language K, M, and then W, as a reminder. Whatever was going on, Will could handle it. I reassured myself he was kind, mature, and wise, for a nine-year-old. The fact that he'd learned ASL so he could talk to his friend Dak was a perfect example. I was proud of him.

At my reminder, his gaze flew to the ceiling, fluttered, and then his eyes closed on a sigh. He'd get through this.

His cousin Lucas was as goofy a kid as could be, and hyperactive in a way that I knew would irritate my quiet, pensive boy. I saw Will wince every time Lucas zoomed his airplanes in wide arcs wherever he went, making me fear for Mom's vases of dried flower arrangements and Will's peace of mind. But Logan sat quietly through dinner, oblivious to his parents' bragging, and seemed like a nice kid. Smart and serious, a good student, and well-behaved, at least that I could see.

After dinner, Mom said, "Why don't you three boys go up to Will's room to play."

Will's look of panic told me something, but I didn't know what.

"I'd rather stay here," he said. "I like listening to adult conversation."

"Nonsense," snipped Stephanie. "We don't want children underfoot when we're trying to relax after a meal. Go on up."

At Will's wide eyes and mouthed *computers,* I explained, "We just unpacked all the school supplies for the year, and they're all over his room. Go up first and tidy a little, honey." I jerked my chin to send him up to tuck our new purchases safely away.

He shot up the stairs, slipping on the hall floor in his socks and crashing into the old umbrella stand with a bang. I flinched. I had to speak to Mom about her waxing. One of these days, she or Dad would fall and break a hip.

"Just give him a couple of minutes, boys."

Poor Will. He hated anyone in his room, touching his stuff. Except Dak. I moved through the remainder of the evening distracted by fantasies of the nice apartment we'd move into, soon. All by ourselves. I tried not to be resentful of Mom and Dad. They were who they were, and I knew what Will and I were getting into. My plans wouldn't be possible without their help, and I had to remind myself of that.

We only had to put up with feeling like a pathetic charity case for a year, maybe two. I could tolerate it, knowing I had not yet made up for my mistakes. But it broke my heart that Will had to suffer with me. The day I was once again in control of my life couldn't come soon enough.

Chapter 5

Jeannie

"I AM NOT JUMPY," I insisted to Quinn, who sat across the wide low coffee table from me.

"Are so." She smirked.

"He's just helping out with these." I gestured to the large bag I'd carried our two new laptops in.

"Sure. And he's not hot on you," she deadpanned. "At all."

I swallowed. "Oh, no, no, no, no." I shook my head. "You think?"

"He's not even trying to be subtle about it. Come on, Jeannie. Why are you playing dumb?"

"I'm not playing dumb," I said, sobering. "Only I–"

My heart rate ratcheted through the roof the moment Phoenix pushed through the café's door. I thought I was ready, but suddenly, the moment I set eyes on his gorgeous brick wall of a chest and sequoia-like thighs, my throat thickened, as if my heart had actually jumped up and got jammed in there. He wore a simple navy-blue t-shirt, and my blood heated at the way it stretched across his broad sculpted chest and huge biceps, my mouth going dry and my brain exiting the room.

Why was I so fascinated with the ink that decorated his arms and neck? My mind circled round and round the thought—*I want to see more.*

The silent look—with a rakish lift of her sandy brow, narrowed eyes, and a teasing side-grin—that Quinn gave me was… *So that's how it is?*

In reply, I replied with innocent bug eyes implying…*I don't know what you mean!* But the skeptical curl of her mouth belied the truth of that.

Of course, I knew what she meant. I just didn't know what I was going to do about it. My attraction to Phoenix made me feel stupid, and the thought of having 'the talk' with him had mushroomed into an impossible feat. Maybe with some exposure, the novelty of the new-and-improved Phoenix would wear off. Maybe in time I wouldn't dissolve into a melted puddle whenever I saw his broad shoulders and strong arms, or become a speech-impaired imbecile when he looked at me with those deep sea-green eyes that saw right into my soul. I wished my feelings were just anxiety about what his existence meant. But that would be a lie.

My body was telling me something different. *I want him.*

Oh, my God. I can't believe I thought those words. My poor sex-starved body! My face exploded with heat that I knew was as obvious to him as it was to Quinn.

My heritage didn't disguise my emotions, blasting them onto my pale cheeks like a neon marquee. Look at me! I'm embarrassed. I'm turned on. Weirdly, these two things looked similar from the outside. I think. Anyway, at the moment I was both, big time.

Phoenix

I had a plan. One step at a time. After Jeannie's no-reply on the weekend, I gave her a few more days to wonder what happened to me. Maybe even start to miss me. Then I texted.

ME: *Bring your new laptops to the café today. I'll set them up while you visit with Quinn.*

I'D LEFT Mom and Bess without resolving their dispute. If Mom had a new man in her life, I could kind of understand why she was scared. It was already upsetting enough that Bess was off to university. Too many changes, too many losses. It was hard for some people. And Mom had suffered plenty of losses in her life.

She and Dad had been happy together, once. I truly believed he'd been the love of her life. And the fact that he'd been away a lot while she was raising me was difficult enough. But when he'd returned, a broken man, and she had to continue living with him, nursing him, and praying that the man she married returned to his husk of a body, it had killed something in her.

I don't know if she'd dated at all in the past seventeen years, but I kind of thought not. Or not seriously. With everything that had gone down with Dad, and me mostly away, she'd hunkered down to raise Bess and lick her wounds.

If she'd finally opened up enough to actually fall for someone new? Well, I wanted to help that happen. She deserved to be happy. But I had to tread carefully. Mom was a determined, independent woman. She wouldn't tolerate me meddling in her life. Although I wondered if she felt I'd be offended if she dated someone other than Dad. Somehow, I had to persuade her to loosen her grip on Bess.

Finally, a reply came.

JEANNIE: *Okay. I checked with Quinn and we can do that this afternoon. Does two-ish work for you?*

YES!

I shot off a quick confirmation.

Jeannie sat with Quinn on the big sofa when I approached the café just before two o'clock. I scanned the mostly empty café as I entered, frowning. Quinn needed to drum up more business. This couldn't be good.

It was a great place, though. She'd done an amazing job setting up a funky modern vibe in the old heritage building. I liked it here. It was very inviting and hip. And the coffee was excellent. My eye caught on the virtually barren display case. Could do with more food choices, though. Maybe that'd attract more customers in the afternoons. I'd be ready for a snack by the time I was done here.

"Hi, Phoenix," Quinn called.

"Ladies."

Jeannie shot to her feet as I lifted my hand and strode towards them. The closer I got, the more flustered she got, until she was staring at my shoes as I came to a stop in front of her, her face flaring.

"Hi, Jeannie," I said. "Did you bring your laptops?"

"Mhm. Yup," she replied in a squeaky voice. She handed them over in their brand new boxes. " I hope we didn't screw anything up. The literature is still in there. We couldn't make sense of it."

I chuckled. "It's okay. I won't need it."

Jeannie nodded, her gaze swimming over my body, her face sixteen shades of red, with hot splotches on her neck and breastbone. *What are you thinking about, you sweet, dirty girl?* I didn't believe it was the computers.

Quinn said, "It's quiet now. You can work at this long table. Do you want a coffee or something?"

Suppressing the wide grin that pulled at my cheeks, I said, "A bottle of water would be good. Thanks."

I pulled the computer boxes out of the carry bags and opened them. Pretty basic equipment. I guess she really was on a tight budget. "It won't take me long. Just relax. Go back to whatever you were doing." I reached out and touched Jeannie's arm, but withdrew my hand when she flinched and sucked in a breath.

"I was wondering if you'd let me buy you dinner?"

Her surprised gaze shot to mine, wide, her pupils dilated, and I held it for a moment, trying to reassure her, searching deeply for some reason she was so skittish around me. "Oh. I…um…I don't know. When?"

I shrugged. "Anytime. You let me know what works for you."

"Oh. Well… I'll have to see if…um…I…" She averted her gaze, licking her lips, and her right hand fluttered and rubbed the elbow that I'd touched as if I'd burned her.

"Just think about it."

"Yeah."

"Actually, come with me upstairs for a minute, Jeannie," Quinn said as she stepped away. "I have something for Will."

"Mhm. Okay," Jeannie mumbled, tearing her gaze from me, following Quinn like a lamb.

I wondered if she'd return with a no or a yes. She sent off confusing signals. She obviously liked me. But something curbed her interest.

I was curious about her kid. Quinn seemed to have met him previously, but Jeannie had never brought him to the café, to my knowledge. And the day I'd given her a lift, she'd made a point of keeping him away from me. I guess she was just a careful, protective mother. I could appreciate that. She seemed to think I was scary, so who knew what she was thinking? I tilted my head, scanning her features for clues. I'd have to work to reassure her that my intentions were honourable.

Removing the computers from their packaging, I kept my smirking face averted. Quinn and Jeannie were so obviously going to talk about me.

After they left, I got to work. I set up the laptops, almost without thought. This was basic for me, allowing my mind to ponder.

Jeannie seemed so shy now. Was it just around me, or had life knocked the wind from her sails?

I remembered how she was in high school. Or how she'd seemed to me. Completely different. She'd been a star student, pretty and popular, dating the top athlete. She was part of a circle of cool friends. To my eyes, Jeannie had been the bomb. Everything that I dreamt of in my sad, lonely world. Everything that was out of reach.

Not surprisingly, I'd been extremely unpopular. A virtual exile at school. In order to survive, I'd assumed a tough appearance and attitude. I'd had to. After Mom and Bess moved out—and before that, really, which was partly why Mom left—the kind of people who came to hang out with Dad at the trailer were… Well, at twelve, they'd scared the shit out of me, too.

It didn't take much bullying, harassing, and kicking

around to figure out I had to fight or run away. Well, that's when I really came to understand fight or flight. I was determined to stay, so I had to fight to survive the consequences of my choice.

Dad's acquaintances—I was loath to call them friends, he wasn't capable of friendship anymore—were either dealers, thugs, or other seriously damaged drug users. Dirt poor, tough, angry guys that he either attracted or felt some affinity to. I'll never know.

But they all thought the skinny kid who cooked and cleaned and dragged his passed-out dad's ass to bed every night was hilarious, I guess. And I didn't get much mileage when I tried to intervene on his behalf when it was obvious they were ripping off the psychotic old wreck. I'm sure he would have sent me to the liquor store if I looked halfway old enough. Or maybe he had just enough pride left that he hadn't.

Not that I particularly wanted him to get a better deal on his drugs or liquor. But funds were tight. His military pension was all we had to live on, never enough. And if he foolishly squandered it, or lost it, there'd be nothing to pay the rent or buy food. So I learned to fight to protect our home, Dad, and myself.

And eventually, when I'd toughened up and learned more about the world, and grown an inch or two, I'd bought and sold too. Just weed. After seeing what it did to Dad, I would never deal in harder stuff. But dealing weed gave me enough cash of my own that I felt safer. And still, Dad or his cronies could easily catch me off-guard and steal from me before I hid it. So I learned to fight, too. Inevitably, other tough kids invited me to join their gangs, but I managed to exist on the periphery, minding my own business. Staying, for the most part, out of trouble, despite appearances.

Anyway, Jeannie had been way, way out of my league. But I was so drawn to her. From afar, I'd craved her sweetness. Her innocence was like a balm to my bitter, cynical little heart. Yet despite my tough-guy act, I was shy to the point of paralysis whenever I was near her. I daren't approach—and could hardly speak.

Honours math class had been a gift from heaven.

I'd always been good at math. I loved it. The clean, clear logic. The rules that could not be broken. The order and linearity. So opposite to my life, where everything was broken and upside down. So when my grades landed me in Honours Math, alongside the brilliant Jeannie, I stuck myself to her side like shit to a blanket. She was confident, kind, and gentle, and eventually, probably because she took pity on me and my silent worship, she spoke to me. Gradually, over the next three years, we grew comfortable with each other—and shared stories.

So that's how I learned that under her glossy veneer of beauty, she too was weighed down by a broken heart. That part of why she tried to be so good at school, and everything else, was to make up for the loss of her little sister, and the sense of responsibility and guilt she felt over that.

That's how she learned that under the gritty armour of toughness that I wore, lived a soft, troubled, broken heart, too. So, against the odds, we'd become genuine friends. Or math friends, anyway. Math class became a bright orb of joy in my otherwise joyless and insecure world. And I could tell she really liked me too and was happy to spend that little bubble of time with me. Even though that friendship never crossed the threshold into our everyday worlds.

Her mom used to teach elementary school and then sometimes subbed at our middle school. Even when I was sixteen, I knew hanging out with me wouldn't go over well with Mrs. van Bellen. She'd been polite when we'd met at the house last week. Probably mostly shocked that I still existed or didn't even remember who I was. I wonder if her old perceptions would percolate into her consciousness and pose a problem.

Maybe it was stupid to carry a torch for a girl for so long. But even now, when I'd lived through so much, and had more than my fair share of life experiences, I still felt warm all over at just the thought of Jeannie van Bellen. But the way she looked at me now? With obvious admiration and attraction? Well, no lie, that did give me some hope.

Now, I'd do anything to return to that place where Jeannie and I could be alone in that intimate bubble of understanding. But she was so reserved. So nervous. The tables had turned, and now it was my turn to be the confident, kind, and patient one—and draw her out of her shell. And just in case grad night was the issue, addressing those events had to come first.

Jeannie

Ugh! *I'm so hopeless!* Clearly, I was being punished for past sins.

Somehow, I had to get up the courage to meet privately with him, and have 'the talk.' But every time I came near him, I dissolved into a quivering puddle of goo, half nerves, half tingles all over at his intimidating and spectacularly sexy self.

All I could do was nod like a bobblehead doll at his overwhelming presence. So confident. So big, brawny, *and* brainy. So quietly intense. Staring at me with those eyes. At least the eyes were familiar, reminding me of the kind, lonely boy in high school, who stared at me with such longing and poignancy. *Stand down ovaries.* How would I get past all of that and broach the subject of our shared, if fleeting, past? Not to mention our complicated, interconnected future, whether he chose to stay or flee.

Once upstairs, I flopped onto Quinn's beat-up old apartment sofa like a rag doll with a huge sigh, groaning in disgust.

"Drink?"

"Tea?"

"M'kay." She shuffled around in her little kitchen, putting the kettle on and getting out mugs, and I noted how tired she seemed. Her shoulders were rounded, and she dragged her steps, her limp more pronounced than usual.

"You want help?"

"Nope. You sit."

I knew what it was like to be that tired. I was glad she could afford part-time help at least, so she could step away from the café now and then. She seemed stressed, and I hoped her business venture wasn't too much for her. She'd confided in me that she was just barely covering her mortgage and bills, and then only with Parker's rent to help.

Once she'd brought over two steaming mugs of our favourite lemon herbal tea, I sat up to make a space for her next to me.

"I'm so happy we can be together like this." Before picking up my mug, I took her hand in mine and squeezed it, giving her shoulder a nudge. "Long distance just didn't cut it."

She squeezed back, nodding. "Shut up, would you? You'll make me tear up." She released my hand and hid behind a big slurp of hot tea and a loud "*Aaahhh.*"

I laughed and picked up my own tea, blowing on the hot surface. In high school, this had been our favourite girl-time drink, when we did homework, watched movies, or had sleepovers. Neither Quinn nor I had ever been big on liquor, though we'd sometimes join our friends by having a beer or something stronger.

I guess that's why I'd completely lost it on grad night. My tolerance was so low. The consequences of that reckless behaviour I was still paying for, which was one reason I still drank very moderately. Being out of control was something I couldn't afford as a single mother and didn't enjoy, anyway. I had too much responsibility—and too much work to accomplish to get to where I wanted to be—for that kind of thing.

"What does your café need, Quinn? Is there anything I can do to help? Are you on top of your books and such?"

"I think so," she said, gazing out the window that over-looked the bay beyond. "That's not a problem, though you can certainly look them over and see if there's somewhere to cut costs. And check over my tax filing. But really, it's just start-up growing pains. I'm really hoping the exposure I get with my pop-up café at the Faire draws more new customers in."

"I think your location is amazing. I'm kind of surprised you don't get more curious walk-ins."

She shrugged. "People need a reason to deviate from their routines."

"Maybe a stronger online presence. Some kind of catchy branding. Have you talked to Deanna?"

"A little. It's only that I'm not good at that stuff, and I can't afford to pay someone to do it."

"She'd comp you while you get established, I'm sure."

"She would. But I don't like to impose. She has her own business to run, and she's been supporting Julian a lot this year."

"What about more focus on your water-view patio? It

doesn't seem well used yet. How can you lure customers in to enjoy that?"

She squinted out the window, pensive. "I guess photos would be good. But I need money to make the improvements I want, and I'm not there yet either. It takes money to make money. That's why my food menu is so limited."

"Some kind of…event? Music? A themed thing?"

"I'll see. First the Faire. Maybe that'll kick start business."

I nodded, wondering if I could spare the time to help her with Instagram. It wasn't really my thing either. In fact, I'd specialized in stealth privacy these last ten years.

"I could bake cookies," I offered.

She laughed. "Right. I don't think so, Jeannie."

I wished there was more I could do. "Well, I'll work at the Faire, anyway. You'll need extra servers, won't you?"

She pulled in her lips and nodded. "That would be nice. Thanks. And it'll be fun to hang out together in the park for a few days, with everyone there."

"It will. I'm looking forward to it. I've been so busy getting us ready for September I haven't really had a summer holiday."

"Mmm." She slumped into the sofa. "I can't remember the last time I had a holiday."

"Once we all get settled, we should plan a group trip. Camping or something like we used to. Maybe next year."

"That would be fun. This summer's going by too fast, what with the reunion, and all the Faire planning going on."

We sat in silence for a few minutes, just enjoying our tea and each other's company. Finally, Quinn said. "I wonder how your boyfriend's making out with the computers?"

"Quinn! He's not my boyfriend." What was it with everyone and their assumptions?

"He sure wants to be," she teased.

"Oh, no. No, no, no."

"This is a good thing! I mean, you both return to Port Cam, and there's insta-chemistry. It's rolling off of you both like steam off of hot pavement."

"Oh, no, no. How could that be a good thing?"

"You're both available, and he's sweet, hot, smart, and sex-on-a-freaking-pogo-stick, yet you're avoiding him." Quinn nodded enthusiastically.

And I nodded along. So far, she was correct.

"He's obviously very into you."

"Is he though?" I wondered why. Did he have a hidden agenda? Was he as sweet as he seemed? Hot, I couldn't argue with. So hot he could have any woman he wanted. So why me?

"Oh, yes. I'm pretty sure of that." She said this coyly while fluttering her eyelashes thoughtfully. "I'm thinking you and he knew each other even better than you let on. He's obviously carried a torch."

My heart lurched at her words. "Well. I couldn't even think about…that."

"Why not?" Quinn sighed, incredulous, tucking her chin.

I swallowed thickly, my gaze burrowing into the freckled face of my bestie. "Well. So many reasons." I cleared my throat and flipped out a hand, counting them on my fingers. "We're just settling into a new home. I'm super, super busy getting ready for the school year. Will and I are both starting new schools and have to focus on that. Phoenix is very…large."

She laughed. "I'm not convinced."

I stuck out my thumb, counting number five in my list of reasons. "And he's… He's in the…military and… Um… Probably won't be here long? And… Uh…" I tapered off, silenced by the steady, penetrating look Quinn levelled at me. "He could die? Again?"

She shook her head. After a long moment of silence, she took my hand in hers and pulled up my pointer finger. "And he's Will's father, and you're terrified to tell him."

After staring into each other's eyes for several weighted breaths, my reply squeaked out like a frightened church mouse, along with the start of tears. "Yes."

"Oh, honey."

"How did you know?"

"No one knows you slept with him except you…"

I nodded.

"Him."

"Yup."

"And me."

"Mhm." I'd told her about grad night, on a long, late-night phone call when I'd first got to university and had been wracked with homesickness and loneliness for my friends.

"It's not rocket science. Just biology."

My heart skittered at being found out. "You've always known?"

"Suspected. The timing. And I know you, Jeannie. You are not the kind of girl who moves to a new town for university and hooks up with a random guy in the first month." She pulled her lips between her teeth and shook her head. "Who else would it have been?"

"Why did you never say?"

She jerked a shoulder. "I figured you'd tell me when you were ready."

"Or I had to," I said morosely.

Her voice dropped. "You've got to tell him."

"I know that," I hissed. "Why do you think I'm stressed?"

"It's forgivable that you didn't when you thought he was dead. But now you have no excuse."

"I know. I know."

"When?"

I exhaled, my nostrils flaring. "Soon," I said, determined.

"It'll be okay." She patted my arm. "He's a good guy."

I swallowed the thickness in my throat. Maybe he was. It felt like such a huge risk. Opening up my life, my private affairs, to someone who was really a stranger. The moment he knew, I'd have to answer a million questions. Nothing that was mine would be mine anymore. Or not mine, alone. And sharing wasn't something I was used to. Not to mention everyone else knowing my business.

"Remember when we were in grade eleven, and we all went to that New Kids' concert?"

"Yep." I remembered. That was in the time I considered 'before.' The time of innocence. The time of freedom from responsibility. "That was a great night."

"You were so in love with Jordan."

"Mhm. And you were gonna marry Donnie. Right? He was going to whisk you away to Paris or London."

"Yeah." She sighed. "Do you still have your Jordan doll?"

I snort-laughed. "I don't think so, no."

"Too bad. Might be worth something on Etsy."

"What's your point, Quinn?" I pressed my lips together, trying not to laugh.

"Phoenix kind of looks like Jordon, don't you think? The way his dark hair falls onto his forehead." She flicked her long chestnut hair forwards over her face. "Even better because…muscles! It's like a dream come true."

I couldn't contain the laughter by this point, and

doubled over, my face in my palms, shaking. "You're ridiculous!" I squeaked into my lap.

When we'd calmed down and dried our tears, she hugged me and said, "We have to adult now."

I bugged my eyes at her. "I'm the one with the truncated adolescence."

"You know what you have to do. And I'll be here for you, no matter what happens."

Jeannie

When Quinn and I returned downstairs to the café, Phoenix was finished, the laptops all packed up in their boxes. He sat with his massive arms crossed over his broad chest, with his eyes closed.

Disarmed of his penetrating deep gaze, he seemed softer, gentler, more innocent. In his resting face, I could for the first time see traces of the determined, vulnerable boy I had known. Was he asleep?

I stopped a few feet away and shot a questioning glance at Quinn, who shrugged.

Serenely, his eyes opened. "Let me know if you have any questions or hit any snags when you use them."

I nodded, stalling. "Were you sleeping?"

"Just a catnap."

How was that possible, sitting upright like that?

The corner of his mouth twitched in an almost smile, acknowledging my frown of confusion. "Acquired skill."

"You want a coffee now?" Quinn asked.

"No thanks. Gotta head out," he said, and I lingered, waiting for him to repeat his dinner invitation, but none came. Had he given up already? So easily? He mustn't be that interested, after all. Or maybe he just wanted to renew our friendship, and I'd gone all hormonal. What a tease. Or maybe I was being a jerk.

"Thank you so much for doing this." Determined to do my moral duty, I lifted my chin and said, "I feel like I should buy you dinner."

He barely moved, but I caught the slightest hint of surprise on his face, and in the minute tilt of his head.

"To thank you. For doing this." I nodded, grabbing the handle of the bag and hoisting it off the table.

After a beat, he replied, "That would be very nice. I'll text you about the details."

LATER, at home, Will and I sat side by side on his bed with our laptops open, poking at keys.

"Looks good?"

"Yup. He installed all the apps I need for school. Did you tell him?"

"No. He just figured it out, I guess. He's pretty smart."

"Who is this guy? Is he your boyfriend?"

"Will! No, of course not."

"Why not?"

I raised my gaze to rake over his sweet, smart-alecky face with a wide-eyed 'mom' look.

He pulled a funny face at me and returned to playing around on his new laptop. "Thanks, Mom," he murmured, and my heart swelled.

I stifled a laugh. "You're welcome, honey. I hope you have everything you need now for an excellent school year."

"I'll be fine."

"You will." Would he though? My darling, clever kid. I wish I could be sure he'd settle in and be comfortable in a new place. I dreaded the potential flare-up of anxiety that could undermine his academic success.

"So, this weekend, at the Faire?" I opened.

Will lifted his gaze, eyes narrowed. "What?"

I smiled. "I'm going to be helping out Aunty Quinn with her café as much as I can. And probably work a couple of shifts at Julian's pop-up restaurant during the busiest times."

He shrugged. "Okay."

"I know you're old enough to take care of yourself, but I need to feel comfortable knowing that you're safe. There'll be thousands of people there. It'll be crowded. And…"

His expression morphed into one of infinite exasperation and annoyance. "And what?"

"I've arranged with Uncle Brandon for the boys to spend the long weekend here. And I've spoken with Grandma about spending time at the Faire so she can be your go-to person when I'm busy."

"Grandma?" His voice rose to a squeak, and his green dappled eyes rolled up to the ceiling. "There goes my fun. Right out the window."

"No need to be melodramatic. You'll have plenty of fun. Grandma's going to be busy with all her garden people, anyway. But she'll have the car there, make sure you all eat real food, have changes of clothes, and all that stuff."

His little shoulders rolled forwards, and he let out a low, rumbly groan. "Mo-oooom."

I leaned over and planted a kiss on his dark hair.

"I'm sorry. Please be nice to Logan and Lucas. Maybe if you get to know each other better, you'll come to like them more."

He whimpered. "Doubt it."

"Be friendly! You're the oldest. You can be the leader."

"I tried that. Logan's a jerk. He only talks about Animal

Crossing and brags all the time about his rich friends at school and all the expensive stuff they have. And Lucas is an idiot. He never shuts up. Just babbles nonsense non-stop. It gives me a migraine."

I chuckled. "Please try. It won't be all the time. I'll be with you when I'm not working. We'll do stuff too."

"It's like…all vegetable farmers, right?"

"There will be many things to see. You guys can visit the petting zoo, go swimming, canoe in the lake, watch the musicians, and explore the park."

"That sounds all right, I guess." Then he fell silent, poking at the same two keys on his keyboard over and over.

"What are you fretting about?"

"Are you going to make me go to the same school as Logan?"

"Oh, honey. Not a chance." I wrapped an arm around him and pulled him close for a hug. "Even if it's what we wanted, I can't afford private school tuition. At this point, I'm hoping I can earn and save enough money to help you with university, buddy. And anyway, the school you're registered at has an excellent reputation. It's the same one I went to at your age, but it's got some great new programs these days."

"Okay."

"You'll be able to make new friends. And best of all, you get to choose them."

He sighed. "It's okay, Mom. I'll do it."

Chapter 6

Phoenix

THE RESTAURANT I'd suggested for dinner with Jeannie was meant to be elegant but not uptight. Trendy but relaxed. I wanted good food and a classy feel, but enough quiet that we could talk. Maybe I was overthinking this, but I was short of time and my expectations were high. Ten Acres fit the bill, with light, varied food that even Julian would approve of, and Jeannie had agreed. Also, I'd asked Julian for a recommendation, so I was pretty confident.

After ordering wine and browsing the menu awhile, I said, "I'm really glad you agreed to see me. I've been looking forward to spending time with you ever since I knew you were home."

"Sure. Me too," she said, unconvincingly, and took a sip of her water, watching me with her huge haunting grey-blue eyes with their dark halo that had always fascinated me. She was so pretty, so perfect.

I felt a smile pull at my lips. "Jeannie."

She blinked and looked up at my face, and her anxiety was written there plainly.

"Are you upset with me? Or afraid of me, for some reason? Have I done something to make you think...?" I shrugged. "That I'm untrustworthy? Have I ever done anything to hurt you, Jeannie?"

"No. No, no, no, no. Of course not."

"I hope you know I wouldn't. Ever. I want... Is there some reason you seem to be afraid of me? I'm not aggressive or..."

"Oh! No. Um. You..." She gestured vaguely at my middle, causing me to glance down, in case my buttons had popped open, or I'd already spilled food on myself. "You do look a little dangerous." She laughed nervously, her gaze flitting around, and then scratched her cheek with her knuckles, her colour rising.

Calmly, I held still, lowering my voice to a whisper. "I thought you liked what you saw." It would be a lie to say I wasn't chuffed when I caught her looking at me admiringly.

She sucked in a sudden breath, and her eyes shot up to meet mine.

I scanned her features, wishing I could touch her, stroke the delicate curve of her blushing cheek, the freckle-dusted line of her pretty nose, trace the cinnamon arc of her surprised brows.

"I do," she squeaked.

I don't think I was completely successful in hiding the smile that tugged at my mouth.

She lifted her napkin to dab her moist lips. Then waved her hands, palms out, in a flutter. "I'm sorry I'm so bad at this. I really don't have much dating experience. I'm such a nerd."

"Don't think of this as a date then. Just dinner with an old nerdy friend." I smiled at the colour that inevitably flared on her pale cheeks. Maybe a little wine would help her relax.

She made a tiny noise in her throat and dipped her chin, like she'd tried, but failed to laugh at my joke. "Right." I think she knew my intentions were a little more than friendly.

The waiter arrived with our wine, and we ordered our meals. After the rigmarole was done, and we were alone again, I studied her. "I know my size can intimidate people. But I really am still the same nerdy guy you used to know in school."

Her sweet, bowed pink lips quirked to one side as she cast her gaze over me, and tilted her head. "I highly doubt that. You've changed a lot. I mean, I wouldn't have recognized you."

"I meant on the inside. Obviously." I lifted my arms, palms out, chuckling.

"I wondered about that too, though. You've obviously experienced a lot. But when did you grow so much?"

I pushed out my bottom lip. "I shot up at about nineteen, twenty. I wasn't even eighteen when everyone graduated so my growth spurt came after. The food in boot camp was better than what I was used to."

She sobered, undoubtedly remembering some of the hardships I'd hinted at then. Though no one knew how hungry I'd been.

"Why did you…?" She hesitated.

"Let everyone believe I'd died with Dad?" I finished for her. It's what everyone wanted to know.

She nodded, her cinnamon brows lowering, and her grey-blue gaze peering steadily at me for the first time, unwavering and wide.

"Before, I'd had to deal with a lot of…crap." I narrowed my eyes, smirking, to lighten the mood. "I'd been fending off my dad's shady friends since I was twelve, you know?"

"I remember." Her voice dropped to a soft whisper, sympathy shone from her eyes, and something flipped in my belly. Sympathy was something I'd had to do without.

"Yeah. So, even though I was freaked out, there was a part of me that could clearly see the fire was my chance to start over. I wasn't even graduating with you guys, because I'd missed so much school. So I knew that moment was a turning point."

"I can see that," she said. "You didn't want to get dragged into that shady world. I know how much you liked school, and how frustrated you were that you had to juggle that rough stuff and missed out credits for grad."

"Yup." I smiled, sadly. My frustration about not graduating was partly why I'd got wasted on grad night, with everyone else celebrating around me. "It wasn't ideal, but I saw a window and, at seventeen, it seemed like it was all or nothing. I wanted it all. No compromise. So I jumped at it."

In a tiny voice, she asked, "Who died, then? In the trailer with your dad?"

I huffed out a breath. There were things about that night I'd never told anyone, ever. Even though the authorities had eventually found me and questioned me, I'd played dumb. I shrugged and told her, "Some junkie that came around. Fortunately, he was young and skinny like me. And there were no dental records to straighten out the confusion. Nobody missed him, I guess."

The waiter arrived with our meals at that moment, putting an end to that morbid topic.

I didn't need to share the fact that Dad had apparently shot him, and then himself, or maybe he'd shot Dad, and set the fire. At least that's what I think happened. I had only a few minutes before the flames engulfed the trailer, and I barely escaped out the bedroom window. I could hardly stand to remember that night myself.

"Hey, enough of that. *Bon appétit.*" I changed direction while we each tucked into our food. I watched her eat her trout for a minute, glad to see she had a healthy appetite, then cut into my chicken breast. "Did you like living in Kingston? Were you sad to leave?"

Her gaze slid to the side while she thought. "Not so much. I had a lot of acquaintances and clients, but no really close friends."

"After ten years?" How was that even possible?

She pulled a face. "I was always working or taking care of Will. Not much opportunity to socialize as a single parent. Or date. And not many people our age want to hang out with a teen mom and her snotty-nosed kid."

"Somehow I doubt your kid was allowed to be snotty." I chuckled. "What about Will's dad? Did you meet him at college? Is he still there?"

Her eyes and mouth flew open, and she gasped softly like I'd said something shocking, and then she coughed, choking on her mouthful of wine. I reached across and patted her lightly on the shoulder blades.

"You okay?"

She nodded. "Sorry. Wrong pipe." Once she recovered, she replied, "He was never around. He…disappeared."

I frowned, wondering what that meant. Was he a lazy deadbeat who wouldn't acknowledge his child or help out? How had she met such a loser? Probably a student, some young tool, too irresponsible to step up. Fire flared in my gut at the injustice. "You were never married then. You don't get financial support from him either?"

She stared at me like I'd just stood on my chair and done a jig.

"I'm sorry. I don't mean to pry into your private business. It's just wrong, that you have to carry the load by your-self. It riles me up."

She nodded. "Thanks. Well. I had no choice. So I did it."

"I think you're amazing, to take that on. But…" I hesitated, not wanting to be too nosy. "Wouldn't it have been easier to come home and live with your parents? You were still so young."

She tsked. "Financially maybe. But it was complicated. I much preferred to be independent."

I let it drop. Obviously, something had changed, since she'd now decided to come home and sacrifice some of that independence. But I'd asked too many questions already.

Leaning my chin on my hand, I smiled. "I'm really glad we're both back in Port Cam. It's so nice to see you."

I could stare at her beautiful face all day. My eyes traced the sweeping slide of her straight nose, the honey-tinged clarity of her pale skin set against her dark auburn hair, shiny as a racehorse. I couldn't decide if I loved the tiny cleft in the middle of her chin more or the larger indentation between her nose and full, bow-shaped upper lip.

What was that called again? I'd obsessed over it, and remember looking it up. Phil-something. It meant love charm. That much I remembered because I'd been convinced she'd cast a spell on me as I stared at her every chance I got. All I knew was I wanted to trace them both with the tip of my tongue—and many other soft places too. My dick stiffened at the mental images, and I shifted in my chair, stretching.

"Are you staying, then? Have you decided?"

I pulled my mind out of the gutter. "Not yet. Not offi-cially. But I do like being here." I smiled. What would she think if I told her it was partly up to her?

"Oh. Where were you before? Or where else might you go?"

"Mostly I've been working out of Ottawa. The base nearby. But I've been overseas a lot. No real home base to speak of."

She frowned. "That sounds hard. Do you have work friends here?"

"They're all over. I mean we were deployed together, a lot. And trained together. But my closest buddies have dispersed now. Settled down."

"So it's Ottawa or Port Camosun?" She laughed. "No contest, right? I sure won't miss Eastern winters."

"No. Though I'm as often in a hot dry desert as there. So this is lush to me."

"Tell me where you've been."

I turned my face to the side and scratched my eyebrow with my thumb. "Everywhere."

"You can't say?"

I took a bite of food and shook my head. "Not specifically. But I've been to every continent. Every ocean. Every climate."

"Okay. Wow. What can you tell me?"

Swallowing, I told her, "If I do stay, I'm going to buy a boat."

"What?" That put a big smile on her face, triggering memories of her as a laughing, confident teenager. "A fishing boat?

"A sailboat. I learned to sail with my dad as a kid. And I...have a few skills. The Navy has a little private marina, so I'd have a place to keep it. And it's so pretty here, to get out on the water. Just chill and soak in the blue sky."

"Sounds nice," she started, then blinked and leaned closer, appeared puzzled, then shook her head as if having an argument with herself. "Is world travel why you joined the Navy?"

"Not really. Though I like it. No, I wanted to study engineering. It was the only way."

"Oh. Of course. I forget you actually went to college, after all. So would you leave the forces, someday?"

"I could. I have multiple specializations. But I really love what I do. I'm at the top of my game. It's challenging. Important. I think civilian work would be boring, in comparison. Not many people can do what I do."

"Tell me something you would do, so I can picture it."

I hummed. "Well. In vague terms, maybe sneak into some place where we weren't welcome, and scout out the tech, the lay of the land, the ordnance, and other gear, and report in so the brass know what's what. Plant some signals. Interfere with bad guys' business. Sometimes blow shit up." I smiled a little. "It's pretty high tech, but physically demanding too."

"It's mind-boggling to me."

"Other times, we just escort some fat cat around, make sure nobody assassinates him." I licked my lips and went in for more food.

"Fat cat…like…the…um…prime minister?"

I shrugged, eyes wide.

"Oh, my goodness. It makes accounting seem like the dullest work in the world."

"I'm sure all the businesses you work for think it's both important and brilliant. I bet you're great at it, too."

"I like order," she said. "I like to take someone else's chaotic mess and make everything organized and logical. Tick all the boxes."

"Me too."

She pished. "Yeah. Right."

"It's true. I have a lot of protocols and rules to follow. The military is a highly structured work environment."

"I suppose."

"But also…unpredictable. I like that. Never quite knowing what's coming. Always having a new problem to solve. The rigour."

"Aren't you ever afraid?"

"Nah. I'm a badass. You don't want to mess with me." I grinned.

She smiled, her eyes sparkling with humour. "Aaaand… we've come full circle."

She surprised a huff of laughter out of me. "You have nothing to fear, Jeannie. Unless…"

She froze as I reached across the table and lightly traced a fingertip along the backs of her left knuckles. "Unless?"

"Unless you're afraid of being adored." I met her gaze, telling her with my eyes how serious I was, how desperately I wanted her.

She let out a little inarticulate squeak, withdrawing her hand with a visible shiver and dropping her gaze. I felt it too, the promise. We were going to be spectacular together. If I could get past her shyness.

I moved my hand to lift my glass. "I always had a crush on you. I guess you never knew."

"Oh, no. I—don't know why…" That made her blush like crazy, as I knew it would. "I thought…" She pulled her lips between her teeth, then shook her head, reconsidering whatever she was going to add.

I grinned. "Couldn't compete with that Zach, though. The guys were jealous of him, and all the girls were jealous of you. He was such a stud."

Her laugh was weak and embarrassed, and she cast her gaze down to her lap. "I was so naive." She lifted her hands to cover her face for a moment. Not quite the effect I was going for.

I needed her to talk. Give me clues. Was she still hung up on Zach? Did she think I was just making moves on her? Or was she embarrassed about grad night?

"Innocence is underrated," I countered. "Nothing to be ashamed of. It was one of the things I liked best about you."

Why couldn't I tell if she remembered our night together? She never let on, even a hint. She had drunk a lot. How did a guy refer to something like that without sounding like an ass? *Hey, babe, remember the night we both got shit-faced, and I accidentally took your v-card? And then my dad died, and I ran away? What a night!*

Shit. This was harder than I expected.

Jeannie

I swear, I tried. Every time our conversation veered near, and I thought I had an opening, he'd take it somewhere else, or he'd do something flirty. His dark sea-green gaze pinned me, making me feel so exposed. So seen. So weak in the knees. I swear nothing escaped his notice. He seemed to be handling me with kid gloves like he thought I was delicate. But at the same time, weaving his hot, sexy, confident charm around me like a spell, melting my panties.

I didn't know which was worse. His probing questions about Will's father, his teasing confessions of his high school crush, or his outright sexy flirting. At first, he seemed laid-back, but his intense focus permeated every moment until I could hardly draw a breath. Somewhere on his travels, Peter Corbin had grown from a reserved teenager to a very sophisticated people manager. I was aware of his orchestrations even as I felt the sway of his powerful personality. I felt like a yo-yo on a string, twitching and spinning, completely at his mercy.

And each time I missed my chance to raise the subject, my nerves wound tighter, my fears growing like inflatable monsters in my head. Did he really like me as much as he seemed to? Would his interest evaporate the second he learned the truth? Would he be angry and storm off? Or would he try to control me and take my son away? I didn't know if I was coming or going. But I did know that Phoenix had some mysterious power over me. Something that rendered me stupid and weak, enraptured, and it scared the hell out of me.

Somehow, I made it through dinner, during which he asked gentle questions about my life in Kingston and told amusing anecdotes about his life in the Navy. A little warm and fuzzy from the wine, I hung onto a strand of sanity so I could answer his questions and maintain a semblance of civil conversation. But my experience of the evening was as fragmented as my attention and my emotional state.

Finally, he drove me home in his sleek, shiny black truck. I turned to face him.

"Thank you for a lovely dinner. I'm glad we could catch up."

It was too dark to properly see his eyes. His firm jaw flexed, and his lips twitched ever so slightly to one side. Was that a smile? How was I to read him?

"You're welcome." He dipped his chin so a little band of light from the streetlight moved up his chiselled face, but still, his eyes remained in shadow. "I hope we can get together again soon."

Afraid to say anything, afraid to be too reticent or too eager or just plain awkward, I nodded. I reached for my door handle, and before I even figured out how it worked, he'd leapt from the truck and rounded to my side, swinging my door wide and reaching a hand in to help me dismount from the high seat.

"Careful, now."

I lurched a little, jumping down, and his big hands flew to my sides to help me land and steady me on my feet. The feel of his grip, strong and sure, on my body, was shocking. I felt light as a doll, and utterly safe beside him. I was so used to being the adult with Will. The taller, stronger, more able one. There'd been scant opportunity for me to feel small, or let someone else help me, in such a long time. The feeling was utterly disorienting.

"Thanks."

Then he walked quietly beside me as I went to the door. There were still lights on, both upstairs and down, and I wondered who might be watching from behind a curtain.

Sighing, I stopped on the low stoop and turned to face him. I needed to say something. This was my last chance. "Phoenix…I…Have a good night."

"You know." He bent his face lower, holding my gaze, his eyes flicking between mine. "I wouldn't mind if you called me Pete. Just you, though. No one else." His lips pulled in slightly.

I drew in a breath, unsure what to say. He made the offer like a kind of gift. Something precious, secret, and intimate. He seemed vulnerable and a little shy. I only smiled softly in acknowledgement.

Wordlessly, he studied me for a moment, his gaze dropping to my mouth, then reached forwards and dragged his fingertips up my arm from my hand to my shoulder, triggering an all-over shiver. Then he touched me under my jaw with a gentle fingertip. Oh, my God. What was he doing? I wasn't…I couldn't…

But then he lowered his face close to mine, his dark gaze

searching, waiting, seeking permission. My lips parted slightly in involuntary invitation. I felt his warm breath on my face before he lightly brushed my lips with his firm mouth, like the dusting of a feather. It wasn't even a real kiss. His eyes slid closed, and he made a low, deep sound in his chest as if he'd been anticipating this for a long time. He veered to my cheek, just to the side of my mouth, and pressed his lips closer as his finger tipped my face higher, gently so I could pull away if I wanted to. The urge to stretch myself up to meet him, craving more pressure, more connection than the teasing touch he offered, was powerful. I felt his lips tighten into a tiny smile against the fine hairs of my face.

Then he whispered, his words tactile on my skin, "Philtrum. I remember now."

"Wha–?"

Before I could express my question, he'd darted his tongue out and dipped it into the indent above my lip, sending shivers racing over my skin in a shock wave. I gasped, and he took advantage of my open mouth to lick into me lightly, just grazing the inner edge of my upper lip, tickling a little and drawing another bodily shiver out of me.

When he withdrew, I sighed. At that moment, I'd have happily curled up in his lap and let him lick me all over.

What was I doing? I stepped away, feeling heat rush under my skin.

He straightened, then lifted a finger to gently trace my mouth. "You have very sexy lips."

I swallowed, unable to meet his eyes. "Good night… Pete." And then I slipped quickly through the door.

Chapter 7

Phoenix

THE DAY after my dinner with Jeannie, I made my way—along with a bunch of other guys, including Zach, Tate, JJ, and Parker—to Bear Lake Park to meet Julian to help set up the Farm-to-Table Faire grounds. The park was centrally located, just off the highway, with plenty of space in a large flat field, with scattered trees all around. There were two large parking lots, a groomed hiking trail all around the lake, and a dock and wharf for boating and water sports.

Exhibitors and vendors were responsible for their own tents, tables, and gear, but there was a bunch of general stuff the organizers had to do, including assembling the main stage, a few smaller marquees for things like tickets, first aid, information, and various tents and banners all over the field.

Julian's friends had come out in numbers, and there were also some casual labourers, but it seemed to be mostly volunteer help. While Julian explained what needed doing, I scanned the area, looking for opportunities, obstacles, problems to solve. It was easily going to take a couple of days to get it all ready.

A flatbed truck took up one end of the parking lot while a crew unloaded rented blue plastic portable shitters and carried them off to the designated area, opposite the regular toilet block, to support the additional crowd.

Julian handed each of us a printed copy of the site plan.

"Maybe you guys can divvy up the common booths and stuff I've marked up on here. There are ladders, ropes, and tools in the back of my truck and in Matt's." He pointed at a tall guy with unruly brown hair. "If you need anything you can't find, or have questions, you all have my number. Or ask Arnie, Noah, or Hanns." Julian swung and pointed at three other guys clustered by the parked vehicles. "They know what's going on."

I remembered meeting Noah and Matt at the reunion. Guys around our age, strong and capable. Arnie was a little smaller and older, but gnarlier. He had the look of a farmer. And the last guy, Hanns I presumed, was older still, with a closely trimmed white beard.

It was like setting up a camp in the field. Ammo, Mess, Bunks, Shitters, etc. Pretty familiar.

I studied the map to see if it made sense, memorized it, and launched into action. "Let's work together to shift materials from the trucks to the different zones," I told the group. "Then once we have things staked out, split up into teams and double down on the assembly."

Everyone was okay with that, and we broke into movement. After a chaotic couple of hours or so of men shifting gear around—special ops they were not, a bit like herding cats—I settled in with Zach to hammer together the perimeter fencing and frame for the field kitchen of Julian's pop-up restaurant, which was in a prominent location so the diners had a view of the lake, and were close enough to hear the main stage music. Everything would be built rough, and then dressed up afterwards with fabric, banners, and paint.

After answering Zach's usual barrage of questions about training—and deflecting his curiosity about my missions, which endlessly fascinated him—we veered to talk about our friends.

Quinn had arrived with Jeannie, and JJ drifted over to help set up the pop-up café with them, or at least lean on the counter and chat. They glanced over, noticed us, and waved. The rest of our gang was at work today.

"Hey, Big P." Zach nudged me. "You're so uncool. You can't stare at her all the time, man. I swear you've never picked up chicks before."

He didn't have a clue about base bunnies. Which I suppose meant he was right. I'd never had to work for it. But I wasn't trying to make moves on Jeannie for any shallow or purely physical reasons. I wanted so much more than that.

I was determined to move on with my plans since my free time was running out soon. But after more mixed messages from Jeannie last night, I needed more intel. I pressed Zach. "Are you sure she's not still interested in you?"

"I really doubt that, dude. She hasn't even spoken to me. What does that say to you?"

"That she's waiting for you to make a move?"

"Nah. Seriously? No way. She hasn't even looked at me."

I wondered if that meant she was still hurt, resentful, or really didn't care. "Maybe you're still interested in her?"

"Not," he spat. "She's not my type. Never was, really."

I studied his face. He seemed sincere. "Then why did you date her?"

He shrugged. "Why does any seventeen-year-old guy do

anything? Some combination of peer pressure, hormones, and…opportunity?"

That sounded like the truth. Though obviously not the opportunity he'd been looking for at seventeen.

"But you were together for two years or something. If you didn't like her, what was in it for you?" I lifted my end of a long board.

"Oh, I liked her well enough. She helped me with schoolwork. And she was soft." He smirked, shifting the two-by-eight on his shoulder, and turned. "She felt good."

It was stupid, but a surge of jealous rage thrummed through me, and I wanted to smash his face for touching my girl. I laughed at myself. She wasn't my girl. Not yet, anyway. And he obviously didn't get very far with Jeannie.

"She was too good for your sorry ass."

"She thought so anyway. You know, I don't even remember making a move on her. Somehow, we just fell in together. That's what I mean about peer pressure. Other guys thought she was hot. I mean, she was cute but so uptight. She was the smartest girl at school, and all she talked about was exams and college." He shrugged. "That's it. We looked good together."

I tried not to roll my eyes at his flip attitude. "You had such a soft life, dude."

"Fuck you." He held the board in place while I hammered a couple of nails, and we were silent while I made noise. "It wasn't really. My mom was getting sicker every year. Dad was a total prick who pushed me into soccer whether I wanted it or not."

"You didn't like soccer?" I asked, surprised to hear the note of resentment in his voice.

"Never got the chance to ask myself."

"I guess that's what you get when your dad's the coach and phys ed teacher."

He hummed in agreement. "Wasn't as bad as your situation, I suppose."

"Truth."

"Anyway. Why are you so hung up on Jeannie? And just do it already? Why quiz me?"

"Always liked her." I thought for a minute. "Didn't expect to ever see her again. So I want to make sure you're not in the way."

"Trust me. I'm not in your way, Big P." He scoffed. "As if I could."

"But I'm also looking out for Jeannie. Would you please talk to her? I know it's an old wound, but clean up your messes. Man up."

Zach groaned but reluctantly agreed as we carried on with our work.

Jeannie

After the second straight day of setting up her café at the fairground, Quinn seemed satisfied. Everything was exactly as she'd wanted.

"It's just as I'd imagined," she told us. "All I have to do is bring in the coffee machine and supplies tomorrow. Then we'll be ready to go."

After final setup tomorrow, the Farm-to-Table Faire that Julian had been planning for months would finally kick off.

"It looks good!" I said. "This is a great location."

"It's so weird," Quinn said. "Having my own café in Old Town was my dream. But this temporary setup seems twice as exciting right now."

"I'm excited, and all I'm doing is waitressing. There'll

be crowds," I added. "And it is an awfully big opportunity to build your business quickly."

"True," she'd said, standing back to survey our work, hands on her hips.

Having strolled around to survey the park—which had been transformed in two days from an empty field dotted with large cottonwood, alder, fir, and cedar trees along the shore of Bear Lake, to a festive setting filled with tents, stages, and booths—we'd concluded the Faire was going to be a smashing good event. I was glad I'd have some time to relax with Will before the hectic school year began. And hang out with my friends, too, of course.

I was nervous though, since everyone's families would also attend the Faire, and this would be Will's first full immersion into my circle of friends. And the first time anyone but Quinn had a chance to meet him and get to know him. I was proud but also scared. To me, his resemblance to Pete was pretty obvious. But maybe to others, it wouldn't be. He had my freckles and my chin. Anyway, I'd make sure he'd be busy with Logan and Lucas when I was working.

In the late afternoon, we located Ruby and headed downtown for dinner out with the girls.

Ruby, Quinn, and I met up with Deanna, Rainy, and Bethune at the restaurant. Deanna had been planning a Kick-Ass Chicks girl-squad night on the town for weeks. Between conflicting work schedules, fairground prep, and school year organization for me, this was the first chance we'd found to get together since the reunion that I'd missed in July. She'd reserved a large tatami room at Shizen Izakaya, her favourite Japanese restaurant downtown. We six were now snugged up around the table, shoes off, making ourselves at home in the cozy private space.

"Why couldn't Aislin be here again?" Ruby asked for the third time. "Everyone was supposed to be available."

Deanna shook her head, pouting. "Some last-minute work thing."

I suspected Aislin just didn't want to do a big crowd. She never did. Also, I wasn't sure what her take was on Japanese cuisine. She was very particular about her food. And we had indeed become a bit drunk and rowdy after several bottles of saké as well as beer. With built-in childcare, I'd been indulging quite a bit lately.

The remains of our enormous feast of sushi, tempura, and yakisoba were strewn across the centre of our table.

Annoyingly, a piece of *gomae* spinach had adhered to the glossy wood in front of me, and I kept dragging my arm through it. It was really bugging me so I took a paper napkin and, dipping it in saké to wet it, scrubbed the spot.

Rainy leaned towards me, bumping my right shoulder. "That stuff's expensive. Don't waste it."

"It's dirty," I complained. "I don't like dirty." And anyway, there was no shortage of saké here.

Ruby said, "You're such a mom."

"That's my name," grumbled Quinn.

"Hey!" Deanna flopped sideways drunkenly, sliding the shoji screen door open and leaning out into the aisle. "S'cuse me, ma'am. Miss? Can we get a wet rag o'er here, pleash?"

"S'okay. I got it." I waved a hand and swigged the rest of my saké.

Our waitress returned with a clean wet rag, a fresh stack of paper napkins, and a discrete smile for the gang of drunken women she'd been politely serving for the past two hours plus.

"And bring another couple large saké," Deanna said. "Pleash," she murmured.

"No! No more," Ruby cried.

"Yes, more," Bethune whined, trying to fill her cup and discovering only drops, peering sadly into the empty vessel, her eyes out of focus.

Oh, boy. I wiped the table with the rag.

Quinn bent forwards, squinting blearily at the tabletop with one eye closed. "You mished a spot." She jammed a finger down next to a smear, and I tried to focus on it.

Was that a reflection? My eyes were getting blurry, and I rubbed them. "I think ish bedtime," I croaked, wondering where my voice had gone.

"No way. One more round," Deanna insisted, reaching across the table to fill our little ceramic cups, splashing the expensive saké all over the place again.

"Remember the first time you ate raw fish, Dee?" Bethune said, giggling.

Deanna pulled a face, retching, either fake or real, I didn't know. "I think tha's the day I decided I was vegan." She, of course, had limited her consumption of sushi to the vegan options. Not even tamago passed her lips. But she was pretty familiar with what to order, and so we'd all sampled the tofu dumplings—and cucumber, avocado, shiitake, and seaweed maki—alongside our fish options.

"You don't know what you're missing, girl." I loved sushi so much, but could hardly afford it normally. And also, it was so much better on the West coast than where I'd been living. It would be so nice to finish this degree and get a real job, for once. My mind filled with visions of sushi every week.

Tonight, I'd completely satisfied my craving. Or at least I'd stuffed myself silly. I eyed the few pieces of tuna and salmon on the plates in front of me longingly, but shook my head, knowing it would be unwise to eat anymore.

"I think I'm in love," crooned Bethune softly, apropos of

nothing, except the meandering conversation we'd had all evening about men and relationships.

"With who?" Rainy demanded.

"Whom," interjected Ruby.

"This new guy I met at the job fair."

"Aaand?" I prompted.

"He's cute," was all she said. Then burped and added, "I made him recruit me. I have a job interview next week."

"What?!"

"That's amazing, Beth!"

She bobbed her head, grinning like a Cheshire cat, her red hair flopping forwards over her dark glasses. "I hope so." She swung both arms up into the air, smashing into Quinn's head. "Fingers crossed."

"Hey!" Quinn rubbed the side of her face with a frown. "Ow."

"For the job or the man?" Ruby asked.

"Sorry, Quinnie." Bethune grabbed Quinn's face between her palms, squishing her cheeks, ignoring Ruby's query. "I'm sorry!" She leaned close, examining Quinn with bleary eyes.

Quinn's cheeks were flushed bright pink, either from the saké or the woman-handling.

"Did I give you a shiner?"

"Why can't I meet my soulmate?" bemoaned Rainy, emptying her cup.

"Not again, Rainy. You don't want a man!" said Deanna, outraged, refilling her glass. "You spend half your life evading the dumb dicks your mom sets you up with."

"That's 'cause they're dumb dicks," Rainy clarified, setting us all off on a fit of giggles. "Doesn't mean I don't want a nice, hunky dude to spend my nights with. Just need one that'll support my independence and career."

"I think Peregrine'll do that," murmured Bethune wistfully, slumping on her elbows.

"Who?"

"Someone as tall as Shiva." Rainy was on a roll, stretching her long, thin arm up to the ceiling. "Taller than me—"

"Tha's a tall order," said Ruby, sniggering and falling backwards, catching herself with an arm.

Undaunted, Rainy went on. "With shoulders wide as a truck! And dreamy dark eyes with long lashes like a cow." She swayed to and fro, caressing her own bony chest, and hugging herself.

"Sounds like my type." Deanna nodded sloppily, sighing. "Maybe we can share."

"What about intelligence? I thought that's what you cared about most, Rainy."

Quinn shoved Bethune off of her, sending her careening into Deanna, who flopped into the screen door. "You can have any guy you like."

I snorted. "Behave!"

At the thump, the screen door slid open a few inches and our waitress peered in. "You want more saké?"

"Yes!" Bethune and Deanna shouted, surprised by the offer, while Ruby and I both said, "No!"

"Jus' one more," said Deanna, smiling coyly as she righted herself.

"Hey!" Bethune raised both hands, palms out, fingers flayed. "Drop a finger if you've had sex with more than… um…five lovers."

We all groaned at the childish party game, but as everyone complied, I lifted my hands, too. Everyone lowered a finger except me and Quinn.

Rainy swung her head my way. "Seriously, Jeannie?"

I made a face at her. "Who would I have sex with? I sleep with a nine-year-old in the next room."

"I know someone who wants to—oof!" Bethune stopped abruptly when Quinn's elbow connected with her ribcage.

"Okay. Who's slept with more than two people? Any gender," Bethune pressed. Rainy dropped a finger. Everyone stared at me.

Rainy peered at me. "Two?"

I shrugged. "Actually only one."

"Will's dad is the only guy you've slept with? Really?"

I nodded. "Well, okay. Technically two. But it was dreadful. Lack of opportunity, mostly. But also, it's rather fraught for me."

Deanna gawped. "Wow. Unimaginable. How can you live without sex?"

"I love sex," Bethune murmured.

"Me, too," Deanna told us. "Especially with big, beautiful men."

"Like Zach?"

Everyone groaned.

"No!" Deanna protested. "I mean, Zach is cute, but… we're just friends. And the sex is—"

"Don't tell us!" Rainy shouted, covering her ears with her hands. "La. La. La. That is something I can go to my grave without knowing."

"I was only going to say that it's comfortable. Between Zach and me. We only do it when we're sad."

"Is that why you slept with him on grad night?" I couldn't stop myself from asking, curious.

"I slept with him because you wouldn't," Deanna said, as if this made any sense at all.

"I was a virgin!" I hissed, slurring, as if this were a secret. Hah! "An' Zach was so insistent. He nagged and pushed. I almost gave in a few times but…it jus' didn't feel right."

"He was a virgin, too," Deanna told us. "That's why I gave in on grad night. He was so desperate. And he was toasted. And sad and crying, *she doesn't love me*, and I took pity on him." She made an upside-down smile face and shrugged, leaving the room in gawping silence. In all these years, apparently, she had never explained herself.

"Is that why you sleep with him now?"

Deanna nodded slowly, bobbing her head up and down as if answering the question for herself as well. "Mhm. Yup. That and being shit-faced drunk myself."

"Like now?"

Quinn leaned across Bethune to pet Deanna's head like a cat. "You have to stop doing that, DeeDee. Tha's so bad for you."

"I know. I know, okay?" Deanna straightened her shoulders and sniffed loudly. "An' for the record, Jeannie. I'm sorry, okay? I'm really sorry I slept with your boyfriend. I was only trying to help," she wailed, tears streaming down her cheeks.

I felt tears welling in my eyes, and my heart hurt. I pulled out of the pit under the table and crawled along the bench behind Quinn and Bethune until I was beside Deanna. Then I wrapped my arms around her. "S'okay, Dee. I's okay. I don't care anymore."

Bethune and Deanna both leaned towards me, enveloping me in a hug from both sides. "Poor Jeannie."

"Jeannie's got something going on," Bethune said, and Quinn smacked her arm.

"Shut it, Beth!"

"Sorry. What?"

"Anyway, sex is cheap," drawled Deanna, slurping her saké. "It's true love that's imposhible to find. That's all I want. Someone to love. Nothing less will do." Her blue eyes stared sightlessly at the wall behind Ruby's head.

"Me, too!"

"I love you, Deanna," Rainy said.

"Me, too," I added. "I love all of you."

"So much."

"Ruby, you're the only one of us that's found romantic love," said Quinn.

"Can't argue with that. Not everyone meets their soul-mate in high school, though, Quinnie. You will all find yours someday. I just know it." She pulled her legs out from under the table and slid open the screen door. "Speaking of Julian, I have to get home. Tomorrow's a big day."

"Speaking of Jules," said Rainy, making puppy-dog eyes at Ruby. "Any chance he'd come and get us with his van?"

Ruby and Quinn burst out with, "No way!"

"He's got enough on his plate without playing taxi driver for us all."

"We'll all have to get real taxis then."

"I can call Zach—" Deanna suggested, only to be inter-rupted by another chorus of opposition.

"Not. A. Chance. Sister," said Quinn, pointing a finger at Deanna. "Not in this condition."

"Why don't you call your boyfriend, Jeannie?" Bethune taunted.

Rainy nodded. "He would drop everything and come for her, wouldn't he?"

My heart lurched at the thought. Call Phoenix? "Oh, no, no, no. I couldn't do that. What would he think?"

"He'd think his damsel's in distress, and he'd race over here to save you, darlin'."

My cheeks flamed at the idea of it. But it would be nice to see his handsome face. Speaking of big, beautiful men.

My thumb moved over my phone screen before I had a

chance to think it through or talk myself out of it. I'd been thinking about him all evening. The way he flirted with me at dinner. The way I sunk into the deep sea-green of his eyes, like a rock to the bottom of the ocean. The feel of his big, strong hands on my body and his lips covering mine. I sighed.

And…well, I did have a good reason to call. It wasn't for me. My friends all needed to get home safely.

A little voice in my head said, *What's the big deal, Jeannie? What are you so afraid of? Honestly, Jeannie, you make such a fuss over little things. There are far bigger problems in the world than whether you feel embarrassed around Phoenix.*

Like, for example, when was I going to tell him he was a father?

Well, not tonight. That's for sure.

In the meantime, I could live a little. Sometimes I thought I might have forgotten how. You'd think I was forty, the way I carried my responsibilities around. What kind of life was that for a twenty-something?

My best friends obviously didn't have this problem. Apparently, they'd all had multiple lovers, a few failed romances, and what was the big deal? They were just young women living their lives, gaining experience, and learning about life, the way they should be. Right?

And they didn't look, or act, broken, as if every wrong turn was the end of the world. Things didn't always work out according to some grand life plan. Why couldn't I just let go for once and go with the flow?

Another voice… Was it on my other shoulder? Anyway, in a scolding tone, it said, *Right, Jeannie. The two times in your life when you actually let go and had fun, something catastrophic happened. And those events did indeed change the entire course of your life! You can't afford to take risks.*

I shushed that stupid voice. I wasn't sure which was the

devil, or whose advice I should listen to, anyway. But I knew what I felt like doing right now. Feeling reckless, I forged ahead, clicking Phoenix's number. Should I phone? Or text first, maybe? He was probably asleep.

ME: *U up?*

OH, my goodness. What does that mean? He's going to think it's a booty call. I guess I shouldn't have been surprised at his near-instant reply.

PHOENIX: *I'm up. What r u doing tonight?*
  Me: Can u call me?

I HAD to set him straight, like, immediately, if he was thinking what I thought he was thinking. What an idiot. Me, I mean. My phone rang almost instantly.

Aware there were five pairs of eyes on me, I squeezed mine shut. "Hi?"

"Hi, there."

"So. Um…you know that big black truck of yours?"

After a beat of silence, during which he was probably thinking I'd lost my marbles, he prompted, "Yeah?"

"Well…I was wondering how many seats it has."

A murmur of complaint rose from my audience.

"What are you saying?"

"What does that matter?"

"Deanna can sit on my knee," and "Just ask him already."

"Ah, ha. I see now. What have you girls been up to?"

"Shushi," I told him. "And some saké." And then, ridiculous person that I was, I burst into a fit of giggles, which set off the other girls like hyenas.

"Are you needing a lift home, Jeannie?" Phoenix asked into the noise.

"Yup. Yes. Well, not only me." I fell silent, waiting.

"All of you," came his response as he put the puzzle together. "Would all of you be needing a ride home?"

In a tiny, tentative voice, I answered, "Yes. Is that something…um…you could…?"

His voice dropped deep and slow and soft, warming my blood and sending shivers all the way down to my toes. "For you, Jeannie. Anything. Tell me where you are."

"It's um…Shizu Izzy Kazoo? Or, maybe…Izen Shizoo Kazen?" My efforts to pronounce the unpronounceable Japanese name was drowned out by another chorus of helpers, and I guess somewhere in there, someone said it right.

His voice sounded tight when he asked, "What street are you on?

"Mm…Fort?"

"No, Government!" Rainy countered.

"Broad Street!" shouted Bethune.

"Okay. I will find you. I can be there in ten minutes. Can you all stay out of trouble that long?"

As he signed off, I heard his low chuckling and thought that was possibly the first time I'd heard him laugh.

Chapter 8

Phoenix

FORTY MINUTES LATER, after meandering all over town and
dropping off Bethune and Rainy at Rainy's apartment, and
then Ruby and Deanna at Deanna's condo on the point, I
pulled up outside of Millhouse Coffee in Old Town.

"Wakey-wakey, girls. We're home."

Jeannie jarred awake, blinking. She'd been slumped on
Quinn's shoulder in the crew seat of my truck. "Where's
everybody?"

"Everyone else is safely tucked in bed at home. Just you
two party animals left." I hopped out and opened the jump
seat door, leaning inside to reach across and unbuckle both
of them.

Quinn stirred awake, squinting, then groaned. "Oh my
God. Oh my God. I can't remember the last time I drank
that much."

Jeannie speculated, "Grad?"

And then Quinn burst into hysterical laughter and fell

out of the truck. Fortunately, I was standing right there and scooped her into his arms.

"Where is everybody?" Quinn mumbled.

"Peter Piper dropped them off," Jeannie mumbled, sloppily trying to climb out of the truck.

That's all I needed was her doing a faceplant on the sidewalk while my arms were full of Quinn. I restrained her with my elbow. "You stay put, Miss. I'll get this one inside and return for you, okay?"

She settled timidly, blinking up into my face, folding her hands together on her lap like a Sunday school student. "Okay." Then her face split into a wide, sparkling, silly grin that made my heart lurch, and she continued staring at me.

Oh, Jeannie. She was adorable.

I half carried, half guided Quinn to the front door of her café, then waited while she rummaged in her little bag for her keys. And rummaged. And rummaged, handing me all sorts of weird objects in her search.

I was on the verge of calling Parker when she finally stood upright, holding them high. "Got 'em!"

I took them from her to unlock the door. I didn't need to stand out here at zero-dark stupid waiting for her to find the keyhole. Once inside, I led her to the sofa and dropped her there. A rapid beep sounded.

"The alarm! The alarm!"

Shit. "Where is it?"

"Behind the bar. Shide panel, there." She flung a wobbly arm over the back of the sofa in the general direction.

Once I found it, I barked, "Code!" hoping she wasn't asleep again. I didn't need to go hacking security systems right now, though I would if I had to. Damn it.

"Sheven Sheven Five Five."

I punched the numbers, my mind already deciphering

the meaning of the code. So obvious. The alarm light went off. Okay. Good. Now for Jeannie.

When I returned to my truck, she was standing outside, slumped against the side door, staring up into the sky.

"What do you see up there, beautiful?"

"I woke up all alone," she said dreamily. "Except for the stars."

Instead of hustling her inside, I embraced the opportunity to be alone with her for a few precious minutes. I leaned beside her, folded my arms over my chest, and looked up. The night sky was clear, perfect for the Faire, with a young crescent moon hanging like a good luck charm. Pleiades, Perseus, and Cassiopeia were the most obvious stars out tonight. I spotted Mars and Jupiter and was searching for Saturn in the southeast when Jeannie spoke again.

"They've kept me company many a night," she said softly. "When I was all alone." She seemed wistful and more sober than before. She shivered.

"You chilly?" I slipped off my jacket and draped it over her shoulders.

She gripped the collar and pulled it up to her cheeks, inhaling deeply. "Thank you. Smells yummy. Like you and…licorice?"

"There might be some in my pocket," I huffed a laugh. "Good nose."

"You're awfully nice," her low, soft voice sending dangerous tingles of awareness through me, making my dick stiffen. Then she hiccuped and leaned into my side. Okay, maybe not quite sober.

I lifted an arm over her shoulder and pulled her a little closer, holding her upright. "You okay, really?"

"I'm fine."

"You ready to head inside?"

"Yup." We made it four or five steps towards the door, and she stumbled. "Oops." And then I waited while she bent over, suffering a fit of giggling accompanied by incoherent mumbling.

"Jeannie?"

Her eyes, when they lifted to meet mine, seemed inexplicably sad and worried.

"What's the matter, sweet thing?"

"I'm sorry. I keep screwing up. Over and over and over." Her eyes went glassy, as if she were about to cry.

Oh, hell. It was time to put this girl to bed. I bent to scoop her into my arms, eliciting a gasp of surprise.

"I can walk. I can walk. I can walk. Put me down."

But we were at the door in three more strides, and she was light as a doll, so I put her down only when we got there, and then led her inside, holding gently onto her arm to steady her.

"Quinnie, Quinnie!" she suddenly called out. "Where are you?"

"I'm over here," came Quinn's muffled voice from the sofa. She was face down on the cushion, arms and legs flopped every which way.

"Are you sleeping?" Jeannie asked, stumbling over and falling on top of her.

"Oof! Maybe I was."

"You're warm," Jeannie cooed, crawling into the gap between Quinn and the sofa back, burrowing in beside her.

Quinn rolled over and wrapped an arm and a leg around Jeannie.

I stood looking down at them, shaking my head.

"I love you, Jeannie," mumbled Quinn, burying her face against Jeannie's neck.

Jeannie giggled. "That tickles!" Then she relaxed into the embrace and gazed up at me over Quinn's shoulder with eyes that couldn't possibly have been able to focus properly. "You look like Thor."

"What?" Quinn mumbled.

"Not you. Phoenix is standing there, tall as a mountain, with his big muscly arms across his hunky chest, looking like some kind of Marvel superhero god person."

"Pardon me?" I coughed a half laugh. She was ridiculous. They both were.

"Oh," Quinn mumbled. "You like that Superman thing."

"He's so handsome," Jeannie hissed in a bad stage whisper into Quinn's hair. Then Jeannie sighed again, wistfully.

"Ah, an' he knows it too," said Quinn helpfully.

"Ahem. Can I help you ladies upstairs to bed?"

Quinn shot up suddenly, almost knocking Jeannie to the floor. They were half on the sofa, half off, their limbs entangled. "Oh! We were just talking about you." She rubbed her eyes.

"Shish, Quinn! Shut your mouth. No, we weren't." Jeannie waved her hand quickly in denial, then smashed her palm over Quinn's mouth.

Then Quinn lost it, bursting into hysterical giggles, dragging Jeannie under with her.

"Is that so? And what were you talking about?" I asked, suppressing the grin that pulled at my mouth. Maybe this saké worked as a truth serum I could use to my advantage.

"Bethune ish of the opinion that you're thirsty for Jeannie."

"Is it a subject of debate? Have I been too subtle?"

Jeannie blinked up at me with her bleary eyes.

"You know what Jeannie told ush tonight?" Quinn asked.

"Mm. Nope."

"She told us that she's only slept with—" Jeannie's hand covered Quinn's mouth again as she leapt on her friend, tackling her to the floor.

They landed with a thud and a grunt. There'd be mystery bruises tomorrow for these two.

"Shut it." Jeannie hissed, digging her fingers into Quinn's mouth. "I'm gonna wash your mouth out with soap. Betrayer. You're not my friend anymore."

They wrestled clumsily on the floor for a minute or so.

Quinn howled, "Ow! My mouth! You broke it," then started crying.

Something I'd never seen before. Interesting.

"But I love you, Jeannie Beanie."

"I love you too, Quinnie."

I rubbed a thumb across my eyebrow, chagrinned. Um. This night had gone TARFU fast.

"I missed you so much. I'm glad you're home."

"Me too, Quinnie." She planted a kiss on Quinn's mouth, snuggling closer.

They both leaned against the sofa, wedged in between it and the coffee table like contortionists.

Quinn returned her kiss, taking her face between her hands, squishing her face between them. "Aren't we still besties?"

"Aw, I didn't mean that. I love you, Quinnie."

Maybe there was no room for me in this love affair. "What was that about Jeannie's sex life?" I teased, laughing.

"Nothing! Nothing at all," Jeannie yelped.

"Ah. You never mind," Quinn said as Jeannie flopped across on top of her.

They slid down the side of the sofa onto the floor.

"Tha's secret," Quinn added.

Then they suddenly went quiet, only the sound of their even breathing remaining.

Were they asleep? Seriously?

It felt good to be needed. I sighed and smiled, and went upstairs to the apartment above the café to wake Parker.

Jeannie

"Oh," I groaned as I opened my eyes and sharp blades of light stabbed my brain. "My head."

"How did we get here?" croaked Quinn from somewhere over my shoulder.

I gingerly lifted my head off the cushion to squint at Quinn. I was sprawled on her sofa, while she leaned in the doorway of her bedroom, looking like road kill with her copper hair in a tangled mess like she'd been through a dryer cycle on high heat.

Parker, sitting at his gaming desk against the far wall, slipped headphones from his head, chuckling. "You don't remember anything?"

Flashes started to recur to me. "Oh my God, we didn't."

"We didn't what?" Quinn murmured, shuffle-limping towards the kitchen as if her hips and feet hadn't yet remembered how to work properly. "Is there coffee? Oh, thank you, little brother." She poured two giant mugs. "Who drove us home from the restaurant?"

Fearing confirmation of what my memory fragments told me, I asked Parker in a whisper, "Was it really Phoenix? We wouldn't let Deanna call Zach and then, oh shoot…"

"Don't sweat the details, Jeannie. It was all done in a gentlemanly manner."

"I fell asleep on the sofa downstairs. I'm fairly sure," offered Quinn as she handed me my coffee. "After that?"

She pulled a confused face and slurped her coffee, slumping down beside me.

Parker told us, "You both did, and I was all for leaving you there all night. But Phoenix insisted on bringing you both up here, which I'll have you know I wasn't interested in doing at two-thirty in the morning when I was very happily sound asleep in my bed."

"He woke you?"

"Yup. And you owe me, Blue. If it weren't for the fact that you have a lot to do today to get ready for the Faire, I'd have left you there for your customers to gawk at through the window." He snickered.

"Thanks a lot, Red."

"But…" I pondered the missing details, aghast. "You carried us upstairs?"

"Phoenix did, and he made it look easy. And tucked you in," Parker added, teasing.

"Oh, my God," I gasped, taking in the pillow and blanket around me on the couch. I would die of embarrassment. I must have looked like a wreck! Was I drooling? Did I talk in my sleep? What did I say?

"And kissed your brow sweetly," Parker added, snorting. "Man, that dude has it bad for you, Jeannie."

My heart pounded, and my stomach twisted in a stew of panic, excitement, dread, and—I didn't know what else. Maybe it was the saké coming back to haunt me.

Parker faced his computer, and we sat for a couple of minutes, the only sound the clicking of Parker's keyboard, the desperate slurps of our coffee going down and the screech of seagulls out the window over the harbour. Slowly, I started to feel human again.

But as my brain woke up, so did more memories of our trip home last night. Oh, my God. What the…?

"It's true. I've got a million things to do," said Quinn,

suddenly alert, cutting into my spiralling thoughts. "Are you two coming with me?"

"I'm heading over now," Parker said, removing his headphones, standing, and picking up his keys. "See you later, ladies."

"Oh my goodness. What time is it? I have two appointments this morning!" I said, my mind finally snapping into focus.

"Where?" Quinn asked.

"I have to drop off some papers at my advisor's office at the university, and then I'm meeting an education consultant at Will's school at eleven o'clock."

"Okay, well, it's a quarter to ten. I need a quick shower, and if you help me load up my car with the coffee gear, I'll drive you to the University and wait for you and then drop you off at Will's school before I head out to the park to unload. Okay?"

"Okay. Okay, sounds like a plan." We guzzled our coffee and burst into action.

On the way to the university in Quinn's older model Prius—because of course, Ms. Green drove a hybrid—we rehashed our night of indulgence, and in particular Deanna's revelations. I felt good about that, but would think more about it later.

I didn't even have a spare moment to contemplate how lovely it would be to be a full-time student on a university campus come next week, finally, even though I'd be a mature student. After I jogged through the leafy concourse to the business building and dropped off my forms, clenching my teeth at my splitting head, and we were settled in the car, Quinn started pressing me on the paternity issue.

I really wasn't in any condition to think about that, especially after how the night had ended. I'd tried to deflect with queries about Parker and Jae Soo's plans, but she pressed on.

"I feel as if I'm being cornered," I complained from the passenger seat as we drove into the city centre.

"You are. If you hadn't stalled, you wouldn't be in this position. It would have been easier to pull him aside the moment you found out he was back. What have you got to lose?"

My muscles tightened with the stress of it. I had so much to lose. My pride. My autonomy. My child? She didn't understand. Or maybe she did, but it wasn't easy at all.

"It's not as if I expected it!" I said when Quinn started grilling me about my dinner date with Phoenix two nights prior.

We'd been alone. I had the perfect opportunity. That had been my sole purpose in going. How had I screwed it up?

"Things were weird," I tried to explain, without giving away too much. My face heated with a flush. "He was all romantic and flirty and sexy, and it felt amazing to just be on a date with a nice, smart, handsome guy for once in my life. He makes me stupid!"

She laughed. "But…"

"I know, all right?! I know."

She reached across to cover my hand with hers. "It's only that… I hope, really hope, that something happens with you and Phoenix. But the longer you keep your secret, the harder it's going land."

I sighed. "I know that, too," I said, my voice small and defeated.

"Just pick your time. Be the brave and strong woman that I know you are. The Faire starts tomorrow. And everyone is invited to the volunteers and organizers' dinner tonight. Maybe you can find a window."

"Yes." I nodded, determined. "I will. At the very least, I'll make a date to talk."

"Just get it over with," she added as she pulled up in front of Will's school to drop me off. "And then you can get laid!"

And I punched her arm.

<hr>

Jeannie

"The thing is, Ms. van Bellen," the counsellor—an ostensibly kind, matronly woman in her fifties named Elizabeth Scranton—went on, "Given everything you've told me about Will, as well as what his records tell me, I'm concerned we don't have the resources here at the school to give him the support he needs."

We sat in a modern administration office at the school, with brightly coloured upholstered chairs, sleek tables, and window blinds on the full-wrap glazing. Whatever money they had once had was obviously spent on this glamourous new building. Somehow, I'd been fooled into thinking that meant more resources for the kids.

But no. I'd heard the same arguments before, in Kingston.

"He really is incredibly smart," I countered. "You can see from the psych assessment that the issues with his math stem mainly from anxiety. I'm more than capable of tutoring him at home so he can keep up with the curriculum, but..." I'd booked this meeting feeling optimistic, excited even, at the possibility that this new school would be a better place for Will. And with help, he'd settle in and finally start to make progress in the areas where he lagged behind. But my hopes were deflating as rapidly as a popped balloon.

"I'm sure your son is very clever. All kids are in their own ways." Ms. Scranton's mouth pressed into a thin line. She adjusted her glasses and shuffled the stack of papers in front of her. "But executive-function disorder linked to ADHD can lead to an accumulation of learning deficits over time that are very difficult to recoup. Falling behind doesn't help the child stay focussed on classroom work or assignments."

"Will doesn't have ADHD. I'm quite convinced his challenges stem from situational anxiety. He's a really sensitive kid, and we've just moved out West and…" I pointed blindly at the file on her desk.

I'd read everything on ADHD, and it wasn't my kid. You knew these things. Will had never had self-control issues. He suffered from some kind of working memory short circuit when engaged in certain tasks. And that invariably triggered a panic attack.

"You can see he doesn't have the same problem in all subjects. It's specific to math. And sometimes writing essays. But in everything else—"

"Nevertheless, there's only so much help he can receive at school. These problems predated the relocation, as well, so I fear there's more to it. As I've said, he can have a quiet room for tests, he can have extra guidance with his problem subjects, and a little help with time management, but the level of oversite needed is beyond our resources. And what I feel he really needs is counselling."

And round and round the discussion went. I knew Will needed something. I just didn't know exactly what. And though I'd been given the impression when I registered Will at this school, that they would be able to provide the support he needed, we'd ended up here. Which was basically where we always ended. Nothing had changed.

"Perhaps there's someone in the family who can give you a hand."

I didn't quite know how to respond to that. "Like, for instance…?"

She cleared her throat, stalling. "I'm certain it can be very challenging as a single mother, but is there no one? Is Will's father not—?"

"No." I cut her off, preparing to leave. "There really isn't anyone else who can help." I wouldn't allow myself the luxury of thinking about Phoenix.

Could he help? Would he even want to? Could I let him? It was all too much. Too threatening. Too confusing.

I thanked her for her time and left, feeling, as ever, that the fault was mine. And mine alone. There had never been anyone else. Somehow, I was failing as a mother. I could count on no one to help, and there was no one else to blame.

Chapter 9

Jeannie

IN THE AFTERNOON when I was finished with my school meeting and had dropped in at my parents' house to change my clothes and check in with Will, I borrowed Mom's car and returned to the park to see if Quinn needed any last-minute help setting up the pop-up café. And maybe to see if Phoenix was still around. It would be nice to thank him in person for his help last night, however embarrassing it might be. I should have brought Will with me to see the grounds, but I was stalling with the introductions until I'd had the talk with Peter—Phoenix—Pete. Why couldn't I decide what to call him? Maybe because our future was so indeterminate.

When I got there, though, I couldn't believe the trans-formation, not just with Quinn's stand but with the entire park, which had somehow been pulled together into a beau-tiful festive setting that was missing only the crowds that would flood in the following day.

Quinn's café was the first in a row of food vendors along

the curving path between the info and welcome booths by the entry and the lakefront. As I approached, I saw Zach and Parker at each end of the long Millhouse Coffee banner that spanned the rear wall of Quinn's coffee bar. She had set up her espresso machine and coffee grinder and had her refrigerators plugged in, and I could see all her supplies neatly stacked in rows. In lieu of her usual glass case where she displayed food, she had old-fashioned mesh umbrellas on the long countertop. It was simple but charming.

"Would you like a coffee? she asked when she saw me.

"I absolutely would."

Round tables and plastic chairs were arrayed in front of her bar, and I sat down with my Americano to watch the guys fuss with the banner.

Quinn stood beside me, arms crossed, barking orders. "Lift your end up a little, Parker. Just a touch. Nope, that's too much. There. There. No."

"Zach, don't move," I chipped in.

"You have to lift yours now," Quinn said. "Okay. Okay, that's level. Perfect. That's it. Tie off before it slips." She turned to me. "What do you think, Jeannie?"

"This is amazing." I gestured with my arm in an arc towards the parking lot. "When people come in and pick up their maps at the info booth, some are going to start by browsing all of those grower exhibits along the front and others are going to be drawn down the main path here. And your café is the first thing they're going to see. So I'll bet tons of people will grab a to-go coffee and then wander around exploring the park and the exhibits. And then they'll return because they'll already know that you're here."

Zach and Parker climbed down off their ladders and folded them up, stacking them to the side. They flopped onto chairs at my table, and Quinn brought them each a coffee.

Parker winked at his sister. "Thanks, Mom. Tastes just like home."

Quinn laughed. "I hope so."

"Everything looks fantastic, guys. Are you all done, then?" I asked.

"Yep. That should be it. What's left is just for the individual vendors and exhibitors to set up. You should walk around and have a look," Parker told me.

"I will."

"Hey, Jeannie?"

I looked up at Zach—and thought he was having a hard time meeting my eyes. He had a tight and earnest expression on his face while he twisted his coffee cup around and around on the tabletop, like he was worried about something. "You got a minute to talk?"

"Of course, Zach." What could this be about?

"Bring your coffee. Let's walk to the lakefront."

I shot a wary glance at Quinn, and lifted my brows, but she pulled a face to indicate she had no idea what this was about. I rose and lifted my coffee and said, "I'll see you in a bit," and followed Zach to the path.

We strolled slowly for a minute or two without talking, and I scanned left and right admiring the neat rows of booths with their colourful signage, the tents both large and small positioned in between with scattered tables and chairs so people could sit down and eat or drink the food they had bought from the various vendors. The banners above the booths showed off a bakery and pizzeria, and people selling organic sausages and vegan rolls, barbeque meat on sticks, juices, seafood, preserves, cheeses, and chocolates. My mouth watered just thinking about the variety of good things to sample starting tomorrow.

"We haven't had a chance to catch up yet," said Zach suddenly.

"No. That's true. It's been a surprisingly busy summer since I got to town. How have you been?"

"I'm good. Been training a lot. Learning a few new moves from Phoenix." He shot me a meaningful glance, as if this information affected me in some way.

When I said nothing, he continued while looking straight ahead.

"How are you doing this season? Are you enjoying pro ball?"

"Meh." After a moment, he seemed to reconsider. "That's not fair. We're ranked third in the league, but we had more draws than wins this season, which is frustrating. I haven't been playing my best lately. That's why I'm focusing on training in between games. Try to recover some strength."

Memories flooded in. Conversations with Zach invariably revolved around his training and game stats, with occasional complaints about his family. While I, on the other hand, was more focussed on school work and my plans for the future. Not a lot of common ground, between Zach and me.

"We tied against York last week, and I return next week for another game," Zach told me. "I'm hoping to do better."

"In York?"

"Yeah. We fly back and forth. The October game'll be at home, though, so you guys can come and watch if you like."

I nodded. I knew Zach was a dedicated pro soccer player, but I had always struggled to feign enthusiasm for the sport. "It must be hard to be out of town so much. How has your mom been?"

"Oh. Same, I guess. It's ok. Hana and I spell off my

dad. We make it work." His arm twitched. "Look, Jeannie, that's not what I want to talk to you about."

I looked at him. "Sounds serious. What's up?"

"Well, it's not serious. I don't think. But…um, I've been encouraged to sort of…follow up with you because… Hmmm, some of our friends want to make sure that we aren't carrying around any old baggage. So, um…"

"Are we talking about grad?" Again? Will people never let that go?

"Yes?" He sounded a little confused. "Don't you want to talk about it?"

"Not especially. Do you?" I waited to see what direction he wanted to take.

"Yeah. No, not really. Okay, well." He spread his hands as if smoothing them on a desk. "I just need to officially apologize for being a jerk-off teenager and hurting you. I shouldn't have done that, and I want to make sure you didn't suffer any lasting damage because of my behaviour." He rattled off what sounded like a rehearsed speech. "And also, you know, I want us to be comfortable with each other. As much for the gang, you know, as ourselves."

Oh, Zach.

We had come to the end of a row of vendor booths and the sparkling blue lake opened up in front of us. The park we stood in was dotted with tall fir and cedar trees, but along the beach stood a row of old weeping willows, their bright-green leaves hanging low to the sandy ground, providing dappled shade for swimmers and picnickers. This really was a beautiful setting for Julian's Faire. I couldn't wait to see the crowds filling the space tomorrow. I hoped for his sake and for Quinn's that it made all their dreams come true.

I stopped walking and gestured to a bench under one of the willows, and Zach nodded, so we sat, facing the tranquil blue water of the lake, with the low rays of afternoon sun dappling its surface.

Zach really wasn't a bad guy. And as for the consequences of his actions that fateful night, I really couldn't hold him responsible for my own emotional meltdown, my bruised pride, my drinking binge, and certainly not for any of the events that followed, never mind the fallout.

"It was so long ago, Zach. I can barely remember that night. And I wasn't hurt as much as you might imagine. I hope that doesn't bruise your ego. I was mostly…embarrassed, I guess?"

He looked at me with his brows pulled together, lines of worry bisecting his broad forehead, and I could see his regret was sincere. His mouth quirked to one side in an attempted smile. "I guess we're on the same page then."

I smiled and nodded. "Let's just put this behind us, shall we? I'm sure every eighteen-year-old has done things they regret, and that they've learned from, myself included. That's part of growing up, isn't it?"

"I suppose."

I turned to face him. "We shared some fun times, and we're both very lucky to have such a wonderful, supportive group of friends who care about us."

He nodded, looking chagrined. After gazing out at the lake for another few moments in silence, he said, in a soft voice, "I really did like dating you. You made me look smarter by association. You were way too good for me."

Laughter burst out of me. "You made me look good, too! Much cooler than I am. And all the other boys were short, skinny, or acne-ridden. You were cute, and I was impressed by your muscles. You were the first real man I'd ever seen."

That made him laugh, and turn a bit pink, and I was glad to see he was capable of humility. "I'm assuming you're discounting movie stars. I remember you had a big crush on Henry Cavill."

I still did. Blushing, I deflected. "We had a lot of fun that first summer, flirting, hanging out at the beach, swimming. It seemed like we were meant to be together."

"I guess we were both the best at something, and everyone expected it. That's the way I look at it now."

"You're right. It's history. So you can stop worrying, or tell whichever of our friends to stop worrying. You and I are going to be just fine. Okay?"

"Okay. Hug it out?"

We stood up. I smiled and leaned forward to slide my hands around his gigantic torso. My God! Though Phoenix was as big and strong as one of the giant cedar trees, Zach wasn't that far behind. His long arms came around me loosely and patted my shoulders. I squeezed him once, twice, and he mimicked my movement, carefully. I laughed and squeezed him again and then we leaned away and smiled into each other's eyes, all awkwardness forgotten.

"Come on. I'll show you Julian's pop-up restaurant and the main stage. We hung the banners this morning." He gestured to the left, and we strolled that way, sipping our coffee in the dappled sunlight.

Once we'd wandered around Julian's place, which was vacant, we passed the main stage, where two or three guys were stringing cables. I realized one of them was Phoenix when he stopped at the edge of the stage and lifted a hand in greeting.

"Big-P, my man!" Zach waved, laughing. He really did have a bit of hero worship going on.

I waved and smiled, too, but Phoenix looked busy, so we continued on. Before we turned away, he pulled his phone from his pocket and shook it, which I took to mean, he'd call later. Or something. If he didn't, I would. It was time.

After Zach took off, I strolled the lakefront alone, enjoying the peaceful view, and then found and followed a narrow trail that led into a treed area. The undergrowth was thick and lush with indigenous plants, many with bright yellow and frilly white blossoms in the shady canopy of the trees. The air was humid and sweet-smelling, and I experienced a momentary feeling of peace and contentment.

I felt glad and grateful that Zach had pressed me to have that conversation. I might have—who was I kidding, I definitely would have—avoided it. But we'd smoothed over any residual hard feelings about our relationship, which it seemed someone had been worried about. And now…all was well. With the lingering tension over Zach and Deanna cleared up, I had reason to be hopeful. Not everything that had happened in the past turned out badly.

Phoenix

I'd been playing the events of our date, and perhaps even more, the uninhibited mess that was Jeannie after she'd been out with the girls, over and over in my mind. Which was the more relevant data? The reserved, cautious, inexplicably nervous woman from last weekend? Or the silly, flirty girl from last night? Somehow, these were both a part of the woman I had set my sights on. Both seemed to be attracted to me, open to spending time with me, but also reticent. In no way had I been given an open ticket. But I hadn't been given marching orders either.

At Bear Lake Park, I'd found Julian and checked in to see if there were any last-minute jobs that needed doing. I'd ended up helping with the stage since it fell well within my arena of expertise.

As we were wrapping up the lighting and sound setup, I paused to look out over the lake from my elevated position.

The sky was mostly clear of clouds, and the temperature was balmy, with a gentle breeze wafting in off the lake.

That's when I saw them. Jeannie with Zach, sitting together on a bench overlooking the lake out beyond the concert zone and Julian's pop-up restaurant. Even from this distance, I could pick Jeannie out of a crowd. And that big blond lumbering idiot beside her could only be Zach.

It shouldn't have caught me by surprise. I'd asked—no, pretty much ordered him to talk to her. That's all that was happening, right? But seeing them side by side, talking intimately, and then standing, hugging, laughing, pushed some button inside me.

The green monster I'd known so well in high school raised its ugly head and let out a nasty growl. Then, I'd had plenty of reason to be jealous of Zach. Though I knew better, because no one's life was that simple, he seemed to have everything I lacked.

We were friends despite our differences. His family was whole. His dad coached athletics at our school. Even at seventeen, Zach was tall, good-looking, well-built, well-fed, and well-loved. And on top of that, he had Jeannie, who I'd adored at arm's length. How could any kid in my position not envy that?

That's why, on grad night, I'd been in the wrong place at the right time. That night, lacking a diploma and sensing the end to even a half-assed attempt to be normal and included, dreading whatever life had in store for me next, I'd felt more like an outsider than ever. While all my classmates were celebrating, I'd been watching from the margins, as usual. I'd gone to the party, because why the hell not? And I'd gotten fairly sauced in a low-key, depressed way, while everyone else shrieked, danced on tables, fell in the swimming pool, and puked into their shoes all night long to a party soundtrack of Kesha and Bruno Mars and Rihanna.

Like the creeper that I was, I always sensed where Jeannie was. Often hooked under Zach's big-muscled arm, or in a clutch with her girlfriends. But suddenly, it was late, sometime after three, and I realized something was happening. There was a flurry of agitated movement. I felt the mood change. Then there was Jeannie, fleeing outside, upset, dashing past me. Something was wrong.

She was ranting, mumbling to herself in an angry voice. And gripping the neck of a bottle. That did not seem like Jeannie. Or a good thing.

I didn't hesitate. She couldn't walk around by herself at this hour. And something was very off. So I tailed her. She walked, stopping every few steps to drink from the bottle in her fist, waved her other hand around, continuing to gripe out loud, and then stomped on.

After a few blocks, she turned and went through a gate into a little pocket park between two huge heritage houses. Morris Park, it was called, named after some old timer who donated the land. There was a copse of huge old oak trees and rolling grass on either side of the wide walkway that snaked through the park to the next street over.

Once in the middle of the park, Jeannie's angry steps slowed, and she began to weave. Whatever she'd been drinking was starting to take effect. I closed the distance between us, but hung back, waiting to see what she'd do next. Then she stopped walking, tilted her head up and seemed to be studying the night sky through the overhanging canopy of branches, thick with leathery green leaves, some of which had already fallen to the ground, crunching under my shoes. She swayed slightly, then turned to a large tree and stepped towards it, wrapping her arms around the broad trunk.

I heard a sob then and knew she'd been crying all along. She rolled against the trunk leaning against it, then stuttered slowly to the ground, with her legs outstretched on the grass.

I stepped closer, standing a few feet away.

Finally, she glanced my way. "Who's that?"

"It's me. Pete," I answered quietly.

"Oh, hey, Pete." Her voice was soft, sad, slurred. She patted the ground beside her. "Have a seat, my friend." Then she took another huge swig of the bottle.

I did as she bid, sitting close but not touching her. She handed the bottle to me. I took it, sniffed, and winced. Vodka. Not my preferred beverage, but at this point, I didn't care much, so I took a drink, setting the bottle down on the ground away from Jeannie. She, it seemed to me, had had enough.

"What's up?"

She filled her lungs, let out a long quivering sigh, and then burst into tears again. I tentatively lifted an arm, and she leaned into me, pressing her face to my chest. I tucked her in and she snuggled closer, whimpering against my shirt.

Through fits of tears and wailing and shaking, she gasped out the story bit by bit. I came to understand that earlier in the evening, Zach had led her upstairs to one of the bedrooms to make out. The party was at Deanna's parents' huge mansion, so there was no shortage of rooms. So far par for the course. Then he'd started pressing her for sex, which apparently had been an ongoing theme of their relationship. And she'd always resisted.

"I thought I wanted to. My friends were all doing it. But it just didn't feel right, so I could never."

"That's okay, Jeannie," I'd reassured her. "You should never do it unless you really want to. You're a good girl. Zach's wrong to push you."

She nodded, tears still leaking sadly down her wet cheeks. "I know, too good," she gurgled. "But tonight he wouldn't give up. He's wasted. I think he wanted to celebrate grad, and…"

My heart kicked up, imagining the worst. "Did that fucker force you?"

Now her head swung in a huge, exaggerated pendulum, and my pulse eased off. Thank God. Not that.

"No, no, no. I don't think he'd do that. But he wheedled and begged, and then he got annoyed and started griping at me. Saying I was leading him on. Saying I didn't love him. Asking me why I was even dating him if I didn't want to have sex with him." She turned her face up to mine, her eyes glistening in the faint light. "As if that's the only reason to date someone, you know?" Her voice dipped to a whine, rose at the end in a pathetic squeak.

I nodded, patting and then squeezing her arm.

She cuddled closer, wrapping her arms around my ribs, returning my embrace. "You'd never push like that. I know you wouldn't."

That shocked me. I didn't think she even saw me that way. My voice cracked when I replied, "I wouldn't. I respect you, Jeannie."

When another minute or so had passed in silence, I asked, "And then you left? Is that what happened?"

"Nope. There's more." She pulled her knees up and twisted towards me, half leaning on my legs, sloppy from drinking now. "After we argued, I came downstairs and talked to Quinn. And Rainy. I don't know. A while later, I didn't see Zach anywhere, so I thought I'd find him. Make up, you know?"

I hummed, encouraging her to continue. When she did, I learned that she'd gone upstairs again, searching for Zach. First in the room where she'd left him, then others, until she finally found him. Flat on his back on Deanna's bed with her astride him, riding him like there was no tomorrow, grunting and moaning, hard at it. They didn't even notice her peeking in, and she was so shocked, she stared a full minute before withdrawing and closing the door.

Jeannie was full-on bawling again, her arms tightening around me. "In truth, I don't even know why I was dating him. I'm so stupid." She reached across me for the bottle, drinking from it again.

I shook my head. I guess I'd wondered too, sometimes. Knowing them both, they sure weren't compatible. But then, they looked good together. I'd wondered, often enough, whether they were getting it on, and if that was the main reason. It was good enough for most teens.

"It's okay, Jeannie. You're a good girl. Forget about that douchebag." I soothed her, stroking her arms and back, relishing the feel of her silky hair under my fingers, the softness of her curves against my body. I was half bewildered to be in this situation, able to touch her for the first time. "You're heading off to university. You don't need that asshole in your life. And your heart will heal from this." I bent my head to press a kiss on her head. So soft. She smelled like flowers. I stayed there an extra moment, just letting her hair brush softly against my cheek.

"I don't know if my heart is hurt or just my pride," she said in a thin voice, thumping on her chest.

I don't know how long we sat like that, touching, cuddling. Her weeping slowly, finally ebbing. I thought she was growing sleepy, and wondered how I was going to get her to the party house, or maybe home, if that's what she wanted.

Then her hands began to caress my side, my back, sliding around to feel my chest through my shirt. I sucked in a breath, shocked by her touch into sudden arousal. I squirmed as my erection grew stronger, pressing into the side of her thigh.

She shifted her weight, turning to face me, pressing herself even more against me, nuzzling her face, her lips against the hot side of my neck. "Pete," she whispered.

I swallowed, my throat as dry as the crumbling oak leaves under my ass. "You feeling better now?" I whispered, afraid to break the spell. Afraid for this magical moment to shatter.

"Mm-hmm," she hummed, sliding one leg over my thighs, straddling me, her face still pressed to my neck. I felt the wetness of her open mouth on my skin, the slippery slide of her tongue behind my ear.

Holy fuck! What was happening?

"Jeannie?" I tested. "Do you know where you are?"

"Mm-hmm," she breathed against me, undulating in a slow sensual wave, pressing her soft round breasts against my chest, against my wildly pounding heart, grinding her hot center onto my ever-hardening cock.

I felt my pulse there too, trapped between us, thumping.

"You know this is me, here," I croaked. "Pete?" I wanted to cry. Any moment now, she was going to wake up and jerk away, shocked at her mistake.

"If it weren't for Zach, maybe you and me could have gone out."

"Oh, now you tell me." I laughed, nervous, and disoriented.

She lifted her head, her hands holding my neck from both sides, peering intently into my eyes, her face inches from mine. "Would you have?"

Her hair had fallen forwards over her shoulders, and I gently pushed it back. "In a heartbeat, Jeannie." I sobered, gazing into her eyes, dark, shadowed, gleaming in the night. "You're beautiful. You're amazing. And you're too good for me."

She shook her head a tiny bit. "You're nice. You're a good person, Pete, in a bad situation. You have a kind heart. I always knew that." Then she rocked my world by tilting her head and closing the distance between us to press her soft, soft lips against mine.

I was dying. This was Jeannie. She was kissing me.

"I don't always want to be a good girl, Pete," she murmured against my lips. "Ever since Bonnie died, I've been so damned good. I'm tired. It's not that much fun, you know?" She raked her fingers through my hair, holding my head as she angled her face to mine.

My brain circuits were frying. In a flash, something electrifying sparked between us. My desire for her flared like a bonfire out of control. I took her face between my palms and returned the kiss. The kiss. I'd always remember this moment as The Kiss.

"I want…" she said between kisses, her breath hitching in surprise.

She felt it too. Her lips parted, she deepened the kiss, and I pressed closer, delving into her heat with my tongue. She met me, tangled her tongue with mine, and explored my mouth with skill and passion belied by her innocence. I felt a groan rising from my chest as my hunger grew wild. My hands slipped down, digging into her curves. When I lightly and tentatively stroked her breast, she let out a soft high moan and arched her back, pressing it harder into my hand. Jesus. We'd gone from a gentle, tender embrace and a chaste kiss to a passionate, frenzied groping make-out session in moments. I gripped her hips, palmed her ass through her summer dress, hiking her higher and tighter against my hardness.

We broke apart, gasping for breath. In the darkness, our gazes met, our breaths mingling in sudden, shocking intimacy. I glanced around, praying no one else walked this way. But it was late. The neighbourhood was dead silent.

"Jeannie?"

"Pete. I…" She blinked, her lips parted. She licked them, holding my hypnotized gaze. "Pete, I want this. I never felt this need with Zach. But suddenly, I can't wait."

"What? Are you serious?"

In answer, she hiked her dress up to her waist, crossed her arms and yanked it up and off, tossing it to the side. My breath whooshed out of me as the sight of her round breasts rising from their nest of a sheer, pale-coloured bra, pink or lavender. Miles of her soft, white skin filling my vision.

"Jeannie, no. You've been drinking. You're upset."

"No, Pete. I know what I'm doing. I want to feel this. With you. You and me. We understand each other. This is right. Right now." Then she kissed me again, grinding herself against me, driving every last coherent thought from my mind. Somehow we ditched my pants, rolled around on the grass for a bit. I stroked her with my hand, my fingers feeling her swollen heat, her ready wetness as she gripped me eagerly. And then the details blur. I only knew that we were joined, and it felt inevitable and right, and we rode that wave of intense feeling right to its blissful end.

Something happened that night that I still couldn't explain fully. Despite all the traumatic events that followed, that precious hour or so alone with Jeannie, and the connection that we felt, had made an impression on me that had stayed. It had changed me.

I was a bit too drunk, too sad, and too stunned by what was happening to fully understand it at the time. But I remember suddenly having this thought. Like… *Oh, so this is what it's all about.* Something like that. That feeling, more than anything, is what stayed with me through the years. Yet

I still didn't know if she remembered that night, or all of it. What we'd done. She hadn't quite let on, and I was afraid to raise it.

Now, the more time I spent around Jeannie, the more I saw of her, the deeper my fascination grew, and the stronger that feeling returned to me. I knew it was partly the unrequited crush I'd had on her my entire adolescence. An opportunity missed. But she really was adorable. Sweet, smart, caring, responsible. And so perfectly beautiful and sexy. I even saw a few hints of the spark she'd used to have —when she'd thought the world was her oyster, before life's hard knocks.

It had to be her son that hindered her. Not literally, but in some emotional or practical way. What else had changed? I understood that she'd want to protect her kid from casual strangers. It made sense that a responsible, loving single mother wouldn't take lightly the impact random hookups with men might have on their child's well-being. Not a woman like Jeannie.

But this was me. And we'd shared…that.

And I actually liked the idea that she had a son. I wanted to be part of her life, no matter what. I'd like to start a family soon, anyway. Maybe she'd be game to have another baby right away. Though I supposed her MBA was her priority right now. So maybe not.

I was getting ahead of myself. As usual, if I planned a mission, I was confident I'd succeed. I could easily visualize the end game. But truthfully, time was ticking on, and I'd made precious little progress.

Ah, Jeannie. What do you need from me?

If things didn't work out with Jeannie, maybe I'd be better off starting over in Ottawa. Meet someone new. It would be awkward, painful even, to continue hanging out in the same crowd forever if I had lingering feelings for Jeannie. I couldn't imagine them disappearing now. What if she hooked up with a new guy? Watching that would kill me.

I didn't have any further intel for Unger despite my looming deadline, yet I felt the need to bounce some thoughts around. It was just after 16:00. Still time. After checking in with Julian, and while driving to the base from the park to shower and change for the volunteer dinner tonight, I used the hands-free function on my phone to call Vice-Admiral Hempell.

Or Uncle Ted, as I'd used to know him, growing up. A younger colleague to my father's father, he'd been a mentor to Dad during his own Naval career. And he'd worked so hard helping Dad get—if not literally, then figuratively—back on his feet after his accident. No one had pushed him harder, or rallied more resources to help Dad deal with his surgeries, physio, and PTSD. And no one had supported Mom and me more than he had.

So when I signed up at seventeen, a homeless ghost, with desperately high hopes and not even a high school diploma to hang them on, it was Uncle Ted's counsel I'd sought first, and he'd steered me right all the way. There was no one whose advice I'd rather seek than his when I had tough questions to answer—or had lost my bearings.

"Sir," I said in greeting when he picked up his private line.

"Peter! My boy." His booming baritone rumbled through the line.

"Hope I didn't wake you, sir." He was in Ottawa, so three hours ahead of me.

"I'm not that old yet." His familiar laugh, like a barking seal, warmed my insides.

"Or disturb your evening," I suggested.

"Just a little light reading before bed." Which likely meant confidential mission reports. Or directives from

CSIS, the security intelligence branch. Or *War and Peace*. "When will you be coming to visit your favourite uncle?"

I snickered at his prod, indulging in our usual banter. "Uncle? You're far more like a grandfather to me, sir. Much older and much, much wiser."

He laughed again. "I suppose you want some free advice, you young smart ass."

"If you're handing it out, sir. I'm a little skint right now." I paused, drew a deep breath, and let it out. I'd arrived on base and pulled into the officer's housing parking area, shutting off the truck. Relaxing into my bucket seat, I said, "I imagine I'll get some no matter what I say."

He just snickered softly, putting an end to our banter and creating a quiet space for me to unload whatever had prompted my call.

There weren't many people who'd known me all my life and, moreover, known my parents and everything we'd gone through as a family. Not for the first time, I thanked the stars for Ted. I wasn't sure where I'd be today if not for his steady, guiding hand.

"You're aware Lt. Robinson has transferred to Halifax?"

"Mm. I recall something about that." As if any detail escaped Ted's rigorous oversight. "And your other friend?"

I sighed. "Lt. Damien Meskew. He's staying at Dwyer, but planning to apply to CSOR, out of JTF 2, so…"

"So you'll likely be running missions with fresh blood."

"Yes, sir. But it's not that. I've worked with just about everyone in the units at one time or another. It's not missions I'm worried about."

"You're not thinking of quitting, are you?"

"No, sir! Not at all."

"Something personal, Peter?"

I hummed my agreement. "I've been on leave in Port Camosun. Time's just about up. And Chief Unger's waiting on my decision regarding a transfer to the Pacific. Or…not."

The rough, gravelly sound that came through the line was just Ted's way of acknowledging he understood something, but it resembled a growling bear. "How's your lovely mother?"

"She's good, actually. Bess is starting university. Can you believe it?"

"Little baby Bess? Well, knock me over with a feather."

I told him about Mom's new secret man-friend.

"Good for her. Good for her." He breathed slowly. "Everyone's moving on with their lives, eh?"

"Yup. Yes, sir. Seems so."

"And so what does Peter Corbin want?"

I sighed. "There's this woman…" And I told him all about Jeannie. Our past, and my desire to rekindle something with her, but my lack of time to pursue it. My lack of data.

"She requires a gentle touch, then." He confirmed. "And you have to make a decision."

"That's pretty much it."

"Nothing is certain in life, Peter. All decisions are made without certainty about the future, even if we sometimes fool ourselves into thinking we have it."

"Yeah, but. This feels…" I shrugged, as if he could see me.

"Trust your gut, boy. I do. You have good instincts." He covered the receiver and cleared his throat, speaking to someone on his end in a muffled voice. "Excuse me. I have to let you go. One last thing." I waited through his thoughtful pause. "You have unfinished business in that town. That in itself might take some time."

Chapter 10

Phoenix

"Hey, everybody!" Julian hollered from the front of the buffet. His face was alight with happiness, flushed from exertion in the kitchen, and his eyes a little shiny from fatigue.

Tonight was a kind of soft open for the Faire, with many of the exhibitors present, putting the final polish on their displays, while the gates were open for any early birds. But tonight, Julian's pop-up restaurant was just for us.

The buzz of lively conversations ebbed as people gradually realized he was speaking.

"I'm so stoked you were able to join us tonight for the pre-launch of the first annual Port Camosun Farm-to-Table Faire."

A burst of enthusiastic applause and whoops and cheers rose.

"None of this would have been possible without you. Everyone here has played a key role in making this dream come true." Julian stepped forwards, closer to one of the tables near the front. "I'd like to send out a special thank you to the core group of inspired and passionate sustainable foodies who joined me in imagining an event like this. And from that idealistic beginning, put in hundreds of hours of tireless work, planning, and expertise to take this event from dream to reality."

Jules stepped around the organizers' table, shaking hands, squeezing shoulders, and accepting warm pats from various friends. "Matt. Arnie. Elinor. Hanns. Reuben. Sarjit. And all the local farmers and producers who told us what they wanted this to be."

"And of course, this is the first public, but not the last time you'll hear me say a heartfelt thank you to all of our corporate, government, and private sponsors. Ethan. Suzanna. Noah. Leon. The Fraser family. Everyone here tonight."

Then Julian came to stand at the end of our long table. "Thank you as well to my family, Ruby, Molly, Mom, and my amazing group of friends, with a special mention for Deanna and Nia, without whose marketing expertise I'd still be an idealistic but obscure farmer."

This elicited a flutter of laughter. It seemed many here were aware of Julian's recent rise to Instagram celebrity status.

"Tonight's gathering is meant as a thank you to all of you who contributed to this Faire. To all of the sponsors, planners, marketing experts and promoters, to our exhibitors, and all of the volunteers who helped with laying out the grounds, building booths, setting up tents, hanging banners, stringing cables, and every other job that goes unnoticed but is an essential component of a successful event like this. Enjoy tonight's festivities and the next few days. I encourage you all to participate fully and enjoy every aspect of the Farm-to-Table Faire."

While he spoke, Deanna, of course, bobbed around taking ample photos and videos to post on the socials.

The dinner Julian had put on for tonight was simple but delicious since he obviously was swamped with other preparations for the days to come. Some of the dishes we enjoyed were the same as those that his Faire menu would offer. The ample salads, salsas, and spit-roasted meats accompanied by freshly baked bread were rustic but delicious.

He'd hired all kinds of kitchen staff and waitstaff to support the Faire effort, and everyone was getting a trial run tonight. Julian had told us that he and his partner had been interviewing and vetting potential staff for their new permanent restaurant that would be opening in the autumn at the Ragged Mountain Resort and Spa. I suspected that the owner of the resort, Ethan Garwood, who was also a major sponsor of the Faire, had picked up the bill for the pop-up restaurant kitchen staff.

Around our table sat our entire group of friends and a few extras who'd been brought along to help out in various volunteer capacities. It was a clamorous and festive environment. Though I did notice that all the girls who had overindulged the night before were a little subdued tonight. I was feeling a little delicate myself—and sticking to drinking soda.

I was also determined, for once, to find time alone with Phoenix to have the conversation.

People were pretty casual about staying in their seats since the meal was laid out as a giant buffet, and most had gotten to know each other over the last three days. Between courses, everyone moved from table to table or stood around talking convivially. The lakeside setting was beautiful with late afternoon sun sparkling on the rippled surface of the water across which a gentle breeze blew, ruffling the dangling branches of the weeping willow trees. The energy level was high.

Keeping my eyes peeled for Phoenix, I returned to the buffet for a second helping of the scrumptious salsa and roast pork shoulder. Scanning the crowd, I finally spotted him seated with a bunch of guys I didn't know, presumably people he'd met while setting up the grounds.

He drank from a bottle of beer and tossed his head back, laughing at something his table mates said, and I caught my breath. He so rarely smiled, never mind outright laughed, that it took my breath away. His level of hotness jumped tenfold when he relaxed and let go of his steely, watchful control. I wondered if he was very different when he was at work, surrounded by his familiar naval colleagues.

After picking up a glass of raspberry soda, I moved in his direction. Before I got three steps closer, I was intercepted by a tall, lean, and handsome man with a coif of wavy brown hair falling over his forehead.

"Hi there. I don't think we've met before."

I blinked in surprise. "No. Should we have?"

"I don't know. Maybe we were destined to meet right now."

I scoffed but couldn't help a gust of laughter and felt my face heat at his implied flattery.

He offered his hand to shake, smiling broadly. "I'm Noah, Noah Saddler, a good friend of Julian's, and a Faire sponsor."

I sipped my soda, ignoring his hand.

"I own Port Cam Harbour Heli-tours. I noticed you sitting at the table with all of his classmates, most of whom I met at the reunion. But I don't remember seeing you there."

"Oh. No. That's because I missed it, but I was in the same class. You're very observant."

His gaze danced over my face and shoulders, obviously trying not to stare directly at my chest. "I think if I'd seen you before I would've remembered, that's all." He raised his dark eyebrows in expectation and stared at me until I twigged that I had dropped my end of the introductions.

"Oh. Sorry." I lifted my glass in lieu of a handshake. "I'm Jeannie. Jeannie van Bellen. I just returned to town a few weeks ago."

"I'm very pleased to meet you Jeannie van Bellen. I hope to see more of you around the Faire over the next few days. Maybe we can get to know each other better."

Without my having noticed his approach, Phoenix suddenly appeared in my peripheral vision, blocking the light and hovering like a tank about to invade an unsuspecting city. I flinched and glanced at him.

"Hi, Phoenix. I was just about to come looking for you. Have you met Julian's friend, Noah?"

Stoic as ever—the friendly smiles I'd seen on his face not minutes ago having vanished—Phoenix stared menacingly at Noah, nodded in a macho way, and grunted a low-key greeting.

"Can I talk to you for a minute, Jeannie?"

"Oh. Uh-huh. Sure." I turned to Noah. "Excuse me. I'll see you around the fairgrounds, I guess."

He smiled. "Absolutely. Nice to meet you, Jeannie." His effusive enthusiasm had dampened under Phoenix's threatening watch.

Embarrassed, I wiggled my fingers in a farewell wave and walked with Phoenix away from him.

Lowering my voice to a hiss, I said, "What the hell is your problem? I'm not your property, Peter Corbin. That was incredibly rude. Why couldn't you just join us in friendly conversation?"

"That was not a friendly conversation," groused

Phoenix. "That was a blatant come-on. Can't you tell the difference?"

Hesitating to consider his question, my lips pursed, because apparently I couldn't, I still stood my ground. "He's a friend of Julian's," I finally retorted. "He wouldn't do that. And anyway, he was perfectly gentlemanly. Where do you get off stomping around like a bear defending his den?"

He didn't deign to reply.

What a bossy, controlling, know-it-all. I was equal parts annoyed and flattered by his possessiveness. We walked without speaking to the outer ring of tables and stepped away from the lights.

"You wanted something?"

He stopped and faced me. "Yes. You." He stepped closer, his gaze a hot caress that slid from my eyes to my lips, to my neck, shoulder, breasts, and down. And then he took my hand in his and held it lightly. The gentleness of his touch directly contradicted the hungry possessiveness of his gaze. Every spot he looked at seemed to crackle and burn under the heat of his survey.

"You said you were just about to come looking for me. Why?" he asked.

"Uh, yes. I wanted to talk to you about…" I couldn't do this here. How did I do this at all? "I…um…wanted to thank you. I'm completely embarrassed that you had to see Quinn and me in that condition, and I suppose all of the other girls, too, but I don't remember much. You were a real hero responding to our SOS and chauffeuring everyone home safely last night. I don't know…what I might have said or done, but hopefully nothing too obnoxious."

That broke him. His grouchy demeanour melted away to reveal the warmth of his teasing half smile, and the sparkling all-seeing intelligence in his deep-green eyes. My insides went woozy at his sweet expression, and I fought the urge to touch the irresistible crease at the corner of his wide mouth.

"It was my pleasure. You can call on me anytime."

A wave of heat swept up my chest and face, and I was grateful for the semi-darkness for concealing my embarrassment.

"You…were very cute," Phoenix said, lifting my hand to his lips and softly kissing my knuckles. "I hope to see more smiles on your face, like I saw last night. It made me happy to see you relaxed and having fun."

He lowered his hand with mine still loosely in his grip and led me further away from the pop-up restaurant towards the lakeshore. "I guess you and Zach had a chat?"

I pulled up short and frowned at him indignantly. "So it was you who put the pressure on poor Zach. I thought he was going to lay an egg."

"Don't know what you mean," Phoenix said, shifting his gaze to the water. "I only happened to see you sitting together when I was working on the stage wiring."

"Un-huh. Sure."

His head twitched slightly in my direction, his brows hitching up in challenge.

When we got to the edge of the water, Phoenix turned to me, his gaze softly and hungrily sweeping over my face and body with clear admiration shining. The mild summer breeze drifting onshore ruffled my hair. He released my hand and gently caressed my hair, combing it away from my face, behind my ear, and over my shoulder, sending shivers racing over my skin.

With his other hand, he placed one fingertip above my lips, in the little divot he'd mentioned the other night, and dragged it to the corner of my mouth over the dimple in my chin. Then, tilting his head, his gaze following the path of his finger, he traced my jaw, drawing a line down my neck and across my collarbones, sending darts of heat spiking through my middle to set fire to my core. I had never felt so seen, admired, or wanted by anyone in my life. Whatever he intended to do to me, at this moment, I was his.

"Ah, Jeannie," Phoenix said and let out a deep, slow breath. "I want to run up a mountain for you. I want to lift a thousand pounds. I'm filled with the powerful desire to conquer worlds on your behalf. To pave your path with diamonds."

Oh my goodness. I couldn't process this. What was he doing to me? My mind was cotton fluff. My will had turned to molten liquid.

"Was there something you wanted to say to me?" Phoenix murmured softly, his breath washing over my skin as though I were swimming in warm water.

"No." My voice was a mere breath. "Nothing that can't wait till tomorrow," I heard myself deflect because I couldn't bear the thought of interrupting this sweet, sensual moment.

After walking with Phoenix along the lakeshore for several minutes, I excused myself to go home, to tuck Will in for the night, I'd said, because I hadn't seen him all day. Though my real reason was to remove myself from over-whelming temptation.

No sooner had I got in the door when my phone rang. I kicked off my shoes, hooked my bag on the newel post, dropped down to sit on the second to last step, and answered the call.

"Did you do it?" Quinn's voice burst out of the speaker excitedly. "I saw you go off with him, but I got distracted so I didn't see anything else. Did you have the talk? Is it done?"

Reluctant to invite her criticism, I rubbed my tired eyes with my knuckles, sighing. "No," I finally answered.

"Aw, Jeannie," came Quinn's reply, thick with disappointment. "You're never going to be able to move forwards and start dating him properly until you get past this."

"Who said dating Phoenix was my objective in all this? I just have to do my moral duty. That's all I agree to. What happens after that, well, I just don't know. My priorities are Will and school, as you know, Quinn. I don't have the bandwidth for anything beyond that."

"Don't get all huffy and righteous with me, van Bellen."

I could tell she'd had a few drinks and was feeling feisty.

"I know what you want. You want that hot man. And I'm telling you that you can have him. You can have it all. Just step up, for fuck's sake. Don't ruin this."

"I will. I meant to tonight. I really did. I can't explain how hard it is and how many weird, disorienting things keep happening to make it impossible." Was it possible that I was subconsciously trying to sabotage any chance of a relationship with Phoenix by undermining his trust in me? "I'll tell him tomorrow. I swear."

When I got off the phone and started up the stairs, I found Will sitting on the top landing, waiting for me.

"Hi, Mom." His voice was raspy, as if he'd been asleep and only woken when he heard me come in.

"Hi, honey. Were you eavesdropping, mister?"

"How do you know a phoenix?" I'm sure his mind had gone to Harry Potter, and he was mighty confused.

"Phoenix is the name of a guy who I went to school with," I reluctantly replied. "One of my gang of friends."

"Are you dating him?"

My heart flew to my throat, pounding wildly, fuelled not a little by guilt. "No, honey. No, no, no, no. I'm not dating anyone. You don't have to worry about that."

"I'm not worried," Will said matter-of-factly. "I'd like it if you started dating, Mom. You've been single forever. It'd be cool to have a dad like other kids. Are you going to intro-duce me to him?"

I was dumbfounded at this response from my nine-year-old son. "Um. Well, if and when I ever start dating someone that I think is worthy of meeting you, then, of course, I will introduce you."

"What about this Phoenix guy? Is he nice?"

"Yes," I squeaked out softly. I swallowed, realizing I'd really hit a wall here. "He's very nice. And maybe you'll meet him at the Faire."

Jeannie

"I'm exhausted already." Quinn flung herself onto the plastic chair beside me, her hand automatically wiping the tabletop with the damp rag in her hand.

I'd arrived at her pop-up café for my volunteer shift with her, having sent Will off with Mom, Logan, and Lucas to explore the Farm-to-Table Faire.

I watched them wander away, weaving in and out of the growing crowd, grateful to have some time to myself. I had a lot to think about—and decisions to make. I scanned the park, part of me searching for Phoenix, wondering how to make a private conversation happen in this crowded place.

"It's a good exhaustion, though, right?" I took a sip of my coffee, then caught Quinn's gaze. "The more people you're exposed to at the fair, the more people will recognize your café and come in when they see it. Even better if they pick up a card and come by out of curiosity."

"True. All true. And this extra work is just for a few days. I truly didn't expect attendance this big."

"Julian must be thrilled. The Faire is a huge success

already. You'd think it was the only event in town this Labour Day weekend."

Julian had estimated about five hundred people could comfortably wander the fairgrounds before it got annoyingly congested. But people would tend to come and go throughout the day.

Quinn nodded, and I could see through her exhaustion that she was pleased not only by this success for Julian but also by the potential boost to her own fledgling business. "You're sure you don't mind working a shift or two?"

"No way," I insisted. "It'll be fun. Will is getting to know his cousins, and he has Molly's kids to run around with, too. I think he and Charlie are going to hit it off. They're not so young that they can't be trusted on their own. Anyway, Mom is buzzing around the Faire like a Queen Bee, with all her gardening people. So she can keep tabs on them. It's nice for me to get a break for myself."

Across the lawn, two women approached our table from outside the café barrier, one tall and blonde, the other short and dark-haired, the latter pushing a towheaded toddler in a huge stroller.

Quinn looked up. "Oh, hi, Giselle. You made it."

The petite tawny-skinned woman behind the stroller smiled a brilliant white smile. She was a stunning natural beauty, with the delicate features and shiny dark hair I'd always envied.

"Hello, Quinn," she said. "Do you still need my muffins?"

"You bet I do." Quinn shot out of her chair and through the gate to them. "You have no idea how much I appreciate your help. These locusts will clean me out faster than I can restock."

The young woman withdrew a large rectangular plastic container from the lower rack of the giant deluxe stroller and handed it over to Quinn. "I hope they're okay. There are a dozen each of blueberry and chocolate chip." She spoke in a lilting accented English that I recognized as Filipino.

"Thank you so, so much," Quinn gushed. "You're a life-saver, Giselle."

"No problem at all. You know I love to bake," replied Giselle. "And you know what we talked about," she added. "This is a good test, right?"

Puzzled, I glanced at the blonde woman, and I suddenly recognized her as Zach's older sister Hana. My eyes bugged in surprise and delight.

"Oh! Hana! I just realized it's you." I stood up and stepped to the barrier, while Giselle carried her container to the counter with Quinn, the two of them chatting like old friends.

Hana blinked at me, and I watched her face morph from confusion to recognition. "Jeannie, is that you?"

I laughed and answered through my wide smile, "Yup, this is me."

"Zach didn't mention that you were back in town," Hana said.

That didn't surprise me. If I were Zach, I suppose I'd want to erase any association he had with me. Or maybe he simply didn't care anymore. But we'd been together long enough in high school that I knew his sister well. I'd spent plenty of time at their house.

Hana was four years older than we were and had gradu-ated when we were in the eighth grade. Neither she nor Zach was particularly on my radar at that point. But a few years later, she'd returned to give a career-day presentation that had such a profound influence on me. She was a woman in STEM too—science, technology, engineering and mathematics. A chemistry whiz. I had followed her career religiously, as she'd always been a bit of an idol to me. Very early, she'd shot up the ranks of a successful biomedical company and was now its president.

Because my own parents' career ambitions had been relatively modest, I hadn't until that time imagined anything grander for myself. But from then on the sky was the limit, and that's when I began to dream big dreams. The dreams that I had ultimately messed up.

I tried to deflect her comment about Zach not mentioning me by saying, "I haven't been in town that long. I've only seen him once or twice at Quinn's café, and we've all been so busy getting ready for the Faire. How are your parents? How is your mom doing?"

She filled me in on her mother's chronic health situation, which had not unexpectedly gotten progressively worse in the last decade. She'd been plagued with severe fibromyalgia for decades, and I knew the whole family suffered with her. In high school, Zach's mom's condition had preoccupied him as he, his sister, and their father had to spend enormous amounts of time and energy supporting her and running the household. That's one reason I'd spent so much time at their house, hanging out with Zach, helping him with math and science, and taking care of his mom.

Though she'd be frailer and obviously older than she had been, I was relieved that she was still around. Mrs. Chapman was a sweet woman who'd been deprived of an active life, and my heart bled for her.

"I'd love to catch up with your mom sometime," I said.

"You might be able to sooner than you think," Hana replied. "Zach is bringing her to see the Faire. If she's feeling up to it. It could be anytime."

Glancing down at the little girl in the stroller, I realized she had the definite look of a Chapman, with her ultra-blue eyes and cloud of golden curls. "Is this your little girl?" I asked Hana, belatedly acknowledging the child.

"Yes," Hana replied brightly. "This is Winnie. She's three." She bent to the girl and said, "Say hello to Jeannie, baby."

The cherub-cheeked girl squinted up at me curiously. Her hands and face were sticky with crumbs and streaks of blueberry muffin, the remains of which lay on a paper napkin on the tray of her stroller.

I squatted down to smile at her. "Nice to meet you, Winnie."

She waved a hand at me. "Hi."

"Are you still working full time?" I asked Hana, wondering if her career had been compromised to mothering.

"Oh yes, I haven't slowed down at all, actually. Our company has doubled in size in the last three years, and I'm busier than ever."

Oh, the luxury of dual parenting. "Is your husband at home a lot?"

"No. He's away more than I am. Kyle is a geologist, and he goes up North prospecting for long stretches of time. I don't know what we'd do without Giselle living with us. She's more of a mom to Winnie than I am," she added, laughing.

"Hana," I chided. "I'm sure that's not true."

My mind processed all the puzzle pieces. Hana's situation was more aligned with the life plan that I had drafted for myself. Education and career, then marriage and family. But I had got the bits all scrambled: family, then career intermixed with education, which I was still interminably pursuing. I wondered if, when you did it my way, there would ever be the time, the energy, or the inclination to squeeze in romance and marriage. Or had I passed that station for good?

On the other hand, looking at the sweet three-year-old in the stroller making mud pies out of her blueberry crumbs, would I have been content if I'd missed out on so much time with Will when he was this small? Could a woman have an ambitious career and raise a family without compromising somewhere?

I swung around, coming back to the moment, just as Giselle returned with her empty container.

"All set," she chirped happily. "We can go now."

Quinn limped up and handed a blueberry muffin on a paper napkin to me. "You absolutely have to try Giselle's muffins."

Eager to oblige, I accepted the offering and took a bite. The sweet, soft, buttery taste of blueberry and vanilla burst in my mouth—and as I chewed, the just-right crispy-chewy edges dissolved. I moaned and nodded at Giselle.

"Hey, Sis." We all turned to see Zach sliding up, casual in faded, ripped jeans hanging low on his lean hips, and a grey tank top with a giant Under Armour logo, his muscled shoulders and arms on display, showing a golden tan from his time outdoors. "Hiya, Winnie, baby." He bent to chuck his niece under her sticky chin and plant a kiss on the top of her tangled blonde hair.

Then he lifted his gaze to meet mine, and we smiled at each other.

"Jeannie." Quinn shot me a glance and strode to her counter with her rolling stride.

When Zach's gaze dropped to the muffin in my palm, I swallowed, licked my lips, and offered it to him. "Want some?"

"Won't say no to food." He ripped off a big chunk of my muffin and stuffed the whole thing into his mouth while laughing. Then his eyes widened, and he smiled through his chewing. Before he'd finished swallowing, he licked a finger and raved, "Wow. That is the best muffin I've ever had. I want to marry that muffin. Or the person who made it so I can eat one every day!"

Hana and I glanced at Giselle and at each other in turn, and I'm not sure whose blush was hotter, mine or Giselle's. Before any one of us could speak to the talent behind the muffin, Phoenix strolled up.

"There you are, bud," he said to Zach. "Been looking everywhere for you." He caught me looking him up and down, also spectacular in a navy-blue t-shirt, his inked biceps bulging.

My pulse skittered, remembering his focussed attention the night before.

The corner of his firm mouth quirked. "Hi, Jeannie. Enjoying the Faire so far?"

I nodded wordlessly, swallowing.

"You here with your son?" he asked, lightly.

"He's with my mom. Somewhere," I choked out as if I wasn't dying inside. I waved a vague hand, though I could still spot the boys through the crowd at one of the booths.

He nodded, then nudged Zach. "Let's go."

"Thanks for the snack," Zach said to me, appearing clueless about the muffin's origin. "Gotta head to the gym. See you, ladies." He hadn't even looked at Giselle, as if she were part of the stroller or another tree in the park.

Hana asked, "I thought you were bringing Mom today?"

He replied, "I am. Later. We'll be back."

"Don't slack off, Zach."

He scowled at her dismissively. "Who do you think relieves Dad when you and Kyle are both out of town, Sis?"

"Alright, alright." She blinked slowly and waved him off,

and the two men ate up the grass with huge strides as they disappeared towards the parking area.

My first chance of the day to talk to Phoenix was gone. I hoped I'd have an opportunity later on.

I said goodbye to Giselle and Winnie, then said to Hana, "I would love to have a coffee with you sometime and hear more about your company. When you have time, of course."

"Happy to."

Quinn returned and handed a clipboard to me. "So, here's the schedule. Sign up for as many shifts as you want. We need all the help we can get."

Chapter 11

Phoenix

"WHAT YOU LOOKIN' so hard at, Lil' Birdy?"

I didn't need to turn my head to know whose voice addressed me. That nickname came only from one man. Monty? What the fuck was he doing in Port Cam?

I turned slowly from my scan of Bear Lake, and the people boating and jumping from the long wooden dock that reached out into it. I'd strolled the park, keeping an eye out for Jeannie's mom—hoping for a glimpse of Jeannie's kid attached to Mrs. van Bellen—but struck out.

"I thought you ghosted me, you mongrel prick."

He tossed his head with a loud, unreserved belly laugh. His dark dreads, longer than I'd ever seen them, bounced around his head, while his teeth flashed white against his light-brown skin and dark beard. Mercurial, that was my friend Montez Borges.

Monty sauntered up like it was no surprise to find him this far north. "Damien told me you were out West.

Thought I'd ride my Harley up and see what kind of trouble you're making."

I shook my head, stepping away to survey him. His eyes were hidden behind a pair of mirrored aviators. Scary dude to see when he wasn't laughing.

"You still can't grow a proper beard." I reached forwards as if to grab his scruffy beard.

His arm snapped up like a whip to knock mine aside. With my other hand, faster than him, I shoved my palm against his face, avoiding his shades—and took a friendly fist to my gut that I was totally ready for. We tussled a bit more and ended in a back-slapping bear hug.

He bumped my fist. "The Aztecs are beating the fuckin' Conquistadores this time."

He was a mix of Mexican, African-American, and Caucasian. Despite my patchy beard ribbing, I'd always thought he was the best-looking of my buddies.

"What's with the long hair?" I asked. "Don't tell me the brass in San Diego approved that mess."

"Nah." He hesitated, his gaze drifting past my shoulder to the lake. "Gone civvy street. A few months ago."

I had nothing to say to that. I took a deep breath, let it out, and gripped him by his shoulder, squeezing in understanding. It was a big move, and one that, maybe, was hardest for him. Monty and I had started out together, and he'd been one of my closest friends and allies through all of our training and early deployments.

But then, heads big with our own power and skills, we'd all decided to go for JTF 2. Monty didn't make the cut.

After we'd separated, he'd been dissatisfied with what the Canadian Forces offered him. Being a citizen of both Canada and the States, he'd opted to transfer to San Diego, where his dad's family lived. With his training, he'd have been welcome anywhere. That had been five years ago.

We'd always stayed in touch, but he'd gone silent this past year or two.

"What are you doing now?" I asked.

Scowling, he tilted his head and shrugged both shoulders in a kind of fluid full-torso roll that was signature Monty. I half expected him to break into dance moves.

So much attitude. That, I recalled, had been part of his problem. Of all my Navy buddies, Monty was the one whose past was as dark as my own. But Monty let things get to him. He carried a lot of anger on his broad shoulders.

"Thought I'd try private security. Been doing a little contract work in California, and it suits me alright."

"Do I know the outfit?"

"Nah. Moved around. But I want to start my own unit."

"There?"

He did another shoulder roll. "Dunno. Loads of competition from other vets in California."

"What about your family?"

"Too much baggage. Rather make a fresh start."

"What about up here? You're still dual, right?" I asked, referring to his dual Canadian-American citizenship, courtesy of his parents.

He nodded. "You thinking of staying, then?"

I drew in a chest-filling breath and let it out as we turned, shoulder to shoulder, to watch the low-key activity on the lake. "Yeah, maybe. I've got to file the papers in a few days tops."

We watched for a while, kids splashing and paddling all around, squealing and laughing, people swimming and sunning on the wharf.

"What's the dilemma? Your mom's here, right? And your sister?"

I nodded slowly, once. Would that be enough? I felt Monty's gaze, studying me.

"What else?" he asked.

I glanced at his face, then returned my gaze to the lake with a smirk. There were three boys crashing around in a green canoe, drawing everyone's attention. Two around nine, and a little blond one in the middle.

I rubbed my brow. "There's a girl."

"Girl?" He said after a long pause, drawing out the word, lifting at the end.

Before Monty had a chance to quiz me further, one of the older boys stood up in the canoe, gripping the gunnels, and started rocking it. At first, I thought he was losing his balance, but then it became clear he was doing it on purpose to get a rise out of the others.

Monty squinted at them. "What the hell is that little fucker doing?"

The smaller kid screamed like a crushed cat, whether from excitement or fear, and stood as well, waving his oar wildly. The gunnel dipped, taking on water. People on the dock shouted directions to stop messing around—and arguments ensued on board. But the older kid continued rocking the canoe until it was clear it would capsize at any minute.

Monty snorted. "Stupid kids. Is there a lifeguard on duty?"

"I dunno." *That canoe was going over and—* Before I could finish the thought, I was running.

Monty's boots thumped the ground beside me. By the time we got to the beach, the three boys were in the water, flailing and screaming. Monty paused, but I kept running, eating up the wharf's wooden boards in long strides until I reached the closest point—and launched myself into the water.

Phoenix

"What do you think you're doing?" Jeannie snapped at me, her face bright pink as she hugged her torso in a white-knuckled grip.

Not much shocked me, but I'd never seen her angry so I was speechless. And despite my good intentions, somewhat embarrassed.

We had an audience. Not only Monty, standing off to one side with a smirk on his face that I wanted to punch, but the three dripping wet boys I'd dragged out of the water and heaved onto the wharf, with their eyes wide and mouths gaping like freshly caught carp. One of them, apparently, Jeannie's son.

And of course, all the people who'd been playing in the water and on the dock and the beach. They were gawking, too.

Jeannie's blue eyes burned into mine like fiery flames. "Do you honestly think," she gasped, "that I"—she jabbed herself on the breastbone with her pointer finger—"would fail to teach my own *son* to swim?" Her voice had climbed an octave from the start of her question, registering just within human hearing range by the end. "You. Should. Know. Better."

She wasn't making sense. How was I to know that random kid in the canoe was hers? "Slow down Jeannie—" I attempted.

But her mother interrupted by bustling up and wrapping a blanket around the three boys. "Come to the car, boys. Let's get you out of these wet things."

The kid with glasses and a mop of dark hair plastered to his head, apparently Jeannie's son Will, cast a beleaguered glance up at me, mouthing, *sorry, man.*

I smiled at him.

His grandmother swept him and his two cohorts away with a reprimand. "What on earth were you thinking, boys? I never would have let you…" Her voice faded as their foursome moved out of earshot.

"Jeannie? I'm sorry. I didn't know who they were."

"You know things. Secrets," she hissed in a stage whisper.

I raised my palms in supplication. She was, I presumed, referring to her little sister's drowning. I got it. "But—"

"I know we don't know each other anymore, really," she added, frowning. "*Phoenix.*"

I closed my eyes, shifting from foot to foot, my feet squelching in my sopping wet sneakers. This was oddly reminiscent of the discomfort and humiliation of SOAC—special operations assaulter course. I wanted to laugh.

On the other hand, I liked strong, confident women, and Jeannie, in her mama-bear role, was proving herself to be a formidable opponent. I found this encounter oddly stimulating.

"Will has had swimming lessons since he was nine months old, for goodness sake."

I suppose I might have extrapolated that Jeannie—smart, capable, confident, stubbornly independent Jeannie—would turn out to be a ferociously protective and proud mother. I couldn't help but admire her. But I still needed to explain.

"Jeannie—" I tried again. "I didn't know he was your kid."

"Give it up, dude," Monty muttered under his breath.

I shot him a death glare.

He pulled in his chin. "This is the one, right?"

I grunted.

"Do you always poke your nose into other people's business, and just—" She windmilled her hands before tucking them around herself. "Just jump in and *rescue* people?"

Uh. "That is literally my job description." Monty snorted. But Jeannie wasn't ready to listen to my point of view just yet. Maybe Will falling in the lake actually did scare her.

"Jeannie," I said again, speaking more softly, moving closer.

She finally stopped for a breath, her chest heaving, the colour in her face high. Her fury, or panic maybe, had ebbed, and she just scowled at me now, appearing close to tears.

"I'm sorry. I didn't know he was your kid, okay?" I dared to take a small step closer, so I could lower my voice even more, just above a whisper, for her ears only. "We didn't see a lifeguard on duty, they weren't wearing life jackets, and my instinct, and my training, led me to act first and ask questions later."

Her gaze searched my face. Her tongue darted out to moisten her lips, and she frowned, puzzled like my words were finally sinking in.

"You didn't know Will was my son?"

I shook my head. "I didn't stop to ask his name as the canoe was capsizing. I just saw three kids in trouble." I shrugged. "And I was a bit far away for conversation, anyway."

She groaned softly, her gaze downcast and locked on the ground at our feet. "Oh. My God. I'm sorry. I…I…over-reacted."

Now we were getting somewhere. I took another small step closer, getting inside her personal bubble, and whispered, "I'd never do anything to hurt you, Jeannie." I lightly touched her arm.

She blinked up at me. "Who's we? You said…" She glanced around.

"Ah. My buddy Monty." I stepped back and gestured to him. "Jeannie, this is Monty. Monty, Jeannie. We just happened to be standing here, looking out at the lake."

Monty strode forwards and held out his hand, and Jeannie took it briefly. I could see her assessing him, and maybe thinking he was even scarier than me, with his shaggy beard and dark sunglasses.

"Nice to meet you, Jeannie," he said. "Phoenix has told me about you."

That made her smile falter, and she glanced at me. "Oh?"

I half-smiled, rubbing my brow with a knuckle. "About a half hour ago." I gave Monty a dirty look. I'd get my revenge on the bastard another time.

"Have you got a few minutes? Can you come for a walk with me?" I asked her.

"I should really see if Will's okay." She seemed uncomfortable again.

"We won't be long. Come on."

She conceded, and with a friendly goodbye wave to Monty, she fell in beside me, as I led her towards the trail that snaked around the south side of the lake, in amongst the trees.

I glanced over my shoulder at Monty. "Later, bud," I said, trusting he'd be around long enough for us to properly reconnect.

Chapter 12

Jeannie

AFTER A FEW MINUTES OF SILENCE, me floundering in embarrassment and anxiety about walking and talking with him, I conceded, "You really do swim rather well." I should tell him he was Will's father now. Now was the perfect time.

Phoenix chuckled. "Swimming is part of my training."

"I've never seen anyone move so fast. You're like a…torpedo."

"Look. I'm really sorry if I pissed you off. It was completely unintentional."

"I'm sorry too. I can be overprotective of Will. It's been just us for so long, you know?" I darted a cautious glance at his face, then away again.

"No problem."

Our path wound around the end of the lake. Shaded by the trees, it was a private, peaceful, romantic setting, with ducks splashing in the shallows and wildflowers blooming under the forest canopy.

When we passed a flowering shrub, he snapped off a fluffy, bright-pink bloom and handed it to me with a flirty half-smile. "So I'm forgiven?"

I laughed. "Yes. Thank you for helping Will and the boys, but you shouldn't pick wildflowers, probably."

"I'll take my chances on there being no wildlife police around here. But whatever happens, you're worth the risk."

My pulse sped up like a runaway train, half from his sweet flirting, half from my own desperate thoughts. *Now, Jeannie. Tell him. Tell him now!*

Before I had a chance to find the words to start, Phoenix reached over and took my hand in his. My breath caught in my throat, my brain freezing. As we continued down the path, his thumb brushed softly over the back of my hand. It felt nice. So nice that my chest hurt and my eyes burned with inexplicable tears. How sweet it would be to have this. To be normal.

He gave my hand a gentle squeeze. "I haven't made it a secret that I really like you. I always have, you know?"

I hummed. "Yeah. You said."

"But I'm getting mixed messages from you. Are you wanting me to back off? Am I annoying you in some way?"

My breath rushed out in a gust. "No. No, no, no. That's not it at all. I like you too. I do." I swallowed thickly, summoning courage. "I only…think we should talk about grad night. I wanted to, last time, but somehow got too nervous."

"Grad night," he rumbled in reply, giving nothing away.

Okay, it was up to me to press on.

Before I could, he said, "Do you remember it?"

Shocked at the question, I dipped my chin and said, "Of course I do."

"Are we talking about…?" He left his question hanging.

I nodded quickly, making a face. God, could this be any more humiliating? "It was my first time. I guess… I guess that was obvious. I never meant to use you or…" I squirmed uncomfortably. I didn't even know what I was trying to say.

He squeezed my hand again. "Trust me. I did not feel used." A grin flashed across his face, then disappeared. "I was worried though, because you hadn't said anything."

"There was never an opportunity. I mean, as far as anyone knew, you'd died that night. So, it was my secret to keep. I thought."

He nodded. "Fair enough."

"What happened. With us. It's not the kind of thing you blurt out when you haven't seen a person for ten years."

He seemed relieved. "I've been afraid to mention it."

"Oh. I see."

"Do you regret it?" he asked, and when I studied his face, I saw tension and a hint of apprehension, as if my answer was the most important thing to him.

I had to answer honestly. "It's complicated. Yes and no. It wasn't ideal, obviously. Do you regret it?"

He said, emphatically, without hesitation, "I don't. But I do wish I'd had a chance to be with you under better circumstances. I didn't mean for things to get out of control. I know that's exactly what you didn't want. It was the reason you and Zach argued. You were so upset. I only wanted to comfort you and keep you safe."

"I know. Because of everything that happened after, we never had a chance to talk. We never saw each other again. I always wished I could have apologized, too. I was a mess that night. And you were always such a good, supportive friend to me. I was grateful. And later, sad."

"That's not what I intended. Or wanted. I hope you know that." He glanced at the lake, pensive, then said, "I'd been pretty bummed about not graduating and had a fair bit to drink, too."

"I do remember taking the lead." I couldn't meet his gaze, my face hot, the details returning to me the more we spoke.

He stopped walking and turned to me, lifting our joined hands between us and cupping mine in both of his. "You. Were. Amazing," he rasped, his voice a near whisper. His gaze caught mine.

And I fell into the dark bottomless window of his eyes and was swept away to those blissful moments together years ago, both of us wrapped up in each other, lifted out of our melancholy.

"I'll never forget the feel of you."

My breath hitched at the heat and intensity of his words, the way his eyes held me, piercing and unflinching. I couldn't help but believe he meant what he said.

"The thing is, Jeannie. That memory is very, very sweet to me, and I've treasured it through plenty of tough missions. Thinking about you has helped me endure some dark and lonely times."

His confession moved me deeply, and I tried to imagine all the challenges and even horrors he'd been through in the last ten years, and him holding thoughts of me in his mind like that. It was disorienting. Of course, I'd thought of him too. But so differently. Naturally. Because I knew something he didn't.

Now, I didn't know how to respond. This wasn't what I'd expected to hear. Not the direction I thought this conversation would go.

With his other hand, he stroked my face. "That's why I'm so stoked we're both here, now. It's like a dream come true for me. I thought by now some lucky bastard would have won your heart. So I'm sorry if I've come on too strong. I want you to know that. When I thought you didn't remember, that kind of freaked me out."

"No," I breathed the word out, aghast. "I would never forget something like that. It's just that, I always wished I could have told you how…" Aagh! What was I saying? I felt a whoosh of heat to my face and kept my gaze on our joined hands.

He waited patiently, and I forced myself to go on.

"How special it was for me, too. It was nice," I finally blurted out. *Nice!* How pathetic I sounded. "I wish I could have told you that I'm not sorry it happened."

Despite the unexpected outcome, that had always been true. He'd been gentle and sweet, and our mutual passion had made it memorable in a good way, even though we'd ended up together for the weird, sad reason of me finding Zach having sex with my friend. I was always happy Pete had been my first.

"And I always wished I could have made sure you were okay." His broad chest rose and fell with a breath and a sigh. "I'm glad we can talk about it now. I hope you know I didn't follow you that night with any idea that would happen. I was worried about you. But circumstances…"He pulled his bottom lip between his teeth, thinking. "I can't regret it. I liked you so much, and you were there in my arms, so trusting and willing. I couldn't…exactly control myself once things got heated."

"I know. And when I saw you again. I really didn't know what to say. I'd thought you were gone. Long ago."

"Everyone did, but for you, I guess, it was different."

I nodded. Understatement of the century. This was it. My moment to tell him about Will. "More different than you know. I—"

But he cut me off with, "I used to look forward to math classes so damned much. They were my favourite hours of the week. I dreamt of asking you out, but I knew it was hopeless. There was Zach, and naturally, you didn't see me that way. You would never have accepted me."

My face pulled tight with a mix of chagrin and shame.

"No. Don't argue, Jeannie. You're not stupid. A girl like you could never have gone out with someone like me. I didn't have anything to offer you then."

"You did though. And I liked you anyway. You were smart and funny. And you were my friend. A better friend than many, since it was you who followed me that night to make sure I was okay."

"Thank you. I think that's partly why I liked you so much. You weren't caught up in appearances like other kids. You were kind."

"And you're being far too sweet. The truth is, you're right. I would have been too afraid to date you. Your situation was dark and frightened me. Sometimes, when you came to school with bruises or a cut lip, I worried about you. That you wouldn't survive."

His brows pulled together and he nodded in acknowledgement of my fears. "There were times I worried too. But I was determined to get my diploma. I was seriously pissed that I missed out on the credits and didn't graduate with everyone else." He turned and slipped his fingers between mine again, and we walked on. "My dad had been getting worse, and unpredictable things were happening. I never knew when there'd be a situation out of my control."

"I guess what happened later that night, the fire, was the crisis you'd always feared."

He nodded. "Worse than my worst nightmares. I imagine no one was surprised when they heard I'd died."

"I'm glad that you're alive and that you made up for lost time. Look at you now."

He stopped again, dropping my hand and cupping my shoulders in his palms, gently caressing me. He dipped his chin and caught my gaze with his darkening, intense stare, and I felt it as if he touched me. "I wanted so much more of you, Jeannie. I still do. And I hope that now…" His firm lips twitched to one side in a cocky smile, his eyes crinkling. "That you think I'm better equipped. Better…suited."

This wasn't going in the direction I'd intended. How could I steer the conversation back to grad night? And what happened after?

Pulling me closer, his hold on me tightening with emotion, he looked at me with a question in his eyes, the light and dark shadows beneath the trees mingling with his natural green in a mesmerizing dance. I could smell him, too. His crisp, masculine, soapy scent carried on the fresh lakeside breeze. My knees weakened, and I swayed towards him, drawn by his irresistible sex appeal, every cell of my body screaming yes. The contours of his mouth drew my gaze, my fingers itching to feel the shape of him. I was captivated by his skin stretched taut over the contours of his muscles and his massive frame. Like a boa constrictor, he was pure undiluted power, and I wanted it so badly my nerves were singing like plucked wires.

Then, before I could say anything more he combed his fingers into the hair at my nape, sending a shiver cascading down my spine. Angling my head, he dipped his head to mine, covering my mouth possessively with his. His mouth was hot and sweet, his lips firm and masterful. Oh, my goodness, he was such a good kisser. My thoughts scattered and flew into the treetops like birds.

A little helpless sound escaped from my throat against my will as I surrendered to sensation, caught in the shared sensual space of our fused mouths, and it seemed to light a fire in him. His hands came around me and pulled me closer, slowly but hungrily. My soft and willing body moulded to his hard one, sending overwhelming sensations racing through me, tingling, zinging, and heating my blood. If this is how he could make me feel with one kiss, I could only imagine the skill he'd acquired in bed. My mind stuttered with the possibilities.

Phoenix's large hand cupped my ass and pulled me tightly against him so I could feel his hardness, his need. The feel of him pressed against my hot centre made me throb, and my leg slid along the outside of his tree-like thigh. Something inside of me desperately needed him. He gripped my thigh, pulling it higher. His hips put more pressure, more heat, more hardness where I wanted it.

Like lightning, he broke our kiss, shifted our bodies, and I found myself pressed up against the rough bark of a big tree trunk, his hands effortlessly holding my legs around his hips as he pressed himself against my molten centre. Rocking his hips, his mouth quirked and his chest heaved in a breath. "You feel so good, Jeannie." His head shook a tiny bit, as if disbelieving, and he resumed kissing me.

My centre pulsed and throbbed with need, my limbs clamped around him, holding on for life. His mouth dropped to my neck, where he kissed, licked, and sucked in time with the thrust of his dry humping against my core. I heard myself whimpering with a need that rose higher and higher. Oh, God, he drove me to the edge.

I remembered how he'd been on grad night. His focus, his gentle attentiveness, his leashed passion. And the scent of him, doing something primal to me. Because I'd never thought of him that way, it had caught me by surprise. It's partly what cut me loose and made me crazy for him then. Why I'd suddenly, desperately wanted to go all the way with him. I could never have said, exactly, why *not* Zach, only that it didn't feel right. And then in a flash, there was Peter and he felt so right. The missing mystery ingredient.

As if he sensed my frenzy, or felt the same out-of-control drive, he growled, then loosened his grip and gently lowered me to the ground. His kisses turned feathery, sweet against my neck, my ear and cheek, my lips and then my temple.

A rustle startled us and we both looked along the path. We were no longer alone, as an older couple walked in our direction, just visible through the trees.

"We have to stop meeting in parks like this," he murmured, and I laughed breathlessly, dropping my forehead to his broad chest. He planted a kiss on the top of my head.

I lifted my face to look up at him, still abuzz with need, my gaze tracing his handsome features. His high, rectangular forehead, smooth dark brows, sharp cheekbones and straight, flared nose. His lips, wide and well defined, both masculine and sensual, hard and soft, so tempting. So skilled.

He wasn't much like he'd been before he filled out, and yet the more I looked, I could see now the superb genes had always been there, waiting. I began to see the connection between the gifts he'd given my son, the teen I'd known, and the man that stood before me now.

Now I could understand how it happened. When Zach was all over me, pressuring me to have sex—I felt like I was resisting a force from outside. But that night, when Peter held me, comforted me, stroked his hands over me—something awoke inside of me. Suddenly, there was a force inside of me, compelling me closer to him. A force I had no control over. A force I didn't even want to resist—even if I knew how. That's how it happened. That's how Will was made. Now here we were again, and my body was going berserkers again. Melting. Coming apart. Trembling with desire. My mind no longer coherent. Simply riding the wave of feeling.

Acknowledging we couldn't go on doing what we'd been doing, Phoenix stepped away, leaving a gap of a few inches between his hot body and mine. He stroked my hair, his gaze bouncing around my face, lingering on my mouth. "I got carried away," he whispered by way of apology. "I want to touch you so badly." His jaw clenched, and the corner of his mouth twitched in an almost smile.

He might have felt what I felt, but he appeared to be cool and in control. Damn him.

I was so not cool. So not in control. I had to get off this runaway train. I pulled myself together, straightening my clothes, smoothing my hair, sliding away to put more space between us. "I'd better get back. I'll see you later."

His smile was tiny but conveyed a confident satisfaction that did nothing to lessen my attraction.

Shit, shit, shit. I stepped away, nodded and stomped through the trees toward the fairgrounds, mumbling, "I'm sorry," to the muffled sound of him chuckling softly.

***

Phoenix

Taking my time strolling to the fairgrounds to give Jeannie some space, I had to admit I was feeling pretty good. I hadn't meant for any of that to happen. I was not in the habit of mauling women in public parks.

But when Jeannie pushed the subject of grad night, and obviously wanted to get it out in the open, which I'd been agonizing over, some trigger was flipped.

For both of us, I think. Talking about that night—those

experiences that only she and I knew about—brought us closer and awoke some sleeping giant. We both felt it. And now the memories that had haunted me had a very fresh, very visceral new life.

I thumbed open my phone and texted Monty.

ME: *You still kicking around, bud?*

I HOPED he'd stuck around so we could have a beer and catch up. I hadn't meant to bail on him earlier. It had seriously been a couple of years since I'd seen him.

When we were young and naive, Monty had been one of a gang of very intense, cocky bastards in the Navy who figured if we couldn't make the cut for JTF 2, then no one could. So we trained together like maniacs, hoofing miles and hauling loads, pushing each other to climb higher, hold our breath longer, scout in the dark, and uncover and conquer our individual phobias. Because if you had a weakness that you still hadn't overcome by then, for sure JTF 2 testing and training would beat it out of you. We all thought we had what it took.

And most of us did. There were a few other guys who tried out with us but didn't make it. But nobody went through that without bonding for life. I still knew all those guys. But our core unit, we wanted it bad.

And Monty was part of that. But, despite being the most badass of badasses, Monty didn't make the cut. It all came down to the psych testing. He was strong enough, for sure. And smart enough. But somehow they cracked him. He didn't talk about it, but I figured it had something to do with his little brother being shot by cops when he was a teenager. He carried some kind of resentment towards authority. Everyone in his family still carried the burden of that loss.

It was after that his folks moved the family up to Canada since his mom was Canadian.

My phone buzzed.

MONTY: *You work things out with your girl?*

Me: Maybe

Monty: Been running errands, back at my crib for a snooze. I'll head to the fairground and meet you after a shower. About 15:00?

Me: Copy that. Rally at the tavern.

I GLANCED AT THE TIME. It was just after 13:00 and I had some time to kill. I wasn't super interested in all the displays unless they were going to feed me, and I'd already done a bunch of that earlier, tasting samples of local cheeses and preserves along with baked goods. So I strolled around the lake to the dock area where the kids were boating and swimming earlier. I'd barely caught a glimpse of Jeannie's kid. By the time I'd realized he was hers, her mother had herded the three boys away to change their clothes, looking like drowned cats.

I was still curious. How could I not be?

On my way back to my viewing spot from earlier, I passed through different themed areas. Aside from growers, gardeners, and food producers, a row of local artisans who used local materials, like wool and dried twigs, as far as I could tell, wound up the central path towards the parking lot.

Ruby had partnered with a local shopkeeper who sold supplies and taught weaving, spinning and knitting classes, and was giving a couple of workshops on the Peruvian toques she'd learned to knit out of alpaca hair. She'd gained a bit of weight, and looked better in just the few weeks we'd both been in town. It was either Julian's cooking or jumping off the stressful roller coaster of reporting from war-torn countries that had done it. Or a bit of both, I figured. I was happy for her.

I swivelled to scan the park for other things going on for kids. The lost and found, arts and crafts, and nature education tents were close to the fixed play equipment, making it the *de facto* kid zone. But nothing programmed seemed to be happening right now. I knew there was a petting farm and livestock area in an open field further away, up a path through the trees. Maybe it had drawn the afternoon crowds. I'd check it out tomorrow.

Beyond the kid zone was a kind of spa area with a big tent where people were doing yoga, getting massages, and I don't know what else. I saw Deanna over there earlier behind a booth full of pretty smelling bath things, cosmetics and oils. Which, I guessed, had something to do with her blog and social-media brand.

It was interesting for me to find out more about what some of my old classmates were up to. When I saw them at the café, they didn't necessarily talk about their work, so I hadn't learned much so far. Other than Zach and Tate, and Bethune who'd just got a new job as an architect, apparently, it was all pretty new-age-y looking from my perspective. All of it, really, was other-worldly in its alienness. Which I suppose was ass-backward. It was my life and work that was alien. It's just all that I knew.

Reaching my spot, where I could see the water activities through a wide gap in the scrubby shoreline trees, I stood in the shade, arms crossed, and just watched. A few stalwart swimmers splashed around, and a couple of kids lounged on towels in the sun, but most people seemed to have moved on to other activities.

"Hi."

I turned at the childish voice. "You talking to me?" I asked, identifying the source.

Jeannie's kid stood about ten feet behind me. He wore a t-shirt and cargo shorts, the pockets of which seemed to be stuffed with all kinds of gear. I kept a tight rein on the grin that tugged at my mouth. He looked like one of my squad, heading out on a mission.

I smiled a little. "It's the excellent swimmer."

I guess I didn't seem too threatening. He stepped closer, lifting a hand in an awkward, nerdy wave. "Yeah. I'm Will," he said, shoving his glasses up.

"I gathered that."

He kept coming closer, a little at a time, until he stood beside me, just a few feet away. I studied his features, looking for signs of Jeannie. Other than a healthy sprinkling of freckles on his rather pale flushed skin, glasses, which I'd seen her wear for computer work, and a little dent in his pudgy chin, it was hard to tell. His colouring was different. Dark-brown hair, dry now and dishevelled in a messy nest, instead of reddish like hers. And his eyes seemed darker than blue, but from here, through his reflective horn-rimmed tortoiseshell glasses, I couldn't tell.

"You Phoenix?"

I nodded. "Mm-hmm."

"Is that really your name? Like Fawkes?" He bent to pick up a stick and tossed it towards the shallow muddy water trapped between roots and fallen logs at the marshy edge of the lake.

Of course, I knew what he meant. I'd read the first Harry Potter book when it came out. But we'd been in senior high already. By then life had gotten pretty hard, and reading books about magical kids didn't make a lot of sense to me. I suppose I ought to give them another try since it was such a big deal. Given my nickname.

"Have you read all of those books?"

"Of course. Who hasn't?"

"Me." I shrugged. "And yes, some people call me Phoenix, mostly in the Navy, but my parents named me Peter. In the military, guys tease each other a lot, and it's tradition to have a nickname."

"Why do they call you Phoenix?" He screwed up his face, scrunching his nose to lift his glasses higher on the bridge.

"Because…" I narrowed my eyes and watched for his reaction. "I died in a fire and came back to life."

He seemed like a pretty sharp kid. And he was Jeannie's. I wondered if she'd mentioned me to him.

"Cool," was what he chose to retort. "How'd you pull that off?"

"It was a ruse," I replied. "A magic disappearing trick."

"Nice."

I scowled and shook my head. "It wasn't very nice, really. Other people died in the fire."

"Oh. I see." He kicked a pebble. "Sorry about my mom's meltdown earlier. That was pretty embarrassing."

"For me, mostly. I stepped out of line."

"It was no big deal. You meant well. She can be a bit intense."

"It's understandable. She's your mom. She's just watching out for you. She doesn't like it when someone else barges in. Does it bug you?"

"Sometimes." His narrow shoulders hitched up to his ears. "You swim pretty well, too."

"You wanna sit down over there?" I gestured to a sunny park bench on the lawn.

He nodded, and we strode over and sat down. We could see a more open vista of the lake from here. The row of willow trees along the shore glowed bright citrus green in the afternoon sun. It was a pretty place. I put out my hand, and he shook it. Not bad for a nine-year-old.

"Nice to finally meet you, kid. Your mom talks about you a lot," I lied. Not to me, anyway.

"Really?"

I nodded. "How you liking it out West so far?"

"S'okay."

"You don't sound super thrilled."

"I like it here. But it's different."

"Yup. I was based around Ottawa. I understand the differences."

"And I'm used to us living by ourselves."

"So the grandparents are cramping your style?"

He twisted his head to peer up at me with a screwed-up face as if he was checking to see if it was okay to admit that or to find it funny. I smiled to let him know it was.

"They're pretty…weird."

"The older you get, the more you realize everyone is, in their own way."

He let out a snort of illicit laughter, doing a faceplant, then shoving his glasses further up his little button nose with the flat of his hand, leaving finger smears all over them.

I pulled them from his face and polished them on the hem of my t-shirt, holding them up to the sky to check, buffing once more and handing them over.

"Thanks!" he said and slid them on, blinking owlishly.

Hazel, I decided. His eyes were a kind of greenish-brown colour.

"You leave anyone special behind in Kingston?" Was I fishing for intel on the sperm donor? Did I doubt Jeannie's word that he'd never been around? I couldn't let go of the idea that the guy was a deadbeat. Even if they didn't want to be together, you just didn't do that. You had to man up when a kid was involved.

"My best friend. Dax." He sighed.

"That's rough. Meet anyone new here? Who were those boys you were canoeing with?"

He let out a surprisingly world-weary and mature groan. "Cousins."

"Aah."

"You're pretty cool."

I shrugged. Assuming that was even true. "I wasn't always."

Instead of querying me on my implied uncool past, he blurted, "Are you and my mom dating?"

Whoa. Where would he get that intel? "That's a…tricky question."

"Why?"

I shook my head. This guy was persistent. And smart. "We went out for dinner once."

"I know. I was looking out the window when you brought her home."

I nodded, rubbing a palm over my stubble. Does that mean he saw the kiss, or, as I thought of it, the almost kiss? In retrospect, it didn't compare to today's encounter. I checked in with the interesting array of visceral sensations that merely remembering kissing Jeannie sent ricocheting through my body. I sighed. I wanted so much more.

Then realizing the time, I checked my phone. "I gotta meet a buddy. I'm going to have to head out. You okay?" Strangely, I didn't want to end this little chat. I liked this kid. Not even, or not only, because he was Jeannie's kid and if I was serious about pursuing Jeannie, then I had to be serious about her son too. They came as a package.

"Yeah. Catch you later," Will said with another little wave.

He was chill. Observant and clever. He reminded me of how I'd been, or thought I'd been at his age. Before Dad's accident. It gave me a glimpse of what it would be like to be a father. To be some kid's hero, mentor, and protector. Just like my dad had been for me. Before.

Chapter 13

Phoenix

I FOUND Monty loitering around the entrance to the tavern, hands in pockets, looking as dangerous as ever in his mirrored aviators. The almost-full tavern was fenced off, for licensing, and nestled in between some tall trees, equidistant from the main stage and Julian's pop-up restaurant. A series of local folk musicians had been rotating through sets on the stage throughout the afternoon. At the moment, a rocka-billy trio stomped out some lively hillbilly tunes with a banjo, washboard, and fiddle.

"Hey, bud." I slapped Monty's shoulder as we wove our way through the tables and chairs, looking for a spot to sit.

While Monty went to get us a pitcher of draft, I scanned the crowd, wondering where Jeannie ended up after our walk. Eventually, I spotted her at a table full of women further into the tavern crowd. Sitting with a few of the other girls from our group. Deanna, Bethune, Rainy, Quinn, and a Black woman who I'd seen with Deanna but hadn't met. Jeannie caught my eye, and I waved.

Reflecting on my impromptu chat with Will, I felt a compelling draw to him. In my line of work, especially since I moved around so much, I didn't spend a lot of time with children. I couldn't help wondering what the last ten years were like for Jeannie, raising the boy out East all alone.

Because of his age, he reminded me of myself when I first came to a kind of self-awareness. Halfway to adulthood, in an awkward child's body. My mind kept returning to that time in my life before Dad was injured.

As if a cruel reminder of my past, I caught sight of Zach near the front of the stage, pushing his withered mom in a wheelchair. That was hard for Chapman, always had been, but at least he had the rest of his family sharing the load.

I closed my eyes, enjoying the feel of the warm sun on my skin, letting the buzz of conversation fade as I evened out my breathing.

There had always been stretches of time when Dad had been deployed for weeks, and that was always hard. But I grew up understanding what his job was about and why that was necessary and important. When he was home, he was so fully present, so engaged and happy to be with us, that we all lived every day as if we were celebrating a holiday. I grew up with this intense gratitude and awareness of our good fortune.

Maybe that's why his accident hit us so hard. There was nothing good about that. But we all expected our previous good times to go on and fought so bloody hard to bring them back. Sometimes I wonder if that put even more unrealistic pressure on Dad to be more than he was ever able to be again, when he left more than half of himself overseas, body and soul.

But before all that, life had been grand, and I'd been convinced that I had the best father in the world. He was my hero. I worshipped him and I really thought there was nothing he couldn't do. My trust and faith in him were absolute. In those days, time with my dad was the highlight of my life. I liked school well enough, and I was a good student, but I couldn't race home fast enough when dad was there. In those days, we lived in a proper house, just a few blocks from Jeannie's. A sweet one-and-a-half-storey stucco rancher. In the big backyard, we did projects, built forts, fixed cars, threw a ball, or played games. I believed my engineering nature, my love of an active life, my comfort in my body, and my confidence in my own ability was born and nurtured at that time.

So I couldn't help but wonder about a boy like Will, growing up with an amazing mom, no question, but with no dad at all. That had to leave some gaps in the boy's understanding of the world.

We lost that house that I grew up in, about two years after dad came home. He'd been in hospital for a long time before he came home. He'd had his legs smashed in an explosion, badly, and later amputated. Both of them, so that left him stuck in a wheelchair for the rest of his life, never able to walk again. It was no small thing to lose both your legs. He had surgeries and physiotherapy for months. The goal, of course, being double prosthetics. Though what was available then was a far cry from the state-of-the-art bionic legs that were being developed now. And, as we later found out, Dad underwent considerable psychotherapy to address his PTSD and depression.

Now every soldier returning from deployment went through mandatory therapy. Mostly, this was routine. The point being, of course, to catch early any problems that might have arisen and intervene before those problems grew.

But what happened to Dad, that was never going to be

routine. He'd suffered so many losses. As part of an UN-backed peacekeeping operation in the midst of the Balkan conflict, his unit had unexpectedly come into conflict with hostile forces. Several men in his unit had died, and he always felt a sense of failure for letting that happen, as well as the loss of his close friends. He'd been their commander and never forgave himself for every decision he'd made, every mistake. And he never felt whole again.

Over the course of a few years, he'd lost his strength, his status, his house, and finally his spouse. There was nothing left for him, and he fell into a terrifying abyss that he couldn't escape. That was why I stayed. I couldn't leave him or he'd have had nothing but emptiness. And he didn't deserve that.

"Here you go." Monty woke me from my snooze, setting the pitcher and glasses down with a thud, and rocking the folding table. He poured two glasses, and we toasted to our reunion.

"If you decide to stay here, it's not so far to visit San Diego," he said, licking foam from his lips.

Sipping the cool, refreshing beer, I nodded. "True." That would be some compensation for being so far from Damien, who I'd only see on occasional missions and visits to Dwyer, and from Carter, who was on the opposite coast.

"Where's your girl now?"

I gestured with my elbow to the table a few feet further along in the tavern. I glanced over. The women were deep into the wine, it looked like, with racks and stacks of bottles and plastic cups littering their table. And deep into the conversation.

I was happy to be able to catch a glimpse of Jeannie's shiny auburn hair when she tossed back her head, laughing, flicked her pale hand, and know she was letting loose and having fun. Which gave me a warm, happy feeling in my gut. Hopefully, they wouldn't drink so much they'd need to be to escorted home again tonight. I wondered if she was thinking about me, at least some of the time. Because I couldn't get her out of my head.

Memories of our last few encounters played on a loop in my mind—her sweet scent, the softness of her pale, freckled skin against my fingertips, the way her body responded to my attention, all mixed up with thoughts of her kid and her hard life.

I had to call Unger in a few days with my decision. Though things were still uncertain, I felt pretty good about my chances. Pretty good about calling Port Cam home again.

Tomorrow, Mom and Bess were coming over for the day —to see me and attend the Faire. And I'd persuaded Mom to bring her boyfriend along so I could meet him. Some progress had been made with regard to Bess' university residence, and I hoped to lock that down this weekend.

And with Monty suddenly showing up, willing to stay in touch even though he was a civvy now, it felt like a sign. A sign that I should stay and make it work, no matter what.

"Hey, can you put her out of your mind for an hour?" Monty laughed, kicking my shin under the table. "I have to head down tomorrow morning."

I laughed. "Yeah, man. Sorry. I'm happy to see you." And we set to catching up on our work and life over the past couple of years, and gossiping like girls about our mutual friends and their domesticity.

"The best would be to run my own shop, but I need to build a reputation in the business first," Monty eventually said, about his contract work in private security. "There's work, and then there's the interesting, well-paying work. That's what I want."

"Have you thought about moving back to Canada?"

He shrugged. "Depends. We'll see how it goes."

A slim guy in dark sunglasses with a ball cap pulled low over his face ducked through the crowd and dropped into the empty chair beside us. He grabbed my half-empty glass of beer and chugged it.

"What the fuck, buddy?" barked Monty, half rising out of his seat.

I stayed him with a hand, recognizing the weirdo who'd busted in and now sat hunched over, hiding his face.

"Having some security issues, my friend?" I said to Tate with a chuckle.

"I'm good. I'm good," he gasped, breathing heavily and licking his lips. "Thanks for the cover, man."

"This," I said to Monty, "is my friend Tate. Tate, this is Monty Borges, a buddy from the Navy. Lives in San Diego now."

Tate, still keeping his face hidden, stuck out a hand for Monty to shake. "How you doing, man? Nice to meet you."

Monty reclined into his chair and raised his brows at me, looking for an explanation.

"Tate here's a movie star." I smirked. "Maybe you can get him to hire you as a personal bodyguard. He seems to need protection from his fans whenever I see him."

Monty's face screwed up painfully. "Like I said, there's work, and then there's the kind of work I want."

We laughed, and eventually, Tate decided whoever was hounding him had moved on, and he relaxed. "Let me get you fellas a fresh pitcher." He turned in his chair to flag down a waiter. And somehow, magically, one immediately appeared at his elbow, and he ordered, not even having to get up. Some people had a charmed life.

Tate launched into an entertaining story about something funny that happened on set last week, drawing more stares from attractive women sitting nearby, who may or may not have recognized him, but left him alone. He really was a consummate performer, and soon even the grumpy Monty was laughing out loud at his antics. Then he moved on to telling ridiculous stories about our time in high school, and we reciprocated by telling tales from our training days. And so we wiled away the afternoon in the sun, lazily drinking beer and entertaining each other with tales of our varied adventures.

Until I noticed Will approaching the tavern with Jeannie's mom and nephews. He saw me before he spotted Jeannie and started waving and shouting. I excused myself and strolled towards her table. I was only going to get her attention, but as I approached, I overheard her talking to Rainy about some problems with Will, his school, and something about anxiety. In my few brief encounters with her son, I'd seen no evidence of that, but it concerned me.

I lingered, so as not to interrupt their conversation, and veered towards the barricade that surrounded the licensed area. I waved at Will and pointed towards Jeannie, and he started hollering for her, finally getting her attention. Then I hung back while she spoke to her mother, only sidling up when it looked like they were about to say goodbye.

Chewing on what I'd heard, an idea had surfaced as I watched them together, a way I could help her and spend more time with her and Will—and maybe even win her trust and help her let me into her life. I lingered to say hello to her boy before daring to voice it to Jeannie.

Jeannie

In the afternoon, after a few hours slinging coffee and selling muffins for Quinn, I spent a couple of hours with

Will in the science area, and the kids' crafts tent building models out of sticks and getting face painting done, while Mom went home for a nap.

Afterwards, I browsed the food vendors' booths alongside Deanna, her friend Nia, and Rainy, who'd shown up after a client meeting. We'd been meandering and sampling foods and beverages from local producers for over an hour —Deanna doing more photographing and live-streaming than actual eating, while Rainy and I indulged in every delicious thing we could find, especially free samples.

After a circuit of the fairground booths, Quinn appeared with Bethune in tow, saying two of her helpers were running the café for the rest of the day.

"Hey, ladies. Who wants to check out the tavern? They're having a tasting event right now. All local wineries, breweries, and distilleries."

"Sounds amazing. Let's go," said Deanna, and we all strolled together across the park, weaving in between exhibits, tents, and a second, or maybe third, wave of attendees.

The thought of cool beverages after the heat of the sticky late summer day did sound appealing.

In the arts and crafts area, we found Ruby sweating in a colourful toque in the heat, with a bunch of people knitting and doing weaving demonstrations on a big loom.

"We're heading for the tavern next," I said. "Come with. You look like you could use a cold one."

She said she was due to help Julian at his pop-up restaurant. With everything going on, we hadn't seen much of her lately.

"Julian has reserved a big table for tomorrow evening, so we can all eat dinner and hang out," she told us.

Deanna, busy on her phone, said, "I'm trying to get A to come to the park. She's been resisting."

Rainy said, "She'd hate these crowds. Maybe she'll come tomorrow."

The remaining six of us spent the late afternoon in the tavern. The wine tasting event came and went and we'd gone through several bottles of wine after that. The conversation was wide-ranging as everyone got their turn to fill Deanna's friend Nia in on the relevant history.

Deanna and Nia shared a very impressive virtual slideshow of the brilliant photos and video clips that they'd taken of every corner and every aspect of the Faire, even many they hadn't posted yet. They walked us through the social campaign, and their methods. Their skill and knowledge were formidable. With this quality of promo and the resulting crowds, no one who had joined this Farm-to-Table Faire could possibly regret their involvement.

As the afternoon turned to early evening, the tavern filled with people. I felt more relaxed than I had in I don't know how long, lounging in the dappled sun and shade, drinking with my friends.

Bethune was excited about her new job. She told us about this guy she was crushing on. She'd attended a career fair a couple of weeks ago where all the architectural and engineering graduates, interns, and other job-seekers gathered with representatives from the local firms, a few global ones, a smattering of institutions and governmental departments, like education, housing and healthcare, and anyone else that was scouting for talent. Since she was in the market for a new permanent job, the timing couldn't have been better.

Apparently, this super-hot shy guy was there as a scout for one of the larger local firms where Bethune was quite keen on working. And somehow—the details were confusing—she coerced him into an interview, for herself and several of her girlfriends. And then last week she'd interviewed with the principals and been hired on the spot to start next week along with one of her friends. She was ecstatic.

"I got six job interviews and three offers, but I'm totally sticking with this firm. It's my top choice."

What was less clear was her gushing about this guy who'd recruited her, who she swore she'd fallen in love with on the spot and would marry despite the fact that he wouldn't speak to her. Or something like that. The wine was making all of us a bit fuzzy.

"Romance is in the air," Deanna sang, flicking her long, pink-tinged blond hair over her shoulder dramatically.

"For some of us," Quinn deadpanned, sliding her gaze to me, and I shushed her.

"What's been going on with you and Phoenix?" Rainy asked, smiling. "You had your big date with him, and then…? Details, come on."

I shook my head, tight-lipped. "We caught up a little. He was the perfect gentleman," I offered, trying not to think about more recent developments even as my skin tingled at the memory of his kisses.

There was nothing gentlemanly about the way he lifted me and pressed me against that tree. Nor about the hot hard heat that exploded between us at the mere memory of our encounter grad night. My body had been in paroxysms of zings and shivers and hot flushes every time I let myself think of either.

"He did chauffeur us all home the night we went for sushi," Quinn added slyly. "And he carried Jeannie upstairs at my place and tucked her in."

"Awww, sweet!" Deanna raised her glass. "I can't wait to hear what happens next."

My face flushed hotly at the memories, and I planted it in my palm with a groan. "I'm still so embarrassed. Why did we drink so much saké?"

In the midst of this teasing, I noticed the very man come into the tavern enclosure with his tough-looking muscle buddy from out of town, the two of them looking like Superman and Iron Man respectively, sans the suits. After they chose a vacant table a few feet away, Phoenix noticed us and lifted a hand in greeting. Tensing, I waved and waited for him to come over, but they settled in to drink beer, mostly ignoring us. The tension eased, as I concluded he would be leaving me alone for a while.

"He's looking at you," Deanna said under her breath from beside me.

"He's always looking at her," Quinn said, chuckling.

I tried not to look, but I was obliquely facing them, and couldn't help but see the men engrossed in lively conversation. Or fail to notice Phoenix's watchful gaze on me more often than not. If I chanced to catch his gaze, his sexy lips tightened ever so slightly, his dark eyes creasing at the corners, sending tingling sensations scurrying through my nerve endings at the memory of our kiss on the path. My blush was starting to feel like a permanent fixture. I rubbed my hot neck with fingers cool and damp from condensation on my glass.

I withstood further teasing from my friends about Phoenix's attention. They pried for juicy details about each of our encounters. I couldn't bring myself to share anything about our most recent tryst among the trees on the trail. That was too fresh, too hot, and too confusing.

Collectively, they were not only supportive but enthusiastic about this new romantic development for me, with many asides about the many, *ahem*, fringe benefits that this arrangement would provide, causing my reliable face to flame. Only Quinn, through occasional sympathetic eye contact, knew how fraught this situation was for me. Her looks of disapproval grew stronger with each passing day.

Not long afterwards, Tate joined the guys, still trying to go incognito, but simultaneously flirting shamelessly with the waitstaff and other patrons who sat nearby and showered him with attention. Which was endlessly amusing for Phoenix and his friend, who didn't look like he was suffering either. Now that Monty was laughing, he wasn't so scary. Rather handsome, really.

I shook my head indulgently, watching their antics from the corner of my eye, while also doing my best to ignore them.

Rainy bemoaned the fact that her life was over. Instead of continuing with her strategy of periodically setting Rainy up with her Port Camosun friends' sons, and any other husband material that they could collectively scrape up, Rainy's mother had decided to take matters into her own hands.

Apparently, the indomitable Mrs. Saraladevi had just informed Rainy that she was arriving next month for an extended visit. The daughter of a close friend was getting married, and the entire family would have to attend, including the matriarch. Rainy supposed her mother didn't trust her and her two brothers to attend and do a proper job of representing the family.

In addition, she would be in town to celebrate the Indian holiday of Diwali. Rainy, naturally, would be expected to accompany her mom to these big events, as well as an endless circuit of house visits to her old network of friends in the community. She would be expected to dress and behave the part of the dutiful daughter.

This was a role Rainy had successfully faked via weekly video chats for the past six years, so she was understandably disturbed by the impending disruption to her life.

Moreover, Mrs. S would be arriving with her relatively new husband, the stepfather Rainy had met only at their wedding in Jaipur about seven years earlier. And together they were bringing his nephew, someone Rainy really couldn't even recall meeting at that wedding. He was a property investor now, evidently, and they made it no secret that they felt he would be an excellent matrimonial match for Rainy. They didn't clarify how his business in India and her counselling and diversity advocacy career in Port Camosun were meant to align geographically, but Rainy foresaw much conflict and many tears ahead. Furthermore, she had no interest and no intention of marrying some traditional stuffed shirt from India that her stepfather and mother had chosen out of desperation.

To make matters worse, they were bringing with them an addition to the party. One of her stepfather's sons was coming along to pursue some business interests in Canada, and as a companion to his cousin. She wasn't sure which son it was, but she distinctly remembered disliking all three of them during their brief encounter at the wedding. Though her mother liked to refer to them as her stepbrothers, Rainy preferred not to think of them at all. One of them, she recalled, had been a misogynistic and arrogant asshole to her during the reception. Him, she would happily never see again, never mind think of as family. She liked her own two biological brothers just fine, thank you very much.

"I just want to be left alone to live my own life in peace," she cried. "Do I really have to get married before she'll leave me alone?"

"That's all I want, too," I commiserated. "Living with my parents is killing me, and it's only been a month. How will I survive two years of this?"

"Did you say you want to get married?" Deanna teased.

"That's not what I said! I want my own home, that's all."

"It'll be worth it, Jeannie," Quinn soothed. "It won't be

long before you'll be done with your MBA and get a great-paying job and have your independence again."

I sighed, sipping more wine, then Bethune, with twitching eyebrows and weird glances at the table two over, piped up with, "Or you could just get married and live with your hunky new husband while you finish school."

I punched her arm, causing wine to slosh all over her hand. "Beth, you traitor!"

"Whoa-whoa-whoa!" she cried, licking her hand sloppily and laughing. Though Bethune had been the first and fiercest to pursue her professional career, about which she remained passionate, she'd always been the hopeless romantic among us.

Parker and Jae Soo wandered by, hollered greetings to us, and joined the guys' table with much back-slapping and guffaws of laughter, and I stopped paying attention to them.

"How've you been, really?" Rainy nudged me with her bony shoulder. "You seem low."

I shrugged. "I'm okay. Preoccupied, I guess. I had the most frustrating meeting with an education advisor at Will's new school the other day."

"What happened?"

"I'd heard they were so progressive, and had dedicated resources for special needs, so I was optimistic going in." I spun my wine glass on the sticky tabletop. "But basically, they told me he needs counselling for his anxiety, not just tutoring in math. They think it's a big problem. And they feel they don't have the resources to help."

"I'm sorry, sweetie. That's rough. Do you want me to ask around my colleagues for someone who specializes in kids?"

I pulled a tight smile. "Not sure there's any point, but thanks. I don't have the budget for counselling or tutors.

And anyway, I'm sure a little extra help with math is all he needs."

"Mom!"

Talking about Will made me think I was hearing his voice, but he couldn't be here in the tavern. "I'll just have to make sure I spend the time with him to ensure he doesn't fall behind."

"Isn't that him?" Rainy said, glancing over my shoulder.

"Mom!"

I looked up, suddenly realizing Will was, in fact, calling me, as if conjured by our conversation. He stood at the barrier, jumping up and down and waving his arms wildly. My mother was with him. Logan and Lucas were behind her.

"I'll be right back," I said and walked over. "Hi, Will, honey."

"Hi, Mom," he said.

Oh, my goodness, he looked like a motherless urchin. His eyes were glassy, his clothes filthy, and his face smeared with whatever sugary thing he'd last eaten.

"Oh, there you are, dear," Mom said, glancing at me and then whipping around to face the boys. "Stay here, Lucas!" she shouted. "We're leaving. Don't run off!" Then to me, "Oh, my Lord, these kids will be the death of me. I can't keep up." She flapped her free hand, the other weighed down with multiple carry bags and a tangled, sandy blanket. "I'm taking them home. They're filthy and tired, and we've all had about as much as we can take."

I'm sure she was referring to herself. Her curly grey-red hair frizzed out above her ears, and her shoulders sagged.

"Okay, Mom. Thanks for watching them. Did Will have any dinner?"

"Oh, you know. This and that. There's nothing but food here," she said dismissively, and I assumed I was correct that his main food group today had been sugar. "Go fetch your brother, honey," she said to Logan, while Will resumed waving and jumping around.

"Do you need a ride home?" Mom asked.

"No, I'm fine, thanks. I'll catch a ride in with someone."

Suddenly, Phoenix was standing beside me, and I realized Will had been waving at him all this time. My heart catapulted out of my chest as the two of them fist-bumped over the fence.

"Hey, my man," Phoenix said, reaching over to ruffle Will's already messy mop of hair.

"Hi, Phoenix," Will hollered, his voice hoarse and manic from being overtired and excited.

I turned to glare at Phoenix, a question on my face, and fear stabbing my chest like an icy spear. How was this happening? "Excuse me?"

Phoenix tilted his head my way, the shadow of a smile tugging the corner of his wide mouth. "What? We're buds. We chatted by the lake earlier." After a pause, he added, "After you took off."

I spun to Will while gesturing at Phoenix. "What are you doing, talking to strange men in the park, Will?" It was my turn to sound shrill and off-balance.

"Thanks," muttered Phoenix, under his breath.

"He's not a stranger, Mom. He's Phoenix, who jumped in the lake before. You know him."

"Yes, *I* know him," I countered. "But *you* don't."

Will scratched his forehead, screwing up his face at my logic.

"Come along, Will. Grandma's leaving," Mom said, exasperated. "We'll see you at home, dear. Or likely at breakfast, since we're all about to collapse."

"Goodnight, honey." I gave Will a hug across the barrier. He smelled terrible, like a wet dog mixed with something cloying and over-ripe. Part of me felt guilty for consigning responsibility for him to Mom so much this weekend, but I'd promised my friends I'd spend time with them, and I was long overdue for a break.

"Have a bath before bed, please." He probably wouldn't but I had to at least ask. Shaking my head, I waved them off, then stood with my arms crossed, waiting for an explanation.

"Why are you pissed, Jeannie?" He approached me.

I grunt-sighed, curling forwards in defeat, dropping my head, my attention caught on the ink vining its way up his exposed muscular calf. "You should have waited to be introduced. It sets a bad precedent."

"Granted. I'm sorry. I thought it was cool."

I tsked and faced him, to find him standing, solid as a tree, his hands in the pockets of his shorts, smirking at me.

"He's a cool kid. I like him."

I bloody well hope so, since he's yours, I felt like blurting. But no. That would be bad. So bad. Why was I being so cowardly? I'd had too much wine today and felt spinny and light-headed. My stomach twisted and rolled over, distinctly nauseated now—all the wine and weird food I'd consumed all day having a row all of a sudden.

All I could do was stare into his frustratingly handsome, smug, unsuspecting face with a tight smile and wish the earth would swallow me whole. Tomorrow would be the day I told Phoenix. And I really meant it this time.

"Hey, so…" Phoenix said, touching my shoulder lightly. "I didn't mean to eavesdrop, but I heard you telling Rainy about Will's challenges at school."

"What?" My pulse ratcheted up. How the heck did he even hear what I'd said? "That's not— We're fine. I've got everything under control. Why would you bother —?" I sputtered.

"Hey," he demurred, lifting both palms, face out. "I said I *didn't mean to*. I'm sorry. But now I can't stop thinking about it and wondered if I could help somehow."

"You?" Even as I challenged him, a part of my mind whirled with self-recriminations. I could maybe ease up on the territoriality, given everything. "Why would you want to?"

"It's just that I've decided to stay. Here, at the Pacific HQ. And when I'm not on a mission, I'll have some free time. And, you know…" He shrugged. "Math. It's my thing. Maybe a fresh perspective would help him. I could make it fun, lessen the pressure."

"Why would you want to spend your time doing that?"

"Because it's important to you. You'll be busy with your own school work. And I care."

I swallowed, overwhelmed by his offer. I should be feeling flattered and grateful. Instead, I was awash in panic, dread, and an irrational desire to push him away and restore my world to its former, tidy state. "But your work…"

"It's true. I never know when I'll be out of town, but it's usually only a week or two at a time. And I work cheap," he added with his signature almost smile. "Maybe even for a home-cooked meal."

I stood, wordless, certain my mouth gaped.

With an inhale, Phoenix went on. "I thought, you know, since he doesn't have a dad, maybe it would be good for him to—"

I pulled my lips tight and peered up at him, and he stopped talking, as if he knew he'd gone too far.

"Jeannie," he whispered. "It just makes me so mad that his real dad is such a useless prick. There are laws, you know. You shouldn't have to carry the burden yourself."

"My son. Is not. A burden." I bugged out my eyes. I was mental. He was only trying to help. But this situation was so fucked up I couldn't think straight. Why was he saying this now? I felt suffocated.

"I'm not saying that," he countered. "But if you're feeling stressed, with the move, your school, and everything else, it's not going to help him. I'd like to help lighten your load, that's all."

What would he say when he discovered that *he* was the so-called deadbeat dad he kept referring to? That it was not only his duty but his right to be involved in Will's care? My gut swirled with adrenaline, heat rushing my body in waves. I didn't even know how to deal with that.

I flapped my hands. "I can't do this."

Except for the past month, I'd carried this responsibility all on my own. I also called the shots. I decided what was best for my child. And I didn't know how to begin sharing that with anyone, let alone his actual father.

"I don't even know what this is," I hissed, waving my hand between us. "And you're making a ton of assumptions."

"Okay. I'm sorry. Maybe just think over my offer when you're calmer."

Did he just imply that I wasn't calm? At my laser-sharp stare, he stepped away, dipped his chin and murmured, "We can talk another time." Then spun and returned to his table, leaving me reeling with confusion, doubt, and fear.

I had thought, maybe, when he found out he was Will's father, he might offer support money, especially given his job and lifestyle. I honestly thought he'd have no interest in hands-on parenting or family life. What single, twenty-nine-year-old guy did?

Now, he was offering… I don't know what, or why. This whole romantic seduction complication was disconcerting, and I didn't know how I felt about it all. Suddenly I was spiralling from hysterical and irrational to feeling the press of tears. I must really be overtired.

Despite my agreement with Rainy that I wanted my career, my freedom, autonomy, and the respect that doing it all myself would bring, having him hovering nearby, expressing such earnest interest in me and Will, made me quite melancholy. Like Bethune, I too harboured romantic longings and dreams, and felt an ache whenever I interacted with Phoenix, who was hot, caring, and sweet. He didn't deserve my bitchy outbursts. In a perfect world, I could have both. But how was I to disentangle this mess and figure out what he wanted, what I wanted, and why?

Chapter 14

Phoenix

AFTER BEING DRESSED down by fierce mama bear Jeannie yet again, I retreated to the safety of the guys' table and the innocuous, ridiculous conversation with Tate, Parker, JJ, and of course, Monty, who I could tell was supremely entertained to get to know these yahoos who I'd grown up with. He knew, of course, about my family, and the circumstances that led to me joining the Navy. But in all our time together, it had never occurred to me, actually, to spend time describing this motley crew.

Much later, after scarfing piles of chips and sausage rolls in lieu of a proper dinner, we called it a night. Tate went in search of Julian and Parker, and Monty and I parted ways in the parking lot after exchanging promises to stay in touch this time.

On my return to the base, I cruised past Jeannie's house, checking to see if everyone was tucked in safely, lights out. While I was in the neighbourhood, feeling nostalgic and a little melancholy, I drove the few blocks to have a peek at my old house. It still stood, basically unaltered but for the colour of the stucco and trim, white and dark green instead of grey and navy blue the way it had been in my youth. A solitary light burned weakly over the front porch, illuminating a stack of yellow plastic crates.

Pulling up at the curb, I stayed awhile, letting mental movies play from my sweet and untarnished childhood days, the memory of my dad's booming laughter providing the sentimental soundtrack.

Suddenly, a white SUV pulled into the house's driveway right in front of me. A man in a suit hopped out hurriedly, opened the hatch, rummaged, and pulled out a large rectangle. At first, I thought I'd caught the current owner returning home. It was late, but soon his purpose became clear. He used an auger to dig a hole in the front lawn, lifted a post into the hole, tamped down the earth around it, then hung the board. I realized it was a sign. Once done, he put away his tools, and as he reversed out of the driveway, his vehicle's headlights swung across the yard, illuminating the sign brightly for a moment. It was for sale.

Huh.

That set my mind to whirring over possibilities. Perhaps that sign was meant for me. Perhaps I was meant to put down roots here, and some higher force was telling me what I needed to hear.

On the way home, I couldn't stop the spin of memories, dreams, and worries. What happened to my dad could happen to me. I thought of it often. That brutal truth rode the shoulders of every warrior. Though I'd spent the past ten years studying, training, strengthening, and preparing for every possibility, something unavoidably shitty could still happen to me.

But I swore, no matter what, I'd come home, and I'd

keep my shit together. Even if my body was blown to bits. I'd be ok. I'd still be me. I'd never abandon my loved ones.

Jeannie

Later that night, as I prepared for bed and calmed down and sobered up a little, I thought about seeing Will with Phoenix, the way they were joshing around. I felt tears burning my eyes as I lay my head down in the privacy of my childhood bedroom. I couldn't help but feel a mother's guilt that I couldn't give Will everything a child should have. I couldn't be everything he needed, though I tried so hard. Did every parent feel this helpless and inadequate?

It could be so good for Will. He needed a father. I knew he did.

Phoenix could be so good for him. I had to be willing to compromise—to share Will with Phoenix. If once he knew everything, that's what he wanted. Phoenix was kind and responsible. I had to trust him to do the right thing. But I wondered how he'd react when I finally told him the truth. His life, like mine had been ten years ago, would be irrevocably changed. Would he be as curious and accepting of Will as he was now? Or would he freak out?

The strong attraction I felt to him grew each time I saw him, and nothing he'd done lessened my admiration. Even when he was being a bossy know-it-all or pushing his nose in my business, he did it out of kind-heartedness and responsibility. Was I being selfish in my reasons for getting closer to him, looking for an easy solution? Could I trust myself not to use Will as an excuse to draw Phoenix even closer than he already was? To be more than he was ready for?

However caring, helpful, and open to Will he seemed now, he might change. It was something that felt completely outside of my control, and it scared me.

Even so, I knew I had to be brave. I owed both Phoenix and Will the truth and was ashamed of my cowardice. Whenever I was with him, his attention and flirtation seemed to turn me into a giddy girl. I hadn't felt that kind of attention in so long that I was a little drunk with it.

Naturally, my mind drifted to high school, especially on grad night when everything had changed.

Just once in my life, I'd let go and done what I wanted, instead of what was right and good and expected of me. Just because it felt wonderful, and it was about me and my needs. And though the consequences changed my life, I could never forget that time with Pete. I'd felt sensations and emotions that night that I hadn't felt before or since. Feelings I'd buried but had now—after spending time with him and being the object of his interest and desire—awakened like a sleeping beast.

Was it wrong to feel this way? To want something for me, again, just because it felt good?

Pete…Phoenix…and I had always felt something I couldn't express in words. Strong empathy and understanding and connection. Even with the full-on disaster of grad night, in so many ways, my being with him was the one bright and focused point of light and rightness.

Thinking about that night, I could more clearly recall how sweet and tender Pete was, how he'd held me as I cried my heart out. How he murmured words of comfort in my ear. That I deserved better. That I deserved to be loved and cherished. That if I were his, he'd never pressure me to do anything I didn't want.

I remembered how he'd peppered soft kisses on my wet cheeks and on my hair, to comfort me, until I lifted my face to his and put my lips on his mouth, tenderly. And then somehow our embrace of friendship had turned heated, and then frenzied until we'd been scrambling to get our clothes off, to get our hands on each other's bodies. Until things were happening so fast, that I wasn't thinking at all. Only doing what I knew we had to do.

I know it had been more me than Pete that drove us onward. His words—*Jeannie, no. Jeannie, stop. Jeannie, why? This isn't what you want.* And my words of response, born of absolute certainty—*Yes it is. This is what I want.* Because it had been. I had never been opposed in principle to having sex, only that when it came to it, with Zach, it never felt right. But then, in the dark, in that moment of shared sadness and mutual comfort and intimacy and trust with Pete, it had felt right.

I'd always reflected on that moment of certainty, as my life spun out of control afterwards. Even as I made the decision to keep the baby, drop out of school, and go the distance alone. Even in the weeks and months of fear, loneliness, exhaustion, and desperation through my pregnancy, Will's birth, taking care of a newborn alone, making all the decisions, and doing all of the work.

I'd never once blamed Pete or held him accountable. Even if he hadn't died tragically that night, I don't think I would have had a bad thought about him. I hadn't even regretted that he'd been my first. Only that we'd been young, drunk, and careless—and had foregone protection in that frenzied moment. I wanted to tell him these things. To reassure him somehow. To share that for me, it had been the best first time.

Except… It wasn't that simple. How did I go from there to, by the way, we made a baby that night? You have a nine-year-old son.

Phoenix

After leaving the Farm-to-Table fairground, after my last encounter with Jeannie, seeing her with her kid, so fierce and strong and committed, I'd been lost in thought. She might be pissed at me. I could take it. But I was filled with awe and admiration for her. My heart ached and swelled with an intense desire to…help, to protect and provide and care for her. To make her mine and keep her safe.

After stopping to look at the old house, I spent a long time deep in my memories of Dad. Growing up with him as my shining beacon of strength and rightness, and abruptly being abandoned. Sure, he came home after his injuries, but he was never really present again after that and I guess my mourning for his loss started then. Switching roles from child to caregiver. Trying so hard to nurse him back to health, to be something for him that I was ill-equipped to be, that I was far from ready for at twelve years of age. Yet so determined.

It had been a long time since I'd felt this desperate urge to ease someone else's pain. Once Dad was gone, and I'd surfaced from the shock and pain of his loss, I'd experienced a strange lightness. After I signed up for the Navy, I contacted Mom through Uncle Ted to let her know I'd got out safely, that it wasn't me in the fire. And I'd felt free for the first time.

Sure, as it turned out, free to work fucking hard, free to be disciplined and dutiful, responsible and tough. But now everything I did was about me. Or it started out that way. You didn't spend a decade in the military thinking only about yourself. Your purpose became bigger, and you became a part of something larger than yourself. You became a teammate, a unit leader, a warrior ready to sacrifice for your country. You never again thought only of yourself.

But this was different. My feelings for Jeannie were so tender, so powerful and vulnerable. I had to take some time to ask myself how much of this feeling was about me. Seeing her again awoke in me a strong desire to repair something that had been broken long ago. To finally have something that was an essential part of who I was, yet had had ripped away. It was a way to be whole again.

That same feeling of lightness, happiness, and hope had filled my heart on grad night, in a small way. After my surprising and mind-blowing encounter with Jeannie in the park, I held little hope that this would mean the start of anything long-term with her. We'd touched each other in that way, perhaps because we were at a cusp between childhood and adulthood, between home and away, between known and unknown. Maybe that moment was all we would ever have. But I'd ended the night with the determination that the end of high school would not be the depressing and hopeless change that I had previously expected.

I'd made a decision. Instead of feeling hopeless, I would return home and find a decent job or some way to make money other than dealing weed. I'd work hard all summer to get my diploma since I wasn't that far off. The school counsellor had told me I could do it with summer school if I put my mind to it.

The grad ceremony wasn't the important thing. I had to keep my sights on my future and get into university. In my situation, I would likely qualify for military family scholarships. And worst-case scenario, I wouldn't be the first student to have to work my way through school to achieve my goals. I'd done harder things. If I could catch Dad in a lucid moment, I would talk to him. I'd share my plans and hoped he would support me, at least by giving me the space to pursue my dreams of becoming an engineer.

But after grad night as I'd approached the trailer park, these thoughts fizzled and evaporated like vapour into the summer night. The orange glow of fire illuminating the night sky in the direction of my home, black smoke billowing upward, chased every thought away and turned my gut to stone.

My memories of the events that followed remained sketchy and fragmented at best. I'd been so flooded with fear and adrenaline, I'd acted on instinct.

Running full tilt towards the trailer, I found it already engulfed in flames. Its flimsy boards and tin siding had burned like kindling. At that hour, there was no sign of anyone else around. The neighbours were fast asleep or oblivious. I saw no indication that anyone had helped my wheelchair-bound dad get out. I remembered grabbing a blanket from a neighbour's clothesline and wrapping myself in it before crashing through the door into the flames.

The place was in shambles. The first detail I noticed was Dad's wheelchair was knocked over. Barely able to see through the dark smoke and heat, I stumbled around until I found Dad curled up on the floor beyond it. Bending over him and shaking him awake, the details came at me like reflections in shards of a broken mirror. Throughout, the frenzied beating of my terrified heart. Dad was bleeding, barely conscious, had been shot. But he came to, groggily, his eyes glassy, red-rimmed, and out of focus.

"Peter?" he croaked. "Petey. It's over, son. I'm flying now." A huff of wheezy laughter.

"What?! Dad? Dad, what are you saying? What happened?"

"I'm—so—proud of you. Remember that. Pete—y?"

In between trying to make sense of his gasped and mumbled words, I felt around in the dark. I was shocked to find his Glock handgun lying on the floor beside his hip, as well as spent casings.

"Who did this, Dad? Who shot you?"

He limply lifted his hand, gesturing towards the kitchen before his arm flopped to the floor.

"What?" I scrambled through the smoke, debris, and tipped furniture, shocked to discover another body.

Facedown in our kitchen, lying in a pool of sticky blood. I rolled the slight man over to discover the face of one of the dealers Dad dealt with who frequented our place. A nasty piece of shit, he went by the name of Wiley, but I didn't know if that was his actual name or a nickname. He was obviously dead, blood seeping from a wound in his chest. If Dad had shot him, his aim was still true, despite being weak and drug-addled. But who had shot first? Dad or Wiley?

I hurried to Dad and tried to get him to wake up again. His wound was less well aimed. The blood that seeped from beneath him came from a gunshot wound lower and to his right. His breath was thin, reedy, and wet sounding. As though his lung had been punctured.

I grabbed my phone from my pocket to call 911, but Dad's hand shot up with surprising strength to knock it from my hand, sending it careening across the room into the flames that ate up our living room furniture. Fuck!

He grabbed my wrist. Then he lifted his other hand, and I saw that he gripped an empty syringe. That's when I noticed the rubber hose tight around his leg. How much had he done? Was he like this from the wound or the drug?

"It's okay, Petey. I've had enough. You're free."

"No! Dad, we have to get you to the hospital!"

"Get out of here, son. Save yourself." And then, with a long wheezing sigh, he went limp.

Crying out, hysterical, I leaned close to him, holding my ear over his mouth and nose, praying for the sound of a breath, however faint. I pressed two fingers to his neck to find his pulse, however weak. I found nothing. My dad was gone.

I didn't have long to deliberate about waiting for fire-fighters and police to arrive or getting the hell out of there. Perhaps it was my dad's last words or maybe just survival instinct kicking in. I'll never know what drove me through the rest of that dark night, but I got out.

The front door I'd come in, next to the kitchen, was now a solid wall of flame. The roof was a red skeleton through which I could see the night sky, about to collapse. With one last glance at my beloved dad's body, knowing there was nothing more I could do for him, I bent low and dashed down the narrow corridor to his bedroom at the end, lifted a chair, and smashed out the small window. Then I leapt down into the dark, landing hard and rolling away.

Rocked by terror, shock, and grief, my only other memory from that night was a burning need to survive.

Chapter 15

Phoenix

"Hey, my man," I said to Will, who I'd discovered with his face pressed to a wire mesh fence around the alpaca and goat corral at the Faire's petting zoo. "What you looking at?"

Startled, he recoiled. "Oh. Hi, Phoenix."

I stepped up beside him, setting a hand on the fence. "Aren't you afraid of getting spit on?" I asked.

"That's a myth. Mostly. And it's more likely to happen with llamas than alpacas. That's Julian's alpaca, Nutmeg. The brownish one. And next door are his friend Arnie's alpacas. That's where Julian got his from. He didn't want it, but Ruby likes it."

I nodded. "Okay, then."

He went on. "Alpacas can be dangerous if they're scared. They kind of bump you. They can knock you over. Nutmeg hasn't seen other alpacas since he moved. Charlie says everyone's trying to talk Julian into getting another one."

I smiled. "Who's Charlie?"

"Um. Julian's nephew." Will pointed across the pen to a boy about the same age as Will with dark curls, standing with a little girl and a man in coveralls, tossing hay into troughs with a pitchfork. "That's him there and his sister Sunny and their dad."

"Are you here with them?" I asked, wondering who was supervising him.

"Yup. For now."

"Where are your cousins today?"

He shrugged. "With Grandma, I guess." He sighed, dropping his gaze. "I needed a break from Lucas." He made a face. "Well, Logan, too. He's eight, but sometimes it feels like he's younger."

"Why's that?"

We strolled along the fence towards some goats, and Will reached through the fencing to scratch their bony heads.

"Their dad, my uncle Brandon, and my aunt Stephanie came to the Faire today, but… I don't know…" He pinched up his face. "They didn't like it or something, and then they had to go work, so they left, and Logan started crying."

"I see. Didn't you feel sorry for Logan?"

"Not really. He was being a brat. And I don't like…" He shot me a wary glance. "Um… Well, Aunt Stephanie isn't my favourite person, so…"

"Seems like you boys are spending a lot of time with your Grandma this weekend."

"Yup." He sounded weary. "Supposed to meet them at Quinn's soon and go for lunch with Mom. I don't mind it that Mom's helping Quinn and stuff, but I'd rather be with her or alone than… You know."

"I do know. Being a kid is tough when you can't make your own choices most of the time."

"Hey, so do you like music?"

He sure was chatty today. "Of course. Who doesn't?"

"What kind?"

"Different kinds. Rock. Blues."

"Indie rock? New age? Like Nirvana or Oasis?"

"Sure." I shrugged. "You listen to that?"

"Yes. I like nineties rock covers and new bands with that sound. So there's this local indie-rock band headlining tomorrow night on the main stage called the Zolas. They've won awards and stuff."

"Ah. That's cool. So you're going to be there?"

Will bent to pick up a fist full of straw and held it out for a small spotted goat to gnaw on. I reached through the mesh and gave the little guy a good scratch on his withers.

"That's the thing. Mom's working at Julian's tomorrow, and then, I guess, all you guys are going to be there. So that leaves me stuck with Grandma and…you know…*the cousins*." He put air quotes around 'the cousins' since that's how we'd been referring to them. "Well, I think Grandma's going to make us go home, so I'd miss the concert."

"Ah. That sucks." Now I understood.

"Yeah. D'you think you could talk to Mom about it?"

"I can mention it. Maybe she can come up with a solution. Someone you could stay with."

He nodded, smiling, and grabbed another handful of hay. After shoving it through the fence, he suddenly said, "You look like my dad."

I choked on spit and cleared my throat, stalling for time so I could think my way through this. Who the hell was he talking about? I thought the guy wasn't in the picture. Was there a man in Jeannie's life, after all? Some guy that looked like me? Is that why Will reminded me of myself as a kid? My heart did a flip. "Excuse me? What?"

My hand curled on the goat's fur, and I was floored by

the strength of my visceral response. I didn't want there to be anyone competing with me for Jeannie's attention. Or Will's, for that matter. I wanted to be the man in their lives. And this realization shook me and almost made me dizzy.

Scrambling for focus, needing more information, I asked, "What does your dad look like?"

"He looks like you."

In the seconds following, my mind spun while my stomach churned. *What the fuck?*

Then he added, his gaze kind of far off and unfocussed, "At least, I figure."

My pulse skittered and slowed, and I could breathe again. I frowned, puzzled but also… Relieved? "You figure?"

"Yeah. When I used to see my friends' dads at school, and other dads at parent-teacher nights and sports days and stuff, I always wondered… Could that guy be my dad? Or that one? I wondered what my dad would be like. So I looked at myself, and other kids and their dads and I thought, *Maybe that one, or that one.* You look like how I supposed my dad would. Kinda like me, only grown up, and bigger, obviously."

I swallowed, my tongue suddenly thick and too big for my mouth.

Huh. "What else did you imagine your father would be? Besides looks, I mean."

Will glanced down, his smooth little brow furrowing the slightest bit, studious, and at that moment I saw only his mother. Serious. Thoughtful. Smart.

He pushed his glasses up with his finger, crinkling his nose. "Well, big obviously. Old, I guess."

Thanks, kid. I laughed to myself.

"And…" He screwed up his mouth, trying to express

something that maybe he had never put into words. "Strong and smart. Like someone I could go to for help with stuff."

My heart pinched and tumbled in my chest. Fuck. Isn't that the truth, buddy? "Isn't your mom all those things?" I asked, even though I knew the answer in the marrow of my bones.

"Ye-ahhh…" he dragged out his answer, clearly searching for some other explanation. "But she's not a guy. There's guy stuff, you know, that you want someone older and smarter to tell you. And show you. But also… someone who's cool to hang out with."

My brows shot up. "Like me?" I thought of myself as fairly cool these days, as opposed to when I was in high school. Then, I wasn't cool at all. Just faking it. But I'm not sure I ever—

Interrupting my own adolescent thoughts, this wise little kid said, "It would be awesome if my mom got married someday, so I could have a dad. Someone who's calm and can deal with problems. A dad should be someone you can go to with problems, who can just make them all go away. Or at least take care of your mom so you don't have to. You know, so you don't have to worry that everything'll be okay all the time."

That knocked the wind clear out of my sails, and I had to think a bit to come upon the right response. The conversation I overheard about Will's supposed anxiety, and how it was interfering with his success at school, hit really, painfully close to home.

"Are you a worrier, Will? Do you worry about your mom?"

He pursed his lips and screwed them to one side. "I guess I am. Because Mom is. And when she worries, I get scared, and I worry. And I always wished there was someone who could take her worries away, so I could"—he took a big breath and let it out—"relax."

My breath whooshed out of me, and for a couple of powerful thuds of my heart, I wanted nothing more than to be the man who lifted the worry from Will's small shoulders, as well as the sweet, delicate shoulders of Jeannie, so neither of them ever had to worry again.

My phone pinged. Damn it. I checked it, and sure enough, Mom and Bess had arrived at the Faire.

"I've got to head to the main gate to meet my family, bud."

"Can I walk with you? It's time for me to go, too."

"Sure. Maybe you should let Charlie's dad know?" I gestured to the man, supposing he was nominally in charge.

Will nodded and ran over, exchanging a few words with Charlie, and got a nod from Charlie's dad, who lifted his gaze to peer at me for a moment. I nodded and lifted a palm in greeting, and that seemed to do the trick. Then Will returned, and we strolled along the gravel path through the trees back to the main park area.

While we walked, we didn't speak much. Will peered into the leafy treetops, at the birds, squinting when a ray of sunshine penetrated the cover and hit him in the face. He scuffed his feet along in the fine dust and gravel, making marks. I let the silence unfold softly. Sometimes, not talking was best.

I wanted to ask him about his math problems, and what made him feel anxious at school, but I didn't. Jeannie made it clear I'd overstepped again, so I had to wait for the right time. For now, I just wanted to be here.

Phoenix

As Will and I strode up alongside Quinn's café, I saw Bess and Mom loitering just beyond the edge of the tables. A few customers lined up at the counter, and Jeannie was busy serving them beside another young helper.

"There he is!" Mom's happy greeting rose as she spotted me, alerting Bess, who ran at me and threw herself into my arms.

"Peter!"

I gave her a hug and kissed the top of her dark head, setting her down. "Hey, Bess."

"The trip over go all right?" I asked as I kissed Mom's cheek and gave her a squeeze, too.

She was stylishly dressed in a flowing sky-blue shirt over white leggings, her hair perfect, with a full face of make-up, as she always was, despite the ostensibly casual setting. She turned her face and returned the kiss, and I discretely checked my cheek for lipstick smears.

"Yes, fine, fine. It's been ages since I came over here. My goodness, the city's grown." She looked around. "This is quite the big deal! I had no idea."

Given our family history, I wondered if Mom had ever revisited Port Camosun, and what she'd have to say when she learned I was moving here again. But that announcement was not for today.

"Yeah. Don't get dirty." I chuckled. "Have you looked around yet?"

"No. We just arrived and wanted a coffee." She flicked her hand towards the café.

"I'll get it for you. What do you want?"

"It's okay. Mr. Barnes is getting our drinks," Bess said, catching my gaze and making googly eyes and a goofy smile to not-so-subtly clue me in.

"Ah, I see." The boyfriend did come. I slid my hands into my pockets. Will hovered at my elbow, so I introduced him.

"Will, this is my mom, Angie Corbin, and my sister, Bess Corbin. This is my buddy, Will van Belen." I tousled his hair.

Bess made a friendly greeting and shook Will's hand, while Mom stared at him thoughtfully, her brow lowering. "Hello, there. What name did you say?" She looked up at me.

"Will. Van Belen. He's the son of my friend Jeannie from school. Maybe you don't remember, but we were in honours math together for a few years."

"You were in honours math?" Will piped up, looking up at me.

I nodded.

"Yeah, he's a real smarty-pants. He's an engineer now," Bess boasted, hooking her arm through mine, and I felt my face pull into a smile.

I'd get a big head with all this hero-worship going on.

"But…" Will said. "I thought you were in the Navy?"

"I am. You can be an engineer in the Navy. They paid for my education. And now I pay them back by doing all kinds of cool stuff with electronics." Like scouting terrorists, surveillance, and explosives, I thought. More than he needed to know.

"Cool."

"Here you go, ladies." A slender, slightly stooped man, maybe in his fifties, strolled up with a cardboard tray of drink cups.

Bess grabbed a frosty brown smoothie in clear plastic from the corner.

The man steadied his load and held it closer to Mom. "That's yours, love."

"Thank you, Greg," Mom said, her gaze flicking to me, then down to her cup. "Lovely."

"This is Quinn's café," I said. "Do you remember Quinn?"

Mom pinched her lips. "Was she the twin? That red-haired girl that broke her leg so badly when you were in grade four?"

"That's the one."

Once Mom's boyfriend had dispensed with all the drinks but his own, I offered my hand. "Phoenix Corbin," I said as he shook it.

"Greg Barnes," he replied with an easy smile. "So you're the famous Peter I hear so much about. Nice to finally put a face to the name."

"That's me. Though I shudder to think what these two have told you about me."

"All good things, I assure you. They're both extremely proud of you."

"He's the coolest," Will added, and everyone laughed.

Then *the cousins* ran up, crashing into Will, who bumped into Greg, who nearly dropped his hot coffee.

I put a hand on both boys' shoulders to steady them and pull everyone apart. "Easy, boys. Hot drinks here."

"See?" Will squeaked, shoving Logan further away.

I didn't know if he meant, see Phoenix is cool, or see Logan's immature.

Then Mrs. van Bellen sauntered up, blowsy as ever, in cropped pants and a floral top. "Come along, boys. Jeannie's waiting. Time for lunch."

"Eloise?" Mom said, and Jeannie's mom looked up at the sound of her name.

She blinked at Mom for a beat, then glanced at me for reference. "Oh, it's you, Peter. Angie Corbin? Is that you?"

"It's me. How have you been?"

"Ah. Getting older, you know," she blustered, smoothing her frizzing hair.

She looked quite a bit older than my well-groomed mother, who worked in cosmetology and used every potion and procedure known to modern science. Though I supposed Mrs. van Bellen probably had at least six years on Mom since Jeannie's brother was older.

"We haven't seen you in such a long time." So much was left unsaid in the beat of silence that followed Mrs. van Bellen's words.

"It's been almost sixteen years since I moved to Vancouver," Mom replied. "And this is my baby, Bess, all grown up. She'll be at UBC this fall."

Mrs. van Bellen eyed Bess. "Well, you don't say. Good for you, dear."

"Okay, I'm ready to go," Jeannie announced, bouncing out of the café with barely a glance for me. "Hi, honey," she said sweetly, hugging Will, who wrapped his arms around her middle.

"Nice to see you!" Jeannie's mom said as the van Bellen party moved off for their planned lunch, waving.

"Don't forget what we talked about," Will called over his shoulder as he walked away.

I gave him a thumbs up, narrowing my eyes after them. But it might be tricky pleading his case if his mom wasn't going to talk to me.

"Sorry I didn't introduce you, Greg," Mom murmured to her boyfriend under her breath. "She's as flighty as ever, that woman."

I got a coffee from Parker, who'd relieved Jeannie at Quinn's café counter, and we proceeded to stroll the park, letting them choose what they wanted to see. Progress was slow, because Mom never moved quickly, stopping to touch things and chat with people. She and Greg walked hand-in-hand, ahead of Bess and me, and I marvelled at how seamlessly she'd integrated her new man into our family gathering. Nary a word.

As we fell behind a few feet, I was able to ask Bess questions about them. "Progress is being made, apparently?"

Bess jiggled my arm excitedly. "Yes. It's like all she was waiting for was permission. At least they're not sneaking around anymore. Your talk helped. He comes over for dinner now and hangs around quite a bit on the weekends."

"Right. On to phase two."

After browsing several stalls where I trailed after Bess as she zigged and zagged from one booth to another, we all stood in front of a vendor selling pizza.

"Are you hungry?" I asked. "We could have a proper lunch at Julian's restaurant. It's just through the trees."

"Let's do that," Mom said, never one to eat street food off of a napkin while standing up.

Then we somehow shuffled partners, Mom grabbing my arm and leaving Bess and Greg to follow us.

"That boy…" Mom said thoughtfully, her voice low.

"Who? Will?"

"Yes. His family is who again?"

"You saw her just now. Jeannie van Bellen."

"So Eloise's grandson. And?"

I waited for her to clarify.

"Who did that girl marry?"

"No one. She's a single mom. She was in Kingston for ten years and just moved home this summer to do her MBA."

"I see." After a long pause, she cleared her throat and said, as if changing the subject, "Did you and Jeannie ever date in high school, honey?"

"Um. No, Mom. I didn't date anyone in high school."

As if she needed reminding of that. "I did like her, though. Still do."

"Uh-huh."

We arrived at Julian's pop-up restaurant and found a table. While we ordered and ate, I told them about Julian's work and how he and a few friends had come up with the idea for, and organized, the entire Faire.

Bess checked his Instagram account and cooed, "Ooh. He's cute!"

"Taken," I said sardonically. "And too old for you, anyway."

"You'd better not be hooking up with men at university, Missy." Mom gave her the evil eye, prompting Bess to go bug-eyed in protest.

Greg was funny, attentive, and solicitous—both to Mom and to Bess—and I was able to retreat and watch the dynamic. I observed several things.

One, that he was a nice addition to the family. I liked him. He was the kind of guy I imagined would be a teacher and become a principal. Gentle and a people person.

Two, that Bess really needed to get out of Mom's house so all of them could have some privacy.

And finally, that I was really happy for my mom. Greg was the most low-key, ordinary guy you could find. After the drama of being a Navy wife, the trauma of losing her husband and home, and the long grind of raising Bess on her own, I imagined he was exactly what Mom needed.

The differences were stark. I could clearly see how Dad's career, even before his disability, didn't suit her temperament. I felt some guilt by association and realized that maybe for her, my joining the Navy too, wasn't the best or the easiest thing. But she'd never once questioned my decision.

And I couldn't help but ask myself whether the career

choices I'd made, while right for me, could ever be a boon to someone else. The life of military families was hard. Did I really want to impose that on Jeannie? Would being with me make their lives easier or more challenging?

After a leisurely lunch, and some extra time lounging and listening to a long-haired singer-guitarist on the main stage, they announced it was time to catch the ferry home.

"I'm glad you could make it over. It was nice having this time together," I said as I walked them to the parking lot.

"I'm glad we made the effort, too," Mom said. "I miss you."

"I miss you too, Peter," Bess crooned.

I pulled a face and squished her cheeks between my fingers, but she still managed to stick her tongue out at me.

I shook my head and released her. "So, when do you move out?" I asked Bess, slyly.

"What?" Mom perked up.

The four of us stood beside a white BMW sedan, while Greg jingled his keys in his pocket. So he had a bit of money. Good. Mom deserved to be spoiled for once in her life.

"Bess reserved a single room at Orchard House on campus," I told her. "And I paid the deposit."

Mom tsked. "Peter Corbin. How dare you go expressly against my wishes?"

I shrugged, and Bess squealed and jumped up and down, again with the arm jiggling. "Mom, you know it's time."

My mom frowned, but at a smile from Greg, couldn't contain her own good humour. "Very well."

Greg popped open the trunk to deposit Mom's shopping bags full of all the things she had to take home.

"Thanks for coming. It was good to see you all." I bent to kiss her cheek goodbye.

Once Greg and Bess were settled in the car, she moved in close for another hug. "I'm just curious, honey. Did you and Jeannie ever, you know? Hook up by chance?"

I recoiled, startled. "What?"

"If I didn't know better." She shook her head, lips pinched, then met my gaze. "Did you?"

My open-mouthed silence was answer enough, and her face well-groomed brows rose up her forehead. "He's the spitting image of you at that age. It's uncanny."

I didn't answer her question, too busy trying to swallow with my paper-dry throat. But I didn't have to answer. The question had been posed. The seed planted. The gears were turning.

As they drove off and I stood waving at their car, my shoes frozen to the spot, I reflected on the things Jeannie had said about Will's father.

He wasn't around. He didn't offer any help. He'd disappeared, for fuck's sake. Will's, my own, and now my mom's observation that he resembled me. And Jeannie's inexplicable hot-and-cold responses to my attention from the very beginning. Her nervousness. Like she was both attracted and afraid of me.

Whisky Tango Foxtrot?!

Chapter 16

Jeannie

"Mom, why are you walking so fast?" grumbled Will at my heels.

The three boys, Mom, and I marched between the booths on our way to the lakefront where Dad was meeting us, having laid out a big blanket in a shady spot under a willow tree for our family picnic. Mom and he had prowled the food vendors earlier for a variety of tasty snacks, and had brought drinks, plates, cutlery, and napkins from home in a basket.

I was mad, partly at Phoenix and partly at myself. He always managed to stick his nose into my business and make me feel inadequate, like I'd been screwing up, or not doing everything for Will that I ought as his mother. I already felt like a failure most days. Phoenix pushed my buttons, and—like a program—I reacted. Whenever I was near him, my brain cells and my calm control seemed to fly out the window like summer gnats.

Maybe my reactions, though, were excessive and triggered by my own insecurities. How could he be challenging my authority when he didn't even know yet that he had a right to?

That was just Phoenix, being Phoenix. The fixer. The helper. The protector.

And I couldn't help but admire him for those qualities.

Argh! I was so frustrated. I opened the picnic basket and yanked everything out, ramming things down on the blanket one after the other. "Sit down here, boys," I barked, tossing a plastic tub at Will. "Clean your hands with these wet wipes before you eat with those hands."

"What's got into your pants?" Mom asked.

Hah! Absolutely nothing. I fumed without answering. That was half my problem. I hadn't had any action in… in…forever! Why did my life have to be so damned complicated that I couldn't even enjoy a sweet, sexy romance with a hot guy without it turning into a bloody drama fest?

I was thirsty, damn it! Horngry. Hot and bothered. And despite the fact I kept pushing Phoenix away, his attentiveness, his caring, and his offers of help were gradually weaving their way into the fabric of my heart. I was falling for him—that's what really scared me. And I didn't know how to stop it from happening. Or if I wanted to.

"Relax, sweetheart," Dad crooned from his reclined position, surveying the lake, doing nothing to help set up our lunch.

Pulling open the various bags and containers of food, I plated up an assortment of things for the kids and myself. Then I sat on the edge of the blanket, silently shoving food into my mouth, stewing.

"Did Phoenix talk to you about tomorrow night?" Will asked, his mouth full of food.

"What? When?" I scowled at him. Why was he suddenly obsessed with Phoenix?

He shook his head. "Nothing."

"Did you see his mother?" Mom asked, then nudged Dad. "I bumped into Angie Corbin. She looks good."

"Who?" Dad said.

"You remember." Mom glared at Dad as if thinking leaving your husband was good for your complexion.

"I don't, actually."

"That poor woman who left her disabled husband who later died in that trailer-park fire with his son."

"Oh, that." Dad took a bite of chicken.

Like anyone missed that news story. But it was ten years ago.

Mom waved her hand in the air. "Well, this Phoenix who's been hanging around, he's their son, Peter. He didn't die in the fire, it turns out."

Dad made a non-committal throat noise, and I wondered if he was even listening to Mom's gossiping. I sighed. Just as well. They were all in for a hell of a shock.

That was part of what hampered me, I realized. Once I told Phoenix, of course, he'd want to be acknowledged as Will's dad. And then who wouldn't find the entire sordid history fascinating? Not just my family—and his, of course—but all our friends. I whimpered into my potato salad.

"He's the coolest guy," Will said, with an earnest expression, trying to be helpful.

Not!

"What's everyone doing tonight?" I asked, hoping to change the subject. I wasn't sure I wanted to hang around the Faire until late. Everything was wearing me down, and I needed solitude, a good sleep, and an evening without alcoholic beverages.

Mom suggested, "We should do something as a family."

"We could go to our house," Logan offered.

"I very much doubt your parents would appreciate that, Logan."

"I'm tired," whined Lucas.

I wasn't surprised. The three boys had been outdoors, in the sun, in and out of the water, and running non-stop for two solid days. Poor little guy. Maybe we ought to ship them home.

"How about a movie at the cinema?" Dad proposed. "Since we're out already. Have a look, Ellie, at what's playing." I'm sure he was thinking of it as an opportunity for a two-hour nap.

"Nobody watches movies at the theatre anymore, Grandpa," Will said.

"Come on, it'll be fun. Something different," Dad cajoled.

The boys sighed and made eye-rolly faces.

Mom pulled out her phone and started scrolling. "Zombies. No. *Minions*."

"*Minions!*" shouted Lucas.

"No *Minions!*" snapped Will, and I swallowed a laugh. He'd be happy enough to watch it at home, with me, another time.

"*Pinocchio?*" Mom mumbled, and Logan groaned.

"I read there's a *Bob's Burgers* movie. Is it playing?" Will suggested.

"Burgers?" Mom looked up from her screen, confused.

"That'd be awesome!" Logan suddenly perked up. "I love that show."

Huh. Finally, something Will and Logan had in common. This could be a good thing. I quickly searched it up, my hope fizzling. "Oh. Sorry. It's already streaming and no longer in the theatre. How about *Lightyear?*"

Logan and Will looked at each other, the scent of possibility in the air. Then they both shrugged and said, "Sure."

"All right, then," Dad said. "*Lightyear* it is."

That would be lovely, actually. I'd bow out and go home all by myself. Run a bubble bath and relax with a trashy novel. Maybe some herbal tea. And think.

I reflected on how much I'd privately admired Pete for his devotion to his sick dad and for his compassion, responsibility and strength—and his self-sacrifice. He hadn't changed. He was such a good guy.

Increasingly, I felt sorry that I was embarrassed to like him in high school, to be his friend openly, when he was so untouchable. How many others in our group had truly understood what he was going through and seen him for who he was? I'd been weak and dated Zach because it's what other people thought I should do. I'd been so shallow then, so pliable.

Not that any of that changed my current predicament.

I was conflicted. I liked Phoenix, maybe even was falling for him, but I was struggling to open up about Will. I couldn't let loose without feeling like I was manipulating and using him. I didn't want Phoenix to think I was angling for financial support or anything like that. But at the same time, I didn't want to keep secrets from him either. The tender and steamy relationship that had been developing between us, built on our shared past, had been hampered by the information that I held in my sweaty palm.

I was so caught up in my thoughts that I didn't even notice his approach until he was right behind me.

"Phoenix!" Will's shout in my ear shocked me out of my mental funk. He jumped up, and I turned on the blanket to see them fist-bump.

Kill me now. I wiped my lips to make sure I didn't have mayonnaise all over them, and slowly turned to look up at him. Way, way up. He stood a few feet away, his massive inked arms crossed over his broad chest, legs spread like oak trees, looking like the Jolly Green Giant. Or the man from Glad. Or Mr. Clean, but with hair. Or some other stereotypical beefcake character. But good, so damned sexy and good.

But there was something wrong with him. His eyes weren't sparkling at me flirtatiously. They were shadowed, like the deepest ocean, brows tugged down into a dark slash. The corner of his firm mouth pulled in, but it was no almost smile this time. His expression was stony. He almost looked angry.

"Can we go somewhere, Jeannie? We need to talk."

"Yes!" I didn't hesitate, but stood up, smoothing my sundress and hair. "Are you okay packing up?" I said, absently, to Mom and Dad.

"What about the movie?" Dad asked.

"You all go. Have fun. I have to talk to Phoenix. And I'm quite tired tonight. I'll head home early."

We stepped away, and he scooped up my hand possessively, leading me across the park in a straight line—as straight as possible given the layout of tents and booths—heading for the parking lot. I felt like I was being taken to the principal's office.

"Are you all right?" I asked. "Did something happen?"

He didn't answer, but led me to a shiny new cobalt-blue truck.

"What happened to your black truck?" I asked as he beeped open the doors and opened the passenger side for me to climb in.

"That was a rental," he said, rounding to the driver's side. "I just bought this."

Wow. He didn't mess around. Didn't he just decide to stay, like, yesterday? He drove in silence, out of the park and down the highway, taking the exit towards the peninsula.

"Where are we going?"

"There's somewhere I want to take you," he said gruffly, eyes on the road.

I sat in silence while he negotiated busy long-weekend traffic, finally weaving through familiar residential streets. We were in the neighbourhood to one side of our old high school, up a rise, close to where Deanna's parents lived. The houses here were big. A mix of heritage houses and newer ones, with views over the ocean in the distance, and lots of huge old trees.

My gut began to swirl with dread.

Shortly, he pulled up in front of a little pocket park about four blocks past the Dunham's place and turned his truck off. *That* pocket park. Morris Park. I stared at it out the window, my heart pounding. I hadn't ever come here again. It was…kind of the same. Mature oak trees didn't change much in a decade, but the path was newly arranged, and there were some flower beds as if the city or neighbourhood association had spruced it up.

"Why are we here?"

He sat brooding for a minute before quietly saying, "Let's get out and walk." He hopped out of the truck and came around, opening my door, holding out his hand.

I took it and stepped down.

Did he want a replay of grad night? He didn't seriously think we'd have sex again in a park, did he? It was still light out, though the sun was setting now, and the heat of the day finally easing off. And we were neither eighteen years old, nor were we drunk.

We strolled slowly down the path without talking. My stomach churned with angst, but at the same time, he was the one I wanted to go to for comfort and reassurance. His physical presence beside me, like a wall of electricity, sent all my nerve endings into overdrive. My hands shook, and my body trembled with the need for him to wrap me in those strong arms of his and hold me.

Then we were there. At our tree.

"They put a bench here," he said with obvious chagrin at the sight. It was right there, under our tree, as if for spectators to our historic tryst.

"Maybe we should sponsor it. Get the city to add a plaque. *Phoenix and Jeannie were here.*"

We both laughed, softly, half-heartedly, awkwardly. Then he turned to me and touched my cheek lightly. Instead of… I don't know what words or questions I expected. He bent his head and touched his lips to mine. My breath shuddered with the pure, clear thrill of it. I wanted him so badly. I clenched my inner muscles as a thrum and tingle of need erupted between my legs, demanding attention. At my indrawn breath, he pressed closer, covering my mouth with his, licking lightly with the tip of his tongue.

With a groaning sigh, he whispered, "Jeannie," taking my waist between his big hands, his thumbs tracing my ribs, teasing the lower edges of my breasts and pressing me up against the bark of the tree. The solidity of his hard body pressing against mine turned my limbs molten, liquid, pliant.

My hands slid up his contoured stomach and chest, revelling in the hot, powerful beauty of him, sliding up around his thick neck, pulling his mouth harder against mine, opening, giving him my tongue.

He met me eagerly, thrusting his tongue into my mouth, luxuriously sliding his around mine, taking me and simultaneously showing me what he had to give. I wanted it. All of it, and I wanted it now, desperately. I was so hungry for him.

He slid his thick, hard thigh between my legs, and I ground my needy centre against him, welcoming the pressure and heat, lifting my leg to hold him tight, tilting myself upward. His hands came to my ass, grabbing and holding me to him as our mouths continued their frenzied dance. A desperate mewling escaped my throat, and he broke the kiss to let me slowly to the ground, reaching between us to cup me with his hot hand, his fingers pressing closely where I ached for him.

My head fell back, bumping the tree, my voice thready when I said, "I need you."

"I wish we had somewhere to go," he murmured, touching me. "You know, I feel like we've barely had a few moments alone together, and I want so much more. I want all of you, Jeannie."

Inching my skirt upward, his fingers stroked me, tracing lines of feverish pleasure along my bare thighs, and between my legs as his hot, wet mouth nibbled and sucked on the skin of my neck and jaw.

Nudging my panties to the side, he stroked me, teased my swollen bean and then slid his thick finger slowly inside me.

I gasped, crying out in shock, "Pete!" as he withdrew and returned with two fingers, stretching me, pulsing and curling his fingers slowly, circling his thumb against my most sensitive pulsing nerves.

Just like my moods, he played my body like a tightly strung, perfectly tuned violin, and my world exploded like the crescendo of a symphony, sounds becoming flashing lights and shooting stars as I cried out.

"I've got you." His hand softly covered my mouth. "Shh. Love. We'll have the neighbours calling the cops in a minute."

I went limp. He held me upright until my senses gradually returned, and I could hold myself up.

"Oh, my God," I moaned, my mind whirling in confusion. "You did it again!" I wiggled out of his embrace, shook myself, and thought, *how was I to keep my wits about me when he turned me into a writhing, helpless mess of desire?*

"Did what?" he asked.

"Ugh!" I groaned, shook my head to clear it, then raced off through the far side of the pocket park.

My parents' house was just four blocks along and around the corner. I needed distance from his powerful effect on my libido. I had to get my shit together. As much as I longed to, as much as I delighted in his touch and wanted to surrender fully to it, we shouldn't be doing this until I'd shared my secret.

I ran. Like I hadn't run since I was a kid. My sandals pounded the sun-warmed pavement. No sooner had I reached the driveway of my parents' house than his new blue truck pulled up to the curb.

Shit! Of course, he'd know where I'd go and intercept me.

I felt myself panicking. I had to tell him. Now.

He strode towards me when I stopped on the sidewalk.

"Jeannie, what's wrong?" Concern etched into his features.

"I couldn't continue," I said, needing to find the right words to begin. I wasn't ready just yet. I had to catch my breath, calm down, and gather my thoughts. I stepped towards the front porch, and he followed.

"What's going on with you? Why did you run off?"

I hesitated for a moment before nodding, finally unlocking the door and leading him into the house.

Phoenix

Following Jeannie into the quiet house, I whispered, "Everyone still out?"

"They all went to see a movie," she murmured, kicking off her sandals in the front hall.

I ditched my shoes too, then waited for her to make the next move.

She stood with her gaze downcast, frowning, then pointed at a spot on the floor with her toe. "Watch this spot. It's slippery." Then she seemed to make a decision and led the way upstairs.

"I would have driven you here if you wanted. You've been acting strange," I pressed as we tread softly up the weathered runner. "Please tell me what's going on."

"I will."

Hesitating at the top of the stairs, she turned right and led me into a bedroom, flicking on the light as she went. It was obviously Will's room, with a narrow rumpled bed, a desk with his new laptop, and a variety of kid's toys and clothes were strewn about. The aroma was a familiar blend of sweet and sour.

She sat on the bed, folding her hands primly in her lap, looking at me. "Sit down. Please."

I eyed the little chair in front of the desk and opted to plant my ass beside hers on the narrow bed, resting my elbows on my knees, staring at the floor.

She squirmed, sidling away a smidge, putting a gap of airspace between our hips and thighs.

"Every time you touch me, I lose my place."

I smiled a little, remembering the way she'd come apart in my arms just minutes ago. I wanted her that way again. Soft, pliant, quivering and begging. I wanted to sink myself into her. "Your place?"

She chopped a hand down on her knee. "My place. On the agenda. On the…the…the to-do list. In my…my life! You scramble my brains," she bemoaned.

I gave her a side-eye. "My brains have been scrambled since the first time I saw you, beautiful." *The truth is I'm falling in love with you.*

She scoffed softly and looked away, a smile pulling at her lips. "Stop. I'm serious."

"I'm serious too. About you and me, Jeannie. But I don't understand your behaviour. I want to rush ahead, but you're hot and cold. You're confusing me."

"I know. I've been thinking about that. About…everything."

"Tell me what's bothering you. Do it," I said. I was tired of this evasive dance between us. I wanted to know what ate at her, and then deal with it. There was nothing as frustrating as a mission without intel or with conflicting data. Your brain stalled out, scanning for the certainty it couldn't have.

Her breathing was rapid and irregular, and she swallowed. Her hands clenched together so tightly, that her fingers had gone white.

"Do you recall that night we had sex?"

I studied her face as if her meaning were written there for me to decipher. I nodded infinitesimally. "Of course I do. I told you so." I narrowed my eyes, peering closely at her, tension coiling and building in my chest. "It was an incredible night. We were both lost in the moment. I came away with the feeling that we had a special connection. You felt it too. We had something special."

"Did it occur to you that we had unprotected sex that night?"

My heart kicked me behind my ribs, like a rifle recoil, momentarily taking my breath away. Was this it? Was she finally going to tell me about Will? "I don't remember even thinking about that. What are you saying? That I knocked you up that night? That—"

She raised her palm to stop me from saying more.

She swallowed, slowly, and lifted her wavering watery gaze to look directly into my eyes. In them, like a storm building on the horizon at sea, I read her strain, her fear, her apology before she spoke.

In the smallest, quietest voice possible, she said, "Yes, Pete. You knocked me up that night." Her breath gusted harshly out of her with the effort to speak, and still, her voice quavered, unsteady, breaking slightly. "We do have something special together. His name is Will. Will. Corbin. Van Bellen."

My face went slack, my eyes unfocussed as I processed her words, confirming what I had suspected after my talk with my mom. While she sat silently, waiting for her words to sink in.

"Are you telling me that your son, Will, is…?"

She nodded. "My son is *our* son."

My throat jammed on the dry sensation in my throat as if I were trying to choke down an MRE veggie burger in the sub-Saharan after an all-day ruck. There was no way to get words past it. All you could do was struggle on, reach for your canteen, and hope to make it to the end so you could draw a clear breath.

So it was true. The half-formed thought that had been floating around my head like a moth, buzzing, irritating, but refusing to land. All the signs pointed here. Will's comments about me, my own observations of him, my mother's shock, and most of all, Jeannie's unsettling unease from the first time she saw me alive.

Beyond that, a gnawing in my gut. A want. Like a hunger for something unnamed.

Sometimes you know something before you know it as if one part of your mind is at war with another. And then once you know it, there's this feeling of *déjà vu*, like you've already heard that somewhere before.

Like I felt now. It took some time for my thoughts to settle. For all the misaligned parts to reorganize themselves into some semblance of order, like a jigsaw puzzle finally coming together to reveal a coherent picture.

"His middle name is Corbin?" Why my mind stuck on that detail I don't know, but it hit me in the gut like a rocket launcher. I felt winded. *I had a son.*

Jeannie was still rambling. I'd tuned out and missed half of it.

"…has never been another man in my life. Any attempts at dating were hopeless and frustrating. I've never had anyone. And I'm so confused, I don't want to complicate our situation by muddling the two issues. I don't know what to do." She clasped my hand between hers. "I've grown closer to you. I care about you, Pete. I just don't know what comes next."

I blinked to recover my focus, studying her face. Pinched and pale, her rusty freckles jumped out, her blue eyes glimmering with unshed tears.

"I'm so sorry. I know I haven't handled this properly. I never meant to keep it from you. Everything changed so suddenly and I…" She stopped as if struggling to put into words her reasoning.

As if I were a program overloaded with data, my mind skipped and skittered over random facts. Jeannie had done this alone. Kept this secret. Dealt with the shock and stress herself. Changed the course of her life, while I'd blundered on, oblivious. As if in some parallel universe, unaware that my future life was shifting too. "Are you okay?"

Jeannie's eyes widened. "Me?"

I shot to my feet, spinning, pacing two steps one way, two steps back. My hands were in my hair, gripping handfuls in frustration. "You've been carrying this around for weeks." I heard my own voice as if from far away. "Years."

Each of our encounters replayed in my mind, and I slowed them down, searching for clues I'd missed. Her welcome home party, our date, her drunken night out with the girls, our moments at the Faire.

And before all of that, our night together ten years ago, the trigger that had set this entire row of dominoes falling, like a complex series of fuses, timers, and switches that terminated in a huge stack of nitro waiting to blow up the skies. The world as I knew it would never be the same again.

And this whole time she held this inside, struggling.

I covered my face, pressing the heels of my palms into my eye sockets, digging my fingers into my hair, and I let out a groan. My hands flew down. "Why now? Why are you only telling me this now?"

"I've been trying. Every minute. I—"

I scoffed. "Not very hard, Jeannie. This…how…" I half gasped, half grunted. I was caught between wanting to understand the past few weeks and needing to make sense of her actions ten years ago. "Why didn't you contact my mom? She would have told me. And she would have helped you."

"You were dead. I was thousands of miles away. Why would I burden your mother?"

"Ah, fuck! If I actually *had* died, maybe she would have been happy to have a grandchild." I threw up my hands, shrugging. "How the fuck do I know? But if you'd told her, I'd have found out, and I'd have been there for you, Jeannie. I'd have done anything for you. You know that, right?"

"Back then… I don't know. I just did what I thought I

had to do. But once I discovered you were alive, I spent the first weeks in shock and have been trying to find the right moment ever since."

"There have been quite a few *moments*, Jeannie." I didn't like the note of resentment and belligerence in my voice. It was unlike me. I swung between frustration and pity, grief and immeasurable joy.

"I know. I've tried and tried, but every time…"

Wow. How could this situation be any more tortured? I was in shock. Cross with her. Stunned. I had developed skills for dealing with shock, keeping my wits about me when all hell broke loose, able to pivot and make critical decisions on the fly. But Jeannie, in two minutes, had managed to crash my system.

"Pete. I'm sorry. I didn't know how. I've been so afraid. I kept trying and failing."

"Jeannie. I'm sorry too," I rasped out. My skin felt too tight, my breath reluctant. I stepped away from her, needing space. Needing distance. "I'm… going. I have to think. I'll be in touch," I choked out.

As I turned to walk out of Will's room, my son's room, I was vaguely aware that Jeannie was weeping. But for once, I had no resources to comfort her. I had to get away.

She followed me downstairs and stood in the open doorway as I stepped out onto the porch and down. But I stopped suddenly before the curb, remembering something, and spun towards her.

"Uh. This is not the best time to say this, but…I promised." I heaved a sigh of frustration. "Will asked me to lobby you for permission to watch the mainstage concert tomorrow night. There's an indie-rock band he really wants to see." I shrugged helplessly. And in that weird moment, I felt oddly like a parent.

Then I grunted, shook my head, and spun away.

Chapter 17

Jeannie

I HADN'T HEARD from Phoenix since last night or seen him all day, and I was a jittery mess, wondering what he was thinking. What would he do? What should I do?

Midday, I dragged myself to the fairgrounds to work a long shift at Julian's pop-up restaurant, as promised. Ruby and Julian's sister Molly were also helping today. Tonight would be the biggest crowd, with the most extensive menu, and Julian and Ethan had hired extra kitchen help as well. There was a ton to prepare, so we were given various jobs behind the scenes before the gates opened.

Will was once again with Mom and the boys. Today was a big day for Mom, who was involved in a large Master Gardener event in the growers' area later on. She had committed to give a short talk and then sit at the booth to answer questions for several hours, a role she absolutely delighted in. The boys were given rein to run around on their own as long as they checked in with me once an hour.

Last night's shared movie experience had been a success, and they had all arrived home about forty-five minutes after Phoenix left. I'd given Will a kiss goodnight and retired to my room, feeling wrung out. The last thing I'd needed was Mom or Will asking me what was wrong. I was sure to burst into tears. But once in bed, sleep evaded me, leaving me tossing and turning half the night, fearful of what the future would bring.

Prompted by Phoenix's parting words last night, this morning I asked Will what the deal was with the band he wanted to see. Smiling, he'd told me all about the Zolas, going on and on about their retro-indie-rock sound and some award they'd won, and I couldn't fault him for his enthusiasm at seeing them perform live.

The problem was figuring out how he could attend since I was committed to waiting tables at Julian's pop-up restaurant for the big dinner shift before joining the whole gang at our reserved table. This was Julian's grand celebration night, and I wanted to be a part of it, even amidst my own problems.

But who would be willing to hang around late and supervise Will and his cousins at the concert?

"What time are they playing?" I asked him.

"From seven to eight-thirty or so. Maybe with an intermission?"

"Are Logan and Lucas interested, too?"

He shrugged. "Don't care."

"Well, you can't wander around the park alone at night, honey. Let's see what we can figure out. That's pretty late for Grandma to be babysitting."

His sigh was of epic proportions. "I'm not a baby."

Before he wandered off, I told him, "Leave it with me. I'll see what I can do."

Molly approached me shortly afterwards while we were wiping down and setting the tables. "I didn't mean to eavesdrop, but I heard what Will was asking about. We'll be staying for the main concert tonight if Will wants to join us. He and Charlie are buddies now."

"Oh, that's so kind, Molly," I said. "Thank you. But it's probably not just Will. I'm certain his cousins will want to stay if they find out he is, and they're a handful."

"We'd be happy to supervise the boys, and even give them a ride home so you can stay and enjoy yourself tonight."

"Really? Are you sure?"

"Absolutely," she reassured me. "Sunny can keep little Lucas entertained, and the three older boys will have tons of fun. It'll be nice for Charlie to have company."

A little later, while we ate an early dinner behind the kitchen, I sent Will a text explaining the arrangement, laying out some rules and setting up a time for Mom to pass the boys over to Molly's husband Jake. Will was ecstatic. Then I sent Molly a link to my parents' address, and she said they'd take the boys straight home when the main set was over. I let out a sigh. With all that I had to do, and all that I had on my mind, not having to worry about Will, or overtax Mom, came as a huge relief.

Then we got super busy. People started filing in for the first dinner cover around five, bringing a festive mood into our orbit. Ruby also acted as hostess, seating patrons as well as waiting tables.

Around six, our friends began filling the long table reserved at the back. At first, I saw Deanna, Nia, and Tate with a date, of course. Then came Jae Soo and Parker. Shortly afterwards, Bethune and Rainy arrived. I'd been assigned to their table, so I could say hello in between bringing them drinks and taking their orders, but could never linger long. When Quinn joined the party, I sidled over with a glass of wine for her to say hello, and through an array of anxious facial expressions and mad-dog eye rolls, I was able to convey that, yes, I had told Phoenix but no, it wasn't settled yet.

We both tensed when he strode in with Zach. Quinn gave me a sympathetic smile and my arm a squeeze of support. After that, I tried to avoid looking at him, but whenever I stole a glance, his dark gaze was locked on me, following my movements like a laser. And his mood seemed sober, sending swirls of anxious tension shooting through my gut.

In the small gaps between serving, while we hovered at the servery and chatted, Ruby asked me how things were going with Phoenix.

What could I say to that but deflect? Hedge my bets. Pretend everything was A-okay and normal.

"He is very sweet and very earnest," I acknowledged lightly. "But I have to be cautious about disrupting Will's life, especially so soon after relocating. Dating has never been my priority as a single mom. And frankly, I'm not sure about dating someone in the military. It's scary."

"I can understand that," Ruby said. "I've been in a similar place. But you need to do things for your well-being too." Under her breath, she confided that Phoenix seemed to have been in all the places she'd reported from, which were all the most unstable, war-torn locations. "Maybe that's obvious, given he's in the Navy, but it seems to me he doesn't have an average Navy job. He's been in the field too often and in too many places. And he's super secretive about it. I strongly suspect he's in the special forces."

"That's even more frightening," I confessed, not really knowing what that meant. It sounded dangerous, though.

She said, "I don't know. Most guys don't do that kind of work. He'd have some serious survival skills." She shrugged, pulling a face. "Maybe it's better than being an average Joe?"

I didn't know. Random clips of news footage and war movies flashed in my mind. All it did was make me even more worried about Phoenix's stability and the risk of his work. There seemed a distinct possibility he could go to work and never return. Or maybe come home a broken mess like his dad.

I peeked his way again to find him, for once, not glaring at me, but in conversation with Zach, his head down. His mood, however, had not visibly improved. What was he thinking? He was like a vault. I couldn't imagine learning I had a child I knew nothing about for nine years and then carrying on as if nothing had happened. I'd be a wreck. But he was stoic, playing his cards close to his chest. Was he biding his time?

I reflected on all the times we'd spent together, and how my perception of him had shifted. When we were alone together, I felt more comfortable. He felt more familiar, as if he were just another version of the troubled boy I'd been friends with but at arm's length. I couldn't help but wonder who he really was now. Why was it so hard to trust him? Why was I now transferring fears about his father onto him? It wasn't fair. He didn't deserve it. But I was a mother, and my first instinct was to protect my child. What kind of father would Phoenix turn out to be? So far, he was an unpredictable quantity.

Now that I'd told him the truth, I would see more of his true character. I don't know what I expected or what I wanted. I just felt apprehension. I didn't want him to pull away. But how did one go from being alone, and responsible for everything, to suddenly having your life tangled up with another's?

Finally, when my legs were about to give out from fatigue, our shift came to an end. Molly bid us goodnight, reassuring me once more that she was happy having Will for the concert.

"Come and sit down. You've earned it," Ruby said as Julian removed his chef's jacket and came to gather her up in a happy, tired hug.

"I'll just freshen up," I said.

"Hurry back," Julian said, grinning. "I'm going to make some announcements you don't want to miss."

"I will. In just a couple of minutes." I scooted out the rear fence to walk quickly to the washroom block, then returned to find our table full and everyone having shifted to make room for Julian and Ruby to sit together. There was only one empty chair, and it was beside Phoenix. Drawing a breath, I pasted on a breezy smile and went to be with my friends.

Phoenix

With Jeannie tied up waiting on the dinner-shift tables for Julian before she was free to join the gang, I was in wait-and-watch mode. I joined the table full of friends, but could only stare at her and think.

As she moved between the tables and the kitchen, she obviously noticed me arrive, and checked on me often, as if she could feel my gaze burning into her. She looked worried and vaguely guilty as if she thought I might be pissed at her.

Was I?

Not really. Maybe I'd experienced flashes of annoyance at how fucking long it took her to tell me the news. But then I'd reconsider and appreciate it was no small task, and she had obviously been thinking about it and planning it. Maybe I hadn't made it easier for her, what with all my attention focussed on seduction.

We had to talk again, that's for sure. It seemed as if she were holding her breath, waiting for me to make the next move.

I'd kept a low profile all day. Mostly for myself, thinking and processing my new situation.

But I'd have plenty of time to sort through the emotions that were swirling through me now, like a desert storm. The sense of loss, of a whole part of my life I could never recover, the irrational feeling of betrayal, the resentment towards my dad, and even Jeannie, and everyone else who'd made my life hard—and my choices narrow.

Objectively, I knew Julian's food was amazing and could see everyone digging in, smell the rich aromas of roasted meat, spicy vegetables, and seasonings wafting around me, and hear people's raving compliments, but tonight I had no appetite. I sat with a single beer growing warm in front of me. I could think of nothing but Jeannie—and Will. My son!

All the signs had been pointing to this. Even my old house being for sale. I couldn't waste another day with doubts or questions or recriminations. The details would sort themselves out. I wasn't quite ready to leap for joy, but there were sensations racing through my blood I'd never had before.

I wasn't a crier. My life had handed me too many sorrows and disappointments, thrown too many challenges my way for me to be soft and give in to every emotion. But all day, I'd felt a thickness in my throat and a tightness in my chest, like someone's boot was pressing there, holding me down. And when I thought of Will, who I'd kept my distance from today for fear of giving away what I knew, I was suddenly overcome with…feelings. My chest flooded with a heat that threatened to explode out of me like unstable nitro.

"What's up with you tonight, Big P?" Zach asked from across the table, a forkful of food hovering at his pie-hole.

All I could do was shrug, tweak a fake smile, and lift my glass.

All this time I'd been wanting something I'd had all along—and missed out on because of my foolish disappearing trick. Why had I never reached out sooner? But then, Jeannie had been AWOL too. For all the times I'd thought of her, it had never once occurred to me that there'd be a place in her life for me. How could I blame her for assuming what everyone else believed to be true? What a clusterfuck.

I felt sympathy for her predicament. My gut told me she was mine, and now I had more reason than ever to make it so. She was my family, for fuck's sake. We'd made a child together. We were meant to be.

But I still had to convince her that this was so.

Obviously, a great many other details of my situation were now self-evident. I was not leaving Port Camosun, that's for sure. Even though I'd already decided to stay, it was now a given. The burning desire and drive to protect Will and Jeannie had hit me like a whole platoon of soldiers on the move, catching me unawares. I would double down on my commitment to both of them. I would do everything I could to help them and keep them safe. I had a great deal to offer. More than Jeannie likely knew.

It required some planning. Ideally, I could arrange

everything before my next deployment. I'd only been realizing that I was falling for Jeannie afresh. And now this. This changed everything. My life would never be the same again.

In contrast to my pensive mood, it was party central at our table. The atmosphere was one of festivity and celebration. Everyone agreed the Farm-to-Table Faire had been an unqualified success. Attendance surpassed expectations, and new alliances had been formed. The future looked bright for Julian, with his Instagram page soaring to new heights of popularity. A solid foundation had been laid for Wild Feast, his new restaurant in partnership with Ethan Garwood.

The Faire would wind down tomorrow, but tonight was the true finale, with every vendor and exhibitor pulling out all the stops with special events and giveaways.

Food services were finally nearing their end, and kitchen staff were cleaning up. I waited for Jeannie to take off her apron and join everyone at the table. But she'd momentarily disappeared.

While I discretely checked around to see where she'd gone, Julian had stepped up onto the main stage, across a small field from the pop-up restaurant.

There was a whole lineup of musicians on the main stage tonight, providing a backdrop of folk, country, and indie rock for the evening festivities. They'd been playing in succession all afternoon and evening—and would culminate with the band Will had told me about. The Zolas.

Julian took the stage, again thanking the entertainers, the organizers, the exhibitors, sponsors, and all the people in the community who came to support, learn, and enjoy their local bounty. "I hope to continue on with my mission," he said into the mic. "And I'm optimistic that I can now count on all of you to be part of that mission."

He paused for the crowds' applause. The restaurant seats were all full, as were those of the tavern next door, and the lawn in front of the stage was nearly covered with people seated in little clusters.

"I also want to make sure everyone in town is aware of my newest venture. If you sampled and enjoyed the food prepared and served at the Wild Feast pop-up restaurant this weekend, then you'll be as excited to learn, as my business partner Ethan Garwood and I are to announce, that we'll be opening the brand new sustainably sourced Wild Feast restaurant in its new permanent home at Ragged Mountain Resort and Spa. This is for you Port Camosun. We hope to see you there!"

The audience, including everyone still seated in the pop-up restaurant who had reason to rejoice at the announcement, broke into applause and cheers, most loudly from the people around me.

"And finally, before I hand the mic to our headline band this evening—who's looking forward to hearing the Zolas tonight?" Again, he paused for the crowd to cheer. "I have one further announcement of a personal nature, which will be of interest primarily to my family." He pointed into the crowd seated on blankets and camping chairs on the grass around the stage.

I thought of Will with an astonishing pang of affection that rocked me. I hoped that he was out there.

"Mom, Molly, Jake, and their kids, and to my friends— that rowdy bunch seated at the long table at the back there." He pointed at us.

Hoots and applause from the table rose even louder.

My skin prickled with awareness, and I saw that Jeannie had suddenly reappeared holding two glasses of wine. In the big shuffle to make space for Julian and Ruby to join us,

I'd made sure the one spare chair was beside me. I didn't want Jeannie avoiding me all night.

With shy and wary glances my way, she wove through the tables and around to my side. She placed one glass in front of Quinn, who met her gaze knowingly. Then she perched on the vacant chair between me and Bethune as if she would bolt out of it and run at the slightest excuse. Darting a glance my way, she faced the stage and took a big gulp from her wine.

"You idiots." Julian laughed. "You don't even know what I'm going to say. Anyway, I… Come here, babe." He gestured to Ruby. "We are excited to share with all of you that we'll have another reason to celebrate together before the year is over."

Teasing catcalls followed this intro, with Zach crying out in a high falsetto voice, "Oh my God, you're having a baby!"

"No, no, no. Shut up, Zach, you goon. My news is…Ruby and I are happy to announce our official engagement!" The cheers and applause were even louder and more generous from all in attendance who likely barely knew the couple. "And we're actually going to go through with it this time. Right, babe?" He pretended to be nervous, and she lightly punched his arm to the delight of our group, who knew that their post-high school engagement had come to nothing after Ruby skipped town.

Ruby sidled up close to Julian and gave him a big kiss to raucous applause and cheering.

Julian took her hand and stepped off the stage with a: "Enjoy your night!"

Then the band began their first number, a cover of 'The Importance of Being Idle' by Oasis.

The bass beat echoed in the thrum of my blood as I turned my attention to the woman beside me.

Jeannie

Julian and Ruby joined our group, and general mayhem broke out as everyone rose to embrace them and congratulations were shouted and whispered among laughter and tears. Phoenix took advantage of the distraction to scoop my hand in his and rise, urging me to slip away.

I was stunned speechless. He'd been glaring at me and brooding all evening. I was afraid he'd never speak to me again, or that when he did, he'd be all shouty and furious.

But he was smiling. His almost smile, that subtle, wry, teasing expression that warmed me all over—and sent shivers and tingles shooting through my squishy middle. Half smiling in that coy, mischievous way that meant… There was no mistaking what that look meant.

But…

Without a word, he led me away from the pop-up restaurant and the crowd, towards the quieter end of the park, mostly empty and darker now that many exhibitors had closed for the night and joined the fun by the main stage.

Phoenix stalked silently and smoothly like a cat, constantly on the lookout for danger and possibility. Eventually, he led me towards the wellness area and into a long closed-up tent where, earlier, yoga classes had taken place. Then to one side, into a smaller tent where private massages were given.

It was not quite dark, though the sun had set. Liminal daylight filtered through the tent's white fabric walls, giving the interior a soft glow. It was possible to see everything, but the colours had faded to soft grey, violet, and muted blues.

Music from the main stage could still be heard, though muffled softly in the distance.

In the space were two padded massage tables and a folding table with supplies. On a rack beside this, a stack of blankets and pillows were kept.

After scanning the room, as if taking inventory, Phoenix stopped his restless movement and stood as still as a hunting lion, his dark gaze coasting over my features while he held my arms lightly. His steady gaze gave nothing away, yet held a soothing serenity I wasn't expecting. Cool, green light bathed me like the calm water of a fathomless mountain lake. Its depths filled with secrets, infinitely patient.

Once his survey was complete, his gaze rested on my mouth, his expression one of longing. "I'm going to kiss you now," he whispered, waited a beat for my consent, and then when I felt my chin lift the tiniest bit of its own volition, drawn towards him by a force I didn't understand, he bent his head and touched his lips to mine. He adjusted his angle, covering my mouth softly with his, nudging my lips apart and sweeping his cool tongue lightly into my mouth.

He tasted slightly of malt and bitter hops and something salty and tangy. Sensing my openness, he pulled me gently against his body, brushing chest to breast, hip bone to hip bone, thigh to thigh. I felt the edge of the massage table against the backs of my thighs, as one of his hands slipped between my arm and ribs and curled around me to pull me closer.

In a breath, I said, "I thought you'd want to talk."

He shook his head, dismissing the notion, peering into my eyes with that honest, naked, deep gaze of his, and returned to stare at my mouth. He had another plan, a different idea, and I couldn't argue. I'd been aching for him.

My hands settled on his narrow hips, resting on the edge of his cargo shorts, my fingers reaching higher, drawn by the heat of his skin beneath his shirt. My need to press my hungry fingers into his firm flesh washed away the droning worries in my mind like grains of sand.

His hands closed firmly on either side of my ribs and lifted, effortlessly raising my feet from the ground, setting me delicately on the massage table as if I weighed nothing. I set my hands on the edge of the firm bed, steadying myself, and he stepped between my legs, his hands sliding down my arms to cover my hands against the cool vinyl of the padding. The breadth and solidity of him brushing the inside of my thighs, breaching that barrier, drew a sighing whimper from my throat, and I tightened my legs around him.

Dipping his head to touch his forehead featherlight to mine, so slowly I felt the tickle of each hair caught between us, his steady gaze lowered, then tipped up, holding mine, so gently, so honestly. His lips brushed the tip of my nose before angling down to hover over my parted lips. My breath rasped. This close, our breaths mingled into a hypnotic bubble of heat, shutting out the outside world before he took my mouth with his, sweeping his soft sure tongue into my mouth possessively as his hands splayed at my back, between my shoulder blades and lower, in the dip above my ass. He pulled me closer and stepped into me in one movement, so the skim of air between us vanished in the hot sigh of his breath into my mouth, pushed out ahead of a crisp, barely audible sound, like a dam giving way before a torrent too powerful to withhold.

My hands followed the thick cords of muscle that formed his sides and back, solid as a tree. He rocked his hips into my centre, pressing his solid erection against my heat. His long sighing groan reverberated, like pebbles slowly rolling over, sending eddies of heat curling into every nook, every corner of my body, swirling, coiling, crashing. The sound of my pulse thumping in my ears mingled with the distant rock drumbeat of the concert.

Threads of my consciousness stretched out, grasping at important thoughts. Will— But I couldn't hold on under the onslaught of sensation. Everything Phoenix did to me was a brand new experience, and one followed hard on the heels of the other, leaving me quaking with need.

His palms slipped around my ribs, his fingers gliding over the light cotton of my dress, his thumbs grazing the sides of my breasts, prompting a soft answering moan from me. I felt his mouth tighten against mine in a half-smile. Gripping me firmly, he rocked me side to side, brushing his chest against my taut nipples, now sharply zinging signals downward at his command. I gasped at the burning need that turned me into soft clay for his shaping.

Walking his fingers down to the hem of my dress, he inched the fabric upward, rocking my body forwards to free it until he'd peeled it up to my waist. His thumbs seared a path along my thighs, the creases of my hips, across the quivering skin of my stomach. Then, in a burst of sudden movement, he removed and tossed his own shirt and returned his attention to stripping me of my dress.

I raised my arms for him to lift it over my head. As I lowered them, he gripped my arms, thrusting my breasts closer to him, forcing my full flesh to rise against his. He dipped his head to softly bite my neck, dragging his tongue along my collarbone. Then his palm caressed the curve of my trapped breasts, and his hot tongue dipped into the space between, licking both breasts at once while rolling his thumb over my tight nipple through the sheer fabric of my bra.

I whimpered as his fingers wrapped around me, and in an instant, he'd unclasped my bra, freeing my breasts. Keeping one hand above my ass, holding me firmly in place, he cupped my breast with the other, lifting it, taking its tip fully into his mouth and sucking hungrily.

I arched my back, keening, responding to the sensations snaking through me and demanding more.

"I've got you, love. I'll give you whatever you need," he murmured as he lay me gently down. "I'll give you everything I've got." Shucking his shorts and boxers in one sweep of his arm, he held a condom packet he'd miraculously retrieved at some point. He sheathed himself, then stripped my panties off while tugging me to the end of the bed. There was no hesitation, no shyness in his movements.

"I'll give you all of me," he said, stroking my thighs, knees, and calves while lifting my legs up. He lowered his face to my belly, dropping soft constellations of kisses before he nuzzled his raspy jaw into the crease of my thigh, his breath hot on my bare skin. Like he had last night, he traced my slick flesh with his fingertips, his thumb dancing teasingly over my swollen nub until, trembling, my hips arched upward, begging for him.

"If you're ready for me, love, just say my name. I'm here for you, and you alone."

Barely able to catch a breath, overcome with a desperate need I had never felt before, I gasped, "Pete. Pete, please. Help me."

"It would be my intense pleasure," he rumbled, as he slowly, surely fit himself to me, then buried himself into me, stretching me, filling me, answering my call, until his hips were pressed tightly to me.

We held still but for our shared tremors, just feeling the rightness, the completeness of our union.

He bent over me, taking my face between his palms, kissing my lips so softly before whispering, "My Jeannie, at last, at last, I make you truly mine."

Then he began a slow, hot rhythm of release and thrust,

undulating his powerful hips, whipping our already intense heat into a frothing, mad, starburst of bliss.

As my fractured bits flew all around and began to settle like sparkling ash from a volcanic eruption, he shuddered, thrusting once more, deep and hard, and gasped, "My God, you're beautiful," as he let out a mighty groan.

Chapter 18

Jeannie

"I THINK I was a little bit noisy," I said, feeling shy as we returned to Julian's pop-up restaurant, holding hands.

"You were very noisy. I liked it." Phoenix's relaxed chuckle rumbled like bass notes, more felt than heard. "A lot."

My body reacted as if he'd plucked a guitar string and sent vibrations singing through my veins. I released a breath, shaking myself a little. My world had just shifted on its axis. Life after sex with Phoenix was…altered. What had I been missing all these years?

I couldn't say what we did ten years ago was bad. It wasn't. It was amazing. But we were young, drunk, and inexperienced. It was nothing compared to tonight.

I reached over to smooth a wrinkle on his t-shirt. "Do we look like we just had sex in a tent?"

Pausing to pull me into his arms, he kissed me deeply with that same confident possessiveness he demonstrated in everything he did. "I don't care." He flashed a full-on, open smile.

It was jarring in its novelty, a little crooked, and completely disorienting to see the flash of white teeth in his stubbly face. They were fairly straight for someone who didn't have the privilege of braces, just naturally uneven, to and fro, like they grew in without quite enough space. It was ridiculously cute.

"I love your smile. Why don't you smile more?"

He shrugged and did a little jaw-jut, like he was self-conscious. "I do when I relax." He quirked one side of his mouth and crinkled his eyes in an almost, maybe unintentional wink. "Like now."

"Ah. I see. So sex makes you smile."

"Sex with you definitely makes me smile."

"I like making you smile. I want to figure out what else makes it happen."

"Be patient. I'll show you." He looped his arm around me, pulling me close, wrapping me up like a trinket in a blanket.

"We should talk," I said, sobering. "I thought that's what you'd want."

He nodded. "Yes, but not tonight. I want to celebrate. And luxuriate. But just know, I'm not going anywhere."

"Until your work——" I started, but he placed his fingertip across my lips to silence me, shaking his head.

He replaced his finger with a peck of his lips and released me.

We'd reached the pop-up restaurant and went first to get fresh drinks, before easing into the crowd at our table. Everyone was standing up, some dancing, mingling and moving chairs, so it was easy to find a spot and try to blend in—as if something world-altering hadn't happened. Or so I thought.

Quinn appeared in front of us, made an ah-ha face at our linked hands, pulled a prudish face, and demanded, "And where have you two been?" She couldn't stifle her grin.

"Just…walking around," I replied breezily.

"Uh-huh. Sure. Okay." She took my hand and pulled me out of Phoenix's grasp.

The band was playing their last set, and the crowd was stirring, a few dispersing early, but patrons at the pop-up restaurant and the tavern had settled in until closing time.

"I'll let you two talk," Phoenix said, smirking, and excused himself.

Without getting into detail, I told Quinn what had transpired, both last night and tonight. We moved a little away from our group, for privacy, but before we had a chance to say much more, we were interrupted.

A man I didn't know approached us suddenly, holding an empty glass. "Evening ladies," he said, weaving a little and leaning in close. Too close for a stranger. "I'm heading up to the bar. Can I get you refills for your wine?" He set his hand on my shoulder.

I immediately shrugged it off. "No thanks. We're—"

"With me," came Phoenix's voice, an octave lower, with a hint of a growl to his definitive statement. He lightly bumped the stranger out of the way with his arm, *accidentally*, and placed his hand on my back. As if any further threat was required after he shot the guy a dark look that sent him scurrying with apologies.

"Macho much?" I snarked, blinking at him and bristling.

His charming smile had gone into hiding again. "He was bothering you, wasn't he?"

"I don't know," I replied primly. "We didn't very far."

"That was far enough."

"That's twice now, Phoenix," I said firmly, my feminist exasperation rising. "You acted like a gorilla."

Quinn's eyes widened as she murmured, "I'll just…" and moved towards our table.

"You don't have to hover and protect me. I can take care of myself. I've been doing it successfully for a long time now."

"But I want to." Dropping his voice to a low whisper, he said, "Your problems are Will's problems, and Will's problems are my problems. Regardless of how I feel about you, or how you feel about me. We're a family now, Jeannie. Accept it. I'm not going away. I'm not leaving you alone again. Ever."

Wow. Was that a promise or a threat? When, in a romantic mood a few minutes earlier, he'd said, *I'm not going anywhere*, I'd taken it as a sweet throwaway line. This was on another level. I swallowed, nodding stiffly and meeting his stubborn green gaze with defiance. "That is a conversation for another time."

His expression was immovable, but with a tiny nod, we shelved it, and then returned to the table and sat with our thighs brushing, but no longer holding hands. I felt sad at the loss of our blissful bubble, a weight in my chest sinking into my stomach like a rock into a lake.

My mind churned. Without even talking about what our newfound connection meant, or how we would manage going forwards, Phoenix had made assumptions and jumped like a paratrooper into my business, standing guard over me as if I were his property. Had I given up my independence? Did I even get a say anymore? I dreaded the conversations that lay ahead. Where would we end up?

But I couldn't dwell any longer on my worries, because a compelling drama unfolded in front of us. Jae Soo sat beside me, his elbows on the table, surrounded by empty glasses and bottles and the messy remains of snacks, his purple-tinged black hair in spikes from thrusting his hands through it. At the moment, his head rested in his hands, his shoulders slumped. Quinn had one hand between his shoulder blades, rubbing circles, and the other on her brother, where next to her, Parker had planted his face on the table.

"I jus' want to stay here in Canada," JJ moaned. "I have ideas. I have irons in the fire."

Phoenix leaned back, sipping his beer, watching from the side of his eye, a puzzled expression twisting his brow.

"What's the matter, JJ?" I asked, querying Quinn with a frown.

"He's getting married," she explained with a tight smile and forced cheerfulness. "In the spring, probably, but the winter will be spent on wedding preparations. And many family gatherings, engagement parties, and dinners. It's a big deal in Korea."

"My only friend is leaving me forever," moaned Parker into the table.

"Thanks for that, dude," said Tate from across the table, a new woman tucked under his arm and pasted to him like wallpaper.

Tonight's companion was edgy with choppy dark hair, piercings, and ink in an off-the-shoulder t-shirt emblazoned with some heavy-metal band. She looked like a rocker, and I wondered if he'd picked her up from the musical lineup or brought her with him.

"That doesn't hurt my feelings at all," Tate added.

Parker raised his head. "I love you, too, man. But..." He gestured to JJ with both palms up, his lips stretched into an exaggerated frown, as evidence. "He's my brother!"

"Congratulations?" I said, "Or condolences, I guess?"

"He's not too happy about it," Quinn mumbled, quirking her lips to one side.

"I'm not at all happy about it," JJ said, sitting upright, thumping his hands on the table. "I've been making plans, working night and day to get my new venture off the ground, and now they do this to me."

"This being…the marriage thing?" I asked.

He nodded, opened his mouth as if to speak, and then let out a long sigh. "I mean I get it. I do. I wouldn't agree to do it if it weren't for my fucking moron of a cousin."

"And who are *they*?" I shook my head, failing to understand, glancing at Quinn for help.

She'd given me some of the circumstances before, in bits and pieces, but it was a complex picture. JJ's father, who used to be CEO of the group of family companies, had died when JJ was about thirteen. Ever since, JJ's training to take over was accelerated while the organization was run by his mother, his father's brother, and a smattering of other relatives. But apparently, a young scion was required at the helm.

Quinn scoffed. "You don't want to get into it. Freaking Korean family business crap. But suffice it to say, some relatives are being difficult, and JJ's arranged marriage to the daughter of a colleague of his father's will…" She shrugged. "Save the day?"

I wasn't sure which of the three of them—JJ, Parker, or Quinn—was more miserable at the prospect of JJ leaving, getting married to someone he presumably had met, and potentially never, or not as often, coming to Canada to see us.

I'd long known that Quinn's feelings for Jae Soo were more than just friendly. She'd confessed this to me intermittently all through high school—and afterwards occasionally in her emails. She refused to let on, however, saying she couldn't come between her twin and his best friend, and JJ didn't feel the same way, anyway. These days, she never mentioned it, and I thought her feelings might have changed. But something about this latest development felt like a nail in the coffin. Like if she had a secret dream, it was about to die a silent death. I shot her a sympathetic glance.

Phoenix pushed out of his chair, saying, "Just going to use the facilities. You want me to bring you another drink on my way back?"

I scanned his face and posture for some clue as to how he was feeling. I nodded, and he faded into the darkness, and I returned my attention to JJ.

"Jeannie?" said a concerned voice.

I glanced up. "Molly?" My heart catapulted into my throat, my pulse galloping like a herd of wild horses. "What's wrong? Is Will all right?"

"I don't know. I was hoping to find him here."

A mad stallion broke free from the herd, thundering ahead, nearly choking me. "What? Why would he be here?"

"That's what I was afraid of," Molly said, wringing her hands.

I jumped up from the table and pulled her aside, but her look of fright had caught Julian's attention, and he immediately joined our huddle.

"What's up, Molls?"

"At the end of the concert, Will and Logan told me they were going to come here and say goodnight to you. And we waited. And waited. I was about to head over to get them, but then Logan returned. Alone."

Hot flushes and cold chills flooded my body. My breath rushed out in a gust. "Oh no. No, no, no!"

"What's going on?" Phoenix returned, glasses in hand.

At our expressions, he set them down quickly and stepped closer.

"Logan said Will had decided to go home with you instead of me," Molly continued. "I thought it was strange, and I didn't like it that he didn't talk to me. Logan insisted you were okay with the change of plans. But honestly, I didn't like the look of Logan. He looked…" She circled a hand vaguely. "Anxious. So I came to check and…" She shook her head in apology, wincing.

"He didn't come here," I said, my voice loud and shrill. "He wasn't supposed to."

"Where's Logan now?" Phoenix asked, his hand lightly circling my upper arm.

"Jake has all the other kids at our truck. They're waiting there for updates."

Julian said, "We have to search the park. Quickly. I'll gather helpers." He rushed away, recruiting friends and colleagues seated nearby.

"It's not at all like Will to go off by himself," I said, my voice trembling. "He wouldn't do that." In a matter of seconds, my mind raced uncontrollably through every possible scenario, some of them very dark.

Phoenix placed his arm around me, squeezing.

"Molly, bring Logan here, please," he ordered.

"It's too late. Jake should take the other kids home. I think I should call the police right away," I said, feeling the adrenaline rush to keep me alert.

"Just hold on, Jeannie. I'll take care of this," Phoenix said. "Molly, what was Will wearing?"

"Uh, blue stripes? Here?" She pointed at her stomach.

"A blue, white, and yellow striped t-shirt," I said, seeing him in my mind's eye. "With a little orange logo." I touched my collarbone with my finger. "Right here. And khaki shorts."

"Let me handle this, Jeannie. I'll organize a quick search first." His voice was calm, emotionless, and very firm.

"You can't search the whole park yourself, Phoenix. There isn't time. It's late." I turned and held Molly's arm before she left. "When did you last see him?"

"As I said, end of the concert, so about thirty minutes ago now. We've been faffing about for a while figuring it out. I'm sorry I didn't catch on sooner."

"It's okay. It's all right. We'll be okay." I felt myself losing it and tried to calm my breathing. I pulled out my phone to dial 911, but my hands were trembling.

Phoenix took the phone from my hand, and I looked up at him, bewildered and frustrated.

"The police arriving will make a scene. It's easier to organize a search if the crowds are all sitting still."

"What if you don't find him?" I pressed. "We need to notify the police."

He said, "I'm better than the police, and I'm already on it. I have a plan."

"No, no, no. You can't. I need to do more." How could I do nothing? How could I leave searching for my lost child to someone else? I was responsible. And I'd let down my guard. Again, just like I had in the past. The moment I did something just for myself, something to feel good for a few moments, disaster happened. I was shaking.

"I'm in this with you, Jeannie. You're not alone." Phoenix's steady dark gaze locked onto mine, and he exuded such absolute confidence that I actually felt my breathing slow and my racing pulse settle to an almost normal rhythm. He took my face between his hands, wiping tears from my cheeks with his thumbs. "Stay calm and stay right here."

"I'm scared," I whispered in a shaky voice. "Please find him."

He wrapped me in his arms and spoke softly into my ear. "I will. I promise. Give me an hour. I know what to do. Trust me, Jeannie, please." He pressed my phone into my palm. "I'll text you the second I find our son."

Phoenix

I felt Jeannie relax in my arms, her breathing slowing, evening out from her frantic panting earlier. She trusted me. When I told her not to worry, that I'd find Will and return him to her, she believed me.

And that did something to me. I'd rescued plenty of people before, from far more dire situations. I'd calmed them in a crisis. I'd had team members put their trust in my leadership, my strength, and my problem-solving skills. But I'd never felt this way before. I'd never cared so much for a person in trouble. It had never mattered this much before, that I deliver, that I keep my word, that I deserve that trust.

Now I had to deliver.

First, I gathered Julian's handful of recruits and gave them each clear, simple, and specific instructions, sending people off on a tight grid with the task of searching areas of the park where a kid might go, hide, get trapped or hurt, especially the lake. I'd memorized the layout of the fairgrounds from when we set it up.

Then I instructed Julian to head to the stage and ask people—in a calm, quiet voice—to keep an eye out for a boy of Will's description. Searching loudly was always a good plan when kids were involved, but mass hysteria never helped.

Molly returned with a very nervous and anxious-looking

Logan in tow, his eyes red from crying. Since he was the last person to see Will, I knew I had to start with him.

"Sit down here. I'll be right with you."

Jeannie balked. "Don't be hard on Logan, Phoenix. He's just a kid, and he's already upset."

I narrowed my gaze at her, gauging her level of hysteria. "No, Jeannie. Logan was the last person to see Will. What he says is critical." I also knew the kid was trouble.

I knelt in front of the seated Logan, lightly took hold of his skinny arms, and looked him in the eye. "Tell me where you and Will went. And exactly where and when you last saw him. Actually saw him."

"I don't know," the kid whined. "Will said he wanted to come here." Logan was crying again. "That's what he said. I believed him."

"But you didn't make it here, did you?" I kept my voice low and soft, my posture non-threatening, but let's face it, I was scary anyway. "Did you leave him?"

He hesitated, his gaze flickering, and I knew he was calculating his response, inventing details. He was definitely leaving something out. "When was the last time you *actually saw* Will?" I pointed at my eyes and kept my gaze pinned on his.

"Uh… Um. Well… We stopped at the… The toilets." His voice rose as if he were delighted with this fabrication. He pointed to a lightly wooded area to the left of the main stage where one bank of the rented porta-potties had been set up.

There might have been a grain of truth in there.

"And did you see him go in one of them?"

He nodded, looking almost hopeful, as though he were off the hook.

I tsked. "And he didn't come out? Which one did he go in?"

That really confused him, and I wondered if he'd ever even seen them, or knew how many there were. "Which one? Do you remember?"

He continued to play dumb, evading my question. "I waited. I thought he'd come out sooner. Then I thought I'd missed him, and so I went back to Molly to see."

"You didn't think he'd come to his mom first?"

I studied his face. His mouth opened, but he didn't reply, his eyes giving away a degree of cognitive overwhelm that was not unexpected for an eight-year-old. Lie detection in kids was trickier since they were less adept, but at the same time, less rational, less able to remember things, and more easily flustered. But I was fairly certain Logan had more intel than he was giving out.

"Okay, come with me. Let's walk the area and see if you remember." I stood up, taking his hand and hauling him off.

I strolled away from Jeannie and the crowd slowly and calmly, with a firm grip on Logan's hand, in case he decided to make a run for it. As if that would solve anything, but that would be his instinct. We headed in the direction of the portable shitters. When we could see them all in a row, I asked again, "Which one did Will go into? Point please."

He scanned the row of bright blue-green plastic cubicles as if he were a contestant on *The Price Is Right*, and I'd asked him to choose a door. "Uh…that one." He pointed at one in the middle.

I knew he was lying, and I'd already directed someone to check all the toilets, but we went through the motions anyway, walking over and opening each door in turn, except the occupied ones. But we checked those too when their tenants vacated as if to prove the impossible.

Then I led him to one side, next to some trees and knelt down.

"Okay, Logan. Here's the thing."

He stared at me wide-eyed as if he thought I was going to toss him into a shitter and leave him there.

"I am a highly trained soldier," I said. "And one of the things I'm really, really good at is knowing when someone isn't telling the truth."

His light-blue eyes grew even wider, filled with genuine terror.

"You know what I'm saying?"

He nodded, and I nodded back.

"I know you're not telling the truth, bud. But I want you to understand something here."

He swallowed, seemingly shrinking in my grasp.

"You're in trouble no matter what. But you'll be in a helluva lot more trouble if you hide the truth. Now I know you boys did something stupid, am I right?"

His little face started to crack, his bugged-out eyes filling with tears, his mouth quivering.

"But the longer we go without finding Will, the greater the chances that something really serious can happen to him. You don't want that to happen, do you?"

He shook his head so quickly that his chubby cheeks jiggled.

"Okay, so now we're going to take a walk. And you're going to show me exactly where you actually left Will, got it?"

Jeannie

I waited, and I worried, while people bustled around me, coming and going. Quinn sat beside me, holding my hand tightly, after forcing me to stop my pacing. Phoenix had made Julian the point person, so all his friends who'd gone off to search reported in, one by one. Nothing had turned up yet.

Rationally, I knew I shouldn't question Phoenix's abilities. If what Ruby had suggested earlier was true, nobody was better able to find Will. I'm sure he had skills far beyond my imagining, and had searched and found people far more lost than Will in hostile environments.

But that didn't ease my feeling responsible. Or lessen my burning need to do something meaningful myself, but everyone had told me to wait. Suddenly I had deep sympathy for the crazed parents I'd seen on newsreels who were distraught and demanding when their children were lost. I, the mother, had still, somehow, managed to lose my child. There was no greater failure.

After another half hour or forty minutes had passed, I desperately wanted to notify the police again. At least they could, I don't know, block off the park access and check cars, maybe?

Did I really believe some villain had snatched my son? What else could have happened to him? Will was clever and had common sense and a strong— As I looked out at the dark lake, I forced myself to recall my outrage the other day. Will was a strong swimmer.

Suddenly, a uniformed police officer approached me, a radio squawking at his belt.

"Are you the mother of the missing child?"

"Wh—? What?" I stuttered. "Yes. Who—? Who called you?"

The officer, a pleasant, bland-faced man with very short hair the same colour as my mothers, smiled. "No one. We've been patrolling the park, monitoring the event, and we noticed the commotion over here."

"Oh." I blinked at him. I didn't know what to say now.

"What's been done here? It looks like you've sent people out searching. That's good."

I nodded mutely, so confused and distraught I couldn't gather my wits.

"Why didn't you call us right away?"

"Um. I wanted to. But—"

"I'll take responsibility for that. I persuaded her to wait."

Everyone turned at the sound of Phoenix's gruff, authoritative voice.

"What did you find? What happened?" I asked him.

"Just a sec." He pulled his wallet out of his pocket and showed something to the officer, who shone his flashlight on it and peered closely, reading for a moment, then did a double-take.

"Oh. I see," was his faltering response. "Is this a…public threat situation, sir?"

"It's a personal matter. Our son went missing for a bit."

"Is there anything we can do to assist?" the officer asked.

Phoenix shook his head. "No. The situation has been resolved. Thanks for checking in."

"N-n-no bother at all." He stepped away to speak quietly to his partner, who then stared wide-eyed at Phoenix.

They stepped further away and looked on, their radios squawking.

I was afraid to ask. With a shaking voice, I asked, "What do you mean, *resolved?*"

He put his arm around me and turned us both to face the other way. Ahead, two boys walked towards us. Logan kept trying to put his arms around Will, who elbowed him away at each try.

"Will?" I croaked. "Will!" I raced towards him, my heart pounding with joy.

"Mom!" he called, when he saw me and ran into my arms.

"Oh, my God. You're safe. I was so scared, baby." I squeezed him tightly, then leaned away to study his face. "Are you hurt? Are you okay? Where were you?" Before he could answer, I'd wrapped him in another hug, smothering his face against my chest.

"I'm sorry, Mom. I'm so sorry," came his muffled cry as he held onto me.

Phoenix met my gaze over Will's head. I realized that he'd done what he'd promised to do. He'd found Will and returned him to me. In just under an hour. And made very little fuss doing it. He also seemed to have impressed the hell out of the local police, who had eventually walked away, their heads bent together in earnest conversation.

A wave of guilt for doubting Phoenix competed with overwhelming gratitude. This terrible episode was finally at an end, and my nerves were beyond frayed. And the very next moment, it dawned on me that he'd referred to Will as 'our son' to the police, in front of everyone.

In the aftermath, things were cleared up quickly. Molly got the essential facts of what happened before saying goodnight. I wanted to take Will, but he said he'd go home with the other boys and we'd follow in Phoenix's truck.

Our friends were incredibly kind and discrete, carrying on with the evening of drinking and socializing as if nothing much had happened.

Some tried to persuade me to stay, saying if ever there was a night when a mother deserved a break, and a glass of wine, it was this one, but I declined.

I wanted nothing more than to go home with Will, get

ready for bed, and curl up around my son, holding him tight. And then there was Phoenix.

Phoenix had done two things. He'd got the whole truth out of Logan, and then solved the conundrum that had stymied the boys, leaving Will in the lurch and Logan scrambling to cover his butt. On the drive home, he filled me in.

It transpired that Logan and Will had gone in search of souvenirs from the band—the Zolas, that Will was so hot on —during the intermission. Phoenix held firm to the idea that Logan had egged Will on, knowing he was a fan, but I'd reserve judgment on that until I could speak with Will alone. It did seem like the kind of stunt Will wouldn't normally try, though.

The boys had noticed three things on their adventures in the afternoon. One was a booth selling CDs, t-shirts, mugs and other band merch from the various musicians performing at the Faire. Secondly, they'd noticed members of the band, along with their crew, sitting at a table in the tavern. And at the end of the main concert, apparently, the band rejoined their colleagues for drinks.

This was of interest, primarily because of the third thing they'd found. Most titillating of all to nine-year-old boys, it was the band trailer parked in the overflow parking lot beyond a copse of trees behind the main stage.

Lacking adequate pocket money, and inadequately supervised, a mistake I wouldn't be making again anytime soon, they'd come up with a scheme. Somehow, in their minds, there was a faint hope of acquiring some free merch if they snuck into the band's trailer when everyone was at the tavern at the end of the set. The fact that this would have been stealing was a topic to be discussed another time.

So giving Molly the feeble excuse of bidding me good-night, they'd snuck away from her, off down the path through the trees to the trailer. Finding the door unlocked, they snuck inside for a quick look around. I'm sure more than half the thrill was the subterfuge, as well as the prospect of scoring some keepsake. Will would have been happy with a wrinkled playbill or a paper coaster to pin to the corkboard over his desk.

That's when everything had gone awry. They'd been alone in the trailer, poking through cupboards or whatever, when they heard heavy footsteps approaching. Not surprisingly, the trailer was *not* left open and unattended. The driver had merely slipped out to smoke a joint. And then he'd returned. Oh, my.

In the seconds they'd had to react, Logan, closer to the exit, had time only to hiss a warning to run and hide, and quickly escaped, whereas the unlucky Will, perhaps more keen to find the merch, had got trapped inside. In a panic, he'd hopped into a closet, holding his breath in terror as the unsuspecting driver came in, took a piss, crashed around, and settled down for a snooze on the sofa.

Logan, hiding outside in the trees, was beside himself. He waited and waited, but the man had shown no intention of leaving again. What could he do? Meanwhile, poor Will was sweating bullets in the closet, afraid to out himself and get in trouble, and just as worried that they'd drive off with him captive at the end of the night. The latter, it seemed to me, was the greater risk, and then he really would have been missing. Until someone went looking for a clean shirt.

Logan, in desperation, had returned to Molly with his feebly fabricated story, the whole time freaking out about Will stuck in the trailer.

Once the truth was out, all it took was Phoenix knocking on the trailer door, having a quiet adult conversation with the chill driver, who thought the whole thing was hilarious, and releasing the trapped jailbird. Unbelievable what kids could get up to. And to think of the fear plus trouble and inconvenience they'd put everyone through.

"Our friends are wondering what's up with us," I said to Phoenix afterwards. It would have been shocking to see Phoenix and I go from awkward flirting and barely dating to the way we were tonight. Obviously a couple. "But nobody said anything,"

"What should they be saying? Let them wonder."

I pulled a face. "I'm sure they have a million questions. You did casually refer to Will as *our* son just a half hour ago."

"They're biding their time," Phoenix said with a wry half-smile, his eyes twinkling. "Until they can catch us alone."

"If that's true, we have to get our story straight."

He tucked his chin in. "Do we need a story?"

I flapped my hands. "I mean, there are details nobody needs to know, so we should agree now what we're going to say when they ask. Because they will."

"What does Quinn know?"

"Just the basic shape of things. Then. And now. No details. And she won't spill. But first of all, I don't want everyone talking about us until we've sorted out Will—and our families."

He nodded. "Agreed."

"Okay. Then, um, keep it simple."

"I think it's going to be pretty clear when we hooked up, given your fight with Zach and the fire in my dad's trailer where I supposedly died. That's a narrow window."

"Sadly, yes."

"Jeannie," he said softly, tipping my chin up with his forefinger. "It's our business. Nobody else's."

I smiled ruefully. "I know. But the girls are going to—"

"Tell them I was irresistibly hot, and Zach just wasn't doing it for ya." He laughed softly.

I scoffed and smacked his arm. "You're no help."

"I'll deal with Zach. You tell the girls whatever you want to. I don't care. As long as—" His brows came down suddenly.

"What?"

"It was consensual. They can't scapegoat me."

I gasped. "I wouldn't! What do you think of me?"

"Not you. But other people might assume."

"Don't worry." I looked up, meeting his gaze. "People know you're good."

He grunted. "But not as good as you." He planted a kiss on my mouth, smirking, as he dropped me off home. I was beat, the stress of the night hitting me like a wall. Before getting out, I thanked him for finding Will for the hundredth time.

"Get used to it. I'll be keeping you safe from now on, always. You can trust me. I'm just as invested in our son's well-being as you are. Nothing is as important to me." He held me close. "I'm here for you too."

I felt tears spring suddenly to my eyes.

"What's the matter, love?"

"I don't know," I said, my voice quavering. "It's all too much."

"Get some sleep. I'll come by tomorrow. We can talk. Maybe, I don't know, go for a walk somewhere with Will. On the beach. Tell him I'm his father."

"No!" I suddenly felt certain, pulling away. "No, I have to do it myself. I... Will and I have to talk about tonight's fiasco first. He'll need both comfort and discipline. Then, I'll know when it's the right moment, I'll break it to him."

He brooded silently for a moment, jaw flexing. "I feel like it's something I ought to do."

I shook my head. "I know you mean well. But you can't just appear in our lives and step into rights or responsibilities on the basis of DNA alone. It takes a lot more to raise a child than that."

He frowned. "That seems harsh since I didn't know."

"I'm sorry. I don't mean it that way. Only that I'll know how to approach it. I know him. You need to pace yourself. Show Will you want to earn your place in his life."

"Didn't I do that tonight?" His expression was challenging.

I nodded, smiling to soften my message. "It was an amazing start."

Chapter 19

Jeannie

THE NEXT DAY, Will was quietly remorseful. And probably just plain worn out. We skipped the last half day of the Faire in favour of a day at home. We'd both had enough. I had heaps of laundry to catch up on—and emails and paperwork for the school year, financial stuff, and insurance. Things had piled up the past week, and we both started classes in two days.

Later in the day, when we had settled into some quiet time, I sat with Will on the deck while we both read, sipping iced tea. We'd already talked about last night when we woke up in the morning, and he'd apologized again for causing trouble.

"Any more thoughts about last night?" I asked him.

"No. Except I told you I didn't like hanging out with Logan."

"It takes two to tango, honey."

"I know, Mom. I just… *Ugh*. Being with him stresses me out."

"Okay. Let's leave it for now, and then, when you're feeling better, we can talk about peer pressure. Okay?"

"I'm not a pushover, Jeannie."

I clucked my tongue and gave him a look.

"Mom. I was just trying extra hard because…" He raised his hands in exasperation. "He's my cousin. Okay. I never had someone I *had* to get along with before."

"I can appreciate that. It's something you'll learn to manage."

My phone pinged, and I flipped over my book and picked up the phone.

PHOENIX: *How's it going?*
   Me: *Fine. Laundry's done. :) Relaxing now.*
   Phoenix: *Did you tell him?*

I PUFFED a sigh through my cheeks.

ME: *Not today. Still fragile.*
   Phoenix: *When? I'd hoped to see him.*
   Me: *I think maybe next weekend. I don't want to upset him before the first week of school. Too many other new things.*
   Phoenix: …
   Me: *I'm sorry. Be patient. Please.*
   Phoenix: *I could be involved at school. Help.*
   Me: *I'll speak with the principal so she knows who you are. For later.*
   Phoenix: *There's stuff I want to talk to you about. Ideas.*
   Me: *Pete! Settle down.*
   Phoenix: *Fine. I'll wait.*

. . .

I WONDERED how long he'd wait, though. I could feel the steam rising off of him. He was chomping at the bit. I'd never seen someone so eager to embrace a new role or take on a load of responsibility. I didn't know what to do with his energy, his pushiness, his opinions about everything.

As to be expected, the following week was hectic and chaotic. No matter how many times you rehearse something in your mind to prepare, the reality is something more.

The logistics of getting out the door in the morning were already enough to sink our ship. I had morning classes at eight-thirty, so I had to drop Will off at school way too early and help him figure out where to hang out until the bell rang. Then get myself on a bus to the university campus. A car would have made our lives much easier, but that cost was not yet in the books.

On Tuesdays and Thursdays, I had a seminar until seven, so again, I had to make arrangements for Will to get home from school without me. Not so easy when you knew not one other parent at the school and didn't have the leisure to hang around after drop off and go for coffee with other moms. I'd never had that luxury, though, so that was nothing new.

Instead, I asked the school principal, and she introduced me to another parent who lived not far from us and was willing to drop Will off. The problem was, that I had no support in case of an emergency, other than my flaky mother. The thought of Phoenix, just across town, eager to help, ran around my mind like a gerbil on a wheel.

What if we became dependent on his help and then he wasn't there anymore? I felt that would be harder on Will than learning to flex a little now by teaching him to think for himself when I couldn't be there for him.

The incident at the park worried me, though. I'd always been there for Will. My own client work, and my part-time courses, had always worked around his schedule. So I'd relied very little on anyone else. But my new full-time load at university was demanding, and at this level, the faculty had little patience for slackers.

Will needed another steady, responsible adult in his life. I'd been fooling myself to think that my mother had changed much since I'd left home. She was more absent-minded and preoccupied with her own interests now than she'd ever been. Dad was almost as bad. And anyway, didn't they deserve a peaceful retirement? It was enough that they'd given us a temporary home.

Also, within three days, I was already buried under a load of reading and assignments, so my evenings were completely eaten up. I just prayed we'd both find our groove, and it would get easier.

Phoenix, I had to grant, had given us space. I hadn't seen him since Sunday night. His texts were regular, but no longer so insistent. And I'd begun to feel guilty for keeping him away when he was obviously excited to get to know Will better and be involved in his life. Had I gone beyond cautious and become petty? I didn't know. But it was time to tell Will.

So on Saturday afternoon, once we'd had a sleep-in and done a few chores around the house, I suggested we head out to the park on the point and wander the trails. Will was game to escape the confinement of the house. The early September day was fine, still clear and sunny, but the air had a new tang that smelled of the coming change of season.

After wandering aimlessly through the trees along winding bark-mulch pathways, sometimes peeking out to ocean views, I suggested we climb onto the big flat rocks and sit in the sun.

"Do you remember when I told you that your father had died?"

Will had been chattering about his new class but stopped abruptly. "Sure. Why?"

"I have something important to tell you. And it might seem like I didn't tell the truth before. So I wanted to start by saying, I believed your father had died at the time. But it's not true. I believed it was true until not very long ago."

Will was silent for a moment before saying, "But you never married him anyway, right? Where is he? In Kingston?"

I let that question go for the moment. "No. I never married him. There was no chance for that. But…we were friends. I don't know what would have happened if I'd known he was still alive." I turned to look at Will to gauge his reaction. He sat very still, squinting out at the ocean, his lips pursed, thinking hard about what I'd said, what it meant for him. "Aren't you curious?"

"Yeah, Mom. Duh." He shot me a sideways glance, rolling his eyes.

I laughed. "Okay. I guess I expected you to be excited. It's big news."

"I'm excited on the inside," my darling son said. "I just don't know if it's okay to be excited on the outside." He screwed up his face, looking right at me. "How do you feel about it?"

"Aw, honey. I'm okay. More than okay. You don't need to worry about me."

"This is kind of a big deal for us, hey, Mom?"

I nodded, my lip suddenly quivering, and I pressed my fingers to them as tears stung my eyes. I drew in a quick breath and said, "Yup."

"What does it mean, then? Do we have to go back to

Kingston? Are you going to make me live with him or something?"

I gasped. "No, sweetie. No, no, no, no. I would never do that."

"Maybe he'd make you. I knew kids who had to, even though they didn't want to."

"That happens sometimes, when couples get divorced. This is quite different." I took his hand and held it tight. "We are not going to Kingston." I filled my lungs for courage. "Because…your dad is here in Port Camosun."

"What? Have you seen him?"

I nodded.

"Mom!" He blinked a few times, his gaze darting left and right. "Have I met him?"

I nodded again, biting on my lips, looking steadily into his green-flecked brown eyes. "It's Phoenix, honey. Phoenix is your biological father."

His face opened like a banner unfurling. "Are you shitting me?"

"Hey! Watch your mouth, mister." I snorted with laughter.

Then he tossed both hands into the air and flopped down, lying flat on the rock, staring wide-eyed and unblinking up at the blue sky. "This is awesome. I have a dad. And he's Phoenix." He sat up abruptly, suddenly vibrating with energy. "Mom! He's so cool!"

I just stared at him, my hand covering my mouth, covering the flabbergasted smile on my face, tears still leaking from my eyes. I was shocked, bewildered, and amused in equal parts by Will's reaction.

"I thought… I worried you'd be scared, or angry, or… I don't know, confused." I shrugged.

"Can we call him? Can we see him? Does he know?"

"Yes. I don't know. And yes, honey, I told him first. He was surprised, obviously."

"Wow. I have a dad! Weird. When did you tell him?"

"The night before your disappearing act."

"Is that why he looked for me?"

I shook my head. "I think he would have helped even if he weren't your father. He's a good guy. But I can't say it wasn't on his mind." I thought of how many times that night and since then he'd said the words, *our son*.

Will scrabbled for my bag. "Where's your phone? Let's call him."

"Slow down. He might be busy. He's at work on the base." I pulled my phone out and texted him.

ME: *Where are you?*

OBVIOUSLY SITTING with his phone in his hand, because his reply came instantly.

PHOENIX: *How'd it go?*
Me: Better than expected.

MY PHONE RANG.

"Hi." The word came out on a laugh.

Will was jiggling and jumping, his face a bright clock, ticking. "Is it him? Is that him?" Will asked, and when I nodded, he shouted at my phone, "Hi, Phoenix! It's me, Will! We're at the park!"

"You have a fan here. He'd like to see——"

"Which park?" Phoenix asked, laughing. "I'm on my way."

I told him and hung up, looking at Will, perplexed. "Well, it looks like I'm the one who should be worried. You guys are going to ditch me and start a new mutual fan club."

Will grabbed my hand and dragged me up. "Let's go meet him in the parking lot." Then he took off running.

"Slow down on the rocks!" I hollered after him, but he was already on the trail, disappearing into the trees.

Short of breath, I caught up to Will a few minutes later just as Phoenix's blue truck pulled into a stall. He must have sped here. Somehow, this was not about me at all, so I tarried to observe them.

The reunion of man and boy, meeting of father and son, was poignant and moving. For all Will's enthusiasm, when Phoenix stepped out of his truck, Will became suddenly shy, stopping, standing, waiting—I'm sure, with bated breath. Perhaps to see if he would be greeted with equal pleasure.

In this first moment, Phoenix didn't let him down. He strode directly towards Will, spoke some quiet words I couldn't hear, set a hand on his shoulder, knelt on one knee, and took my boy in his arms—holding him so closely, I thought he'd never let go.

It broke my heart in two and fused it back together in a new, supersized version bigger than I knew it could be.

Phoenix

Jeannie was cool about bringing Will to meet up with me, to hang out in a low-key way at first. We'd go out for meals together and just catch up on our days. Share mundane details. That first Saturday in the park, she sat and read a book on her phone while Will and I walked in the park and talked. He was so clever and mature for a nine-year-old. And he was taking this, admittedly radical news, in a very chill way, though he had a million questions about where I'd been all his life.

That evening, we went out for burgers and milkshakes. When Jeannie had decided it was time to head home, I didn't argue even though I wanted to hold on to both of them and never let go. It felt as if I had something I'd always dreamt of in reach, just not quite solid enough to grasp. Yet.

The first time I met them wearing my uniform was interesting. I'd come from work and met them at the school so Jeannie could introduce me to the principal and register me with the office in case of an emergency.

Will thought it was cool and asked questions like he always did. Especially about camo—which obviously I didn't wear every day—and what equipment and gear I used on missions. He had the curious and practical mind of an engineer, which made me feel more than anything that he was cut from the same cloth.

Jeannie got all quiet and just looked and looked as if I were someone else entirely. Or maybe as if the fact that I was in the Navy was, until now, a very abstract idea that had suddenly become very concrete and very real.

"I'm still me," I'd teased her, and stolen a kiss when Will was using the washroom.

Though we'd been getting together a couple of times each week, she'd been reserved and kept me at arm's length. I understood that right now she was focussed on Will and his adjustment to me. Testing the temperature of the water. And despite the thrill of our new situation, life marched on.

They both had busy school schedules, piles of homework, and I had now returned to duty, making the necessary adjustments to integrate as part of the Pacific JTF 2 team.

Under Unger's oversite, there was one other Team Leader, an Air Force Major named Roland Laflamme, originally from Quebec. While a senior officer, he was a couple of bars lower than me. At the same time, he was used to being the top-ranking active officer out West, since Unger was pencil-pushing brass. That meant a fair bit of jostling of egos for the first couple of weeks. He knew I outranked him, of course, but being CAF, he still tried pretty hard to show me that he was boss. Until it came time for risk assessment, tactics, and task force planning.

When not deployed, we spent our time reviewing intel, monitoring currently active missions, evaluating performance on past missions to ensure future challenges could be met, analyzing risk, reviewing high-level security data, and liaising with other units—brass, non-military organizations such as CSIS, the feds, and the Mounties. Basically, a ton of reading, analysis, and meetings. The rest of the time, we worked out, conducted specific training and drills, and trained with junior officers and personnel to elevate their skills. I'd always found it interesting and mentally stimulating work, even when not deployed. Though, of course, that's when my training and expertise synthesized in indescribable ways. I loved it.

The last five weeks, while restful, were the longest leave I'd ever had in my career. I'm sure I would have been bored out of my mind if it weren't for Jeannie and Will being in my life.

Now, when I was at work, I thought of them, and when I was with them, I thought of work. My attention had never been so divided.

But for all that I saw her more regularly, I missed Jeannie. I missed touching her, wanted to hold her and kiss her. And I really wanted another opportunity to make love to her like we had in the tent. That had been incredible, but over too soon, and our newfound intimacy was too quickly overshadowed by other events. I had to find a way to change that.

Logistics continued to be challenging. I was still sharing a single officer's bunk. Where were we supposed to go to be private? We hadn't made headway talking to our families yet. And, aside from that, going on a date and leaving Will at home also felt…strange. So for now, I bided my time and enjoyed what we had. We felt, a little bit, like a family. I was aware of the way others looked at us three when we were out in town, walking around or in a restaurant. It did something funny to my insides.

It wasn't long before pretty much all of our friends had asked one or the other of us what was going on. If it was true that I was the father of Jeannie's son. As planned, we were, if not coy, then vague about how it had all happened. My disappearance took centre stage, obviously, and I encouraged everyone to focus on the fact that Jeannie had to cope all on her own, at eighteen, as a mother.

In the meantime, I did everything I needed to formally acknowledge Will as my son. Another man might have resisted or required proof, but I needed no more than Jeannie's word, and to look at Will, to know the truth.

There was legal paperwork, and research into topics I'd never paid too much attention to, such as life insurance policies, extended health benefits, family identification cards, housing allowances, and many others.

I could hear Jeannie's voice cautioning me, saying, *You're getting ahead of yourself, Phoenix*. Which may have been true in one sense. But I had a son now, if not yet a wife, and that would never change. And I believed in being prepared.

I also looked into children's counsellors and tutors available in town. While either Jeannie or I were more than able to tutor Will in math, I thought a separate, third-party tutor might actually be better for him, given his performance anxiety issues.

On that note, I'd gently questioned Will about what triggered his anxiety attacks, and how he experienced them, and was starting to get the picture. Keeping most of what I'd discovered in reserve, for now, I gently offered to help with his homework from time to time. The issue was, I was still *persona non grata* at the van Bellen residence since Jeannie had not yet "found the right moment" to tell her mother the whole story.

Yes, all right. I knew I was pushing for too much, too fast. It's only that, when I saw the right path, when I'd settled on a solution, I needed to go directly there. Of course, I was trained to think outside the box and to adapt to changing circumstances. I was even trained to wait if waiting was the strategic thing to do. I could be very patient when I needed to be. Like now. But my mind was busy laying out a variety of alternative tactics. After all, I was also trained for success.

I took every opportunity to spend time alone with Will. And Jeannie generously made herself scarce by going grocery shopping or sitting with her reading and saying, "You guys go ahead. I'll be right here when you're done," I'd begun to drill down on Will's anxiety.

I'd coached him to, first of all, accept that maybe his worry over certain things was valid.

For example, his mom did stress a lot. Being a single parent, responsible for everything, was a huge job. Jeannie had no support. So it was hard for her to relax. And Will's worry for her was actually the logical, right, and caring thing to do. His feelings were valid. There was nothing wrong with him.

My main message to him was that those days were over. I recalled the wistful things he'd told me at the Faire, about what a dad was for. That I was always going to be around for them both. That they had reinforcements now. That nothing bad could ever happen to them, that I wouldn't be there to help with. If I ever let anything bad happen in the first place. And my mission now was to do everything in my power to keep them safe. Over time, I think I was starting to make an impression on him.

My second tactic was to gently teach him techniques for managing his anxiety. Awareness. Affirmations. Breathing. Reality check-ins to keep his worries in line with actual, likely outcomes, and avoiding catastrophic thinking. And also teaching him to name it when it was happening and ask for help. And then, taking that intense nervous energy and redirecting it towards thoughts and behaviours that would actually help achieve the desired outcome, whether that was doing well on a math quiz or dealing with family drama.

I also taught him to use movement to change his body energy. Sitting straight and standing tall would help his confidence. We threw balls around so I could nudge him out of his head. Finally, when opportunities presented themselves, I taught him mindful meditation techniques. Basically guided daydreams, and breathing, as a way to bring his stress level down.

I didn't know, but I didn't think that he had told Jeannie any of this. She certainly had made no reference to any of it yet.

I'd brought them home one evening after grabbing a quick dinner to find that her parents were both out.

"Come inside for a bit," she'd offered, and the look on Will's face made saying no impossible. Not that I wanted to.

Will sat at the kitchen table and pulled out his homework while Jeannie made tea.

"What are you working on tonight?" I asked him, leaning back to take in the stuffy details of the house.

With a heavy sigh, he replied, "Spelling. And I have this sheet of math problems. They're the worst."

"Don't psych yourself out. You'll be fine."

I tried to leave him to do it on his own. Jeannie set a steaming mug of tea in front of me, then went to the bathroom.

I sat quietly, watching Will in a low-key way, trying not to be obvious about it. His face screwed up as he read the problems, and I could see where he read them over and over, where the point of his pencil hovered over the words. He started to chew on his lips, then the end of his pencil. He wrote and stopped. Erased something. Tried again, sighed, and groaned.

"Is it making it worse that I'm sitting here?" I asked softly.

"No. Yes." He lifted his gaze to meet mine, and they were filled with self-doubt and worry.

"I can leave if—"

"No! Don't go," he said plaintively.

"Do you remember the steps?"

He nodded, his expression shifting to one of focus and determination.

"Take it slow. Homework is for learning. School is for learning. Nobody's judging you, little man."

I curbed a smile, watching him mentally rehearse the steps I'd taught him. Sitting up, breathing, thinking it through.

Suddenly he blurted, "*Viam Inveniemus.*"

"What? Where the heck did you get that?" I laughed.

He'd even pronounced the Latin properly. It was our special forces motto. It meant *we will find a way.*

He rolled his eyes and pointed at my left bicep, where the motto was inked into my skin. Granted, along with a couple of dozen other images and words. But my kid, he'd seen it, remembered it, figured it out.

"I looked it up on YouTube," he said simply, shrugging. "You said I should find a mantra. To focus my thoughts when I was feeling anxious."

Breath whooshed out of me, and pride filled every space until my heart would burst, like helium, making me lighter. Of all the things my kid could have chosen as a phrase to help him through his moments of fear and insecurity, he'd picked the best of all. "You know how to pick 'em, my man."

"What's going on? What's this about?" Jeannie said, coming in, holding a towel.

I glanced up and caught her scowl, then looked at Will.

"It's my mantra." He was so stoked about it I wanted to praise him, but I bit my tongue.

"I gathered that," she deadpanned, then squinted in my direction suspiciously.

"I've been teaching Will a few tricks. To help manage the anxiety." I rolled my lips between my teeth, waiting for the fallout.

"Go upstairs, honey. It's bath night."

"But my homework," he protested.

"You can tackle a bit more afterwards. Maybe the bath will relax you." She raised her brows at Will with a look that brooked no further opposition, and I sighed.

After Will gathered his books and rucksack and stomped up the stairs, she speared me with a look and said, "So. You're a child psychologist now, too? Is there anything you can't do?"

I tilted my head, studying her. "Jeannie. Please."

"Don't look at me like that, as if I'm some kind of lunatic. What's been going on behind my back?"

"It's not behind your back," I hedged, though I had been sly about it. "I've asked Will to describe his anxiety to me and given him a few strategies to help him deal with it. That's it. I promise."

"Yet neither you nor Will thought to mention it to me. That's not sneaky?"

"It wasn't meant to be sneaky. Just something private. Is that not allowed?"

She jutted her chin, grinding her teeth, and frowning at me, the gears in her head working. "No. Not yet. I need to…vet things. I need…to know what's going on."

"Is the problem what I coached him to do? Or the fact that you weren't consulted?"

"I can't very well comment on the first option since I don't know anything about it." She set her fists on her hips.

"But you know about his anxiety. It's been eating you up. The counsellor at school said he needed therapy. What's the harm in starting with something easy when I knew how to help?"

"How? Why do you know…anything like this?"

I rocked my head a little. "Mostly, it's part of my training. Managing stress, fear, anxiety, panic. It's part of the job."

She just stared at me, stony-faced, so I went on.

"And I may have done some extra reading and training in mental health in relation to PTSD." I shrugged. "After what happened to my dad, can you blame me?"

Her face softened, her gaze sliding to the side. "No. I guess not. But it's not your job to fix Will. It's mine."

"It's both our jobs," I insisted. "And I can help. Why is it so hard for you to let me?"

She pursed her lips, stewing in her thoughts, but she slackened and let me pull her gently into my lap. I rubbed her arms lightly with my thumbs, taking it slow—and felt her shiver a little at my touch.

After another minute, I said, "I can also, if you prefer, arrange good cognitive-behavioural therapy for him. I know people in the mental health field in the forces. People I saw as a kid when…When I needed them."

She spun her head and peered up at me, questions swimming in her eyes. "I didn't know that."

"Why would you?"

"Is that why you stayed with your father?"

"No. But it gave me some perspective, I guess, when things got ugly. It helped."

"I'm sorry. You come across as this invincible superman. I sometimes forget that you suffered so much as a kid."

I brushed it off. "Not the point, anyway. But I can't say my sensitivity to mental health issues hasn't been an added focus of my study and an extra skill set that I've worked at."

She nodded, pensive.

"You should be aware, that I—" I forced a smile. "I have the most awesome extended health coverage."

"What did you do?"

"Just some official paperwork. So you can access some extras for Will. If you want." I dipped my chin and bumped her forehead with mine gently.

"Just because I struggle with money doesn't mean I don't do everything I can."

"No one's suggesting that, babe. But stuff's expensive without insurance. And…I can pay for other things. A math tutor." I smiled to soften the message.

"But I can—"

"Yes, I know you can. So can I. Sometimes, though, it's better if it's an outsider."

"Did you sign him up already? Without asking me?"

I shook my head. "Nope. Just did some research."

"Phoenix. Damn you." She pushed off my lap and paced the kitchen.

"While we're being honest here," I ventured. "I should probably tell you that I also added Will as a beneficiary to my life insurance. In case anything happened."

Her expression held a dozen different emotions: disbelief, aggravation, pity, fear, gratitude, and a measure of fury. I wasn't sure which was foremost in her mind.

"I don't want to become dependent on you. And I don't want Will to become dependent on you."

"That's not how I see this. Why would you choose to deprive Will of resources that could help him if they're available?"

"But it's happening. You're swooping in and, and, and taking care of things. Making problems disappear. What happens when you aren't here anymore?" Her voice cracked on the last word.

I stood up and stepped closer. "I'm not going anywhere, Jeannie."

"That's what you say. Maybe you can't…" Her chin began to quiver.

I wrapped my arm around her and rubbed her back. "Even if—"

"Don't even say it!" She turned her face away, pressing her knuckles to her lips, shaking her head.

I stayed silent, waiting for her to speak.

"I've always been responsible for my actions. For my life. Ever since…" Her voice wavered, and she stiffened her chin. "Since Bonnie died, I made sure I never burdened anyone. And since Will came along, I took responsibility for us."

"I get that. But you're being defensive when I only want to help."

"I am. But you're treading all over my territory with your big boots."

I took a deep breath and let it out. "Don't make this a contest of egos, Jeannie. That's not important here. You are so capable it's scary sometimes."

"It's not my ego that's a problem," she said, defensively.

I sat down, to make myself smaller, but also to anchor her in space. She was winding herself up tighter and tighter. I wanted to coach her how to breathe, how to do a reality check.

"You want to be good. Do all the things. Be the best. Not let anyone down. Has it ever occurred to you that Will's anxiety might stem from your own fear of failure? If you let go a little, it might help Will relax, too. You're his whole world."

"I had a plan. I've been working so hard to rebuild my dreams. And my success had to be mine or it…it doesn't count." She was on a roll. And I didn't even know if she was listening to me anymore. "If someone rescues me, then that's failure. Don't you understand? I have to make up for past mistakes myself."

"But rigidity is a weakness and being soft is also a strength." I took her hand and pulled her closer, trying to soothe her. "When I'm on a mission, do you think we head out without a plan? We have truckloads of intel, and we have all the assets. But do you think the situation in the field always goes to plan?" I shook my head. "I'm trained to pivot, make changes on the fly and always, always look at any situation and assess risks and opportunities.

She seemed to run out of steam, and stood looking down into my face.

"You're viewing me as a risk, instead of an asset. I want

you to use me, Jeannie, to achieve your goals. You're still in charge of this mission."

A little crease formed between her soft rusty brows.

"And if the so-called 'mistake' that set you on this path was having a son, then I'm fifty percent responsible. You're doing me a disservice by depriving me of my chance to make up. We can share responsibility. It's high time I made a contribution, don't you think?"

"I'm tired," she said, rubbing a hand over her forehead and eyes. "I think you should go."

I stood up and moved to the front hall.

"Phoenix!" Will called, bouncing down the stairs. "Are you going?"

"I'm heading out. And you have to get to bed, bud."

He took two more steps to close the gap, and I gave him a hug.

"Come for dinner Sunday," Jeannie suddenly blurted. "My brother and his family will be here. We can barbeque on the patio before the weather turns cool."

"Yes!" Will chirped. "Please come."

I turned to peer curiously at Jeannie, with a smile. "I'll be here."

# Chapter 20

Jeannie

BEFORE PHOENIX COULD COME for dinner, or have time alone with Will, I had to explain who he was to my family. Obviously, one did not let one's kid go off with a strange man. Late one night, after Will was in bed, I sat Mom down for a cup of tea in the kitchen.

"There's something you need to know."

"What the matter?" Mom said, blinking at me, confused.

I didn't tend to pin her down like this. It was too much like trying to catch a moth. Exhausting and often futile. I drew a deep breath, choosing my words carefully. "I've invited Phoenix to join us for dinner on Sunday."

She pursed her lips, and predictably, countered with, "But that's family time, sweetheart."

I nodded, swallowing. "Exactly. Will should… Will would like his dad to be included."

"What?"

"Phoenix is Will's dad." At her continued blank stare, I

added, "Peter Corbin. You know who I'm talking about, right?"

"But…how?"

"You don't mean how. You mean when?"

Her lips moved, folded, parted, and then she gave up, nodding.

"Grad night." I shook my head. "Details are not important. It happened. Unexpectedly, obviously. And then, like everyone, I thought he'd died."

A little breath shot out of her, like an airgun. *Pssht.*

"It took me a while to tell him, and then a bit longer to tell Will. But now…I want to include him at a family dinner, and introduce him to everyone. I want you all to get to know him and accept him as part of the family. For Will."

"Are you going to…? Will you marry him?"

"I'm focusing on Will right now. Keeping an even keel while he adjusts to Phoenix. While we get used to having him around. I can't, and I don't want to, make it harder for everyone by including a new romantic relationship into the mix."

"But you already started dating him. You like him?"

I jerked my shoulder dismissively. "I do. Yes. He's a good man."

"Sweetheart. I know you've made a lot of sacrifices. But you have to take care of your own happiness too. Don't let life pass you by. I think this is finally your moment."

My mind took a little detour. This was the first time I could ever remember my mother speaking to me with sympathy. It made my chest tight and my breath short. I pushed on.

"Not at Will's expense. He's my responsibility. I still have a lot to make up for. I won't screw that up by getting involved with Phoenix."

Mom brought her hands together on the tabletop,

linking them and wiggling them, her grip tightening. She'd always had such capable, busy hands, and more often than not, they were clad in gardening gloves, covered in dirt.

Suddenly I noticed the leathery wrinkles, the proud blue veins that traced their bony backs. I peered at her face, searching for verification that she was getting old, and found it in the loose skin under her eyes, and the creases that bracketed her thinning mouth.

"I've never understood why you feel you're inadequate, Jeannie, dear. You're so clever and accomplished. You've always been so determined and mature. I wish you could lighten up and enjoy life more. Have fun."

My head went hot, my neck muscles stiff. "How can you say that? You're the one who made me this way." I didn't mean to blurt out those words. But since my blow-up with Phoenix a couple of nights ago, my thoughts had been on overdrive, grinding and churning. Is this the way everyone saw me? Is this who I was?

Mom was nonplussed. "What did I do?"

In a calmer tone, I explained, "You… You made sure I understood that I was responsible for Bonnie. That it was me who messed up. You never let me forget it."

Mom's mouth dropped open in shock, her eyes tearing up. "What? Why are you saying that? How could you be responsible for the death of *my* child, Jeannie? How could anyone take the blame for that but me?"

Mom confessed that she'd never forgiven herself for not watching Bonnie more closely, and afterwards was always so fearful for my safety. "I might have been overprotective. I don't know. "

I was shocked. I whispered, "I thought you were trying to teach me a lesson."

"Oh, no, dear." Mom patted the flat of her hand against her sternum. "I was grieving. I never forgave myself for losing Bonnie. I was quite depressed for a time, too, numb. I could hardly function. I couldn't bear to lose you too and the only way I could cope was to hold you tight."

I was just as stunned by her reply, outrage bubbling up through my chest like a boiling kettle. "What? You were so hard on me. Now you're urging me to have fun, but then, it was all… *Stay home and be quiet, Jeannie. Clean the house, Jeannie. Work hard at school, Jeannie. It's up to you to make something of yourself, Jeannie. You're all I have left.* You never said anything like that to Brandon."

She tucked her chin. "He was already grown up. I could see where he was going. And he dealt with Bonnie's loss in his own way, along with your father. Mostly by avoiding their feelings, as men are wont to do. But you, you were faltering after Bonnie died. I mean, we all were, sweetheart. My heart was broken. But you… You were in such a dark place for a child. I thought you needed guidance. Some structure. A little push until your sparkle returned."

"My *sparkle*?" Did I ever have a sparkle? "You weren't… punishing me for letting her go out on the lake by herself?"

Mom shook her head, her face a picture of remorse and pity. "No. Of course not. It was you who were punishing yourself, my poor, sweet girl. I felt as though I'd lost both my bright, beautiful daughters overnight."

"But, my God, I felt like Cinderella. I did all that housework, and studied so hard, and did volunteer work, and…"

"I thought, if you kept busy, then nothing bad would happen to you. And… I don't know but, maybe Dad thought you needed to help out." She shook her head. "I think I wasn't quite myself for a long time."

"But I moved away, Mom. I abandoned you."

She nodded pensively. "I was sad about that. But I'd learned by then to let go. I always felt you were strong and independent, and wouldn't tolerate interference in your life.

So we let you do what you needed to do, your own way. But we always wished you'd come home and let us help you with the baby so you could go to school. Of course, we were sad you couldn't follow your dreams. We're so happy you're finally doing that. So happy to finally get to know Will."

My reality was splintering and reforming into new, different images but with all the cracks and misalignments showing. Edges didn't meet up properly. The resulting picture made me feel nauseated. My head pounded and my eyes burned. How could I have gotten such a different, distorted apparently, take on what had happened in my family, in my own life?

"That's why I was so upset for you the other night when Will went missing. My heart was absolutely breaking for you. I knew that feeling of terror. But I also knew how much you'd blame yourself."

What had they all been thinking of me all these years? Did they suppose getting pregnant at eighteen and dropping out of university, sacrificing all my ambitions and plans was some kind of adolescent act of rebellion? That I'd *chosen* to go off the rails like a depressed delinquent? They didn't know me at all!

"Oh, honey. There's no need to cry," Mom crooned, reaching across the table and taking my hands between hers, bony and dry, rubbing her thumbs over my knuckles. "We found Will. Everything turned out just beautifully. You're doing everything you wanted now, and more, and with such grace. You have no idea how proud we are of you."

I wiped my face, shaking my head, sorting my thoughts. "This is not…" I sniffed. "Not how I…saw things." I really needed to call Quinn.

Mom stood and picked up our empty teacups. "And now you have a boyfriend, too. And he's so tall."

I scoffed. "A boyfriend. It's a bit more complicated than that."

She set the cups in the sink with a clatter. "Do you think you can let up on yourself and be happy now?"

I pursed my lips, or maybe I pouted, feeling lighter, but also very, very confused.

Phoenix

"Time to head home, bud," I said, as our video game ended in a spectacular crash with alarms clanging.

"One more?" Will begged.

"Your mom would kill me. I promised to be at the house at 15:30 to man the barbeque."

Will chattered as usual on the short drive over to the house. When on Saturday, Jeannie called to ask if I wanted alone time with Will before the family barbeque Sunday evening, I didn't hesitate. So I'd picked him up after breakfast, and we'd had a few hours to kick around, just us guys.

I let Will set the agenda, and I was sure Jeannie would be thrilled to learn that what he wanted to do first was see where I lived and worked. So we'd headed out to the base for a civilian tour, and I'd shown him my very utilitarian shack. None of that was exciting, but he'd never been on a base tour before, so he thought it was all interesting.

Will asked a million questions about my work, which I could only answer in the vaguest, most generic of ways. But I suppose that's all a nine-year-old really wanted to know, anyway. He was curious about how I'd chosen the Navy, which inevitably led to talk about my dad and his own military career.

"He shipped out in February of 2002, along with tens

of thousands of other troops, into the Afghanistan theatre. His unit was assigned to security and surveillance in the Panjwai region near Kandahar, which is where a lot of Canadians were.

"How old were you?"

"About your age now," I told him.

Seeing him now, so bright and curious, gave me some insight into what I might have been like then.

"Then what happened?"

"It was supposed to be a six-month deployment, and we were used to him being away. But there was more conflict and instability in those early days in Afghanistan than there had been before, for him. Anyway, a few months into his tour, he was part of an early offensive against fierce Taliban resistance around these rural villages, and he led a unit out to patrol an unsettled area where many locals were sympathizers. Long story short, their convoy of trucks was ambushed by Taliban forces, and several marines died."

"But your dad didn't?"

"No, but his friends did, and he was badly injured. He was in the hospital for a long time before he came home. He was eventually discharged from the military."

"At the Faire, you told me about the fire that you escaped from."

"Mm-hmm."

"Was it your dad who died?"

I angled a glance his way to see him scrunching his nose and pushing his glasses higher with his forefinger.

"Where'd you get that idea?"

He shrugged. "I might've overheard Grandma talking."

I sighed. "Then why ask?"

"Well. I guess because…he's not just a stranger now. He was my grandfather. Wasn't he?"

My throat suddenly tightened with emotion, and I

roughed up Will's hair and grunted a "yeah" as we approached the HQ building. "He was."

"Was he a hero?"

"Yeah, bud. Anyone who sacrifices their own safety for the well-being of others is a hero in my books."

When he asked to see where I actually worked, I had to tell him it was a secure area he wasn't allowed access to. Since I'd formally been assigned to Pacific HQ, I'd been given a permanent desk in a secure JTF 2 planning room with the rest of our team, with very high-level security access. But I walked Will around the public areas of the building a bit.

After the dangerous stories about my dad overseas, Will was disappointed to learn that I worked in an office building, with desks, computers, and a big meeting room with tables and large screens for presentations. Not that exciting when you didn't consider the subject of our meetings or the content of those presentations. Seeing military vehicles and uniformed personnel strolling around was, however, itself a novelty.

When he'd tired of that, we'd gone out to buy him a new pair of sports shoes since he'd complained that his toes hurt, and ended up getting myself a pair while we were at the store, along with a couple of workout shirts. Then from the mall, after a hotdog, we went to a video arcade for the last hour. Pretty standard fair for a father and son outing, I guessed.

Will burst into the house when we arrived, and for the first time, I followed him inside, knowing I'd see other members of the family.

Jeannie'd come up with the plan for Will and me to be absent so she could explain the situation to her brother, sister-in-law, and their boys before we arrived.

"It'd be better to get their reactions, questions, and

comments out of the way quickly, without you or Will there," she'd said.

I was happy enough giving Jeannie and her mom time alone with her dad, Brandon, Stephanie, and the boys to share the news so they could get their initial obnoxious reactions out of the way. I wondered how Jeannie's talk had gone with her mother, and how the rest of the family would react to my presence.

"Mom!" Will hollered, racing through the house, and out through an open glass doorway onto the patio. He returned just as quickly. "Mom! Mom?" I intercepted his search in the narrow hall between the kitchen and the front entry.

"Slow down, bud. Where's the fire?"

"Oh, you're here," Jeannie said behind us, and turning I saw her rounding the baluster of the stairs.

"Mom, I got new sneakers," Will said, kicking up his feet.

She made a surprised face. "Go outside and say hi to Logan and Lucas, honey."

"Hi," I said with a smile as she came alongside me. I leaned in to give her a hello kiss, but she pulled away just as my lips glanced off of hers, and set a hand lightly against my chest with a gentle push.

"You're just in time," she said, passing through and into the kitchen. "Everything else is ready so the meat can go on the grill."

Biting my lip, studying her flustered demeanour, I sidled up beside her at the kitchen counter and murmured quietly, "You okay? Don't I get introductions first?"

"Yes! Of course!" She flapped her hands and finally looked up, meeting my questioning eyes with low-grade panic in hers. "I have a lot going on." She huffed out a sigh. "I'm sorry. I just need a minute." She turned to the sink.

I braced my arms on either side of her on the counter and tucked my chin over her shoulder, looking out the window to the back lawn, where the three boys now raced around in a bumblefuck while Jeannie's family sat at a patio table with drinks in front of them, talking among themselves.

"What are you worried about?"

She dropped her head with a soft grunt. "My brother can be such an ass. And he's been trying to wind up Dad ever since… You know, I dropped the bomb."

I planted a reassuring kiss on her head, pressing my front snugly against her back. The feel of her soft curves was a welcome, sensual pleasure. "I knew I should have taken you for a ride before tonight." Lifting one hand, I eased her hair over her shoulder, exposing the side of her neck, and bent my head to drop a lingering kiss there.

Shuddering, she said, "Phoenix, don't," and twisted away, but I caught her reluctant smile. "I can't do that, and this." She arced a hand out, palm up, to indicate everything else. Her family. The dinner.

"Why isn't anyone helping you with the food?"

"I said it was my treat. It's… You know, our day for… Ugh!"

"Well, let me help then. What can I do?"

She relaxed against the counter with a deep sigh. "Thank you. Start grilling, okay? I'll introduce you quickly as we go out, then you get busy. Then maybe they won't mob you with pitchforks."

I scoffed softly with a half laugh. "Is that what's happening?"

She covered her face with her palms, rubbing her eyes. "I don't know. But brace yourself."

She handed me two large platters of raw steaks,

sausages, and chicken, then picked up two serving bowls of salads and led me outside.

"Hey everyone, Phoenix is here!" Setting the bowls down on the table, she continued at a quick, staccato pace. "Mom's already met him, of course. Same for Logan and Lucas. Dad, this is Phoenix. Phoenix, my dad, my brother Brandon, and his wife Stephanie."

"Hello." I nodded at Jeannie's dad, brother, and sister-in-law. "Pleasure to meet you." Since my hands were full of platters, I was spared the awkward formality of shaking hands. Good move, Jeannie. I cast her a smiling glance.

From Mr. van Bellen, I got a stiff, awkward smile of hello. Stephanie just stared at me with wide eyes and a plastic smile like I was a Kraken about to eat her whole. Brandon leapt out of his chair and met me at the barbeque, where I'd turned, searching for somewhere to set down my load.

Instead of offering to help, he moved in close, hands in his pockets, and rocked back on his heels like a tool while I slid the platters onto nearby surfaces. "So…this is certainly an interesting turn of events."

"Is it?" I said, lifting the lid and checking the grill temperature with a hover of my palm.

"Well, sure," he drawled. "All these years and nobody knew who Will's father was. The mystery is solved, eh?"

I cleared my throat and slid a dark glance his way, hoping to scare some manners into him. "Jeannie knew."

"Ah. Yeah. I guess so. But this all must have come as quite a shock to you, man. Every guy's nightmare."

I twitched a shoulder, laying meat on the grill in a neat line with the tongs. "Not for me. It was surprising news. But it's all good now."

"Is it, though?" he needled. "What does it all mean? It's

a kind of awkward situation, you appearing suddenly out of the blue. Part of the family now."

Slowly closing the barbeque lid, I turned to show him my full width and height, scowling slightly as I looked down at him. He wasn't a short man, though I had an inch or so on him. But he was soft. And he wore suit pants and a dress shirt, for fuck's sake, to a family barbeque on a Sunday afternoon. Dressed like that, he obviously never expected to help with the cooking or washing up.

"It's not awkward for me," I said in a low voice. "You mind setting a timer for twelve minutes, man? Just holler when it goes off. I'm gonna say hi to the boys." And I walked away.

What a thudfuck.

Figuring I'd have more opportunity for chaperoned adult conversation while we ate, I strode out onto the stretch of grass where the three boys were malingering, picking up a soccer ball off the lawn.

"I have ten minutes to volley this ball around. Who's in?"

The boys squealed and shouted and raced around, and I kicked the ball to each of them in turn and tried to keep it in bounds when they kicked it wild.

It was fast-paced, pointless and fun, and all of us were laughing when Jeannie called out in a reedy voice, "Phoenix? Are you grilling?" Her expression was tight, and I realized she needed my support tonight more than Will did.

I returned to the grill, aware of all the eyes on me, flipped everything over and decided I'd better stay and make sure the meat wasn't burned. Another ten minutes later, I was heaping the meat onto platters that Jeannie held out, then I rounded up the boys to sit down.

Then everyone dug into the meal.

"I understand you're planning on staying here in Port Camosun, young man," Mr. van Bellen said while cutting his steak into tidy squares.

I swallowed my mouthful before replying. "Yes, sir. That's my intention. It's my hometown."

"Sir," snorted Stephanie softly, then coughed into her napkin, sharing an amused look with her husband.

"Pardon me, Steph?" Jeannie said. "I didn't catch that?"

"Nothing, nothing," she simpered. "Something stuck in my throat." She cleared it daintily.

"How is your mother doing, Peter?" Mrs. van Bellen asked. "And was that your little sister I saw at the Faire?"

"Yes, it was. She's just started at university this month."

"She's smart then. Like you," she replied.

It was Brandon's turn to snort. "If he's so smart, why'd he join the Navy? Why not get an education?"

"I couldn't afford any other option after my dad died," I said quietly, my gut curdling in the way it used to when I'd been sidelined for being trailer trash, and sometimes for being a Navy brat by clueless, flat-faced civvies.

"Don't be such a snob, Brandon. Phoenix is better educated than you are," Jeannie retorted, her jaw jutting, and I shot a tiny smile her way for defending me.

"Oh? How's that?"

"The government educated me in exchange for my service," I said simply.

"He has an electrical engineering degree, for your infor-mation," Jeannie spat, waving her hand in a vague circle. "And a bunch of other high-tech stuff I don't even understand."

If Brandon was shocked, he hid it well and resumed eating his dinner, but I think he was taken aback by that intel. It contradicted his prejudices, and he didn't know what to do with it.

Stephanie jumped in with, "You don't look like any engineer I've ever met." Then she licked her lips, smirking and openly ogling my arms and chest. "That's a lot of muscles and tattoos for a professional."

I cleared my throat softly, tonguing my teeth to disguise my smile at her poorly hidden admiration, and avoided soft Brandon's gaze. "Well, they kind of go with the job."

"I for one am relieved Jeannie and Will have someone strong and capable to take care of them now."

"Mom!" Jeannie said plaintively. "That's not only untrue, it's rude. I'm perfectly able to take care of us myself. As. I. Always. Have."

"Well, be that as it may," Mrs. van Bellen snipped. "It is true that he's strong and smart. And I believe he wants to take care of you, dear. Don't you, Peter?"

"Yes, ma'am. It is," I murmured politely, still holding in my smile. When I received a kick from Jeannie under the table in thanks, I cocked a brow at her.

"Oh, he'll take good care of her, all right," Stephanie quipped, elbowing her husband, and receiving a scowl in return.

"Is it…is it really true?" Logan piped up suddenly. "What Jeannie said? Are you Will's dad?"

"Shh. Logan," Brandon hissed.

But I didn't see the value in pretending that wasn't what this dinner was for. "Yes, Logan. It is true." I shared a smiling glance with Will.

"How come you never said, before?" he kept on, "At the park and…"

My smile vanished. "I didn't know it before."

With his mouth full of food, he chewed thoughtfully, blinking at me. I guessed it might take him a while to figure that one out.

"Mom knew." Will snickered. "Mom knew all along and

kept it secret." He was apparently the only one enjoying himself tonight.

"There wasn't much point in talking about it," Jeannie mumbled, stabbing her salad. Her colour was high and her forehead shiny.

"You told me you're a well-trained soldier," Logan continued.

"I did," I levelled my gaze at him, connecting. "When I needed you to tell me the truth about Will. That's still true, too."

"Oh!" Stephanie gasped.

Mr. van Bellen suddenly said, "Well, all this engineering aside, your work is dangerous, is it not?"

I gave him a steady, reassuring gaze, understanding him fully. I nodded. "I am often in dangerous situations. But I'm well trained to handle them."

He harrumphed softly, as any older man might, who hadn't a clue what war really meant but still had a mature understanding of what it probably meant. I reached under the table to take Jeannie's hand and give it a squeeze, and when she glanced up at me I lifted my brow.

"Most of what goes on now is peacekeeping-related work," I added, reassuringly.

"Ow!" Will yelped suddenly, glaring at Logan and punching his arm. "Stop pinching me!"

"Will," Jeannie hushed him, that crease appearing between her brows.

"Settle down, boys," Stephanie said listlessly, lifting her wine glass. "Darling?"

Brandon flinched and pulled his phone out of his pocket. "Oh. I've got to take this. No rest for the wicked. Excuse me."

"Brandon!" scolded Mrs. van Bellen and then said, "Oh, that boy and his calls," as he scooted into the kitchen.

"That's the real-estate business," Stephanie said. "There are no days off."

Mr. van Bellen, for his part, diligently sliced and chewed his dinner, observing his quirky family with a permanent bewildered expression on his thin, lined face, as if he'd been dropped by some bird into the wrong nest, and said little more than, "pass the salt," when he needed it.

Once the meal was over, and the kids had eaten their duff, I excused myself and called the boys out for another round of soccer. This time, it was even more chaotic, and they all ended up falling on the grass, rolling around, clutching their full bellies. Probably the sugar high. Will tackled me, jumping on me like a monkey, and I good-naturedly went down. But I turned the tables and tickled him until he squealed, and little Lucas cried out, "Tickle me next. Tickle me next."

Phoenix

"Sorry about all that," Jeannie said later.

Dinner was weird, without a doubt. Though I'm not sure how the event might have gone well. I sensed how confining it was for Jeannie and Will to live with her parents, and I burned with the need to fix that.

After Brandon and his family had skipped out, apparently because Brandon had to write up an offer for a client, Will had been sent to get ready for bed and finish homework for the week ahead. Jeannie's parents offered to clean up the kitchen. Jeannie and I relaxed on an upholstered garden swing, talking. Though she'd kept me at arm's length all evening, she was now tolerating my arm around her, and I soaked up the feel and the scent of her.

Her parents' hushed conversation and the clink of dishes wafted out through the open kitchen window into an otherwise silent suburban Sunday night.

Glancing towards the house, she said with a note of sarcasm, "I feel like you're my Prince Charming and Cinderella's been emancipated. Somehow having a man around has freed me from my role of domestic drudgery."

That drew a laugh out of me. At my relaxed reaction, she smiled and touched the corner of my mouth. I turned my head quickly, caught her hand and kissed her fingertip, sucking it into my mouth before she yanked it away with a tiny gasp of dismay.

"Phoenix," she scolded softly.

I closed the distance between us, stealing the moment of semi-privacy to taste her mouth, to pull her soft body into mine.

"Yes, Jeannie?" I whispered, teasing, against her lips.

Despite her protests, her body surrendered to my touch, and she melted into me with a soft moan. My palm slid down her side, following the bend of her shoulder, ribs, and over the curve of her hip, where I held her, deepening the kiss with a sweep of my tongue while I gripped her.

Her knee, and then her thigh, slipped up over mine, seeking contact and pressure at her centre. With a squeeze of her ass, my fingers probed the hot crease between her thighs, stroking her from behind, driven by instinct to find her cleft and enter it. She whimpered, her chin lifting, her head lolling, inviting me to suck the soft, translucent skin of her neck and nibble her ear lobe.

I groaned into her neck, "I want you, Jeannie. I ache for you. You haunt my dreams."

My restless greedy hand pulled her over my thigh, and she undulated, rolling her body against mine as I cupped her round breast, feeling the scrape of her erect nipple against my palm. Her response was immediate and intense, her mouth opening in a sharp inhalation, and releasing a soft cry. My own need intensified, pulsing and twitching. Sweeping my thumb across the teasing, tempting peak, I rocked my hips up against her soft heat, my need driving me towards her, needing to possess her and claim her.

"Pete. We can't," she gasped, pulling away. "Not here."

I sighed and then snickered. My prim Jeannie. What a bundle of contradictions she was. Serious and diligent. Sweet and smart. Beautiful and so sexy, yet she didn't seem to know it.

"If only I had somewhere to take you," I murmured, kissing her with lingering heat, wanting to swim in her, but releasing her, my fingers and hands reluctant soldiers obeying my command.

We sat side by side, me stroking her thigh hungrily but still softly, calming our breath.

"I know you told me about your family dynamic," I redirected our thoughts. "But it's like a psychological war. I'm sorry that you grew up in the midst of that."

From the outside, from my perspective, her family always looked so idyllic. Nothing was quite what it seemed.

"It's annoying for me to watch your family misunderstand and treat you badly."

She laughed. "It's been a challenge. But I'm happy to see Will coming out of his shell. I'm happy he has you now. You've been good for him."

Her words filled my chest with a fizz of warm satisfaction. He was good for me too.

"When I put Will to bed, he told me you talked about your dad. His accident."

I hummed in the affirmative. "Will had questions."

"He's too young to know about things like that. Your family stuff is too dark for him to understand."

"I said he'd been badly injured and discharged. I didn't mention the drugs or…anything else."

"I don't want him to worry about you. He's already anxious. And he's enjoying having you around so much."

"Kids are smart. It's important for families to understand some of what soldiers experience. It teaches them responsibility, empathy, and maybe to give their loved ones some space to deal with stressful situations in their own time."

She sighed, staring into the dark backyard as I rocked the swing slightly with my foot. "It's not something I would have wanted for my son."

"I'm sorry. It's who I am. It's better that he knows that."

"I'm terrified of when you have to go away again. Anything could happen to you."

"It may look, on the surface, like I tempt fate more than most, in my work. But I've spent my adult life working and studying hard to ensure I have the capability to survive unimaginable risks and challenges. I trust myself to deal with anything I encounter, and apply myself to the fullest to not only survive, but to keep my team safe, and to win every battle. I have a better chance of surviving one of my missions than the average person has going to work in an office every day. Better than you, despite your caution. Because I'm prepared. And trained for when things go wrong. Because they always do."

She remained pensive while I gently rubbed her arm.

"I think it's the hard things—our losses and disappointments—that make us who we are. Like you with your family. I never knew how hard it was for you because you had something I lacked."

"I don't know if there's such a thing as a normal family."

"Tonight I was feeling out of my element because I've

spent so little time in my life in domestic family settings. Even growing up, I didn't live in a normal home, at least after Dad's injury. As an adult not at all. It got me thinking about Victorian times for example when men left their calling cards and came for tea to court young ladies. There was so much protocol and so much weight on manners and rituals. A man like me wouldn't know how to survive in a game like that."

"You navigated it well, anyway. But even in Victorian times, they had the Crimean and the American Civil wars, and then the Boer war. The Napoleonic war was a major feature of the Regency era before that. There's always been war and soldiers. Manners and mores come with the times. They just tried to keep most women and children well out of it, so it didn't affect family life at home."

"Maybe. Maybe not. Soldiers have always returned from war, but tried to keep their horrific experiences to themselves. I think it's instinctual to hide it. Bury it and pretend it didn't happen. Because a part of you wishes you'd never seen or done those things. In situations where soldiers returned with physical wounds, those families had to deal with that and suffered. But men have always returned from battle with psychological wounds, and I think they and their families probably suffered more. Because they didn't under-stand it, and they didn't talk about it."

"Isn't that still true today?"

"Yes. But it's better to talk about it. All soldiers today receive a headspace and timing check—I mean spend time with a therapist—after time away, so while it's not a hundred percent, it's better now. There are ways of helping. "

"Wasn't that true for your dad? Could no one help him?"

"They tried. It's better now than it was then. But somehow he'd suffered too many wounds, too many losses, and they couldn't reach him. He retreated inside himself and wallowed in self-recriminations. And self-pity. That ate him alive until there was nothing left of him. Because of watching him suffer I've always been very proactive about therapy. I didn't understand as a child, kind of resented the Navy shrinks poking at me, but eventually, I came to see it for what it was. And I see my job differently I think than Dad saw his. I'm stronger."

Then Jeannie asked the question everyone who knew me wanted the answer to. The question I'd asked myself a million times.

"Why did you stay in such an awful situation when your mother couldn't take it anymore? You were only twelve years old. Why didn't you go with your mom?"

"It felt like the right thing to do. My dad was the most incredible man. So smart. Strong. Charismatic. Everyone loved him. Not least of all Mom and me. When she left…I know it was to keep Bess safe, but I felt her betrayal in my heart, like a knife. How could she walk away from a man like that? Despite his failures, he didn't deserve to be abandoned. I couldn't do it."

She sighed and set her head on my shoulder, comforting me, and I dropped a kiss on her forehead.

What I didn't say was that Dad was a Marine, like me, so I'd been through that. Maybe not to the same degree, but I'd been injured, and I'd lost a friend, too. I was an officer. A unit leader.

But Dad was also a husband. The best of fathers, before. I thought about Will's question earlier. I'd answered in the affirmative. Yes, I believed everyone who sacrificed was a hero.

But the truth was, I never forgave my dad. I'd loved him

with my whole being, and he broke my heart. He had one responsibility. Just one.

To be my hero.

And he failed.

My entire life had been about one thing. Making myself invincible to whatever broke him. Whatever weakness. Whatever flaw. Whatever crack in his armour. I had to fortify myself. I had to be smarter. Stronger. More flexible. I couldn't let anything be that one thing that broke me. Like he broke.

Chapter 21

Phoenix

SINCE I LEFT Jeannie's Sunday night, I'd been in a low mood. Talking, and thinking, about Dad tended to do that. I was determined to be better than him and had prepared myself. But now that I had Jeannie and Will, doubts began creeping in.

I knew, from working with Unger and our unit, that there were a number of hot spots and issues simmering. Soon, I'd be sent out to deal with one or the other of them. They didn't give me my stripes and medals for sitting in an office.

With Jeannie pulling away from me even as she let me into her family and her life for Will's sake, I was dissatisfied. I wanted more. I knew they'd be safe, with the extra financial security I could provide, but it wasn't enough.

Seeing Brandon jump to his client's call on the weekend gave me an idea, and I'd called the realtor for my old family home, arranging to see the place. I'd told him to write up an offer, leaving blanks. I'd made up my mind, sight unseen. Thankfully, I'd applied for a pre-approved mortgage weeks ago, when I'd first had the idea. Of course, I ought to inspect the house before offering, but this city was full of old heritage houses. Old houses could be fixed. And it was more important to me in so many ways, I didn't think it would change my plan. I knew the house, after all. How bad could it be? But I did need some sense of how much money I'd need to throw at it before deciding what to offer.

I sat at my desk and logged into the group chat. A lot had happened since I'd last checked in with my buddies. When I got in, they were all there. I'd looped Monty in since I knew the others would be interested in his status.

"Hey, hey! The chief is here," said Damien, breaking over the general raucous chatter of the others.

We didn't mention the fact that we'd likely see each other soon. This was a social call, after all. The others weren't to know.

"It's the sandy bottom sailor, his-self," said Carter.

"Gentlemen," I said grinning. It was good to see their faces. I'd missed them.

"Phoenix! My man," greeted Monty, fist-bumping the air in front of his camera.

"How are things in San Diego?"

"I'm in LA at the moment. On a job."

"He's guarding a celebrity," Carter added with an *ooh-ooh*. "That's the life, eh?"

I watched Monty's face. I knew it wasn't the line of work he preferred. He was too intense, too tough for that glitzy nonsense. But it was lucrative. Naturally, he was scowling and rolling his eyes.

I got work updates from the other two guys.

When they asked why I was growing a beard, I said only, "I expect I'll be shipped out soon."

"How're things going with your girl?" Monty asked.

"Hm. Complicated," I hedged.

"What's complicated about it?" Damien asked. "You were hell-bent on winning her just a month ago. I expect you've locked that down by now."

I sucked a breath through my teeth. "Yeah. No. Remember I told you she's a single mom?"

"Oh, fuck me," Damien said. "There's a dude in her life after all?"

"You got sidelined by the kid's dad?"

"You could say that." I bit the bullet. "Turns out, the boy's father is…" I paused to swallow, nodding, my voice croaking a bit. "Me."

I'd never heard them so…silent. I even checked my speaker volume in case I'd accidentally muted them. It was like all three of them were rebooting their hard drives because they thought the data was scrambled. The looks on their faces were so funny I took a screenshot so I'd remember this moment.

"Whisky Tango Foxtrot?"

Barely holding a straight face, I said, "Yeah. I'm a dad. I have a nine-year-old son named Will." My face pulled into an involuntary smile just saying those words out loud.

Then reality broke through to the chuggernuts, and they were all talking at once. Which didn't work so well on a video chat, so I heard nothing but broken words and static.

"Way to fast track, brother."

"That's it then," Carter said. "You really are staying there."

I nodded. "Thinking of buying a house, actually. The one I grew up in."

"Whoah!"

"For better or worse, my home is here with my family."

"But the girl?"

"Working on it. Buttering her up."

They were generally sympathetic that the situation required a delicate touch, but also simple-minded enough to think any woman would leap at the chance to hook up full-time with someone like me. If only.

We chatted a bit longer, but other than them wanting details about Will, and to see a picture, which I flashed them from my phone, we wrapped up shortly afterwards with their good wishes for the speedy resolution of my "girl" problems.

I walked out to the general office area, looking for a coffee.

"Commander Corbin, sir?"

I turned to see one of the admins who'd been processing my transfer documentation.

"Corporal Singh. How can I help you?"

"I was wondering if you'll be applying for bachelor housing now that you're permanent?"

"Good question. I'm…just looking into something on the private market. If it falls through, I'll let you know."

Before leaving for my afternoon appointment with the realtor, I checked in with Unger.

"Corbin," he said. "Good that you stopped by. We just got intel that SIGINT Team Four has run into some difficulties in the Sahel. We're monitoring the situation, but I have concerns."

I nodded.

"I want you to review their comms closely and get intimately familiar with their mission objectives. All the tech. I might need you to bail them out and finish their job."

"Yes, sir."

On the way to meet the realtor, I reviewed what I already knew about the SIGINT mission. The team had been dropped in Chad, and then, under cover, made their way overland north and westward across Chad to an area north of N'Djamena, scouting a chaotic region south of Lake Chad where ISWA threats had been growing. There were roughly twenty-five active militant terrorist groups, as well as mercenary governmental bodies and bandits in that region that made it sensitive, complex, and dangerous. Their alliances and allegiances shifted weekly.

The team's objective was to update ground intel on a remote compound belonging to ISWA, mainly focusing on tech, comm, and stockpiled ordnance and munitions, simultaneously planting remotely monitored signals around the perimeter. I could see how they might have gotten caught in some cross-fire. But that was tomorrow's work.

For today, I had a house to buy. Regardless of Jeannie, I wanted to make a home for my son.

———

Jeannie

The Saturday after the family dinner, I'd just parked in the driveway in Mom's car and hopped out when Phoenix's big blue truck rolled up to the curb. He jumped out and strode over, looking like sex on a stick in workout gear, his dark hair clinging hotly to his neck, his damp t-shirt hugging every bulging muscle on his chest and arms. His stubble was unusually long, several days' worth.

"Hey there, beautiful."

"Hi," I said, unable to stop myself from smiling. "What brings you here?"

"I followed you from the grocery store," he said, moving to my trunk. "Pop it?" he said, and when I complied, he scooped up all eight bags of groceries in his hands, his biceps bulging with the weight, closed the trunk with his elbow, and followed me into the house.

"Thank you," I said, and he set them all down in the kitchen. "You saved me four trips."

His masculine scent filled my senses like a drug I'd become addicted to, and I just ogled his broad chest, his biceps popping as he set down the heavy grocery bags, the complex ink that decorated them dancing.

"Where's Will?"

"Don't know." Tearing my gaze away, I peered out the window to the backyard, in between unpacking the bags. "In his room, probably."

Phoenix pulled his phone out and texted, and two minutes later, Will bounded down the stairs hollering, "Hi, Phoenix!"

"My man," Phoenix greeted him and pulled him in for a chummy side hug.

I was getting used to seeing them together but still taken aback by how close they'd become in such a short time.

"Is your homework done?"

"Almost," Will said, picking up a nectarine off the counter. "Can I have one?"

"Okay. Dinner's in about an hour, though, so don't fill up on snacks."

"What are we eating?"

Moving around to put away items, I listed, "Kebabs, pasta salad, green salad, and buns. Simple. Grandma's out at a thing, so it's just us and Grandpa."

"And Phoenix?" Will looked up, hope shining in his eyes.

I pressed my lips together with a little smile and glanced at Phoenix, who'd just taken a big bite of Will's nectarine, juice trickling down his lips. I lifted my brow. "I guess you've earned it. If you like."

"I like. Since you're offering," he said, chewing and licking juice from his sexy mouth with a tiny smirk, and I'd have put money on that being his plan at the outset. I shook my head.

"You guys have to help, then."

And instead of Will whining that he had more important things to do, he enthusiastically jumped in alongside Phoenix as they bustled around, putting groceries away, lighting the barbeque, and setting the table. I could get to like this.

While Will was outside, diligently placing cutlery—or gut wrenches, as Phoenix called them—around the placemats, Phoenix sidled up and set his hands on my hips, pulling me close, front to front, tipping his face down to catch my gaze with his. "Since you refuse to go on a date with me, I have to finagle ways to get close to you." Then he squished me gently against the counter, tipped my chin up and covered my mouth with his, rocking his hips into me, letting me know exactly how much he missed me. His new beard was half soft, half prickly as it scratched my face, adding to the element of exciting danger I felt when he touched me.

He tasted sweet from the nectarine, and faintly of mint, his mouth warm and firm, possessive.

My body lit up, tingling and clenching muscles admitting what I'd been trying so hard to ignore. His left hand slid up from my hip, holding my ribs, his thumb sneaking between us to stroke lightly over my peaked nipple, sending intense shocks of pleasure shooting down to my core like knives.

An involuntary moan-sigh escaped as I feebly tried to protest. "Phoenix. No."

"Why not, love? Your body's on board. What do I have to do to talk Jeannie into some fun and games?"

"It's just that…"

"I know. Will first. But I want you, too. You're keeping me too far away. When do I get to make you mine again?"

He tried to resume the kiss. Evading him and his question, because I didn't know the right answer, I palmed his furry face. "What's with the beard?"

He shrugged, pulling away and murmuring, "Might need it for my next mission."

My smile fell away, tingles of arousal instantly replaced with a pounding pulse, tension gripping my neck. "Are you leaving?"

"Don't know yet. Soon, probably."

I froze, unable to think of anything to say, my mind spinning with half-formed fears and useless protests. I might have been resisting his romantic advances, but my heart just kept marching forwards into dangerous territory, more and more enchanted with him, more and more attached to him. Exactly what I was afraid of, for myself and for Will.

I sucked in a breath, unaware that I'd been holding mine, feeling panic and irrational tears fighting to escape. I turned away, busying myself with salad prep.

"Don't worry, Jeannie. This is normal. Routine stuff for me. I come and go a lot."

"Mm-hmm," I hummed agreeably, nodding. "Here, chop this, please." I plonked a cucumber and a knife down on the cutting board in front of him and turned back to the sink to wash radishes and lettuce.

He made a soft, humming sound, deep in his chest, and did as he was asked, the methodical clunk, clunk of his chopping filling the space between us.

When everything was ready, I sent Will to fetch Dad

from his shop in the corner of the garden where he'd been tinkering all day. He was in a chipper mood and filled the space with friendly conversation, especially after Phoenix asked about his whirligigs. That got him going, excitedly explaining the details of his current designs and how they delighted him. Will enjoyed describing to Phoenix some of his favourite models, and it was decided Phoenix would be given a tour of the shop after dinner.

Dad was building inventory for a fall craft fair where he'd reserved a table, and planned to donate his earnings to Big Brothers and Sisters, a charity he'd long supported.

"If I'm in town when that craft fair happens, I'd be happy to help you load them up and transport them to the venue," Phoenix offered, making Dad's face light up.

Tonight, he seemed less bothered by Phoenix's tall, dark, and dangerous persona. Maybe he was just getting used to having him around. Or maybe he enjoyed being addressed as sir. Either way, the meal was relaxed and fun, and a spot in my chest grew warm and tight as I enjoyed the evening with the three most important men in my life.

I quickly cleared the table and cleaned up the kitchen while they were in the shop, and shortly afterwards, Phoenix went with Will upstairs to see some things in his room.

About an hour later, Mom had come home tired, she and Dad had both gone to bed, and Phoenix finally came downstairs. I'd been sitting in the living room reading a human-resources textbook, making notes for a quiz next week. So far, my program had been a blend of subjects I was familiar with, such as accounting and finance, and those that were completely new to me, like this one, and operations. I was enjoying it, but the amount of reading required to keep up was massive and sucked up all my free time.

"Did Will get ready for bed?" I asked him.

"Yeah, he got cleaned up and changed, but he's playing a game for a few minutes. I told him to shut it down at ten."

It was a bit late, but since it was the weekend, I let it go.

"Would you like a drink or something?"

"Actually, would you go for a walk with me?"

I set down my books and stood up. "All right. I guess."

I grabbed my keys from the hall table and locked the door on our way out, and as we stepped to the sidewalk, he took my hand and led me to the right.

"Are we going somewhere specific?"

"Can't I take my girl for a stroll on a late summer night?" he asked.

"Phoenix."

"What? Now I can't even call you my girl?"

"No. I mean, it's just…all the romantic stuff."

"Jeannie," he chided, "You are a very stubborn woman, you know that? I am trying to woo you."

"Isn't it enough that you're getting as much time with Will as you want?"

He tilted his head, considering, "Nope. I want more." He squeezed my hand, then said darkly, "I want it all." I laughed, and he added, "I keep thinking of our night together at the Faire. Frankly, hanging around you, and yet not getting enough of you, is giving me a tragic case of blue balls."

I gasped, and we both laughed. I let it go, though my thoughts battled with the usual—it's too soon, and I'm too busy, and Will needs time, and it's too complicated—arguments drowning in waves of longings.

Then we just strolled slowly along the cracked sidewalk under the canopy of old oak and chestnut trees that lined our street, crunching over the scattered leaves, kicking away the acorns and chestnuts that were beginning to fall. Days were rapidly growing shorter. And the nights, while still warm, carried a cool bite and the scent of humus and moisture and the tang of sea air.

"It smells different here than out East, hey?" I said. "Is that where you were before, when you weren't deployed?"

"Yeah. Ottawa area mostly. But I was on the move a lot."

"Are you happy to be back here?"

"Yes," he said, simply. "I am now."

"Now?"

"When I came here on leave, I was undecided. I thought…I thought I might miss my buddies. But since they're spread all over, I didn't know what to do next."

"You wanted to be near your mom and Bess?"

His shoulder twitched, pulling at my hand. "I wanted a home."

He made a series of turns, right, then left, then left again, weaving through the neighbourhood in a zig-zag pattern. We talked about dinner, my dad, Will, school, and our friends.

Until I gestured to the path ahead of us. "Do you have a plan, here?"

"Maybe," he said, huffing a small laugh.

Another few blocks further, along a curving street, he stopped suddenly, turning us to face a cute little white house with a dark roof and a long driveway swooping up the right side.

"This is adorable," I said, taking in the neat front yard with shrubbery and the tiny arched entry porch.

"It has twenty-five hundred square feet and six small bedrooms," he said. He pointed. "Two of them in the roof gable, up there. It includes a suite in the basement."

"I love this style," I said. "Quinn and Parker's dad's house is kind of like this. Around the same era."

"It was built in nineteen fifty-two," he supplied, then

drew a breath. "My parents bought it in nineteen eighty-six."

I gasped. "This was your house?"

He nodded. "Until I was ten."

I squeezed his hand in sympathy. All he wanted was a home, like the one he'd lost. And I guessed, a family to make up for everything else.

"Do you want to see inside?" he asked suddenly, tugging me forward.

"What? How?"

When we got to the front door, he punched a code into one of those key-lock thingies that hung on the front door knob.

"Does that mean it's for sale?" I asked.

"Mh-hmm." He pushed the door opened and flicked on a light in the hall. "It's vacant. Go on in. The realtor graciously gave me the code so I could look at it."

Stepping inside, I noted the empty interior was in much the same style as Quinn's old house had been. Neat coved stucco ceilings, oak floors. A curved archway from the living room into a dining room. "It's in pretty good shape," I commented.

"I have some wonderful memories from when we lived here. It's a great house. Needs fresh paint. And the kitchen is ancient. Same as I remember it." Taking my hand, he led me through, flicking on additional lights. He was right. The cabinets were original, and the sad-looking appliances dated from sometime in the late seventies.

"Ew. Yeah. Has potential though," I said. "Look." I pointed at a cute breakfast nook to the other side of the kitchen and a single door leading out to a good-sized wooden deck fading into darkness.

"The bathrooms are just as bad, all pink and blue. You can't see in the dark, but the yard is large, and there's still a big old oak tree in the back corner where Dad built me a tree fort. It's gone, though."

"You saw it before?"

"I was here a few days ago." His voice was laden with his thoughts.

"It was nice of the realtor to let you come in on your own. Wouldn't it be great if you could live here again?" I turned to smile up at him, and his dark-green gaze locked on mine, intense and filled with yearning.

"It would," he said somberly, his voice dropping low, the vibration sending waves of want through my blood. Sleeping hunger there, awakened by his kisses and touches earlier, simmered, rising, insistent. "Imagine," he said, "you standing right here, making a nice meal for me and Will like you did today. Me coming into this cute little kitchen, holding you against this counter, kissing you like this."

Taking my face gently between his large hands, he covered my mouth with his, sweeping his tongue inside. His taste had shifted from sweet to spicy, and again the drugging masculine scent of his body, so near, did its narcotic work on me, heat twisting through my centre.

My hands wrapped around his smooth solid neck, tangling in the longer silky textured hair at his nape that went with the beard, a scruffy and slightly wilder version of the neat, well-groomed Sailor. He pressed closer, his hands tightening their grip on my sides, sliding down over my hip bones and pulling me snugly against his growing erection.

Pulling away, he turned me and guided me, hands on my hips, out of the kitchen, down a short hallway, and through an open door. "Imagine," he whispered from behind me, his warm breath and soft lips moving my hair softly, brushing my ear. "This could be our bedroom. Wouldn't that be sweet?" His mouth dropped to my neck, speaking close to my tingling skin, sending shivers snaking down my spine.

"It would," my weak voice aspirated, my pulse accelerating.

"If I could bring you here, and lay you down on a big soft bed and make love to you properly," he kept on, teasing me, his mouth close on my neck and shoulder, his hands stroking me from hips to ribs, up to cup my breasts, skating lightly over my curves, aching now for his touch. His fingers found my firm nipples, and he moaned softly against my hair while pressing my breasts together, lightly pinching them both, and angling his erection hungrily against my ass.

The total effect, surrounding me, was overwhelming. His knowing touch, as in all things decisive and sure, in all the right places, his own insistent need, his gentleness and firmness together, wrecked me.

My voice trembling, I whimpered, "We're all alone here. It's really a shame we don't have a bed right now."

Taking my words as confirmation of my desire, he spun me in his hands like a toy top, took one sure stride towards the wall, carrying me with him, and pressed me firmly against it with his huge, hard body. His broad chest crushed my breasts, his quickening breath moved his firmly chiselled abs against my soft stomach, like an eagle's powerful wing. His hips and hardness pressed against my core, fanning the fire of my own need. He pushed a tree-like hard thigh between my legs, giving me pressure where I desperately wanted it. And my legs parted to give him space, to ride him as he rubbed against me.

His hand spread and gripped my ass, lifting me to wrap around his hips, touching my heat to his need, setting off an incendiary explosion of desire shooting through me. And through him, as he groaned and rolled his hips, pushing harder against me.

"Who needs a bed when you have a wall?" he murmured before taking my mouth again, thrusting his tongue in, pulsing, stroking. He set me down, sliding over his hard ridge so my legs trembled and could barely hold me up. "I have to have you, Jeannie. I'm going to fuck you, hard, against this wall, right…right now. If you don't want that, say so or there's no stopping."

"Yes," I heard myself gasp. "I want that. I want you, inside me, right now." I sounded feral, and with an answering animal grunt, he was tearing my clothes from my body while I grappled to peel his shirt from his beautiful chest, fumbling at his waistband.

We tangled arms in our desperation to get at each other, to get naked, fast. He grabbed a condom from his pocket and tossed his pants across the empty room as if he never planned to wear them again.

Then, quickly rolling the condom over his standing length, he came to me again, lifted me again, his ready hardness caught between us, thick and pulsing.

I cast my eyes down, looking at him. "Oh, yes," I whispered on a breath, and he shifted, lining himself up with my center and pushing slowly forwards, stretching my opening.

We both moaned with inexpressible pleasure as our bodies slid together, so perfect.

I looked up at him, his teeth gritted, his jaw firm with the tension of restraint. "Oh, Pete. Do it now. I want you to fuck me hard."

And he did, withdrawing and thrusting forwards with his powerful hips and muscled thighs, my ass slamming hard against the wall with a smack of flesh again and again as his strong hands dug into my thighs, holding me up.

Oh, shit. "Again," I gasped. "More. There."

"Fuck! Jeannie!" he grunted, "This. Isn't. Gonna. Last."

And he did, again, more, harder, and again as sensation

and heat and shudders of pleasure spiralled in and up and through me, building and building into a wild, mindless crescendo. "Oh. God." Our desperate voices mingled as we grunted, moaned, groaned, and finally screamed each other's names in a magnificent supernova of simultaneous release.

Afterwards, he continued to sandwich me against the wall, his legs planted firmly on the floor, his body shaking all over, as our ragged breathing gradually calmed, our hearts pounding against each other through our flush rib cages, slowly settling into a more normal rhythm. Shuddering aftershocks rippled through us.

"You can put me down now, Superman," I said, chuckling softly, astonished he was still standing after all that.

He groaned and did so in slow motion, grabbing the condom and turning to pull it off. "Wow. Thanks for that."

His face was flushed, his expression slack and stunned as I looked up at him, smiled and took his cheeks between my palms, kissing him soft and slow. "Mm-hmm. I'm ruined forever."

Dragging our spent bodies, we dressed without taking our gazes from each other, both of us wearing stupid, satisfied grins.

Phoenix led me into the empty dining room, faced me and took both of my hands in his. I looked into his face, which hid a half-smile, and his dark eyes sparkled with mischief. "So. What do you think of the house?"

"It's a very sweet house. It's a lovely dream to have a home of your own and one so special to you." My voice came out wistful and languid.

"What about you?"

I hesitated, unsure what he was getting at. "I'd love that too. Of course. Some day."

His grin grew wider, pulling to one side.

"What?" I laughed at his playful manner. "Are you actually thinking of putting an offer on it? Could you afford to?"

He drew a breath. "I already bought it, Jeannie. I offered on the spot, and I got it."

"You're kidding me! You bought a house? *This* house?"

He nodded. "I already had a pre-approved mortgage, so I pushed for a fast closing. And, barring any snags, it'll be mine on the fifth or sixth. The widow living here had to go into a nursing home, and her kids were interested in a quick sale."

I was stunned speechless. My heart stuttered with a sudden swell of happiness. He was such a sweet, adorable man, with his talk of home and his sentimental attachment to this old house. I was happy for him and happy that Will would have him nearby, with a home of his own. One that was so meaningful to him.

Yes, I was happy for him, but I realized I was happy, too, that he'd be staying, and that he'd be close. It was getting harder to keep a sensible check on my emotions. It was highly likely I was falling in love with him.

"I paid extra for a really quick inspection and appraisal," he continued. "It's pretty tired, but it's solid. I have plans to paint the whole thing and update the fixtures and stuff."

"You don't mess around once you've made up your mind, do you? I guess this means you're really committed to staying in Port Cam."

"I can't imagine living anywhere else now. I've found what I was looking for."

"A home," I said.

He pressed my hands. "For us, Jeannie. For Will, and you and me."

My ears buzzed, my head filled with bubbles, the room suddenly shrinking. I blinked up at him, confused. "What?"

"I'd love it if we could live as a family. I want to be here for Will and for you, Jeannie. You're my family now."

I slid my hands out of his grip and took a step away, my pulse skipping too fast, tripping, stumbling. My head shook side to side as panic swept through me, and I felt my neck and face heat. "Oh, no, no, no, Phoenix," I whispered. This was crazy. I needed time—and space—to figure out my own feelings.

Registering my reaction, he said, "Wouldn't it be better for him to have a stable home of his own? And you too. You'd be less stressed going to school if you weren't living with your parents."

"There you go again, deciding everything for everyone else."

"I'm not deciding anything. I'm offering a solution. I'm trying to make things better." He bent to kiss me lightly, tentatively. "Jeannie, I'm in love with you. I want us to be together."

Thud, thud, thud. My heart smashed against my ribs in panic. His words ruined me, weakening every last defence. My fears trembled but dug their heels in, resisting the very idea. Contrary to my own growing feelings, I protested, "You can't possibly have fallen for me so quickly. We've not seen each other for ten years and have only been reunited for a few weeks. How can that be possible?"

Unhesitating, he countered with, "But I didn't fall for you in a few weeks, Jeannie. I fell for you ten years ago. You were the only bright light in my dark, miserable world. You have no idea how much I looked forward to our honours math classes and our little bubble of time together, away from all of our friends, and families, and the pressures of high school. And if we happened to see each other outside of school, and you paid me the tiniest drop of attention and were kind, I rode that high for hours, if not days."

I stared at him, dumbstruck, as he went on. Was this even real? Or just his fantasy.

"In all those years apart, and believe me when I tell you I have not led a sheltered existence, I have never met another woman I like as much as you, or that I'm as drawn to, or trust as much. I never forgot you. I thought of you often. Finding you here, now, after all this time, has only reinforced those feelings. Discovering that you and I have a child together…" He shook his head as if he still found it hard to believe. "And that you have no partner or attachment, makes me feel like our seemingly random reconnection was no accident, but fate."

My face exploded with heat at his declaration. Fate? No one had ever said such things to me. I tried to speak, but my lips faltered because my brain couldn't figure out what to say.

"I totally get why you might not have given me a second thought then. Despite our connection in class, I had little to recommend me. I know that better than anyone. But that's not true anymore. I'm…I'm…not that guy anymore. I'm here for you Jeannie. A hundred percent."

"Not quite a hundred percent," my fears whispered, under my breath, insistent. "Your job has a large percentage of you. And I can't accept you as part of my family so soon. Don't you understand?"

It was his turn to shake his head in confusion and denial.

"It's barely been two months since I first set eyes on you. Of course, I knew you were Will's father. But you…you had ceased to exist in my mind. How can I adjust to this so quickly?" I gestured between us. "I like you too, but I don't even know if you and I are a real thing. If we'd even work. I can't trust that you'll be here for us. What if…what if…I'm sorry. We couldn't possibly live together."

The look of disappointment in his eyes shattered my heart. I didn't want to be the one to thwart his dreams of a home and family. But he couldn't strong-arm us to fit into his fantasies, either. I wanted Will to get used to the idea of having Phoenix in his life without imposing an insta-family on him—and risk having it all fall apart.

His throat moved as he swallowed. "I'll respect your wishes. If you don't want to be involved with me, I'll accept that, for now. I only want to be part of Will's life. I want Will to know his father."

"I'm sorry to disappoint you, Pete," I whispered and turned, walking to the door, my heart breaking at the sour turn of the night. "I can't deal with this so suddenly. Your swooping in with your grand gestures and your romantic dreams is all very sweet. But I need to find my own way." I stopped in the doorway and peered at him. "This is my life. My problem to solve. I don't want to be rescued. "

"Rescued?" His voice rose with a choking sound. "Is that what you think this is?!"

"I've been surviving on my own for ten years, taking care of Will since he was conceived." If I gave up now, how would I ever know if I could have done it myself? "I can't give up my independence and autonomy now, just because you happen to fly in on your magic carpet and offer to make all my problems disappear."

His expression had shadowed. His brows formed a dark slash over his flashing eyes. "That's not fair. I would have been there for you from day one if I'd known. You know I would. We'd have been in this together from the start."

"It doesn't matter now. We can't have a do-over. It's too late to change anything."

"I'm not trying to change the past, Jeannie. I'm trying to make the future better. This is within our control."

No. I felt my pulse racing. "That's exactly the problem.

You want to control everything. And everybody. Including me."

"Fine!" He threw up his hands and stalked towards me. "You don't have to live in it." He raked an angry hand through his hair. "I was excited that Will could live in the same house where I grew up. It means a lot to me. But it's my home now, regardless, and Will's second home when he's with me. He'll have his own room and——"

With icy fear in my heart, I said, "Will can't live here. You can't take him from me."

"I'm not trying to——" If I'd actually stabbed him, his face couldn't have registered deeper shock or betrayal, and I knew I'd overstepped. I knew in my heart I'd let my own fears overrule my good sense.

"I was going to add, my door will always, always be open for you," he whispered, barely audible. And for all his guarded stoicism, he couldn't hide the hurt he felt. It was painted all over his face——as plain on his face as the ink on his arms.

Phoenix

Mid-week, when Jeannie had a late class, I picked Will up from school, and we hung out at the DQ nearby, while I helped him study for another test. He'd been doing a lot better and was pleased with his marks on last week's quiz, so we were celebrating with ice cream.

On the way home, I said, "Can you keep a secret?"

"Of course," he said, his green-flecked eyes lighting up with curiosity.

I detoured to my house, pulled up at the curb and pointed at it. "See that?"

He looked out the window of the truck, unimpressed. "What? What is it?"

I decided another approach would work better. We got out of the truck, and I took him to the door, entered the code, and let us in.

"Who's house is this? Are we allowed to be here?" Suddenly he was on edge as if we were doing something illegal.

"It's okay," I reassured him, stalling until we got inside and I closed the door. I gave him a few minutes to get his bearings, then said, "Come with me," and led him up the stairs to the two little bedrooms in the eaves.

He peeked into the empty bedrooms, both basically identical, one with a view over the neighbouring house's low rooftop, the other with a view across the street towards some big trees. I thought that was the better one, personally. It had been mine, after all. But for all I knew a cute nine-year-old girl lived next door now, so, you never knew.

"Which one do you want to be yours?" I said.

"Huh?"

"If this was your house, which of these two bedrooms would you like better?" I spoke more slowly, so he wouldn't trip up on all the conditionals.

He walked between the two rooms a couple of times, looking around and thinking carefully, then stepped into the tree-view room. "This one."

"Why?"

He shrugged. "It feels cozier. I like the way the sun sparkles through those trees. It makes the room feel like it's underwater. I think reading and doing homework in here would feel nice and calm."

Wow. Okay. "That's cool. How have you been doing with your mindfulness exercises?"

"It's good. It helps. When I remember."

"I'm glad. It'll become more like a habit the more you practice. And then one day you'll realize you don't get panic attacks anymore."

Then I told him this had been the house I grew up in, for a while, when I was his age, and his interest in it blossomed.

We went downstairs and wandered from room to room until he'd inspected the whole house. We looked at the back-yard, and I told him about playing ball with my dad—and about the old tree fort.

Then we headed to my truck.

"So the thing is," I said as I drove him to his grandparents' home. "I actually bought that house."

"Are you shitting me?" he squeaked, bouncing in his seat.

Snorting, I said, "I don't think your mom likes it when you say that."

"Don't deflect, Phoenix." He scowled at me. "Can you please repeat what you just said?"

Laughing, I did.

And he let out a loud whoop. "So you mean that really will be my room?"

"I'll live there, and it can be our place, for when you visit me," I said carefully. "And maybe sleep over sometimes, if it's okay with your mom."

The echo of Jeannie's paranoid voice replayed in my mind. I still couldn't believe she'd think that my intentions were anything but honourable, as if I were a hostile force.

"Awesome!"

"But maybe…don't mention to your mom that I showed you the house. Not yet."

"Is it a surprise?"

"She's a little mad at me right now."

"Why?"

"Oh, we have different ideas about the future, that's all. Your mom is used to doing things her own way."

"Did you guys have a fight?"

I rocked my head. "I don't want to call it a fight. We just see things differently."

"Oh."

"Oh, what?"

"That's what you and Mom fought about."

I drew a breath, preparing to explain, deny, or something.

Before I could, he added, "Don't worry. She'll come around."

I chuckled. "A man can dream."

"So can a boy," he said slyly and offered his little fist for a bump.

"I'm trying to line up a contractor to fix the place up," I told him. In fact, I'd narrowed it down to a shortlist and was waiting for quotes, then as soon as I took possession, they could get started. I didn't need to move in until the work was mostly done.

"Next time, we'll go to Home Depot to look at paint colours. Think about what colour you want on your walls."

"Green!" Will said without hesitation.

"That was quick."

"It's my favourite colour."

"There's a lot of greens. We'll look at paint chips, and you can tell me which one you like best. And maybe pick out some furniture you like."

"Whoa. New furniture too?"

"Yeah. But…again. It's a secret."

"Right. Not fighting." He tsked.

I scoffed and ruffled his hair.

As I walked him to the door, I added, "Ask your mom if

you can come with me to Vancouver next weekend to visit my mom and sister. I want to introduce you properly soon."

"So I guess that means you're not coming in today?"

I shook my head, sad to part from him, sad I couldn't give him the home that I wanted to. "Not today, bud."

Chapter 22

Phoenix

JEANNIE AGREED to let me take Will overnight to meet Mom and Bess the following weekend but refused to come with us no matter how much Will and I begged.

Bess came home from university for dinner Saturday evening, but returned to her dorm to sleep since Will and I had taken over her bedroom. Greg came to dinner too but politely excused himself early enough that we had some alone family time to talk. Both Mom and Bess were squirrelly over Will, Mom gushing at how she just knew when she'd first set eyes on him, that it could be no accident that a boy could resemble me at that age so perfectly.

Bess kept repeating, "I can't believe I'm an aunt." And she said, "You're so darn cute," so often to Will that he was permanently pink in the face like his mother.

In one way, I was glad that Jeannie had begged off from joining us, as that gave my family the opportunity to focus on Will and bond with him. There was no question that he was fully welcome into the family fold and that he'd be spoiled rotten for the rest of his days.

Everyone commented on my thickening beard, and I had to explain that it was in case I needed to blend in with the locals when I was travelling, then field a battery of questions about whether I'd be sent to the Middle East, to South America or somewhere else. Of course, I could tell them nothing, but the entire conversation twigged Will's curiosity.

When, later, I tucked him into bed, he asked in a tremulous voice, "When are you leaving?"

"I don't know yet, bud. I'm just getting ready because I've been off for so long. I know they'll need me soon."

"Where will you be going?"

I shook my head, repeating. "I don't know that either. But even if I did, I couldn't tell you. It's against the rules."

"You'll be safe, won't you?" he persisted. "And you're coming back, right?"

"Don't worry about me, okay? I'm tough. And as I told Logan, I'm a highly trained soldier." Though I couldn't see into the future, I knew that only one thing would or could stop me from returning home.

On Sunday morning, we all drove out to the university to see the dorm where Bess lived and walked around the campus. Then we had lunch with Bess before dropping Mom off at her home.

Just before we left to catch the afternoon ferry home to Port Camosun, Mom said, "Oh, before I forget. I have something I wanted to give you." She walked to a wall unit and lifted a banker's box, handing it to me. "It's mostly papers and photos, but there are bits and bobs. Medals and things. I thought it best you should have it." Without saying the words, she managed to tell me that it was Dad's.

Discretely, I opened the box and leafed through the contents quickly, and found it was mainly memorabilia from

Dad, messy piles of photos, a couple of old family albums, Naval papers and things, as well as a sealed, unopened letter, addressed to me that caught my eye.

I lifted my brows in question at Mom, but her expression was closed. I don't know why she'd waited until now to give it to me, and I couldn't say if she knew what it contained.

I'd read it later. His medals and ribbons were in there, and his stripes. Then I found an official letter from the Navy with a seal along with a square box, all of it in a plastic sleeve.

"What's this?" I asked.

"Open it."

When I did, I found a letter of explanation and inside the box was a Sacrifice Medal—Canada's equivalent to America's Purple Heart, awarded to those killed or wounded while in military service. I knew it had been released in 2008, but I didn't realize that Dad, who'd been wounded in mid-2002, was eligible.

"I didn't know about this," I said.

"They presented it to me at his memorial service. I decided not to tell you at the time. I thought you needed to forget and move on. You were still at basic-training camp in Quebec. After I'd informed them of his death, they arranged it. I was surprised, too. I always thought it would have been nice if he'd gotten it himself."

"It wouldn't have changed anything, Mom."

"No. I suppose not."

Though she'd moved on, I knew she still held a tender spot in her heart for the man she'd married and once loved. Dad had been a good man, despite everything.

"You deserve a Sacrifice Medal, Peter," Mom said.

I shook my head. "No."

"Do you regret staying with your dad?"

"No. I'm glad I did. If I'd left with you, I would have carried that regret more. And though it was hard, and ended badly, I'm a better man for it."

"You are a better man, sweetheart. But I'm not convinced it's because you stayed with him."

I shrugged, wondering what my life might have looked like if I had left. Very different, I imagine. Better? I'm not sure. I likely wouldn't have joined up. I probably would never have fulfilled my dream of becoming an engineer. I would have been a burden to Mom instead of helping to support them.

"Do you ever resent me for leaving?" she asked.

"No," I answered, though there had been times when I did. I would never tell her so. "I understand you had to do it for Bess. And I'm glad for her sake that you did." I paused, thinking about Jeannie's reluctance to get involved with me. "Do you ever resent me for following him? For joining the Navy?"

"No, darling." Mom stroked my arm. "Not at all."

Touched, I thanked her and kissed her goodbye.

As I carried the box out to my truck, Will asked, "What's that?"

"Some old stuff of my dad's," I told him. I wanted to look through it before sharing it with anyone.

But all the way home to Port Camosun, I was lost in thought, wondering if maybe Jeannie was smarter than I knew, keeping her life as separate from mine as possible.

Despite all my differences, I was more like my dad than I wanted to admit.

Jeannie

Phoenix was closed up and preoccupied when he returned Will on Sunday evening, even as he hugged Will and said goodbye.

"Everything go all right?" I asked, worrying that something had happened to ruin the weekend.

Will seemed happy enough as he greeted me and bounded into the house.

"Yeah, fine," Phoenix said. "I'll probably get sent out on a mission soon. There's stuff brewing that I have to be involved in. I was thinking that you should line up alternates to pick up Will from school this week and next. Just in case."

"Okay." I nodded, studying his hard expression.

His leaving, going on a mission, was nothing new. For him, anyway. So I wondered…had his family gathering not gone well?

"I'll be off then," he said, stepping off the stoop.

"Will you tell us when you're leaving?"

"If you want." His gaze slid to the side. "It might be better if I'm not around too much for the next while."

"All right," I said, thoughtful. "School will keep us both busy."

I was determined to focus on school and Will and nothing else, anyway. I told myself that was most important right now. But I wasn't sure I still believed it. I also wanted to give Will time with Phoenix, because it made him so happy and seemed to give him confidence.

I wasn't sure if the dark emotion simmering under Phoenix's surface, like vague shapes obscured by murky water, was resentment, sadness, or something else. Like some kind of drawing inward, that happened when he was preparing for a mission. That was one of the reasons I needed to let things unfold more slowly, I told myself. I needed to understand his seasons and his moods.

"Maybe not being around as much is best," I told him, evading his uncomfortable, troubled gaze. "Things are complicated. I have to sort out my own life." After a beat, I added, "I'm not rejecting you, you know. I want you to understand that. This is about me, and the timing of everything."

"It's okay. I understand and respect your wishes. As long as you accept that I have both a duty and desire to do my share to raise our son."

"Of course I do," I said, as gently as I could. "I can't deny I have growing feelings for you, Pete. But I have to look out for Will. I have to guard our future. Not just our material and financial future, but our emotional well-being, our peace of mind and happiness, too."

He pressed his lips together and nodded again, his nostrils flaring.

After a beat of silence, while I studied his face, I shook my head thoughtfully. "The way I see you, standing in front of me, offering me everything that you are. It means a lot to me, truly. You're too good to be true. The missing piece? You chose to follow in your father's footsteps. You have possibly *the* most dangerous job on earth. You can disappear." I snapped my fingers. "Either like your father disappeared." I shrugged. "Or worse, the way you did on grad night. But this time, for real. Forever."

Instead of arguing, as I thought he might, rebutting with proclamations of his strength, his superior skills, his preparation for worst-case scenarios, he just nodded, his expression sombre. "No one can cheat death, Jeannie. Life can't be guaranteed. But neither can it be lived in fear."

That scared me more, somehow. "My life might be a bit feeble, a far cry from what I dreamt, but it's whole and complete. If I let you in, and then you disappear, I'll be left with something less than whole. I'd have a hole! An unfillable hole. One that I'd have to live with for the rest of my life. And not just mine. But Will's." I whispered, "I can't do that."

He nodded. "I can't force you to accept me as part of your life. I can't force you to accept my love. But know this. I'm yours. I'll be here for you and Will. I will watch over you and protect you. And provide for you. Until my last breath. And beyond."

I heard his words, but my fear of loss was too great. "I'm sorry." I was coming to both love and need Phoenix, but as afraid as I was to lose him, would rather struggle on alone than face that loss. It was already more than I could bear.

Chapter 23

Phoenix

Somehow, I was beyond being frustrated at Jeannie's persistent fears. I could put myself in her position. She'd lived most of her life with the fear of loss and its consequences. Her solution, not illogical at face value, was to shrink her life to minimize risk. That was her survival instinct.

I could tell her I was in control, that I was the one whose job it was to keep everyone else safe, and she'd still not believe me.

I couldn't technically argue with any of her points. She'd hit home with her comment about my dad. Even though I knew I was much stronger than Dad mentally and emotionally. Because I'd lived through my own childhood, but also because I'd prepared myself.

My team had suffered a heartbreaking loss, too, when Russell died. And we'd survived it and banded together, stronger than ever. We were there for each other and always present and strong for our families, for our team. And I knew I was largely responsible for that strengthening. So I of course didn't look forward to the losses, whether it was close friends or even my own disability, that might easily come through my work. But I knew I'd survive it and stay strong.

But death? I'd cheated death my entire life. I had nothing to say to that. Despite my diligence, superior strength, and skill, I knew it could come for me at any time. So I had nothing to say to Jeannie.

My heart hurt for her, and disappointment weighed me down, but I had no choice but to agree to give her space.

As I arrived at my shack on the base, my phone dinged with a message from HQ.

UNGER: *Report to me first thing in the morning.*

AND THERE IT WAS.

I knew what this meant. I would be deployed. Could the timing be any worse? And yet, I knew it was coming. I had no choice.

Knowing I was out of time, I sifted through the box that Mom had given me, sorting its contents. I organized photos by subject and date, stacked paperwork giving some history on Dad's career, some correspondence and print-outs of emails, and then tidied Dad's medals and insignia, laying them neatly on top. In addition to the new-to-me Sacrifice Medal, still in its box inside a bag, his older MSM and South-West Asia Service Medals were there too.

All the while, images of our life in the old house flashed through my mind. Each time he was deployed, how I'd felt proud and scared. Every joyous reunion upon his return. And the last time, his return in a wheelchair, his legs wrecked, his eyes dark and distant with pain and the medications he was now addicted to, his spirit broken.

Finally, curious but wary, I held the sealed envelope addressed to me in Dad's scratchy hand. When would this have been written, and why would Mom have not given it to me sooner? For the same reason she gave for not telling me about the Sacrifice Medal all this time? Had she tucked it away and forgotten about it?

I wasn't sure I wanted to read any words Dad might have written to me. Now that I was a father, were there lessons to be learned from him? Or if it were written prior to his accident, would the words and sentiments seem naive, generic, or irrelevant, given all that happened afterwards?

I didn't know, but probably it was not the intel I needed the night before deployment on a mission. I tucked the envelope into my rucksack, put the lid on the box, and hit the sack.

Early the next morning, I met with Unger, got my assignment details, and we pulled my unit together. As I predicted, he'd made the call to send a team in to retrieve SIGINT Team Four in the Sahel region. We would be a four-man Special Operations team, including Damien, who was a SIGINT/EW collection specialist. We'd interpret and complete SIGINT Team Four's original mandate, manning an AN/PRD-13 SSME. The rest of our team was Luekins, an IMINT expert, and McLean, a tactical intelligence specialist familiar with the region, with Arabic, and local dialect language skills. And myself able to exploit computer networks, as well as mission strategy and leadership.

There was overlap in our skill sets, and I'd worked with two of them on missions before, Damien obviously, as well as McLean, who'd leave from Ottawa and meet us in Chad. We'd fly out tonight at 21:00, landing in N'Djamena sixteen hours later, and touching base with AFRICOM JSOC personnel stationed there.

Unlike our neighbours to the south, we preferred to keep a truly light footprint on the continent, but there was no question that having a friendly place to land made our missions feasible. But this counterterrorist work was team-work anyway, a long-term objective.

Once on the ground, we'd work undercover, often at night, to locate the stranded SIGINT team, and move in to assess the situation in person. We'd allocated up to six days on the ground, depending on what we found there. It was not an area where you'd want to spend a lot of time anyway, and I could easily see how the currently deployed team had run into trouble. If all went to plan, we should be in and out in just over a week, ten days tops.

Once the team was organized and we had our gear packed and ready to go, I headed off base to tie up a few loose ends.

Carrying the box of my dad's stuff, I drove by Jeannie's place around 16:00, hoping to catch them just as they were getting home from school.

Jeannie answered the door, and seeing me in my drab uniform, holding a box, I could see the moment she twigged why I was there.

"I thought you'd like to know. I leave tonight."

"That was quick." After gazing at me for a moment, she stepped into the house and called out, "Will. Phoenix is here."

"Some housekeeping before I go," I said, finding it diffi-cult to look straight at her face. "Uh, so, the house. I closed today, so it's mine, but I don't have time to deal with it. I lined up a general contractor to do a few things. I gave him your number. I'd appreciate it if you could be the point person, in case anything comes up since he's starting work immediately. Field any questions he might have."

Her face twitched, and I read regret in her eyes.

I went on. "And if you have any ideas or…preferences, please feel free to give the contractor direction. I'm not much for interior decorating, so I'd be grateful for your help. Just make the call for me. I don't care. I just want it all updated, nice and clean."

She nodded, pulling her lips between her teeth. Then said, "Okay. I'll take care of it for you."

I handed her the banker's box. "This is some family stuff. I wanted to show it to Will, tell him some stories about my dad." I sighed. "I cleaned it up, so you're both welcome to have a look through. There is an envelope in there with the house info, and a set of keys in case you need to…whatever. The contractor has the other set."

Will came downstairs, running across the foyer, his features etched with concern. "You're leaving."

"Yep. I wanted to stop in and say goodbye. I head out tonight."

Will wrapped his arms around me. I picked him up and held him tightly. I spoke into his ear, but also over his shoulder, addressing both of them together.

"Nothing to worry about. This is a routine mission. I should be home in ten days if all goes well."

I felt Will's face heat against my neck like a camp stove, his glasses pressed between us, felt the wetness of his tears. I turned my head to kiss the side of his head.

"I love you, bud. Don't forget everything I told you."

"I won't," he cried. "I love you, Dad. Please be safe."

I nearly lost it at his blubbered words. He'd never called me Dad before. I met Jeannie's gaze behind him, and her eyes were flooded with tears as well. "Just be a good boy for your mom, do your homework, help with chores, keep that pigsty of yours tidy. I'll be back before you know it."

"Okay," he said weakly, and I set him down, while he clung to my hand like he'd never let go. He roughly rubbed at his eyes, knocking his glasses askew, then straightened them. "Dad!"

I looked at him, and memorized his sweet face as he said earnestly, "*Viam Inveniemus.*"

I nodded and replied in kind, "*Viam Inveniemus,*" then looked up at Jeannie.

She met my gaze, her dark-blue eyes swimming with tears, and set one palm along the side of my face, her chin quivering. She scanned my features for a long moment, lightly caressing my cheek with her thumb, then leaned closer, reached up onto her toes, tipped her face up, and kissed me softly. She let me hold her face and kiss her tenderly, slowly, sadly.

I didn't grab onto her and hold her tight, though I ached to. I didn't tell her I loved her, I'd miss her, or not to worry. She knew it already.

"I'll be back, love."

When she pulled away, I nodded and stepped away.

Setting a hand on Will's shoulder, she whispered, "Be careful." Then she closed the door as I turned away.

Phoenix

"What's up, Big P?" Zach scowled, his gaze dropping to my drab combat uniform and returning to my face. "You're not working out today?"

I strode towards him, the soft gym flooring giving under my heavy jump boots, conscious of my incongruous appearance in this place and, for the first time in my career, almost wishing I could stay.

I gave my head a shake. "No. Heading out on a deployment tonight."

Zach stared at my khaki t-shirt, olive-drab jacket and pants, and green beret, looking me up and down.

"Oh, shit." He set the weights down with a thud and came over. "Where you headed?"

"Can't say."

He grunted. "When you coming back?"

I shrugged. "Don't know. I'm done when I'm done. Hopefully no more than a week and a half."

The corner of Zach's lip twitched up. He squinted and glanced down and to the right, processing. "What about Jeannie?"

"That's why I'm here. She knows I'm going, yeah. We're on a..." I sighed, glancing over his shoulder. "A bit of a break. And I know she'd hate it if she knew I was saying this, but...can I ask a favour?"

"Sure, man. Anything."

"Can you keep an eye on her while I'm gone? And Will, too?"

Zach met my gaze, sombre. "Yeah."

"Not in any obvious way. Just..." I pressed my lips together and glared at the bench press to my right. "Just be aware. In case they need a hand or get into trouble of any kind. Just be a friend."

Zach's head bobbed. "I got your back, man."

"Be *just* a friend to her, asshole. Don't get any ideas."

"Nah." He scoffed, then hesitated. "You'll be back, though."

At that, I had to smile, whether I felt like it or not. "Of course."

Chapter 24

Jeannie

THE MOMENT PHOENIX stepped away from the house and jumped in his truck, I missed him. But my feelings had to be shelved for later, because Will was distraught, and I spent the next hour or two comforting him. If I thought to spare him this kind of sadness and worry, it was far too late. He'd already bonded with his father.

At first, we just sat in his room, and I held him, and we talked. About Phoenix, the nature of his work, what it meant to him and to us. Of course, I said all the things to Will that Phoenix had said to me, to reassure him, but I didn't know whether my repeating Phoenix's words helped to quell my inner fears, or Will's outward expression deepened them.

After Phoenix dropped off the box and left for his mission, I thought, *You're a fool, Jeannie. How is this better?* It was better with Phoenix. It's too late now. He already lived in my heart. He was already a part of our lives. My heart was already breaking. I was so afraid for him. It might be routine for him, but I'd never had to deal with anything like this before.

Once Will had calmed down a little, we opened the box and looked through the photos, letters, and medals it contained. Will was fascinated. With this mysterious grandfather whom he would never know, but also, and maybe more so, the idea that he was part of this family legacy. One of a line of Corbin men.

"Dad looks just like me, Mom," Will said.

"He does."

"Did you know him, then?"

The photo that most intrigued him, and I had to admit was compelling, was a picture of Phoenix's dad in uniform with Phoenix as a boy, a little younger than Will was now.

"I don't think I knew Phoenix at that age. I'm not sure why. Maybe we'd been at different elementary schools." But seeing him as a kid, there was no mistaking who he was. It was like looking at Will. It was almost like Phoenix and Will in costume, caught in a time warp. The resemblance between father to son to son was uncanny.

This strange echo of my son's current reality was somehow grounding, and at the same time terrifying. The young Peter at that moment was still innocent, still believing in the invincibility of his strong father, still under the illusion that his life would continue on as it had been on that summer day.

There was a shiny new medal, still in its box, along with a letter in a clear acetate envelope. Reading the letter, it was clear that the Sacrifice Medal had been awarded to his dad posthumously, as the letter was addressed to Phoenix's mom, and explained that the rules for awarding the newly released medal had not yet been ironed out in 2001-2002, around the time Phoenix's dad had been injured overseas. There was a brief description of the events around his mishap. The colleagues whose lives were lost. His efforts to save them and bring them home. His own severe injuries.

Will had to study a map of Afghanistan, find Kandahar, and look at it for a long time.

It was a very different image of a man who, when we were in high school, was more of a shady myth than a real man, a victim surely, the shell of a once heroic father. As part of Phoenix's loose group of friends, we were all vaguely aware of his situation, from the naive perspective of young teenagers. Rumours flew. Some of them, I'm sure, were sensationalized.

My perspective was different because Pete had confided in me, sharing small anecdotes and specific circumstances he'd dealt with, though I suspected he edited heavily. Maybe the sensational rumours were more true than I realized at the time. Certainly, I never thought of his dad as a war hero.

Will wanted to hang Phoenix's father's medals on his corkboard, as talismans, to keep Phoenix safe and bring him home. So I helped him rearrange the pictures and souvenirs and tchotchkes he had there to make room. Then he insisted we print a couple of pictures of him and Phoenix together off of my phone. The old printer my parents owned was crappy, and the resulting prints were pale and sketchy, but they found their place of pride among the other things.

Finally, he was emotionally drawn out and exhausted and agreed to go to bed early.

I took the remaining thick envelope from the box to my own room to look at before I retired.

Inside was the house purchase contract, a survey plan, the realtor's documentation, and related information. There were new insurance papers and keys to the house on a little ring.

Before he'd left, he'd said he'd closed on the house today. It would have probably been disappointing for him to not be able to go there and see it on the day it became his own.

I sighed, turning over the papers, and scanning them with my business mind. He'd paid a good price for the house, given the current market, and paid a substantial amount as a down payment. I guess he'd been saving money for years, perhaps with nothing much to spend it on until now.

Inside another smaller envelope was a copy of a signed and countersigned letter on a lawyer's letterhead that briefly outlined his change of beneficiary on his last will and testament to be his son, Will. My heart swelled in my chest, knowing he'd gone to all this trouble. I was named as a trustee until Will came of age. If anything happened to Phoenix, and he never returned, the family house he so desperately wanted us to live in with him would belong to Will.

Clipped to this letter, a hastily scrawled note in Phoenix's neat handwriting said:

IN THE EVENT *I don't return, the mortgage is insured. If you don't want to live in it, you can rent it out and put the income in a fund for Will's education.*

I FELT LIKE CRAP.

I'd been so unkind. So ungrateful. So obsessed with my own narrow perspective. I'd completely ignored how momentous, how meaningful and how important this house was to Phoenix. He wanted to make a big gesture to prove his commitment to Will and to me. To his family. He wanted to repair his broken past and carve out a better, sweeter future. He'd planned it and been prepared. And he'd acted swiftly and decisively when the opportunity presented itself.

And I'd thrown his thoughtful gift in his face.

Now he was going somewhere across the world, risking his life to keep people safe and make the world better, having done all this for us, while I thought only of myself.

I was not my favourite person at the moment.

He and I had both faced challenges and adversity as teenagers. We'd both lost someone close to us, and we'd both faced losing, or compromising, our youthful dreams. I'd survived by inscribing a tight circle around my world, minimizing risk, taking tiny steps, and letting no one in. On the surface, it looked like he'd run away. In reality, he'd leapt with both feet into a new life, working hard to achieve his dreams and more.

A few days later, I got a call from a contractor named Davie Malloran. He'd started work on Phoenix's house renovations and had been walking the house, taking measurements and making plans, finalizing the specifications. Apparently, Phoenix had been firm on the budget but made only vague mention of the paint colours and styles for fixtures and fittings. But Davie had questions. He'd only allocated a couple of weeks for the work, and he didn't want to mess around. Would I meet him at the house in the early evening to look at some options, and help him narrow down the choices?

So after Will and I got home from school, we ate an early dinner and walked over to the house. That's when I realized that Will had already been there, and had the full tour, including the backyard, which I hadn't seen.

He showed me "his room" and then took me out into the yard to repeat the stories Phoenix had told him from his youth. We spent some long minutes staring up into the spreading canopy of the huge oak tree in the corner, trying to figure out where the old treehouse had been, and what a new one might look like.

I didn't say anything to oppose this plan, as now was not the time. But my mind filled with horror stories from Quinn and Parker's childhood.

It had been a treehouse accident in their backyard that had ruined Quinn's leg. And also, I thought, forged the close bond between the twins—and their hero Jae Soo, who had rescued them both that day, securing for himself the status of hero and idol in their minds till the end of time. In any case, I'd make sure Phoenix built in copious safety features if this treehouse ever came to fruition.

We met and walked around with Davie.

"I brought some paint sample fans. Phoenix said you wanted a green bedroom," he said to Will. "Have a look here." He fanned out the samples on the old kitchen counter, and Will eagerly searched through them. "He said neutrals for the rest, but to listen to you if you had other ideas," he told me.

I smiled, chagrinned. All I could do was imagine what I would personally like, and hope he would, too. "I think the ceiling and cove should be a bright, flat white," I said. "And maybe a warm cream for the walls. Did he say anything about the new kitchen cabinets?"

Davie handed me some brochures, and I considered the styles. This was a luxury I had never experienced. I'd never owned my own home, never had the funds to choose anything except what I could afford. So my kitchens were usually ugly and functional. The best I was ever able to do was a fresh coat of paint and shabby-chic accents. I flipped through the different ideas, considering the age of the house and modern styles. In the end, we agreed a clean, slightly retro style would look best. Not too over the top, since as the original bathroom fixtures attested, pink, blue, and mint green were all the rage when this house was built.

It was fun to make design choices when working with a blank slate. I briefly considered blue and white cabinets and bright red accents, so it felt like a fifties diner, but then thought maybe that would get tiresome. Finally, we went with a mix of white and soft-green cabinets, white laminate with subtle gold stars that felt very retro, white subway tile splash, and a black and white checked linoleum floor. I could picture the counters and shelves stacked with a fun rainbow of vintage Fiesta tableware and Pyrex bowls. I hoped Phoenix wouldn't hate it.

As for the bedrooms, I picked pale off-white shades that made the slightest nod to period colours, such as a barely-there robin's egg blue for the master bedroom, and the palest blush for the bathroom. Will had browsed his green paint options, listening to our meandering discussion, and finally chosen a luminescent moss-green shade for his room he said was the same colour as the light through the leaves outside.

Davie nodded approvingly. "Consider it done. Last thing, some new plumbing and light fixtures. Or I can pick them in keeping with your general concept." Since he and I seemed to be on the same page, I agreed he could do that. "I appreciate your input, Jeannie. It's an added stress making these decisions for a client."

I enjoyed myself. It was impossible to go through that exercise, visualizing each room with fresh paint, cabinets, fixtures and trim without also dreaming of what it would be like to live there. Without my telling it to, my mind began choosing furniture and window coverings, and I imagined browsing second-hand shops with Phoenix and Will, searching for perfect funky accent pieces. I wondered if we could find, or afford, a mid-century modern dining suite, which would pull the spaces together beautifully.

As Will and I said goodbye and headed out, Davie waved us off from the open doorway and said, "Should be able to wrap this up in two weeks if I bring in extra guys. Phoenix said he wanted it expedited."

"Thank you. Let me know if you need any more input or hit a snag."

"Will do."

We walked slowly home under the leafy trees, our heads full of dreams, and I thought at least Will would be able to enjoy having space of his own in the new house. As for myself… I didn't know. But I was softening. A home of my own would be a lovely thing indeed, but only if Will and Phoenix were in it with me.

Chapter 25

Phoenix

For the tedious hours in transit, while I sat idle, my mind chewed on thoughts of Jeannie, mostly. Whose great idea was it to have a family?

I couldn't get them out of my head, Jeannie's words, Jeannie's fears spinning round and round. I'd never been more distracted. Never felt more uneasy. I indulged myself for several hours, slept for a few more, and then I had to focus on the mission ahead.

Finally, the shabby commercial plane that Luekins and I took on the last leg of our journey landed at N'Djamena. We were met by an unfamiliar middle-aged US military guy with two camo-clad soldiers at the airport and escorted by jeep to an unmarked compound on the far side of the airport. The US AFRICOM Operation Nimble Shield base. Local time was 20:00, already two hours after dark, but the heat was intense, radiating off the tarmac as we drove through the unmarked gate.

With seven and a half hours of darkness left to work

with, we gathered our team, quickly organized our gear and changed into inconspicuous clothing. We had to move as far as we could into the target area, suss it out, and find a base to hide before twilight at 05:30.

Damien had already arrived, along with McLean.

"Chief!" Damien barked, and we locked hands, laughing. "You gettin' any action yet?"

"I'll give you some, brother."

"It's good to see you," he said. "You've been a busy man."

Meeting with the operations chief, we picked up what current local intel we could, including the current mood from the leader of the local tactical PSYOP team, and were made aware of what support resources were available to us.

We'd been assigned a local Chadian military jeep driver and guide to take us as far up the Chari River as possible without attracting notice. We took with us only what gear we could carry, as we'd be on foot after that. We'd aim for Douguia, and further, where an abandoned food manufacturing plant might provide temporary cover until the following night.

Our goal was to make our way to an area south of Lake Chad, which provided both scrubby trees, rocky outcrops, and a string of small villages with many abandoned buildings that we could use as cover as we explored the flat ground, zeroing in on the last signals received from SIGINT 4. The coordinates were near one of these villages, between Bédam and Haraze-Al-Biar, on the river near the Cameroon-Chad border.

SIGINT Team Four's assignment had been to locate, scout, and map a fenced compound in the region that had been identified by aerial surveillance, further confirmed by Gray Eagle MQ-1C drone, suspected to belong to ISWA, or possibly Al-Qaeda, where ordnance was being stockpiled, and training taking place. Some of it was likely liberated from Libya to the north. Apparently, their work was mostly complete, with some unanswered questions that we would, if possible, clear up quickly as we gathered the stranded team and extracted them. That was the goal.

All over this region, we could expect to run into ISWA factions, other tango cells with affiliations to ISIS, Boko Haram, or Al-Qaeda, as well as myriad smaller organizations, local bandits and corrupt governments. Basically, there was no one we could trust, had to rely on our own observations to confirm intel, and had to be as invisible as possible.

In reality, it was a long, hot grind punctuated by periodic tense encounters with very bad, often heavily armed dudes whose affiliation was impossible to determine, and occasionally herds of slowly migrating ruminants heading south for the dry season.

***

Jeannie

It had been nearly a week and a half, and I'd heard nothing from Phoenix. I knew he said he'd be away for up to ten days, but I'd thought if he wasn't home sooner, maybe he'd have had an opportunity to send a message. For Will's sake, if not for mine.

Maybe that was foolish, given the nature of his work, and the short duration of the mission. Likely these were fast-paced and intense, the details of which I couldn't, and didn't even want to imagine, though my mind kept revisiting all the scary places he might be, what troubles might take him there, and what might be happening.

Though I knew he couldn't tell me where he was going

or for how long, and also would be out of contact, I worried. Could I deal with this kind of uncertainty and vulnerability as a way of life?

After repeated questions from Will and endless speculations that were spiralling out of control, I finally agreed to make some enquiries. I wasn't sure what I could find out, but I thought I'd try.

During a break between classes, I sat down in the cafeteria and made a few calls. The process of figuring everything out—who in the Navy to talk to, what to ask, and how to explain who I was—turned out to be very complicated. And in the end, though I'd been redirected politely a few times, I was refused any information at all on the basis that I was not family. I came away with the feeling that even if I had been, I could learn nothing much this way—other than that Commander Corbin was out of town at the moment. *Yes, thank you. Very helpful.*

The fact that he was due home soon made no difference. The fact that I was his son's mother also seemed to make no impression. I suspected there were approved channels for getting updates, but I was not in the loop.

That evening, Will had math homework and asked me to sit with him in case he needed some help. But after only ten minutes or so of me leaning in and making suggestions, he sat up straight and said, "Stop, Mom."

"What is it?"

"You're breathing down my neck. It's not helping."

"I don't understand. Explain."

"Phoenix taught me to watch my mind, so I can tell when I'm getting anxious, and try to figure out what triggers it. And then he taught me ways to stop it before I…" He spun a finger around.

"Spiral?"

"Yeah. And since he's been helping me with math, it's

gotten better. But just now I realized, when you do that thing, it triggers me."

"What thing?"

"It's hard to explain. Something about your voice. The way you ask questions and poke at me."

I pulled in my chin, surprised. "I poke?"

"Kind of. Like…" He struggled to find the words. "Like if I don't see it, or get there the way you did, then I'm slow or stupid."

"Aw, honey. That's not true at all."

"I know. I mean, I know you don't mean it that way. But it still makes me feel that way inside."

"Why do you think that is?"

He twisted his mouth to one side and pushed his glasses up his little nose as if he was uncomfortable saying it.

I smiled softly and nodded to encourage him.

"Phoenix said maybe it's because I don't want to disappoint you or make you worry, and that makes it worse."

"Oh, I see." I pursed my lips, frowning a little. "Me wanting you to do well makes you want to please me, and then you get nervous."

"Yeah."

"So what now?"

"I'm gonna go to the other room for a minute or two, and then I'll come back. And while I'm gone, you just… chill. Okay?"

I laughed. "Okay. That's what I'll do. I'll do my own homework, and just keep you company unless you have a question."

He slid out of his chair, went to the living room, and everything went quiet and still.

Mom bustled through, rummaging in her purse and absently smoothed her frizzy hair down. "Oh, I'm so late. I've got to run."

"Did you see Will in there?"

She blinked and glanced over her shoulder. "Oh, yes. He's sitting in there quietly, with his eyes closed." She shook her head. "He's been doing that lately." She shrugged and added, "I'm off then," and slipped out the kitchen door.

After a few minutes, Will returned and sat down and I could almost feel how much calmer he was. I just looked at him, waiting for him to tell me what he needed. Which he did. He explained that word problems gave him the most trouble because he thought about the wrong things, and asked me to demonstrate how I broke down a word problem into useful bits, and not leave anything out, however obvious it seemed to me.

So that's what I did, and he said, "Okay. I'll try that on my own for a bit and let you know how it goes."

Shaking my head, I resumed my own assignment, frankly amazed at how Phoenix's guidance had rooted out the problem, but even more, how he'd given Will the tools to solve it himself.

The next day, we went to school again, but both Will and I were subdued. We both knew Phoenix should, in theory, be back already. Where was he?

That evening, Will suddenly said, "Why don't we call Grandma Angie?"

"What?"

"I have her phone number from when we visited."

Huh. "I could try that. Would you like to talk to her?"

"Uh-huh."

In the end, we decided that Will would make the call, have a chat with his *other* grandmother, and then introduce me, saying I had a question. So that's what we did.

I stayed close and listened to Will's side of the conversation. It was incredibly sweet. By the sound of the woman's voice, she was thrilled to hear from him, and they'd made a connection during their short visit.

"How is Bess?" Will asked, and then listened politely while he got an update. Then he explained that he and his mom were kind of worried about Phoenix and that his mom had a question for her. After some soft-spoken words, he said, "Okay, Grandma Angie. Here she is." And he handed the phone to me.

"Um. Hello?" I said into the phone.

"Hello, dear. I'm Angie, Peter's mother."

"It's nice to meet you, Angie. I'm Jeannie."

"Of course you are. And I'm so, so happy to make your acquaintance."

"Yes. Me too. I'm very sorry I didn't come with Will the other weekend. I was…shy, I guess, and…"

"It's not a problem, darling. We'll have plenty of time. We were so happy to meet and get to know Will, though. We can all get together again soon."

"About that. Um, the reason we… Well, one reason we called was to ask you about Phoe–Pete and… You know. When he's away."

She hummed in understanding. "Will said you're worried about him."

"Yes. It's been ten days. We haven't heard anything."

"I do know what you're going through. And the truth is, it's pretty much impossible to get concrete, useful information. They just won't tell us anything, and extended deployments in his line of work, well…" She hesitated as if trying to find the right words, or perhaps soften her message. "Things get complicated. But it's safe to say, no news is truly good news."

"So, as his mom, you can't call or…"

She clicked her tongue. "No. I really can't help in that way. But I do have some advice for you, darling."

I said nothing, waiting politely for her words of wisdom.

"If you love him, and you want to make a life with him, then I truly hope you do. I've never seen him so happy as he was with Will last week. And I know he has some strong feelings for you as well. Anyway, this is his reality. This is the life he chose. If you love him, you have to accept him for who he is. All of it."

"I've been doing a lot of thinking lately. And I… I guess I'm getting there," I told her.

With her assurances that she'd call me the second she heard anything, at any hour of the day or night, we said goodbye.

Afterwards, quiet again as I tucked Will into bed for the night, I took a hard look at my life, and my apparent inability to find joy and peace because no matter how well I'd coped, I'd always carried my burdens alone. How much sweeter it would be to share the load with Phoenix at my side.

With his dark tousled head on his pillow, Will looked up at me. "I'm scared, Mom. What if he gets hurt?"

I swallowed, my throat suddenly thick. "Me too, honey. But this is who he is. We need him, we want to keep him close, but he's needed more elsewhere right now. We have to be strong. We have to believe he'll be all right. And he'll be home. And we have to know we'll be okay no matter what happens. We have each other like we always did."

Chapter 26

Phoenix

We weren't authorized to engage in combat, so avoiding run-ins, even with the most questionable citizens, was ideal. That didn't mean it always worked out that way. Sometimes trouble comes looking for you.

After lying low through the day and studying the signal data and maps, we were ready to move on at dusk the next night. As we moved out, we were summarily dive-bombed by fruit bats overhead, swooping and screeching through the dimming sky.

"Fuck me," Luekins said, shuddering. "I hate flying things."

"You're IMINT for fuck's sake, Luekins. You *are* flying things," McLean scoffed.

"I'm good with drones. It's those live things with claws and talons that give me the heebie-jeebies. Think I'm gonna lose an eyeball or something."

We set out at a steady ranger's pace for our coordinates, which were about twelve or thirteen kilometres away as the crow flies. Even without night-vision goggles, the going would have been easy. The land was relatively flat, the trees sparse, and the sky big. We were too exposed for my liking, but the upside was we could spot others even faster than they could spot us. And we were pros at disappearing into the landscape like so much dust.

After just over an hour of rucking, we passed the second village after Bédam, sticking close to the agricultural land adjacent to the riverbank. Then we cut inland, through some trees, to an area south of the main road. From here, we were able to follow linear depressions where former oxbows formed oases of trees that provided cover. Animals grazed and snoozed in the cool grottos.

This close to the bottom of the Lake Chad Basin and the Chiri River, there would be scarce high terrain to give us a prospect on our target. But as we approached the target, we found a minor outcrop of rock that gave us a hide site to scout the area, about eight hundred metres distant.

Allowing for all the other bodies in the camp, we picked up a signal from up ahead, in one of a cluster of shanty shacks that lined the crop fields. And almost immediately spotted the problem.

Our target was surrounded. A large temporary camp of squatters had been established to either side. A group of fifty or sixty people, mostly heavily armed men, gathered between the shacks and tents, a few cooking fires glowing. This transient group must have set up camp after our guys had taken refuge in the building. And now they couldn't get out without walking straight into a firefight, massively outnumbered.

The challenge, we could see, was that the camp included not only goats and chickens but women and chil-dren. They did not look like they were packing up and leaving anytime soon, so we had to do this quietly.

After observing their patterns for a day and a night, we found that several of the men drove off every day, leaving a dozen to guard the camp and its inhabitants. We could handle them if necessary, but we had to do it clean, on the sly.

After dark, Damien and I stalked in close through the fields and using thermal cameras, located our guys, who were hunkered down in a half-collapsed shack that their visitors had deemed useless.

"Lost Boys. Ten." We crawled forwards.

"Got your six," said Damien from behind me.

"Oorah. Any Squirrels in this dump?" I hissed into the dark opening.

"Roger that," came a hushed voice. "Op Silver Eye, fow-er zee-ro present."

"Papa Charlie, over," I murmured into my head mic and received a squawk in reply. "Lost Boys found."

"Man, it's ripe in here," Damien said, ducking inside.

We crawled inside, finding them squatting and lying under a collapsed corrugated metal wall and an assortment of cardboard and dry foliage. We identified ourselves quickly and moved on.

"Nice CHU. Seen better, though."

"We were thinking of redecorating."

"How are rations?"

"Black." Meaning they were nearly out. I tossed them a sack with basic supplies and MREs for a couple of days.

"Tango Mike."

"Injuries?"

They gave us a report. "We took shelter here after an encounter with a jeep full of unidentified tangos who tossed an IED our way just for kicks. Stevenson here tried to catch it."

That'd be the guy reclining with bloody bandages

around his thigh and knee. And would explain why they hadn't crawled out themselves.

"You mobile, Stevenson?"

"Not well," he replied. "Leg's mangled."

"Affirmative, assisted walking. What else?"

The fourth guy told us he was weak from days of some mystery fever. "Sobey, here. Mobile but slow as a three-toed sloth," he said.

We got a report on their surveillance and signal planting assignment, picked up their remaining equipment, which had the coordinates of the perimeter and locations of already laid remote signals.

Because of his leg wound, we decided to carry Stevenson out that night and return for the others. We left them with a working radio and crawled out, dragging our baggage.

Then we split into two groups. Damien and Luekins went out the next night to finish planting the last few signals around the camouflaged compound, which lay a couple of kilometres to the northwest, hidden among some trees in a scrubby area adjacent to the marshlands.

Meanwhile, we watched our neighbours, waiting for our window. Once Damien and Luekins returned, job completed, we picked our moment, rucked in what we needed and silently extracted the remaining three, supporting and half carrying the feeble Sobey. Though the meds we gave him had begun to work, he was still weak.

Once collected and regrouped, we planned our extraction path to allow for reduced pace as we'd be supporting the two injured. It would take us two hours to get back to Bédam on foot. We arranged for extraction transport from there, if possible. Some kind of bus or van, with enough space for eight men. We'd know when we got there if they'd come through for us. Worst-case scenario, we'd have to hoof it to Douguia for pick up.

At approximately 03:30, when we should have been either piling into a van or taking refuge from the rising sun, we'd hunkered down to catch our breath and wait for our ride in a thick clump of trees to the north of the road just northwest of Bédam. From this point forward cover was sparser, so this would be the optimal extraction point. If they showed up, but nothing so far.

Just beyond where we hid, a sprawling fenced property lay with numerous small houses and outbuildings scattered. Everything was quiet, but suddenly we spotted a group of bodies and heard a loud commotion up ahead. For an instant, I tensed up, my senses sharpened the way they would on combat missions.

"Get low. Cover up," I ordered the men, and we all flattened out between the trees, on high alert.

We should have been clear at this hour, in a sleepy agricultural area, so these guys were definitely unscheduled visitors. Just our luck.

A moment later, it became clear there was a conflict between two parties, and it was escalating. Maybe an arms deal gone awry or an ideological debate between neighbours.

"Anything, McLean?" I whispered.

"No. It's a local dialect, but too faint to catch any meaningful words. Except they're losing it."

"Roger that." I didn't need to understand Arabic or a local language to read the body language or feel the tension radiating off the group of men. Especially one skinny dude who seemed to be the leader—or one of the leaders—in debate with the others.

In a split second, it escalated. Amid shoving and dodging bodies in the dark, came a sudden burst of gunfire.

Men ran in every direction, towards parked vehicles, nearby buildings, and the copse where we hid.

"Stay down."

More ran towards us. There was a scurry through the trees, this way and that. More gunshots and shouting. I shifted to my elbows, weapon aimed. Everything exploded in a flash of fire and smoke, and I was hurled backwards, slamming into a tree with a breath-shaking thud.

Shaking it off, I aimed my sight on a guy with a rifle rushing towards me, and fired a shot, felling him, just as I felt heat burn my side. Our guys fired a few shots, but it wasn't clear if the locals realized we didn't belong there before they dispersed in a flurry of shouts. Footfalls thumped away. Vehicles revved, their tires tossing dirt and gravel as they sped off into the night. Then it was silent again, but for one jeep in flames, possibly the target of the IED that blew and the crackling of a few tree branches burning from the explosion.

Fuck.

"Damien?" My ears were ringing. "Damien?"

"Roger, Chief." His helmeted head appeared nearby, red light reflected in the lenses of his goggles.

"Anyone hit?" I croaked.

"I'm good," came McLean's voice, creeping nearer.

We crawled towards each other in the dark, my legs all rubbery, counting heads. Scratchy voices yelled through my headset, their words unintelligible.

Stevenson lay where we left him, no worse off, but muttering to himself that he was happier in the collapsed shack. We found Sobey leaning against a tree, too weak to move, his fever spiking from the long hike. One of the other SIGINT team four members, Knox, had caught a passing bullet, just a flesh wound to his shoulder, and their medic,

Krupac, was binding it up. They'd all been spared from the blast by tree cover.

"Where's Luekins?"

His answer came in the form of a groan from a few yards off. We crept over to him, using a small beam light to check him all over. He'd been caught in the blast radius, probably hit with shrapnel. There was blood everywhere. We opened up his clothes, checked him over and found numerous wounds and wrapped him up as well as we could in the bush.

Whatever IED contraption was tossed was neither too big nor toxic. Shitty luck though. We needed to find proper cover to lick our wounds and contact our missing extraction driver. There was no way now we'd be walking far, with three immobilized men and only five to carry them.

Once we were sure it was quiet again and the coast was clear, our noisy neighbours having moved on, we gathered our rucks, propped each other up, and walked slowly around the north side of the village, scanning for a vacant building we could camp out in.

McLean and Damien carried Leukins between them, Krupac supported Stevenson who could hop on his good leg, and I took Sobey, who was so limp I decided to lift him over my shoulders for the hike. My head was still ringing from the blast, and my legs weren't working properly. I kept tripping, though there was nothing on the ground. It was pissing me off.

It took about forty-five minutes, but we finally found a storage building off on its own, on the northeast side of Bédam, and collapsed inside. Luekins was passing out by then, so we laid him out and gave him medical attention first, cutting through his pants and checking for any bleeders we'd missed in the dark.

Once he was patched up and had been given something

for his pain, he got a bit blubbery. "No one's coming for us," he whined. "We'll never get out of here."

"I've been in tough spots like this before and always made it home, kid. Our people know where we are. They're coming." My own voice was faint and fuzzy in my ears, still ringing from the blast.

I stood up to look outside and sent out repeated requests for immediate extraction, but heard garbled words and confusion as if several people were on the radio arguing. *C'mon, people. Get your shit together.*

Finally, I got word that a truck was heading out of Douguia. So we had an hour and a half to wait. I turned to the doorway. The darkened room spun, lights flashing behind my eyelids.

"Chief?" Damien rushed over, hauling me up and helping me further inside, setting me down. "What's wrong?"

I shook my head, specific words escaping me.

"Jesus. He was hit too!" Damien's voice came through the fog in my head. "There's so much of Luekins' fucking blood everywhere we didn't notice. And he carried Sobey all the way."

Ah, well, that would explain the light-headedness. My wobbly legs.

Suddenly someone was getting all handsy, checking for new holes all over me. A sharp pain zinged through my ribs, and the room went dim.

Jeannie

As the days dragged on, I decided distraction was key. A week later, I cleared it with Mom and Dad, called Quinn and arranged a get-together at home, with pizza, ice cream, popcorn, and a movie marathon. When she arrived Saturday evening, Quinn was not alone. Her twin Parker, Jae Soo, Deanna, and Aislin followed her in through the door and made themselves at home in our kitchen and living room.

A half-hour later, Tate slunk in, incognito in a baseball cap and dark glasses, looking both tired and unshaven, like the classic stereotype of a celebrity. He was in the midst of shooting the new season of his popular fantasy series, and for once was not dating anyone. Flopping onto the sofa, he said, "I'm so exhausted, I can't even," to ruthless teasing from everyone else.

We ordered several pizzas and settled in to fill our faces, drink wine, beer, and colas, and unwind. Will, who now knew everyone in the gang, thought the whole thing was excellent fun. Since I'd had virtually no social life, ever, he was fascinated to sit and listen to the adult banter and stare with unabashed curiosity at my assorted friends. It hit home how proscribed our life had been.

We started, by design, with a recent family-friendly film for Will. As I'd suspected during the Farm-to-Table Faire, he really did want to see the new *Minions* movie, and all my silly friends were only too happy to indulge in the latest animated adventure.

Tate entertained us further with credible minion-speak, and if Will had not already attached himself like a mollusc to his father, he might have decided Tate was his new hero. He was, in any case, a new fan and wanted to know all about Tate's show. I balked, but Tate assured me it was more PG than R, but still. Will was only nine, and now I'd have that battle on my hands.

With a full belly, my senses soft-edged from a couple of glasses of wine, and, as I'd hoped, massively distracted by all the company and fun, Will wound down and went to bed around ten. My parents returned from their dinner out, said a polite hello to everyone, and also retired to their room.

I sat wedged on the sofa between Quinn and Parker. Jae Soo and Deanna were on the loveseat beside us. Aislin sat on the recliner on the other side, and Tate sprawled on the floor.

Quinn sat up, her speech just beginning to slur as she said, "Sugar and spice or blood and guts?"

"What?" I replied, baffled.

"What do you need more? To sugarcoat your blues with a romcom or wallow in it with a military-action adventure?"

"Are those my only options?"

"We could watch Tate's show," suggested Parker.

"No alien prosthetics, please," begged Jae Soo.

She went on to propose a variety of films, ranging from *Bridesmaids*, one of my favourites as she well knew, to *The Edge of Reason*, which elicited snide comments from Tate and Parker about how real men fight. Raucous laughter followed, highlighted by Jae Soo's familiar donkey bray. Then came a list of military-action movies most of which I hadn't heard of before.

I sat, frowning, unsure what I really wanted.

Flapping her hands as though it were the last thing she'd want to touch, Deanna suggested, "Let's do a soldier flick. And if we need a cleanse afterwards, we can watch *There's Something About Mary* for laughs."

"Okay," Jae Soo said. "Then I suggest *Black Hawk Down* or *13 Hours*. A hundred and ninety guys in Mogadishu or six secret soldiers in Benghazi." He snorted with laughter, something I felt too heavy to do tonight.

"Oh, the latter has John Krasinski. It's a good one," Parker mumbled through a mouthful of pizza.

Suddenly, I needed to understand…something. Be able

to empathize with whatever he might be dealing with. "Um, that one. The last one."

So that's what we did, and it was awful, gut-wrenching, suspenseful, and heartbreaking. And despite all my nail-biting and hand-wringing, my gasps of shock, and my pathetic endless stream of tears, I felt closer to Phoenix. I understood that I was watching a dramatization of an exceptionally horrific and unprecedented situation.

Was that what it was like for Phoenix? It was so brutal and violent. *Was he thinking of me and Will?* Did he even have two minutes to think about anything but survival? God help him if he had to contend with anything like that.

A tremor and a convulsion of fresh tears wracked me at the thoughts. If I'd told him I loved him, if I'd said yes to living together in his house, if I'd accepted him without reservation, would knowing that give him comfort and reassurance in difficult moments? Or was he, as he'd said to Logan, a highly trained soldier who thought of nothing but doing the right thing and coming home again? I prayed I hadn't weakened his will in any way by denying his dreams.

"How can he do this?" I moaned, and Quinn wrapped me in a hug.

"Sometimes you just have to do things," Jae Soo said morosely. "That's duty."

"But why him?"

"Because he can?" suggested Aislin. "I think he's freaking awesome."

"Because he's a dude. And dudes have to protect."

"That's bull-twaddle," declared Dee.

"It is, and it isn't," suggested JJ, his dimple popping in his cheek. "It's like childbirth. Someone has to do it. You don't have to, but you can. I don't have that choice."

That was just convoluted enough of an argument to shut us all up.

Deanna deflected, getting up to leave. "If Phoenix's anything like those guys in the movie, he's one in a million."

It was true. While the film made the dangers he could be facing all too real, it also gave me a visual, visceral understanding of what feats of strength and endurance he might be capable of. And in a weird way, that was reassuring. Awe-inspiring. But reassuring.

We never got around to watching a rom-com afterwards. After Deanna and Aislin left, and Tate excused himself, saying he needed his beauty sleep, it was just us four left—the triplets and me. Jae Soo got up from the loveseat and wiggled onto the sofa, shoving Quinn over and squashing me into Parker.

Phoenix had been gone ten days. He'd said he'd be back in ten days if all went well. Why hadn't he returned yet? Why hadn't I heard anything from him? Did that mean things hadn't gone well? Or as his mother said, things could get complicated out on a mission, and that was all there was to it.

Suddenly, I remembered that Quinn and Parker were about to be separated from their special person. "I'm sorry I made tonight all about me and my woes," I said. "When are you leaving, JJ?"

"Tomorrow night, sadly," he said, frowning. "I'd love to stay for Julian and Ruby's engagement party on the twenty-second, but I've delayed twice already, and Mother is furious with me." He shuddered. "I have to attend my own engagement parties."

"We're lucky we got to have you this long," Quinn said, equally sad, hooking her arm through his and patting his hand.

Parker had drawn silent, brooding, but with speaking eyes, and I noted his Adam's apple bob a few times as he reined in his emotions.

"Will you visit for Christmas?" I asked, and I looked between all three of them, shaking their heads in unison, like Bobblehead dolls on a shelf.

Jae drew in a big breath and sighed, his head falling forwards. "The wedding is set for late January, so no. I'll be buried in preparations and getting involved with the business before my uncle trashes the whole thing."

"Sounds like you're in for a long haul, then." I wondered if we'd get wedding invitations. Or at least Parker and Quinn. But somehow I doubted it.

This marriage of Jae Soo's was all about family and business, and nothing personal for him at all. It sounded dreadful.

When we were all so tired we could barely keep our eyes open, I said, "You guys can leave. I'll survive."

"What are you going to do about Phoenix's house?" Parker asked.

I shook my head. I'd had too much to drink to trust myself to make decisions or confess my feelings right now.

Quinn patted my head. "Face it, Jeannie. You are already fully invested in him. Since you already love him, pushing him away is just…just…"

"Foolish?" suggested Jae Soo, with sad eyes and a twisted smile.

"It is, isn't it?" I whispered. Quinn's words were true, and the realization that I'd been a fool pressed in on me, making my chest hurt.

"It doesn't accomplish anything, is what I was thinking," Quinn said with a head shake. "If you're trying to save yourself heartache."

"How's that working out for you, girl?" Parker cast a sly side glance at me, his eyelids heavy with exhaustion, and then yawned.

Heartache. That was exactly what I suffered from.

I pushed off Quinn and Parker's knees, standing up. "Off you go. I'll call you a taxi."

As we all stood on the stoop by the open front door waiting for the taxi to arrive, Quinn took my hands in hers and said, "You've got so used to depriving yourself it's become a habit. Nothing in life is guaranteed. Enjoy what you can while you can."

"Well, that goes for all of you, too," I said, thinking about the secrets, sacrifices, and sorrows all of my friends carried in their hearts. I turned to Jae Soo. "I won't say goodbye, Jae Soo, but farewell. I hope you don't regret your choices. And can enjoy what you can while you can. No matter what, I hope we see you again soon." I hugged him and held on tightly for an extra few beats.

He had gone to Korea a million times—and returned. But this time felt ominously permanent. I hoped for the twins' sake it wasn't.

I watched the three of them stumble out to the waiting taxi and waved them off, feeling suddenly eager for Phoenix's return. I might just be ready to take that big leap of faith and try happiness on for size.

Chapter 27

Jeannie

AND THEN, the next day, I got a long-distance call that changed everything and set me into motion. A foreign operator put the call through and patched me through to Phoenix.

"Hey," he said. He sounded awful. Tired, slow, his voice raspy.

"Are you alright? Where are you? I was so worried." My voice got thin and reedy by the end as if crushed between the swell of my heart, relieved to hear from him, and the crushing tension of my ribs holding it in.

"I'm okay. You can stop worrying." He fell silent, and I listened to his laboured breathing. "I'm sorry I couldn't call you sooner."

"What happened?"

"I still can't tell you much, but…" He hesitated. "I'm in a Naval hospital in Sicily. I think they're going to transfer me home in another day or so. I had a little… Uh…"

He was reluctant to tell me he got hurt.

"I want to know everything," I insisted. "Don't shelter me."

He huffed a sigh. "Well, I'll give you details when I see you, but I had to get a few stitches, okay? I'll probably be on medical leave for a few weeks while I heal."

My eyes burned and overflowed with a river of tears that spilled down my cheeks. "I knew it. I was so scared. What do I tell Will?"

"It's okay. I did something stupid, is all. Turns out I'm not Superman after all." He chuckled softly.

I sobbed and laughed at the same time. "I hate you. You're in so much trouble."

"It's so fucking great to hear your voice, love." He clucked his tongue and sighed. "I can't wait to see your baby blues."

I didn't know what to say. My feelings, so conflicted just two weeks ago, were now crystal clear. My heart thudded with the magnitude of the decisions I was making on the fly, at the welcome sound of his voice, at the hope and excitement I felt for the future. Everything had changed. But it didn't feel right to say any of this over the phone from so far away.

"Will you let me know when you're arriving?"

"I will. They'll likely take me to the base hospital for a check before letting me go, but I don't know when."

"Okay. I'm glad you're safe." *I love you.* The words hovered at the tip of my tongue. Soon, I'd say them to him.

We had so little time to get ready, I called in all the help. But first, I sat down to have a heart-to-heart with Will.

He was enthusiastic about my idea. No hesitation. Clearly, the fears I had nurtured didn't bother my son. He wanted to be with his father. He was ready to embrace our little family. He was excited to move into our new home with Phoenix and make the best of our new life together.

Though it felt reckless, unpredictable, and unsafe, I was trilling with nervous excitement too. For better or worse, we were a family, and we loved him.

I realized I was a million times happier having him in our lives than not. And now that I knew I loved him, and Will loved him, I was afraid he'd reject me since I'd pushed him away. I hadn't the courage to tell him we loved him and were anxiously waiting for him to come home. I'd show him soon enough, and never again leave him in doubt of my feelings. Even if we lost him, we would be better off for having had him, than not at all.

I called Quinn, and she recruited the rest of the gang.

We met at Millhouse Coffee and brainstormed. Everyone was excited about my decision to move into Phoenix's house, and on board with my desire to welcome him home there. With a hastily scrawled floor plan on a paper napkin to sort out what was needed, we all dispersed to our homes, or more likely their parents' homes, on the weirdest treasure hunt ever.

Chapter 28

Phoenix

I LAY in a hospital bed at the Port Cam Naval Medical Hospital, waiting for my discharge papers. It had been a long week. Except for the messed-up extraction, our mission had been successful, all objectives met. Luekins was recovering from his multiple surgeries in Ottawa. Damien was there too, with his wife and baby daughter. Everyone had gone home.

It had been the most frustrating deployment of my career. Mainly because I hadn't finished it properly. Because of blood loss and shock, I'd been unconscious for a day while they stitched me up at the N'Djamena Military Medical facilities and from there, put me on a bird for the US Naval Hospital at Sigonella, Sicily. It was deemed the nearest facility with adequate facilities to refine the work, and also because they were sending Luekins there to get patched up. He'd needed more work than I did.

When I'd first awoken, everything had changed. Instead of dark and dirty, I was surrounded by bright white.

"Where…?"

"You're at Sigonella Naval Hospital, son. You're fine," said a calm male voice.

Whisky Tango Foxtrot? "What the hell am I doing in Italy?" I tried to push upright, again opening my eyes to blinding whiteness, and closed them again as firm hands pushed my shoulders onto the bed.

Resigned, I asked, "How'd I get here?"

"You caught a bullet through the ribcage, cracked a rib. No vitals affected. And some nasty shrapnel in your thigh. Fortunately, small junk we were able to clean out, though quite a lot of it. But it turned your femoral artery into a sieve, and I understand you didn't notice it right away. So you lost a fair bit of blood before your buddies got a tourniquet on you."

Shit. What an idiot. I'd been so concerned for Luekins, that I hadn't checked myself. I hadn't felt anything except a bit dizzy. It should have been routine, and easily solved with a field tourniquet, or so I assumed. Major fail on my part, and I let my team down before we were safely extracted.

"Lieutenant Luekins?"

"He's here, too. You'll have to ask someone else about what happened before you arrived here."

When I connected with JTF 2 HQ, I'd been informed that the rest of my team, save Luekins, were treated at N'Djamena as needed and sent home.

I ought to feel lucky, I supposed, but my overwhelming feeling was that I'd let my team down. I hadn't been able to protect them and lead them to safety because of something as careless as not checking myself for wounds after the explosion.

They'd provided a fresh uniform and my old rucksack. All the technical equipment had been taken home from

N'Djamena. After resting there for another day, I'd been released to fly home and got worked over once more by local doctors.

While waiting for a transfer at Sigonella, I went through my rucksack and discovered Dad's letter. In the thick of the mission, I'd forgotten to read it.

Dad had apparently penned it not long after my decision to stay, when Mom took Bess away. It was a strange thing to read, fifteen years too late, and I wondered what Mom was thinking, keeping it tucked away all this time.

It was a simple letter, perhaps composed in a moment of lucidity and, apparently, remorse.

He said he was sorry. He was grateful. He was so proud. And he wished for a better future for me than he was able to provide. He wanted me to pursue the math and engineering I dreamt of, trusting that I'd be brilliant. And lastly, he hoped I would break with tradition and stay far away from the Navy. If only for Mom's sake, he said.

Sorry, Dad.

On the flip side of the single page were a few added lines, slightly less legible, scrawled, perhaps as he slipped to the dark side.

p.s. If you do end up in the forces, as I suspect you will, I'll only add that I hope you do a better job than me. In the end, my greatest hope is that you can forgive me for my failings as a father, and more importantly, no matter what happens, that you accept your own limitations, and move on with the life you deserve. I will always love you. Dad.

My throat tightened with emotion, my eyes burning. Insightful words from a man who never could move on.

I'm sorry.

I sighed. Recently I realized I'd carried the weight of Dad's choices with me on my journey. They'd served their purpose, spurring me on, driving me to succeed. But perhaps I'd carried them long enough.

I love you, Dad.

He must have given the letter to Mom long ago, for it to have survived the fire. Maybe she'd been waiting until I was an adult. And by then, I'd already joined the Navy. Not that she'd known what was in the letter. Or maybe she felt I was better off looking forwards, forging my own path, as she'd said.

I forgive you.

I'd had communication with Unger and a few other HQ brass to debrief, as had my team members. And for now, I'd be on medical leave until my stitches healed.

And my thoughts finally returned to Jeannie and Will. What would they think when they saw me like this? After all her worries and fears, I'd managed to bung myself up. *Brilliant.* This was not likely to nurture confidence, and I felt bad about that, too.

What did it mean for our future?

All I could do was continue to be available and present for both of them. I could be constant in my love and desire to support them. I couldn't force them to accept me as part of their family. I couldn't force them to love me, live with me, or accept my gifts. But I knew I wanted to be as much a part of their lives as Jeannie was willing. Perhaps, in time, we would grow into a real family, whatever that looked like.

One thing I knew, they were my family, no matter what. As long as I was alive, I'd be there for them.

When I hobbled out of my room to check out, I was disoriented to find Jeannie waiting for me in the hospital lobby.

"Hey. What are you doing here?" I limped over and leaned in for a kiss, letting her meet me halfway. Even more surprising, she slid her hands gently around my neck and planted a sweet, soft kiss on my mouth, leaving me a little confused.

I might have been through a lot in the last two weeks, but nothing had changed here. Had it?

"I thought you'd need a ride home," she said and led the way to her mother's car.

Jeannie

"Where are you taking me?" Phoenix said, confused when I turned off the main road to the naval base and wound into a residential area. "Is Will at home?"

I hummed noncommittally, nodding. He could continue to believe I was taking him to my parents' house for another few blocks before I'd have to say anything.

When I turned again, away from the van Bellen residence and towards the Corbin residence, he twigged. "Oh, you want to show me the renos? Now?"

"Yup," I went with his suggestion. "It looks great, but Davie didn't get everything done. He had some questions about…" I shrugged. It was true enough, so I pulled a few random details out. "The laundry room. And the, um, downstairs bathroom. And a few other things."

"Okay?" He seemed a little confused.

We pulled up into the long driveway, and I went around to open his door. I didn't yet know the extent or nature of his injuries, though he was walking slowly and favouring one leg, but it had to be serious if they flew him to a Naval hospital in Italy, didn't it?

He also looked exhausted, and ragged, his hair and beard longer and untrimmed, dark circles under his eyes, small cuts healing on his face. My heart squeezed, so over-joyed to have him safely home again.

As we went up the sidewalk, I said, preparing him, "I took the liberty of getting your belongings from your room at the base and moving you in. I hope you don't mind. Since the work is basically finished, I thought it'd be fun for you to see it right away."

"What?" He narrowed his eyes at me suspiciously. "Who let you into my room at the base?"

"Oh, I…" I flipped a hand. Shit. The last thing I wanted was for him to know that I'd been talking to his mom. "I asked and…"

But we'd arrived at the house.

Phoenix

As she laced her fingers with mine and led me in through the front door, I had to pause and get my bearings. The whole place felt so different. Warmer, cleaner, busier, and more colourful. I stood in the front entry looking around, studying my new surroundings. The walls were now a soft buttery cream, the ceiling glowing white like sunshine on a new cloud, and the wood floors gleamed without a scuff or scratch.

But more strange yet was the fact that there was…furni-ture? It was tacky and sparse, but…

"Where did this stuff come from? Who does it belong to?" I was stunned, grinning. There was an old comfy couch, an ugly old recliner, mismatched coffee and end tables, and old-fashioned floor lamps with wonky shades arrayed around a tired-looking area rug in a hideous green and brown pattern.

Jeannie laughed, covering her mouth with her fingertips. Glancing at her, I caught her sparkling, amused gaze.

Waving a hand in an arc across the room, she said, "It's all borrowed, so don't worry that you have to live with it forever. We raided everybody's parents' basements and garages for the spare stuff we could find."

"We?" I blinked, confused, taking in Jeannie's smug smile, pinched lips, and mischievous, crinkled blue eyes.

"Yes, we," she said quietly, her small voice immediately drowned out by a chorus of shouted, "Surprise!" as people jumped from behind walls, out of the hallway, and down the stairs.

"Dad!" Will squealed his delight and flung himself at me, and wincing, had to brace myself for the impact.

"Easy, bud," I murmured through gritted teeth. "Still a little sore here."

"I'm sorry," he said, aghast at his carelessness. "Where are you hurt?"

I patted my side, and he drew in a breath and set his little hand against my shirt, gazing up at me with remorseful eyes.

"S'okay. I'm so happy to see you." I looked around at the smiling faces of Quinn, Parker, Zach, Tate, Deanna, Aislin, Rainy, Bethune, Ruby, and Julian. And of course, Jeannie, standing at my side, not appearing at all like she wanted to be somewhere else. I felt my heart wobble, and I thought I might be on the verge of a come-apart. "All of you."

"Jae Soo would have been here, but he had to take the red-eye out last night," Parker explained.

I was utterly at a loss for speech. My wish had been only to be home again—and to hold my Jeannie and Will in my arms. This was too much, and I found my throat thick, my mouth wet and salty. I didn't trust myself to speak, but looked at them all, shaking my head in disbelief.

"Sit down, Dad." Will led me by the hand to the recliner, and I sat, and someone put a cold beer in my hand.

"I need a tour," I said. "Is the whole house furnished?"

"Minimally. But the tour can wait for later. Just rest now," Jeannie said.

Over the next hour, I drank my cola, which I'd swapped out for the beer since I was on antibiotics, and talked with everyone, who mingled and moved from room to room, taking turns sitting in the few seats. Julian walked around with plates of snacks, offering them and setting them down on the coffee table, and as I discovered later, on the very tacky dining table now occupying the dining room under a sexy hanging light fixture.

"I like the chandelier," I said to Jeannie, who stayed close to me, one hand resting lightly on my arm, as if she needed to know where I was and prevent me from disappearing. "But this table is hideous. Is that…MacTac?"

"You think?" she said, tilting her head to consider the chunky wooden thing with its heavy carved legs painted bright blue and scarred, patterned surface with peeling patterned vinyl. "Well, good thing you own the light fixture, and the table and chairs can go back to where we found them, in Zach's parents' garage. Or maybe to a flea market, since we hauled it out and cleaned it."

"I think my folks would probably appreciate that," Zach said, laughing.

"Everyone's house got a fall cleaning," Quinn said. "Wait till you see the bedrooms."

"Bedrooms?" I raised my brow at Jeannie.

"We actually stole Will's bedroom furniture from Mom and Dad's house, for now. Until you get…whatever you guys choose."

I hesitated before asking, "What will he sleep on when he's not here?"

Her smile was small and coy. With twitching lips, she told me, "He won't be sleeping at my parents' anymore."

I swallowed, my mouth opening, my chest squeezing with an intense throb of my swelling heart. "What are you saying?"

She gently scooped her arms around my waist, setting her forehead momentarily against my chest, then tipping her head back to look up into my eyes. "We didn't just move you in, Pete," she whispered. "We all moved in."

I smirked, glancing around at our gathered friends, watching us with big smiles. "*All* of you?"

Catching my meaning, she giggled and face planted against my chest again, her face blooming with colour like a rose. "No, no, no. Obviously." Her smile faded when she looked up again, her eyes filled with hope, regret, and love. "Just us three."

Blinking away a sudden burning in my eyes, I just stared at her, my beautiful Jeannie, for a long moment, counting my blessings, overwhelmed with my good fortune. "Where's Will?" I glanced around, searching for our son, and found him nearby, waiting. Opening one arm, I welcomed him into our shared embrace, our little family of three.

"I love you two so much," I whispered, and in return, received the gift of both of them saying, almost at the same moment, "I love you, too."

Still reeling from the past two weeks, which for all our strength and training, broke us down and made us morbid, philosophical, and sentimental for the sweetness of a normal life, I was a little numb. This—my dream, my family, my home—was not what I was expecting to find when I came home to Port Camosun. All I could do was stand there, holding onto my family, surrounded by my friends, and feel profound gratitude.

After another hour of drinks, snacks, and generally boisterous chatter, everyone conveniently had to be somewhere else. They slipped out the door two by two, leaving us three on our own with a very messy house.

Then Will and Jeannie took me on a detailed room-by-room tour, pointing out everything Davie had touched, every paint colour and finish they'd chosen, and demonstrated every faucet and light switch as if they were just invented last week. "The kitchen is very cool."

Will's bedroom was indeed now green, a soft mossy colour that suited him very well. His things were still partially in boxes strewn around the room. "Little man, we have got to teach you to keep your kit tidy."

Then Jeannie led me downstairs and showed me the other two rooms. The front bedroom was bare, awaiting some new designation, but furniture made the master bedroom overlooking the backyard feel cozy.

"I like the colours you chose," I said, limping closer to the bed and sitting on it with an ominous squeak. "I think buying a new deluxe bed is top of the list, hey?"

"Definitely," she said, leaning in the doorway. "This stuff is just a placeholder. We had, like, twenty-four hours to pull it together once I heard you were coming home."

The weird borrowed furniture gave it all a warm, old-fashioned vibe, and Jeannie babbled nervously about hunting down a vintage mid-century dresser and dining suite to suit the old house.

I smiled at her, so beautiful and sweet in a thin white sweater and jeans, her pale skin glowing, framed by chestnut-brown hair draped over her shoulders, her deep-blue eyes sparkling. Suddenly, being home, really home, with the woman I loved, was the most amazing dream I could imagine.

"We…" I said, my voice low and suggestive, lifting a brow, "…have a bedroom all of our own."

"We do." Her smile widened. "But I thought you were an invalid?"

"Oh, I'm sure you'll take good care of me, love." I shoved my aching body up off the bed. No matter how much I hurt, or how jet-lagged I felt, I was staying awake tonight.

We nibbled on a bit more of the food that Julian had left behind, then put the rest away in the new modern stainless steel fridge that smelled of plastic, and tidied up the kitchen while Jeannie sent Will to get ready for bed.

"Do you realize how few opportunities you and I have had to be alone in the past two and a half months?"

She just smiled, blinking innocently, as if she had no clue what I meant.

"I think I'll go say goodnight to my son."

Not long after tucking Will in and kissing him goodnight, I closed the door to our new bedroom, turned down the lights, and slowly, patiently, strategically stripped every last item of clothing from Jeannie's soft curvy body.

She did the same to me, running her hands like feather dusters over me, exploring all the ink she hadn't really seen properly, touching her lips, her tongue, and her teeth to my tingling skin, my flesh growing hard and demanding under her delicious torture. Then she got seriously sidetracked by my ugly raw stitches, which I had to distract her from by laying her down and kissing every inch of her beautiful body, from her ears to her toes, until she shivered and shuddered and begged me to love her.

So very easy to do. Ordinarily.

Which actually was about all the activity I had energy for, so I reclined and let Jeannie take control, make the decisions, and be the boss of me. It was very fine. In fact, it was bliss. She made the gentlest, sweetest love to me, even though the mattress was thin and lumpy, sagged and squeaked whenever we moved, and we laughed as much as we cried.

Epilogue

Phoenix

Jeannie and I parked on the street outside Millhouse Coffee, about to go inside for Ruby and Julian's engagement party. We'd arrived five minutes ago, but were still sitting in my truck while she scowled at her phone, and I looked at her. These days my heart seemed too big for my ribcage.

I waited patiently for Jeannie to finish what she was doing. I could do it all night. I was in no particular hurry to get inside. As long as Jeannie was at my side, I was where I wanted to be. Where I needed to be. Only three nights had passed since my surprise homecoming. Barely any time at all.

But three days and three nights with Jeannie and Will living with me in our new home, three breakfasts, three dinners. Three days and nights of saying 'I love you' and hearing it in reply. And three nights making sweet, tender love to Jeannie in a bed of our own, holding her in my arms all night, had transformed my existence from uncertain to complete. From longing to belonging.

Only one of those nights had been spent on that miserable squeaky lumpy excuse for a mattress that she'd scrounged up from someone's basement. The very next day I insisted we go out and buy a deluxe new bed with a proper firm mattress. I had them load it into my truck and we brought it straight home and set it up. I might have used my recuperation as an excuse for expediting the purchase, but really I just wanted to luxuriate, undistracted, in having Jeannie in a bed of our own.

Once I'd had another week or so to heal up, I'd return to desk duty. Thankfully, I wouldn't be deployed for another several weeks, and I'd enjoy every moment of that time at home with Jeannie and Will, and indulge her every whim as she browsed for the perfect mid-century modern dining suite, and hunted down more colourful vintage bowls for the kitchen.

She seemed to have come to terms with my job, both of us having survived my first deployment apart. Now, she claimed, she was happy for every minute she could have with me.

"Any time now, love," I murmured.

"One more sec," Jeannie said, "I had to log in to check my midterm grades." She bent over her phone, its blue light making her beautiful face glow in the dimly lit cab.

I was so in love with her, I was floating.

Then she hooted. "Oh! Oh. Straight A's! Even in Operations, which I thought wasn't going so well."

"I expected nothing less from you."

She was faster hopping out of the truck than I was. My body had stiffened up and I was feeling my wounds, along with the general fatigue and aches and pains after the exertion of our mission. I was happiest lying in bed with a naked Jeannie spoiling me with gentle caresses, kisses and snacks. But, this was an event we couldn't miss.

Though it was early days yet, my strategic planning mind had already raced ahead to the day, not too far in the future I hoped, when Jeannie and I might also be celebrating our own engagement. But I'd learned at least that one lesson. I'd bide my time. I wouldn't rush her.

On the way to the front door, Jeannie skipped and twirled on the sidewalk, her smile wide. I'd never met anyone so happy to get good grades. But she was smart, my girl, and had high expectations for herself, and what made her happy made me happy, too.

I caught up with her, trying not to hobble like an invalid, but my leg really did throb. At least I could be guaranteed a chair and a beer once inside. I stood, hands in my pockets, watching her complete her happy dance.

She stopped twirling, her flowery skirt settling, and I stepped close, twining my arm around her waist, pulling her against me, my fingertips luxuriating in her softness.

"Are you sure you'll be okay all evening without your cane? Your leg's not hurting too much?"

"Nah, I feel fine. I just have one question."

"What?"

Nestling my face against her neck, I said, "Why did you wear that damned pink sweater?"

Surprised, she stopped, pulled away and looked down, running her hands over her sweet curves searching for the problem, triggering a response from my cock that stood up to attention. "But, it's a party. You told me it was too pretty to wear to school, but this is a celebration so I wanted to look pretty."

"You look very pretty. So pretty. You know I love that damned pink sweater so much. Any man within a mile radius will be disabled. It makes your tits look amazing. I'm going to be walking around with a boner for the next five hours."

With a teasing smile, she shimmied her lush body against mine, guaranteeing my immediate and prolonged discomfort.

"You kill me." I groaned. "I can't wait to get you home and strip that sweater off of you. I forbid you to wear it for anyone but me from now on. "

"Ooh. You're so bossy. You can't tell me what to do, mister."

"I can and I will," I growled, kissing her. "I'm going to peel that sweater off of your luscious tits and lay you down on our nice, firm new bed and fuck you silly. You're going to pant and scream my name."

"Hmm," she said pensively. "Too bad we have to go to this party."

Too bad.

"But seriously. Don't get any ideas. We had to come. It's for Jules and Ruby. Oh! Did you get the gift?"

"Got it." I showed her the gift bag hooked over my finger.

"Good."

Inside, we found a familiar welcoming scene, but a smaller, more intimate gathering. Quinn revelled in her ability to host private functions after hours at her homey café, and Deanna never tired of event planning and decorating with twinkly lights. Julian, of course, had orchestrated the food himself. Though tonight Deanna'd been forbidden from posting any images of the private event on social media.

Ruby and Julian had wanted only their closest circle of friends, along with their own family, to attend. I spotted Matt, Arnie, Hans and Eleanor in the crowd.

Julian's mom, his sister Molly and her husband Jake were there. Their kids, at home with a sitter tonight, were keeping company with Will. An adventure for him on their farm, a little different from the usual, that Jeannie and I were happy to accommodate. Family or not, Charlie was a better friend for him than his own cousins, who he was chafing at.

Ruby's family was here too. Her parents, her brother Isaac and his wife.

Everyone had dressed up tonight. Even I, with my limited civilian wardrobe, had acquired, with Jeannie's help, a new collared shirt and dress pants. She'd warned me I'd need a suit for their wedding and I laughed to myself. Wait until she saw me in my formal dress uniform.

Jeannie leaned close and whispered in my ear. "You know, maybe we could slip upstairs to Quinn and Parker's apartment if your problem…gets too bad." As if to guarantee that outcome, she slid her hands around my middle, stroking my back.

"Promise?" I growled into her ear, then pulled her to me and kissed her deeply.

"Get a room, Big P!" came the instant retort from Zach, accompanied by catcalls and whistles from Tate and a few others.

I released Jeannie, reluctantly, and we joined the party, greeting everyone. But I wouldn't forget her promise to sneak away at some point. Maybe I'd even find a nice solid wall to bang her up against. The music was loud enough to drown out her cries of pleasure. Then again, I doubted I could do that in my current condition.

I sighed. Patience, man. You have the rest of your life.

Thankfully, Jeannie stayed by my side, relieving me of the need to follow her around like a hungry puppy. She'd shooed someone out of the comfy armchair at the gang's usual table so I could sit there, and perched herself on the arm beside me, letting others fetch us drinks and food. Which various friends gladly did. Meanwhile, she kept her fingers entwined in the hair at the back of my head, driving me mad with wanting her.

Across from us, Parker slouched like a sad sack. Quinn stood behind the sofa, her palms framing her twin's face, massaging his pouting cheeks into misshapen funhouse masks of self-pity. His depression at Jae Soo's departure for Seoul bore a closer resemblance to a brokenhearted lover than a best friend. Which was odd, because my instincts told me that JJ had a thing for Parker's sister.

Rainy arrived after us, clearly agitated. She collapsed onto the sofa between Parker and Bethune. "Someone bring me strong liquor," she demanded.

"You look lovely, Rainy," said Jeannie. Rainy did look different. She was wearing some brightly coloured traditional dress, and gold jewelry and seemed to have on a lot more makeup than usual.

Rainy groaned. "Spare me. I'm so uncomfortable."

"Why are you dressed up?" Bethune asked.

With a heavy sigh, Rainy explained that she'd had to come directly from her brother Sam's place, where the family had gathered tonight for the first of a series of dinners and events to celebrate Diwali.

"The minute I picked them up from the airport yesterday we launched into a steady stream of social events. I can barely catch my breath. Today was supposed to be my day off, and I spent it scrubbing my apartment from top to bottom because Krishna help me if my mother finds a speck of dust during Diwali. Then I had to drive all over to pick up the *laddoos* and *Mishra mawa* I'd ordered ahead because there's no chance you'll ever catch me making that shit from scratch."

"Who're they?" asked Tate.

"Mom, stepdad, and…" Rainy shuddered, "two guys our age. Hanuman, a nephew of Krupesh, my stepdad, who has convinced Mom would make the ideal husband for me, and one of his sons." Rainy's voice rose with sarcasm.

"Which brother ended up coming?" Deanna asked, having heard the history before.

"The absolute worst!" Rainy gasped. "I couldn't really remember any of them from the wedding six years ago, but when he walked in, I remembered all right."

"And?"

"Kiran Kamdar. He's the youngest of the three brothers and a total douche. As soon as I saw his face, I remembered he was the one who was such an ass at the wedding."

"And what is your prospective husband like?" asked Bethune, snickering. "Is he a hunk?"

"He is most definitely not. He's a snivelling little brown noser, about four inches shorter than me, and he has no chin!"

"Aw, poor Rainy." Bethune pulled her in for a side hug.

"They expect me to have the lot of them for dinner at my apartment, thus the house cleaning and sweets. And I'll have to accompany them to events and dinners all over town for the next two weeks at least while all the festivities are going on. And then Chhaya's sister Mindy's wedding on top of all that. As if I don't have a job as well."

"Will we see you at all this month?"

She sighed. "I don't know. I might need you guys to call me with fake emergencies to get me out of awkward or boring situations."

"You can count on us. We've got you."

"You have to bring the nasty step-brother and his cousin into the café so we can ogle them," Quinn said, diverted from her melancholy.

"Oh, yeah. I'm sure Mom will insist I entertain them and escort them around. Have no fear." Rainy shuddered dramatically.

"That could be amusing," Tate said. "What role should I play? How can I torment them?"

"I won't have a moment to myself for the next month!"

After Rainy'd had a couple of drinks and calmed down, the gang dispersed and mingled, but Jeannie stayed by my side.

"Are you getting tired?" she murmured softly next to me.

"No," I said. "But I am obsessing about your earlier offer." I reached up to caress her arm, and she met my hungry gaze with a coy smile.

"Hmm," she hummed. "Let me just have a word with Quinn." I tracked her progress across the café, watched her whisper in Quinn's ear, and smirked when Quinn glanced up at me suddenly with an amused grin.

Then Jeannie was back, tugging on my hand. I hauled myself out of the chair, anticipation building.

She smiled at me. "Can you manage the stairs?"

"Hell, yeah. I'd climb mount Everest to get to you, love."

"Somehow I believe you."

She led me to the private door at the bottom of the stairs, opened it and then turned the deadbolt after closing it behind us. Then we climbed, admittedly more slowly and awkwardly than I normally moved, up to Quinn and Parker's apartment at the top.

"What about Parker?" I asked.

"Quinn will make sure we have time."

I chuckled. "How does she know how much time we need?"

"I think she'll be generous."

Instead of borrowing her best friend's bed, she led me to the sofa in the middle of the brick-walled loft space and pushed me down gently with a hand on the middle of my chest. Willingly, I sank down.

Jeannie seemed to have a plan.

"What's on your mind, beautiful?"

In answer, she nudged my thighs apart and stood between them, then lowered slowly to her knees, her skirt flaring out around her, causing my pulse to race. When we were at eye level, she held my gaze as her fingers slid along my thighs to my fly, making quick work of the clasp and zipper, her agile hands caressing and pressing my hard-on as she moved over my body.

"Oh, baby. I love you so much."

"I. Love. You." She rubbed my swelling flesh, wasting no time pulling aside the fly of my dress pants, tugging back the elastic of my boxers and taking me in her sure and determined grip with a welcoming squeeze. My entire being tightened and focussed on where our skin touched, the fucking fantastic sensations rocketing through me like nitro.

"Oh, fuck," I breathed, settling back into the sofa, closing my eyes in pure bliss at what she promised lay ahead. But I opened them immediately, not wanting to miss a thing. Just in the nick of time. Jeannie held me firmly, pumping once, twice, and then opened her sweet mouth to lick the leaking tip.

My breathing accelerated. "Jeannie," I gasped. "I want to make love to you."

"Not yet," she murmured, just before running her tongue along the underside of my shaft and slipping the tip between her beautiful lips.

Then I lost the power of speech, totally absorbed in the sheer, inexpressible joy of Jeannie's loving attentions. When I could take no more without violently exploding, I caressed her hair and groaned, "C'mere, love."

Without protest, she released me, stood and then

kneeled on the sofa, her legs straddling my hips. She lifted her skirt, revealing that she'd somehow forgotten to wear underpants—

"Did you leave home like that?" My voice cracked.

"I'm not that reckless, silly," she said with a laugh and showed me the panties she'd somehow slyly removed while between my knees. And then she sobered, her deep blue gaze holding mine intently, making me feel like a king, as she slowly lowered herself onto my shaft, taking me entirely inside of herself with a long satisfied sigh.

My chest tightened, my throat squeezing as my eyes suddenly burned. "Jeannie," I whispered, giving my head a small shake. How could I find the words to express how happy she made me, not just in this way, in this moment? But in every way, every moment of my life. But I knew I needn't say anything. I knew she knew how I felt about her. As she leaned closer and set her mouth on mine, I reached forward, taking her hips into my hands, holding on for all I was worth as she rode me all the way home.

THE END

DID you enjoy The Phoenix's Unlikely Prodigy? If so, you can leave a review here: The Phoenix's UNLIKELY Prodigy here: My Book

WANT TO READ THE FIRST BOOK IN THE HAVING IT ALL SERIES?
BUY EBOOK ON AMAZON : BeMineThisTime

WANT TO CONNECT WITH ME?
www.maryannclarkescott.com
maryann@maryannclarkescott.com

If you enjoy reading this book, please rate it and leave a review on Amazon HERE. Your opinion can make or break an author's success, and it means the world to me.
Go here to leave a review:

Acknowledgments

Thank you's must go first to my HEA Marketing squad, Donna, Erryn, Jeanine, Natasha, Reshma & Stacy for being part of my process every day, and for helping me to really look at what you, the reader, are looking for in a romance book. Just like me, you love the tropes that help define our genre and this book, and this series, are my response to that. I hope it delivers, and more than that meets all your expectations.

As well, special thanks go to my first, close and final readers of the manuscript: Natasha, John & my editor Jacqui. Thank you for finding and helping to repair those places where the story tripped on my verbosity and bad writing habits. I hope I managed to fix them all, and take full responsibility for those places where my stubbornness or blindness won out. A special thank you goes out to Sayeh H for confirming, for the most part, that my research for my military hero paid off, and I didn't make too many mistakes or take too many liberties with my imagination.

I hope you, my final reader are happy and share the love in reviews. That's really the only way I'll ever know what you thought of my story, so I hope you share your views with me as well as other readers who might be searching for just this story.

Thank you also to subscribers of my newsletter who were part of the creative journey as I shared this manuscript, albeit in a slightly rougher form, chapter by chapter before final edits and publication. I hope you found the experiment fun and 'novel' and enjoyed the story as well.

And finally, thanks to my new crew of characters who've kept me company this past couple of years as I built, piece by piece, my imaginary world of Port Camosun. I hope you, reader, have fallen in love with this crew of friends as much as I have, and stick around as I tell you their individual stories, one by one. It's going to be a bumpy ride, and it's good to have your friends along.

xo,

MA

The Reporter's UNLIKELY
Reunion ~ sample

Julian

Ten years ago, my life plan had been simple. I knew exactly who I was, where I was going, and what I wanted.

I was Julian Michaels, an easy-going, third-generation chicken farmer, and I'd be married to my high school sweetheart with two, maybe three kids, I figured. A dog, of course. A simple, pleasant life stretching as far into the future as I could see.

Then everything came crashing down. My life, my future, my dreams, my faith in humanity, and my self belief.

I learned that nothing is simple; you can't ever really know or trust anyone—including yourself—and life was random. It was best to take things one day at a time. Be adaptable. Take pleasure in simple things.

Even so, I wasn't prepared.

"Julian! Julian!" A chorus of female voices rose to greet me the moment I walked through Millhouse Coffee. Collectively, the voices belonged to two of my oldest and dearest friends: Quinn, the proprietor of the café, and Deanna, my social media mentor. I'd known them since middle school. They were two-fifths of a dynamic group of clever, popular, can-do girlfriends ironically known as the Kickass Chicks. Quinn, Deanna, and Rainy—who was at work—were the only three that stayed in our hometown, and at the moment were the core organizing committee of our tenth high school reunion. I was a mere hanger-on, their mascot if you will. Also, their caterer.

They leapt from their chairs, swarming me as I strode toward the table where their lists and spreadsheets, seating arrangements and menus were spread. I felt my neck and face heat with embarrassment as they batted their eyelashes in slow-mo, made smooching faces, and fake swooned all over me.

"I love you, Julian!"

"You're so sexy, Julian!"

"Julian, will you marry me?"

"Geroff!" I chuckled good-naturedly, peeling their arms from my neck and pushing them away as they giggled. I was a lucky man to have so many warm and true friends, and beautiful women to boot—inside and out.

I could hardly blame them for the teasing. My newest Instagram Live had gone viral, and my following had grown by ten thousand over the week, thanks to the coaching and technical support of Deanna the social media queen. Or influencer, as she was known, with the 748,000 followers of her Dee+Dun Beauty and Wellness profile. I wondered if the explosion of follows for my farm and food page and gaga girl fans qualified me as an influencer now too. All for tromping around my farm with my dog Finnigan and my goats and chickens like the hick that I was. What a weird world we live in.

"Your following, dude!" said Deanna, giving me a side hug.

"Thanks to you. You really are brilliant, Dee. I'm over the moon."

Swooning girl fans who thought I was some kind of rustic sex symbol was not what I'd expected from the new cooking and sustainable food campaign, nor what I signed up for. I felt awkward AF, but if the attention got me the audience I sought for my brand, and the sponsorships and partnerships I needed to advance my cause—and pay for my animals' feed—I could hardly complain. My actual cost of living was very low, since I essentially lived off my land as much as possible.

They sat down and I joined them, sweeping their papers aside and setting down my cloth-covered tin tray in the centre of the table.

"Ooh! What's this?" asked Deanna, pinching the edge of the cloth to peek underneath. Deanna's diet was too health conscious and frou-frou to allow her to enjoy my cooking fully, and Quinn had rather conservative tastes, though she wholeheartedly supported my sustainable, local approach. But I made sure to include all their needs and preferences when planning the menu, as they were a rather spot-on avatar for my target audience. And I aimed to please.

I swatted her hand away. "Hold on a sec. Where's Rainy?"

"Running late."

She was the most adventurous foodie of the group and loved to sample every new thing I came up with. The highly anticipated event was tomorrow night, and it was my food that would grace the buffet and circulate among the crowd. The food had to be superb, brilliant, and eye-catching, as well as on message. I might be attending the reunion mainly to spend time with my closest friends and reconnect with a few old ones, but I had an ulterior motive.

"Have you got the final numbers for us?"

Deanna pulled her hand back, dragged her laptop closer and clicked. "Yes. There were a few last-minute responses." She scanned her screen. "We heard from Alex whatsit. He is coming after all and he's bringing his husband."

"Any more?"

"Mhm. The four from Boston confirmed. Elsa from Montreal is coming. Dean and his wife from up in Prince George are coming down. Oh! I got a call from James Reynold's mom. He died! She just heard about the reunion and finally got back to me."

"Another one to add to the deceased poster," murmured Quinn, rummaging under the stacks of papers and jotting his name on a list.

I vaguely recalled James. "The theatre guy? With the curly hair?"

Quinn added, "Voted Most Likely To End Up on a Soap Opera." She frowned down at her list, scratching her pen through a line.

"Wasn't he friends with Tate?"

"Yeah, that's what I remember, too," Quinn said, her bright features falling. "They were in the theatre club together. I wonder if Tate knows."

Deanna chewed her lip. "She said it was cancer. Throat cancer. How cruel is that?"

"Fuck cancer," grumbled Quinn. "Want a coffee, Julian?"

"Nah, thanks. I've gotta run. My buddy Arnie is delivering an alpaca this afternoon. I have to get back to the farm."

"A what? Alpaca? Is that like a… like a llama?"

I laughed. "Yeah. Sorta."

"Why on earth would you—?"

I brushed her question aside with a shake of my head. I

didn't want the hassle of learning about a new species, but Arnie was adamant.

"And Jeannie? She still coming?" I turned to Quinn, raising my brows in question. Quinn was the only one who Jeannie had stayed in touch with since grad.

Deanna's face lit up. "I am so excited to see her. I can't believe she's not been back once in ten years."

Quinn gave me her sedate trademark smile, and I caught the undertone of sympathy beneath. She knew I'd never ask directly about Ruby, and that Jeannie was a kind of stand-in for my perverse self-indulgent curiousity about the missing fifth member of the clique. "Jeannie was due to arrive from Toronto tonight. But there was some work thing, and she had to reschedule her flight for tomorrow. It's up in the air but she's still hoping to make it in time."

"She'd better goddamwell make it," Deanna grumbled, making a pouty face. "It won't be a reunion at all without her. I'm still mad at her for cutting us all off."

"Not all of us," I said, elbowing Quinn, who shrugged, pulling a face. Being in Jeannie's confidence, she knew things that she hinted at but never shared. Quinn was like a vault.

We fell silent, as though we all were thinking the same thought at the same moment. Which, undoubtedly, we were. It wouldn't be the same without Ruby either, but nobody expected Ruby to come. And they didn't talk about her in front of me, anyway.

Deanna cleared her throat to break the awkward silence. "So. The final numbers are here. A hundred and twenty-six, give or take. Is that close enough for you?"

"Sure. Anyway, I had some ingredient substitutions and re-jigged a few of the appetizers, so I brought some samples for your approval."

"Ooh. Taste test." Quinn rubbed her hands together, licking her lips.

I swept away the covering cloth with a flourish to reveal my latest creations. I pointed to one. "Harissa grilled baby lamb on sumac flatbreads. You should get a little kick and a gorgeous depth of flavour from the roasted spices, but nothing to knock your socks off."

Tentatively, Quinn plucked one stack off of the tray and popped it whole into her mouth. She closed her eyes and savoured it, humming. "Nice."

"Caramelized shallots on slices of gluten-free Hasselback Jerusalem artichokes for you Deanna."

Deanna picked a sample and peered at it for a moment before touching it with the tip of her tongue. She liked the colour and shape of things as much as their taste and so I'd decorated the tops with a dollop of Creme Fraiche and a pretty sprig of chervil. I thought she'd like that, and as she smiled at it and took a dainty bite, I knew she did. She chewed thoughtfully, and I watched her eyes register the lovely silky texture combined with the chewiness of the artichokes. Another winner.

"Next," Quinn said, waiting for the introduction that always preceded my food.

I picked up one of the dessert items. "How about something sweet, Quinny? This one's maple sugar rhubarb mousse in a cardamom crisp, with wild strawberries and a caramel halo." Quinn's eyes lit up and she enthusiastically gave that a go. I sat back, watching them crunch and chew, listening to their moans of delight, knowing I'd knocked it out of the park.

Without warning, Deanna lurched forward with a guttural noise, her big, dark eyes bulging at something over my shoulder.

Deanna clutched at my sleeve as Quinn followed her gaze. As I went to turn around, Quinn grabbed a paper napkin and spit the contents of her mouth into her hand.

What the hell?

"What's wrong? Does it taste bad? What is it?" Had I mixed up sugar and salt? Accidentally dropped chili pepper into the mousse? I didn't do stuff like that. I was exacting and careful; some might say, too precise.

She frowned and hissed, "Don't turn around. Don't turn around."

Deanna let out a long plaintive cry like someone had stepped on a cat. Of course I turned, because whatever had caused this uproar in my girls had to be faced.

Of all the things or people I expected to see entering the café when I turned, it was not Ruby.

My head roared with a whooshing, tidal wave of blood; burning, anguished tears shot from my tear ducts as my throat seized up.

"Did she contact you? Did you know?"

"No. No, I never got a reply to the invitation."

"I thought she was in Afghanistan."

"No, it was Azerbaijan."

I heard the halting exchange between the girls through the thunder in my ears.

I squeezed my eyes closed, opened them wide, shut them again. Surely my mind was playing tricks on me. I'd imagined I'd seen my Ruby a million times over the years. Here on the streets downtown, and even in London, Paris, Rome, and New York; there were times when I was convinced that the person I saw in a crowded restaurant on the sidewalk up ahead was Ruby. But it never was. This, my pounding heart jammed into my throat told me, was undoubtedly Ruby.

Suddenly, we were all on our feet. I don't remember rising. Everything happened at once, in a staccato rhythm.

Deanna rushed forward calling her name, then stopped and glanced back at me, uncertain. Quinn stayed by my side, her fingers digging into my bicep, as though she thought I might topple over without her support. And I might have. I still might.

"Ruby? Is that really you?" Deanna stepped forward.

Ruby, for it truly was her, stood blinking at the bunch of us, disoriented too. Did she come in here by accident? Her lips opened to speak, but she stalled. She reached a hand out, and Deanna clasped then released it.

"Hey… wow… guys. I…" Her gaze skipped across each of us, but kept bouncing back to me, locking on me. As our gazes met, her pupils huge and black, I felt as though I'd fallen into deep space; she seemed as disoriented as I felt.

Deanna stepped back while Quinn released my arm at last, shoving me forward. I stumbled. I didn't know what she wanted me to do. What was I supposed to do?

"Jules?" Ruby's voice reached me, scratchy and faint, like a bad recording. "I didn't expect to see you here. Mom told me about Quinn's new place and I…"

No words came when I tried to find them. Something cottony closed my throat. My eyes burned and my skin was hot and tingling. Confused, I turned to look at Quinn and Deanna. They'd retreated, huddled together like nervous puppies.

"Jules?" Ruby stepped closer and closer. Ten inches away, then eight. I could smell her. Feel her breath on my face. She lifted a hand as if to touch me, but stopped mid air and let it drop. She knew better than to try, this woman who destroyed me. She was part stranger, part lover, part ruination, and it was hella confusing; a storm of emotions swirled inside me.

But then she did touch me. First her palms landed featherlight on my chest, as if gauging my temperature, like a hot stove. Then her arms slid up and around my neck, grabbing fistfuls of my shirt and pulling me closer, tipping her face to the crook of my neck, grazing it with a feather touch. The familiar scent of her, dark chocolate and the cinnamon spice of carnations that I'd loved so much, swamped my senses.

In a flash, my body remembered what I'd fought ten years to forget. The silky feel of her thick hair and smooth skin against mine. My fingers tingled, and my arms ached to grab her and pull her into me, hold her tight. I feathered my fingertips on her back, and felt her ribs and vertebrae jutting, strange in their gaunt hardness. But I could go no further, enveloped by her trembling breath and crushed by the sound of my own heartbeat in my ears.

Suddenly we were at the centre of a frenzied group hug, the other girls rushing us and twining their arms around both of us. Pressed closer to Ruby, our chests, bellies, hips, and thighs connected, a fever of familiar desire washed over me; my body temperature shot up as my skin screamed and nerve endings lit up. Blood surged to my groin in a tidal wave of sexual reverberations. I tried to pull back but was locked into the embrace, painfully conscious of my swelling groin.

They must have all realized they were crowding us at the same moment, because the group broke apart and everyone teetered back a step. My head was on fire.

I drew a breath. Some shards of sense cut through the fog. Finally, I found my voice, a choked, stiff, drowning voice. "Are you here for the reunion?"

She winced and swayed on her feet. Her head tilted to

the left. "No. No, I didn't know. My mom and dad just told me about it." Her shoulder hitched up. "That's why I came looking for Quinn."

I said nothing. Did I honestly expect she'd look me up first? Or at all?

She looked great. Fantastic. Strong, lean, and tanned, her brown hair streaked with gold. Of course, I'd seen her on TV. We all had. So it's not like the changes wrought by ten years in her field should shock me. But they did all the same. In the flesh she looked tired, weathered. Not the incandescent, nubile Ruby of our youth. Tiny lines flared out from the corners of her hazel eyes, and cut into the sides of her full mouth. It was a hard life she'd chosen. I knew that. Still, she was as beautiful to me as ever.

I reached up to rub the back of my head, staring down at my rubber work boots, now painfully aware that I'd come in directly from the farm. I was in my rattiest t-shirt and scarf, my baggiest work pants. I never fussed about clothes anymore, but my skin crawled now with self-consciousness. A deep, crippling sense of my inadequacy swamped me.

"Are all of you going to the reunion?" Ruby finally asked, scanning the group.

"Of course we are. We organized it. And now so are you!" squeaked Deanna, leaping closer. I just kept staring at her, as blood roared in my ears to the sound of her name. Ruby, Ruby, Ruby.

"You're going?" Ruby's big green-bronze eyes circled my features, as if she too were taking the measure of time since we'd last been together.

"Ah… nooo, actually. Nope." Tugging on my scarf, I shoved my hands in my pockets and stepped back to give myself a bit of space. I registered the sharp intake of breath behind me. "Have an alpaca to unpack. Got to get it… settled." This couldn't be happening. I took a step to the side, clenching my hands into fists, and angled my shoulder towards her—like a bull intent on plowing through a fence. Anything to stop me from wrapping her in a crushing embrace, burying my face in her hair, drawing the scent of her skin into my lungs like a life-giving elixir.

"You are too going, Julian." Quinn's quiet voice came right behind me. "You have to go. Everyone expects you."

I twisted to glare at her. "No. Can't make it. Sorry." I turned back to Ruby. "You should though. Since you're back. Everyone will be so excited to see you." My God, I have to get out of here. I stepped around her, forcing myself to put one foot in front of the other until I found myself on the sidewalk out in front of the café. The warm summer air washed over me like a silken veil, waking me up from a dream. A volcano of emotion erupted from somewhere deep inside me; I felt like I was on fire. I had to get away, and fast.

Though anguish and horrible humiliation, and latent rage swirled together in my gut, all my nerve endings stubbornly insisted on standing up together and singing a high clear note like a choir.

Ruby was back.

***

If you missed out on book 1 in the Most UNLIKELY To series, you can grab The Reporter's Unlikely Reunion now. Find it here: The Reporter's UNLIKELY Reunion here: https://www.books2read.com/reportersreunion

About the Author

MaryAnn Clarke ~ USA Today Bestselling author MaryAnn Clarke is a Chatelaine Grand Prize winner and Next Generation Indie Book Award finalist for The Art of Enchantment, first in the Life is a Journey series about young women on journeys abroad who discover themselves and fall in love while getting embroiled in someone else's problems. Her Having it All series is about professional women struggling to balance the challenge and fulfillment of their careers with their search for identity, love, family and home.

Always eager to fill blank pages and empty canvases with ideas swirling in her head, MaryAnn set out to write emotionally engaging stories that walk a tightrope between intelligent Women's Fiction and heart-warming Romance.

A socially awkward polymath with ASD who studied Fine Arts, Urbanism, Architecture and Gerontology at university on both coasts of Canada, she turned to her first love, writing stories, when she realized she could have more fun with fewer rules to follow. When not writing, she meditates while hiking wooded mountain trails, does yoga and Pilates to fend off decrepitude, reads eclectically, contemplates wormholes, experiments with painting abstract expressionism, kills plants and tries not to burn dinner while solving her next plot problem. Now that her chick has flown the coop, Clarke lives on beautiful Vancouver Island, Canada with her husband and cats. Although she knows she lives in Paradise, she still loves travelling the world in search of romance, art, good food and new story ideas.

Get MaryAnn's newsletter and never miss a new release!

Want to receive a FREE book? Join MaryAnn's mailing list to get all new and exclusive Single Dad in Studio 7D. Stay in touch to hear book news, special deals and updates about her new series release schedule.

You can read more about MaryAnn, her books and ideas that strike her fancy at www.maryannclarkescott.com.

Find All of her books on Amazon at
https://www.amazon.com/MaryAnn-Clarke/e/
B01KPSGXNO

Want to connect with me?
www.maryannclarkescott.com
maryann@maryannclarkescott.com

Subscribe & Follow MACS!
www.maryannclarkescott.com
Question? Fan mail? Sure, you can reach me here.

Also by MaryAnn Clarke

Be Mine This Time

Making Room For You

Before You Knew Me

The Art of Enchantment

A Forged Affair

Hiding From Christmas

9 781988 743431